TARGETED

Also by Kendra Elliot

Bone Secrets Novels

Hidden
Chilled
Buried
Alone
Known
Veiled (A Novella)

Callahan & McLane
Part of the Bone Secrets World

Vanished
Bridged
Spiraled

Rogue River Novellas

On Her Father's Grave
Her Grave Secrets
Dead in Her Tracks

TARGETED

KENDRA ELLIOT

Montlake
Romance

Text copyright © 2016 Kendra Elliot
All rights reserved.

Published by Montlake Romance, Seattle

www.apub.com

Amazon, the Amazon logo, and Montlake Romance are trademarks of Amazon.com, Inc., or its affiliates.

ISBN-13: 9781503935044
ISBN-10: 1503935043

Cover design by Jason Blackburn

Printed in the United States of America

To my new espresso machine, which fueled me through this book.
And to the man who watched me fall in love with espresso in Italy and bought me a machine because he knew I'd never buy it myself. He's pretty smart.

1

The scent of death entered his nose.

Mason Callahan sniffed again, but the odor vanished in the cool morning air.

He'd stepped out onto the small front porch of the remote cabin, sipping his coffee and watching the low fog slowly weave through the tall firs, before the smell had reached him. Inside, the other four men still slept; multiple snores rumbled from the bedrooms.

It was the third day of their escape. After years of talking about taking a fishing charter off the Oregon Coast, they'd finally made it happen. It'd taken some major shuffling to assign the five detectives the same vacation week, but it'd been worth it. Yesterday's fifteen-mile ocean boat trip had netted them more big lingcod than they could eat in a decade.

He shrugged and stepped off the porch and circled their vehicles, automatically checking for signs of break-in or low air in the tires. He moved toward the forest, searching for the source of the brief rancid scent, but he smelled only the fresh pine nearly masking the faint smell of ocean. Two neatly stacked cords of chopped wood sat in a three-sided wooden shed. The group had built a fire in the woodstove last night, feeling the chill of the coast that hadn't moved into the valleys. Winter was coming, but Portlanders had experienced a long Indian summer that had bypassed the coast. Mason decided to bring in an armload of wood and fire up the woodstove before the other men woke. He balanced his coffee on the woodpile and started to load his arms.

Death reached his nose again.

Nothing else smells like death. Coppery and putrid and rank.

He froze and then sniffed at the stack in his arms. *It's not the wood.* He leaned forward and sniffed along the woodpile. It smelled woodsy and musty.

His adrenaline spiking, Mason silently set each piece of wood back in its place on the perfect stack. *A dead animal must be nearby.* He listened for the sound of a bear or cougar or another predator, but all he heard was the quiet rustle of the wind in the high tops of the fir trees. He slowly stepped around to the back side of the woodshed, his hand automatically touching the empty space at his side where he usually wore his weapon, and saw the source of the odor.

He sucked in a breath, unable to move. The man's face was hidden by a rubbery covering that had dozens of tiny spikes sticking out of it, but Mason knew he was dead. No one could survive the wide, gaping gash that had opened his neck.

"Denny?"

Mason's vision tunneled as he recognized the shirt Denny had worn to the bar last night and the tips of his thick black mustache poking out from under the odd covering. The ground seemed to sway under Mason's feet, and his fingers went numb.

It was definitely his boss.

Alarms shot off in his head as Mason crouched low to the ground and tight to the woodshed, scanning the area.

Nothing.

He listened harder, searching for a sound, any sound. His gaze jumped from shadow to shadow in the forest.

Silence.

Accepting that he was alone, he took a long look at his friend, fighting the urge to uncover his face, knowing he couldn't disturb evidence. Unable to stop himself, he reached out with one finger and touched the back of Denny's hand.

Ice-cold.

Dammit.

Mason slowly backed around the corner, trying to place his feet where he'd stepped before.

Vacation was over.

• • •

Denny Schefte's vacation cabin sat deep in the woods, ten minutes from Depoe Bay. It was the last week of October, so the tiny coastal fishing town was quiet. Unlike during the summer months, when tourists clogged the main highway, searching for vantage points from which to take pictures of the ocean, the enclosed bay, and the quaint town.

Fish and chips, saltwater taffy, and miles of backed-up traffic constructed Mason's memories of his old coast trips with his son and ex-wife. This trip had been different. The locals were more plentiful than tourists and the roads were clear. Their group had been the only outsiders in the bar last night. They'd gotten a few stares and had one rude drunken encounter. Mason had blamed Ray in his ironed shirts and polished loafers for highlighting the fact that they were tourists.

The Oregon coastal towns were less affluent than the larger valley cities. This wasn't California. Most of the year, the Oregon Coast was cold, windy, and gray, and many businesses struggled to survive.

Tourism was a primary source of income, but the season was extremely short. Mason didn't consider himself a snob; he'd been raised on a ranch in rural Eastern Oregon, but he'd grown used to a Starbucks on every corner and clean silverware in a restaurant. Yesterday he'd bought a cup of coffee from the snack counter in the fishing shop. Probably not his smartest move. He could drink almost any cup of black coffee, but that one had tasted . . . odd.

It was as if he'd bought that cup of coffee in a different lifetime; today everything was different.

Standing next to him in the yard of Denny's cabin, Ray muttered, "How can this be happening?"

Mason watched him wipe his eyes and politely looked elsewhere.

After backing away from the body, Mason had immediately roused the other three men in the cabin. He'd never been so relieved to see Ray's face. His blood pressure had shot up as he pounded on one bedroom door and then another, scared he'd find more corpses. His partner Ray Lusco, and Detectives Duff Morales and Steve Hunsinger, had lunged out of bed within a split second of Mason's yells at their doors. No rubbing of eyes or stretching of limbs. All three men had been instantly awake and alert, ready to react.

It came with the job.

Anger, shock, and then sorrow had shot through them at varying and dizzying speeds. The four of them had reported the death, studied the scene, and walked a fast perimeter. They'd found no indication that another person had been near the cabin. Now they stood a small distance from the body, waiting for the first local police to arrive. They'd reached out to the locals, the closest OSP office, and Denny's boss. Mason wanted to call Ava but was waiting, wanting to be able to tell his fiancée more than "Denny's dead."

"Did he hear something and leave the cabin?" Duff asked. "Or did he just happen to step outside?"

"God damn it," Steve swore. "Could someone have been inside the cabin? Taken him outside?"

Mason shook his head. "We would have heard. Denny's a big guy. There's no sign of a struggle anywhere between here and his room. No scuff marks, no drag marks in the dirt. He walked out here on his own."

"Where's his cell?" Ray asked.

"He usually keeps it in his shirt pocket." Mason glanced back at Denny. "Clearly it's not there now. I didn't see it when I looked in his room, but I didn't dig. Call it," he told Ray.

Steve darted back into the cabin to listen for a ringtone as Ray called. "It went straight to voice mail," stated Ray. Steve jogged back down the steps shaking his head to show he hadn't heard a sound inside.

"It was probably taken and turned off. We shouldn't start messing with anything that could be evidence," Mason stated. "It's not our place to meddle in someone else's investigation."

"Bullshit. This is Denny," said Steve. "We're not going to let the local yokels handle his murder."

"They won't," Mason said with forced confidence. "The murder of an Oregon State Police captain? They'll pass it up to the Lincoln County sheriff, who will probably call Major Crimes in Salem," he added, referring to OSP's primary office. If the command of the investigation didn't immediately move in that direction, he'd prod until it did. Steve was right. This couldn't be left to the locals.

"Anyone know his ex-wife's number?" Ray asked the group.

Everyone shook his head. Mason couldn't remember the woman's name.

"Two boys, right?" asked Duff.

"Yeah, both married and live out of state," said Ray.

Mason had forgotten that, too.

"We need to be doing something," Steve said. "We can't just stand around." He ran a hand through his hair, making his case of bedhead even worse. "What was the name of that bar we were at last night?"

Mason wasn't the only one thinking about the argument Denny had had last night with a local.

"Pete's Bar," answered Ray. "But you can't think—"

"Yeah, I can," said Steve. "That guy had it in for Denny. If Mason hadn't stepped in, someone would have thrown a punch. I don't know what that asshole's problem was, but Denny said it had something to do with his truck. It sounded like it went back a few weeks."

Mason nodded. "But just because someone made a dent in your truck doesn't mean you cut his throat."

Steve's brown stare met Mason's. "You know as well as I do that plenty of people have killed for less."

True.

"Who saw Denny last?" asked Duff. His calm manner had always been a good balance for Steve's temper. The four men exchanged looks. "I went straight upstairs to my room when we got home," Duff said. "Since Denny was the only one sleeping on the main floor, did you guys see him after I crashed?"

"I stayed up and talked with him a bit down there," said Mason. "I noticed it was nearly one thirty when I went to bed. Anyone else see him later? Or hear him after that?"

Everyone shook his head. "I was in bed before one," said Ray. "I didn't hear anything."

"Same here," said Steve. "What'd you guys talk about?" He turned a curious gaze on Mason.

Déjà vu passed through Mason. He was suddenly on the hot seat, the one who had seen the murder victim last. He'd been here before, when one of his informants had been murdered and the killer had set up Mason for the crime.

It'd nearly ripped him apart.

"No work stuff. We just talked about fishing and why he bought the cabin," he hedged.

A faint siren grew louder and the men turned their attention to the end of the driveway. Mason's stomach felt as if he'd eaten too much fiery salsa. It burned and twisted. Ray met his gaze, and he saw sympathy. His partner remembered exactly the hell he'd gone through last December under the magnifying glass of his department.

It wasn't going to happen again.

• • •

Mason forced himself to stand back and watch as officers from the Lincoln County Sheriff's Department and the Oregon state police from the Newport office tried not to step on one another's toes.

"All we need now is the FBI," Ray muttered.

"Not ruling it out," answered Mason. He'd listened to each word and watched every movement of all the officers. No one would be allowed to make an error on Mason's watch.

A Lincoln City patrol cop had arrived first; the population of Depoe Bay was too small to support a police department. The cop was young and Mason bet he'd never seen a dead body before. As Mason had expected, he'd quickly deferred to the Lincoln County deputy and OSP officers who had showed minutes later. The news of a murdered OSP captain had quickly shot up the ranks. The Lincoln County sheriff appeared, dressed in jeans and hiking boots, looking as if he'd just rolled out of bed. He shook all the detectives' hands and looked each one in the eye as he offered condolences. He strode to the body and bent over, staring for a long moment, his hands on his knees as the morning sun glinted off his silver hair. Mason had heard about Sheriff Michael Jensen for the past decade. The man was known for being outspoken and getting shit done. He wasn't an apologizer; he was a doer. If he heard something he didn't like, he handled it immediately. He was blunt and very popular in his county. He came back to the four men and crossed his arms on his chest.

"You want me to call in your Major Crimes Unit out of Salem?" he asked.

"Yes, sir." The four of them spoke at once.

The sheriff twisted his lips. "Usually I'd make a case for my detectives right now. But this one's personal for all of you, right?"

Nods.

"I'd want every available resource on it, too," he sighed. "And I know OSP has a lot more resources than we do."

"We might go higher," said Ray.

"I would," said the sheriff. "If that was my boss and friend, I wouldn't stop at OSP. No offense," he said quickly.

All of them paused as the young Lincoln City cop stopped outside their circle and asked a question.

Mason fully turned, facing the young cop. "What'd you say?"

The cop lifted his chin, looking from the sheriff to Mason. "I asked what's the deal with the Pinhead mask?"

"Pinhead?" Mason repeated. Brief clips of horror films flooded his memory. He'd never watched the movies, but his son Jake had been an addict. He moved over to where Denny's body quietly lay, waiting for the county crime scene techs to start their processing.

Mason stared at the mask that still covered Denny's face. The Lincoln City cop had wanted to remove it when he'd first arrived, but the Portland detectives wouldn't let him touch it.

Mason recognized the character. He'd seen a parade of pop culture horror icons on the TV screen as he passed through the family room where Jake had watched movies for hours on end. He had no idea which movie franchise Pinhead belonged to, but knew it'd been one of Jake's favorites. The mask on Denny's face was ill-fitting, gathered and gapped in several places, which explained why he hadn't recognized it as a mask. It'd looked like a lumpy piece of rubber with lines and pins.

He exchanged a glance with Ray, who slowly shook his head as shock crossed his face.

"From the horror movies?" asked Steve. "I didn't realize that it actually was a mask. I thought it was just a jumbled mess."

"What's it mean?" asked the sheriff.

"Hell if I know," said Mason.

2

Ava McLane pulled open the door of the tiny shop in downtown Lake Oswego. The bells on the door jangled softly, and she stepped into a space managed by someone with much better decorating taste than herself. She was instantly jealous. The owner had a passion for the beachy home decor that made Ava's blood pressure lower and stress flow out of her limbs. Everywhere she looked she saw something she wanted . . . or possibly needed. Pale distressed wood furniture, striking ocean photos, and beach glass in icy blue and green shades that relaxed her brain. She picked up a mesh bag of the glass, running her thumb over the water-smoothed pieces, imagining it in a clear bowl on her fireplace mantel.

She had a purpose in visiting the store. Looking around, she spotted several paintings on a wall near the back of the shop. She made her way through the store, trying not to be distracted by a fabulous weathered chest of drawers that belonged in a home on Martha's Vineyard. She stopped in front of the first watercolor and understood why the owner had featured the artwork.

The paintings of coastlines were striking. Bleak and desolate but deeply engaging in their shades and depth. The loneliness portrayed by the artist's strokes took her breath away. *Am I the only one who sees it?* Or did everyone experience the emptiness?

She stared at the small placard featuring the artist's name. Jayne McLane.

You finally did it.

It wasn't much of an art show, but pride swept through Ava.

I hope this helps you continue to heal.

Ava exchanged one email a week with her twin, knowing her every word would be scrutinized by a counselor before Jayne ever read it. Jayne had been incredibly upbeat and proud of her showing in the home decor shop. Needing to confirm that Jayne wasn't exaggerating, Ava had hunted down the small notice in the local newspaper.

Art show. Jayne McLane's beach watercolors.
10 to 2 p.m. Free coffee and cookies.

She'd told Jayne she'd go, assuming her twin wouldn't be allowed to leave her rehab center. Jayne's doctors were taking her recovery slowly and carefully. Once the gashes on her wrists had healed, they'd encouraged her passion for art, and the result had been these seven paintings.

"These are great," said a male voice beside her. Ava turned to see a man in his sixties smiling at her. "I love the beach."

"Me, too."

He seemed harmless, but Ava wasn't in a chatty mood. She turned her attention back to the art, realizing the one with the rich teal shades would be perfect in her freshly remodeled dining room.

"Know the artist?" her fellow art admirer asked.

"Not really," she hedged.

He laughed. "I just wondered if she was local."

"You'd have to ask the manager," Ava said, unwilling to talk about her twin. Would Jayne be considered local? In the past decade, had she ever called a city her home?

He held out his hand. "I'm David."

"Ava." *Please don't hit on me.* He was too old for her taste.

"I think I'll buy that one." He pointed at the one she'd wanted for her dining room. She bit her lip, holding back her disappointment, and he narrowed his gray eyebrows. "Unless you were going to? You were here first."

She swallowed. "I was considering that one," she admitted. At another time she would have let him buy the painting since he'd spoken first, but she'd already pictured it in her home and knew it was perfect.

He studied the others. "In that case, I'll take that one."

It'd been her second favorite.

He eyed her. "Unless you're uncertain about the first one?"

"I want it." She did. The more she looked at it, the more she saw her sister's sense of isolation in the bleak seascape. But in a good way. A healing way.

"We have good taste," he pronounced. He glanced around the quiet shop. "I'll find a salesperson." He walked off.

Ava exhaled. The man's comments confirmed that Jayne did have some talent—and not just in the eyes of her sister. She wondered what Mason would think of the constant reminder of Jayne in their home. Not that it'd be the first one. She was reminded of Jayne every time she looked in the mirror.

A saleswoman bustled over with David in her wake, clearly excited that two of the paintings had immediately sold. Ava added the chest of drawers to her purchase, along with the bag of beach glass. She avoided looking directly at other charming pieces in the shop, knowing she'd stumbled into a store that spoke to her heart. Her wallet couldn't take the expenses right now. Retail therapy had been an unexpected part of her healing process.

Last Wednesday had been her first time back at the FBI office in two months. It'd been a time of physical, mental, and emotional recovery from being shot at close range as she wrestled with a serial killer. For a long time, she'd wondered if she'd return at all. The trifecta of her injury, a deadly infection, and Jayne's suicide attempt had thrown her into a deep dark pit.

She'd struggled to find her way out.

The quiet therapist who had annoyed Ava last spring had turned out to be a godsend. Ava had thought Dr. Pearl Griffen meek, but there'd been a backbone of steel and a sharp mind under her docile exterior. She'd pushed and prodded Ava until her brain had seen life as it truly existed. Not the contorted version she'd started to believe in.

Mason had stood beside her the entire time, taking his own leave from work and spending hours simply being in her presence. They'd talk or they'd sit quietly. It didn't matter; he was her rock. The message was loud and clear that he was there for her.

In sickness and in health.

She looked at the diamond sparkling on her left hand. It'd felt odd the first week, but now it was part of her. A symbol that she and Mason could handle any garbage their lives threw at them.

Surely they'd been through the worst.

Returning to work had been a burst of invigorating fresh air. Before that she'd spent weeks feeling torn into pieces and slogging through some of the deepest depression and pain she'd ever experienced, but she'd emerged strong and hopeful. She'd been placed back in criminal investigations and assigned a caseload that focused her brain and made her feel useful. Returning had been the right thing to do.

What doesn't kill me . . .

She'd fought her way out of that black pit and was on the right track thanks to Mason and Dr. Griffen. Each day would be a new step in her journey, her doctor had told her; nothing completely goes away. *If you think you're over it, you're deceiving yourself.*

Ava understood. She had a form of PTSD from a cocktail of Jayne's emotional abuse and her own physical trauma. Now it was embedded and woven into the person she was. Forever.

Her phone rang in her purse. Mason.

"Denny's been murdered," he blurted.

"*What?* Are you okay? What happened?" She made a beeline for the shop's door and stepped outside for privacy.

The line was silent for a few seconds. "Yes, we're all fine. We don't know who did it. I found him this morning outside the cabin. His throat was cut." His words were clipped, his tone short, and she knew he was struggling. Her heart broke for him.

"I'm so sorry, Mason. You've worked together for a long time."

A text beeped at her ear, and she glanced at her screen. Her boss wanted her to call him immediately.

Ava suspected it wasn't a coincidence. "Do you need me to come out there?" she asked.

"No. I'm good." He paused. "I just needed to call you. I had to tell you."

She understood; she would have done the same.

The pain echoed in his voice. He was trying to hide it, but he couldn't fool her. She *knew* him.

He'd had some rough moments with his boss, but Ava knew he had a lot of respect and fondness for the man.

"What's next?" she asked.

"The county sheriff passed on the case to OSP."

"Will there be a conflict?" Ava asked, knowing most law enforcement agencies shouldn't handle investigations of their own people.

"I don't think so. This is different and no one's more qualified to handle it than OSP."

Ava didn't fully agree but held her tongue.

"Except you guys," Mason admitted.

"Do you want to me to request we offer support?"

The phone was silent. "I don't know yet."

She heard him cover his phone and reply to someone in the background. "I need to go," he said. "I'll call you as soon as I know more. I love you," he said fervently.

She echoed the three words, ending the call as she worried about his pain. It took a lot to push Mason to reveal his feelings. No doubt all the men with him were experiencing the same thing. A quad of tough cops, accustomed to being the backbone of whatever situation they walked into, had been stripped bare and left dangling.

She called her boss back while making a mental checklist of resources to support the investigation on the coast. Anger focused her. No one murders a cop without igniting the wrath of every police force in the state.

Assistant Special Agent in Charge Ben Duncan answered his phone. "We're keeping an eye on the murder investigation of an Oregon State Police captain on the coast."

"I heard," said Ava. "Do you want me to go out there?"

"They haven't asked for our help, and I don't think OSP should handle the investigation of one of their own, but it's their call. I'm just giving you a heads-up. Fill up your gas tank. You'll be looking at a two-hour drive. Probably more."

Ava knew she had to speak up. "You know the victim was Mason's boss, right? And that Mason was at the coast with him?"

Duncan swore. "I didn't. He was one of the cops staying with the captain?"

"Yes."

Duncan was silent for a few moments. "Your thoughts? Everyone's plate is completely full—too full—except yours. Zander has some time, but I want two people on this."

"If we get the case."

"Correct."

"I don't think my relationship would be an issue. OSP is sending a major crimes team. The first thing they'll do is clear their own guys. Once Mason's name is clear, there's no conflict of interest."

"We might be jumping the gun. They could find their suspect behind a tree within the hour."

"True. But I need to fill up my gas tank anyway."

3

Too many people crowded Denny's property, and Mason struggled to keep track of them all. He positioned himself next to the sheriff's deputy holding the crime scene log, watching as people signed in and making mental notes of each one's department and task. A young Hispanic male joked with the deputy as he signed. Mason stepped closer to read the log.

"You're the ME?" He couldn't read the name. Something Ruiz.

The man smiled broadly, surprising Mason with very crooked teeth for his young age and medical profession. "Jason Ruiz. You must be Detective Callahan. I just got off the phone with my boss. Dr. Rutledge says to tell you hello and to convey his condolences." He shook Mason's hand.

Dr. Ruiz's smile was infectious, and Mason felt his spirits lift for the first time in two hours. Mason chalked it up to the gossip chain that the state's medical examiner back in Portland knew he was there. News of a fallen officer travels fast. Or possibly Ava was making calls, greasing the investigative wheels to the best of her ability.

"Thank you. I'll thank Seth next time I see him—"

"Which you hope isn't too soon," Dr. Ruiz finished the lame joke for him. Probably all medical examiners had heard it too many times.

"You discovered the body?" Dr. Ruiz asked as they both moved behind the woodshed.

"Yes."

Dr. Ruiz studied Denny Schefte as he pulled on his gloves, his booties already in place. Two crime scene techs backed out of the scene, giving the ME a full view of the body. "Does everything look the same as when you first saw him?" he asked Mason.

Mason took a deep breath and looked closely at the gash in Denny's neck and the position of his limbs. "Yes. He hasn't been moved. The blood is drier now. More flies."

The ME glanced at the crime scene techs hovering behind Mason. "Got your pictures?"

"Yes. I photographed the entire scene from the perimeter to the body and took images of the body in its current position," said one of the young women. "We were waiting for you before collecting any immediate evidence from the body." Dr. Ruiz gestured for her to take more photos as he gently used long tweezers to lift the spiked mask.

Mason forced himself to watch.

"Pinhead, I see," said Dr. Ruiz conversationally. "Not one of my favorites, but not the worst villain out there."

"Watch horror movies?" Mason asked. Under the mask Denny's mouth was slack, his eyes open and slightly fogged. The medical examiner palpated Denny's skull and frowned.

"He's got a blow to the back of the head."

Mason wasn't surprised. He'd assumed the attacker would have had to sneak up on Denny to take advantage of him.

Dr. Ruiz moved to the arms and quickly felt all the limbs. His practiced hands rapidly worked the length of the body. He gestured for Mason to help him roll Denny onto his side so he could visually examine his back.

"I've watched my share of horror movies," said the medical examiner, answering the question Mason had forgotten he'd asked. "I think

every man goes through a phase where he can't get enough. Usually in
the late teens, early twenties, I'd say."

"I skipped that phase. My son didn't. He's still a fan."

Dr. Ruiz picked up one of Denny's hands, looking closely at the
nails and wrists. "No defensive wounds apparent, but there's a lot of
dried blood on them since he grabbed at his neck wound. The blow to
the head must have stunned him, not knocked him out cold. With all
the blood, I can't tell if the nails have any fresh flesh under them. We'll
bag the hands and see what we find. Maybe we'll get lucky and there
will be some DNA under the nails. Right now it's too hard to confirm
if he fought back or tried to defend himself. Later I might find some
bruising under his sleeves if he blocked any blows."

Could he have known his attacker? Nausea crept up Mason's throat.

Dr. Ruiz scanned the small clusters of law enforcement. "Where's
the OSP lead detective?"

Mason pointed at a tall blonde woman in a dark green jacket and
jeans who was speaking with Sheriff Jensen. "Right there. Nora Hawes."
She glanced their way as if hearing her name.

"I haven't met her. Know her?"

"A bit. We work out of the same office, but she's only been there two
weeks. My partner Ray knows her from when he worked in Salem. Can't
say enough good things about her." Mason was reserving judgment until
he'd seen the woman work more cases. Ray wouldn't have said she was
okay unless he meant it, but with Mason everyone started at level zero and
had to prove themselves. An endorsement from Ray meant that Mason
actually smiled during the introduction. Mason was surprised OSP had
assigned a Major Crimes detective out of Portland; the Salem office would
have been closer, but maybe it was stretched too thin.

Dr. Ruiz pulled a long thermometer out of his bag and lifted Denny's
shirt. Mason watched as he made a small cut below Denny's rib cage and
slid in the silver sensor to take the temperature of his liver. "I'll go online
and check what the air temperature was here overnight," the doctor said.

"It was forty-two when I found him two hours ago," said Mason. "When we got home last night just before one A.M., it was forty-six."

The doctor slid out the sensor as he looked sideways at Mason.

"I look at the temperature almost as much as I check the time. I keep it on the front of my phone."

Dr. Ruiz twisted his lips. "I'll get the official weather records, but based on what you just said and his current temperature, he died shortly after you guys got back to the cabin last night."

"Thank you, Doctor," said a female voice behind them. Mason glanced back to see Detective Hawes listening carefully. She held out her hand to shake the medical examiner's. He slipped off his gloves and stood to take it. "We knew the window of time was short since the men returned just before one this morning," she continued. "And Detective Callahan found him at six, but it's good to know at what end of the window it occurred."

"I suspect the gash in the neck will be the cause of death, but don't quote me yet," said Ruiz. "The blow to the head was hard, but I imagine that came before the neck, and clearly he touched his neck while it was bleeding. I didn't find any bullet holes or other major injuries during my quick assessment, but I'll know more once I get him back to the center and get a solid look." He glanced at the ground near Denny's head. "I think he bled out right here. Did you find blood anywhere else?"

"No," said Detective Hawes. "No traces anywhere yet." She turned her direct green gaze on Mason and said nothing.

He felt as if he had a target on his forehead. Defensiveness swelled in his gut and he bit his tongue. He didn't need to prove to her he wasn't involved.

Yet.

"I'd like to debrief you now, Detective," Hawes stated. "How about we chat in my vehicle?"

• • •

In the front seat of her Ford Explorer, Mason blew on the cup of coffee that Detective Hawes had handed him. Someone had made a coffee run into Depoe Bay and managed to return with a big cardboard carafe of surprisingly good coffee and a stack of paper cups. Mason wanted to ask where they'd found it.

Not that he ever planned to return to Depoe Bay. The quaint little fishing town had lost its already thin appeal.

He'd met Detective Hawes the first day she transferred to Portland from Salem's Major Crimes. She'd been partnered with Henry Becker, but their desks were on a different floor since the primary detectives' room couldn't fit another desk. The separate floors had made for a slow get-to-know-you period. He'd been out of the office most of her second week on the job, but so far the feedback from the other guys was good. Everyone had commented that she looked like a young Helen Mirren.

Nora Hawes set her coffee in the cup holder and picked up a notepad. He watched her write his name on the first line and felt a drop of sweat run down his lower back.

Christ.

Self-directed anger swamped him. He wasn't an eighth grader who'd been caught breaking school windows; he was a cop whose close friend had been murdered. Detective Hawes hadn't said a word otherwise. She'd been polite and professional. His mind was circling the drain of guilt simply because he was now on the vulnerable side of the interview. He didn't like his position one bit.

"How long did you work with Denny?" Hawes asked.

"Almost ten years."

"You worked with him before he was promoted?"

"Yes. We even partnered for a short while."

"How was that?"

Mason kept his tone light, when he really ached to glare and snap at her. "Good. I'd want him backing me on a call." Hawes nodded at his statement. There were no stronger words to validate another officer.

"What was your first thought when you found him?"

The memory was fresh. "I wondered if the killer was still there. My next concern was for the guys in the cabin."

"They said you scared them to death when you woke them up by pounding on their doors."

"I didn't know what I'd find inside."

"Was the front door unlocked when you went outside this morning?"

Mason nodded. "It was. Surprised me. A cop will lock his doors even in the middle of nowhere."

"The evidence team hasn't found Denny's cell phone yet," Hawes said.

"We noticed it wasn't on him this morning."

"I have a request in to his cellular carrier for the last activity on his phone. They say this is the last location they have for the whereabouts of the phone."

"Someone took it," Mason stated the obvious. "And removed the battery or turned it off. It's probably at the bottom of the ocean by now."

"I agree. So far someone has covered their tracks. We haven't found anything that indicates how they arrived at the cabin or how they left. There's no soft dirt with tire tracks." Frustration furrowed her forehead for a brief second. "What can you tell me about the argument in the bar last night?"

"The five of us were at a table in Pete's Bar. We'd ordered a couple pitchers of beer but they hadn't come yet. No one had drunk anything at that point," he added, meeting her gaze. "Three guys came in and one of them spotted Denny. He came over to the table and started mouthing off about a dent he claimed Denny had put in his truck on a previous visit. Denny denied that'd he'd done it, but the guy was getting pissed and his friend looked ready to start throwing some punches."

"Could you recognize them?"

Mason closed his eyes, clearly visualizing the three men in their twenties. All wore caps, heavy boots, and thick jackets. Facial scruff. One was a dirty blond and the other two had dark hair. "Absolutely."

"What happened next?"

"Everyone at the table had stood as the argument heated. I stepped between Denny and the main guy and told him I'd buy him and his friends a pitcher of beer if they'd leave us alone for the evening and take it up the next day. They backed off, and I gave the bartender twenty bucks to keep them supplied for a while."

"Pretty lame that a twenty quieted them down."

"I thought so," said Mason. "Made me think he didn't believe it'd been Denny who'd done it but felt the need to spout off about it when he spotted him."

"How often did Denny visit his cabin? Did the locals know him?"

Mason shrugged. "Dunno. In the office it seemed like he went to the coast pretty frequently. The bartender greeted him by name last night. I'd say people who live here know him."

"Did Denny dent his accuser's truck?" Her straightforward manner had relaxed him a bit.

She's looking for answers. Doing her job. It was an attitude he understood.

"He told us he hadn't. He'd parked next to the guy's truck when he was in town last month. That day the guy had blown up when he spotted the dent and immediately turned on Denny. Denny told him then that he hadn't done it but could tell the guy didn't believe him."

"Were the three men drunk last night?"

"I could smell beer on the one I spoke to, but I wouldn't call them drunk. They'd had enough to be cocky assholes."

"Sometimes reaching that level doesn't take much," Hawes agreed. She wrote on her notepad and the vehicle grew silent.

"When did you last see Denny?"

"It was about one thirty in the morning when I got to my room. Denny and I had sat in the kitchen alone and talked while the other guys went straight to bed."

Hawes nodded. Mason knew she'd already interviewed some of the men and would be looking for consistency across all the detectives' stories. "I told the other guys we'd just talked about fishing and the cabin. That wasn't true."

She lifted an eyebrow as she waited for him to continue, her pen hovering over her notepad.

"He wanted to ask me about my ex-wife."

Her lips twitched and the eyebrow rose higher.

"His ex-wife had approached him about giving their relationship another try. Both Denny and I are divorced, and he wanted to know what I would have done if my ex had said the same to me." A flush warmed his face. "I'm with someone else now, but I would have considered it if Robin had asked to get back together years ago. She was the one who struggled with being married to a cop and had to break loose—not me. Denny's been divorced as long as I'd known him, and I've never known his ex, Cindy. I wasn't in a place to tell him what to do."

"It depends on the two of them," Nora added. "Every relationship is unique because the people are unique."

Mason agreed. "He turned her down, but I think he was having second thoughts and worried he'd answered without thinking it through. He's had some other relationships, but they didn't last. He wanted to know—" He stopped speaking, suddenly embarrassed.

"Know what?" Hawes asked when Mason didn't continue.

"He wanted to know how Ava and I were making it work. He seemed to think we'd found some secret." He gave a half shrug. "I told him we talk about everything and always keep the communication open." He shifted in his seat. He'd gone from feeling like a target to talking about his most personal relationship. He didn't talk to strangers about this sort of stuff. Hell, Ray was his closest friend and he only got to see the surface.

Ava had opened Mason's eyes. He'd believed he had a solid if slightly boring life, and he was good with that. But during a kidnapping case, she'd been immersed in his life and job. She'd infused oxygen into his simple existence. Once their case was over, he'd discovered he didn't want to go back to his life without her.

They'd had their ups and downs over the past year, but they were definitely in an up part of the cycle at the moment. Wedding plans were being discussed, her twin Jayne was in a good facility, and their damned kitchen remodel had finished only five weeks over schedule.

"Well, Detective Callahan, you've managed to surprise me. I didn't realize men had late-night heart-to-heart talks about relationships." She grinned.

"I thought you knew Ray Lusco."

Her eyes lit up. "You've got me there. Ray is definitely different. His wife is a good friend."

Mason had noticed she didn't wear a wedding ring. A lot of married cops didn't. They didn't want the scum they encountered to have any insight about their personal lives. He didn't ask if she was married; it was none of his business.

"You lied to the other guys because you didn't want to share what Denny had told you in confidence."

"I omitted one of our topics. We did discuss fish and his cabin."

"Did you know much about his ex?"

"No. I've heard about Cindy a bit here and there. Denny didn't bitch about her the way some guys do about their exes." He paused, realizing how little he knew of Cindy's temperament. Was she capable of murder? "He didn't tell me how she reacted when he refused to give their relationship another shot. Has someone contacted her?"

"Not yet. I'll go notify her in person." She made a note on her pad. "Do you know of any bad blood between Denny and his coworkers? I haven't been there long enough to hear any gossip."

Do you think any of the men from the cabin could have done this?

Mason had already picked apart this question. He'd done it first thing after finding Denny and again as Dr. Ruiz did his quick exam. "Between the four of us that are here, no. Absolutely not."

"And back at the office?"

"He's pissed off a few people over the years. Who wouldn't in his position? Enough for one of them to drive to the coast and slit his throat? No."

"Not that you're aware of."

"Not that I'm aware of," Mason agreed. Everyone hid their true feelings. Especially cops. "I could be completely in the dark about a situation."

"Does the Pinhead mask mean anything to you? Was Denny a fan? Had you previously seen the mask in the cabin?"

"I'm stumped about the mask," answered Mason. "If Denny was a horror fan, I didn't know about it. And I definitely didn't see anything like that in the cabin." He strongly suspected the killer had brought it with him.

"Who knew the five of you were coming up here? Did anyone back at the office know? I knew because Denny had asked me to cover some of the schedule."

"Everyone knew. Getting the schedule arranged was a bitch."

She made a notation and then met his gaze, giving a small smile that signaled the end of the interview. "Thank you, Detective. Even though the circumstances suck, it was nice to talk to you more in depth than we have back at the office. And I'll say the standard line about letting me know if anything else occurs to you."

"You couldn't stop me."

Her phone rang and she glanced at it. Mason couldn't help himself and noticed DUNCAN FBI pop up on the screen.

Ava's ASAC Ben Duncan?

Mason decided to stay in the vehicle a few more minutes.

4

Ava tapped her foot in the elevator. She'd arrived at the Portland FBI office near the airport with a full tank of gas and three texts from ASAC Duncan stating he needed to see her in his office the minute she arrived. Her instinct told her the FBI had finally been brought into the murder at the coast, but what could have changed within an hour?

She stepped off the elevator and dashed down the hall to Ben's office, not even stopping at her desk. His door was open. Inside, Special Agent Zander Wells and a female agent she faintly recognized were looking over Ben's shoulder at his computer screen. They straightened as she entered and she felt as if she'd stepped into a cloud of tension.

"What happened? Is it Mason?" she blurted.

"No, no!" Zander held up his hands. "Nothing like that. Relax."

Ben and the other agent echoed Zander's words. She took a deep breath and forced a smile. "There's enough tension in here to make even my sister wonder what's wrong." The joke was weak, and sympathy flashed in Zander's gaze. He knew Jayne's narcissistic personality.

"Do you know Special Agent Mercy Kilpatrick?" Ben Duncan asked. "She's from Domestic Terrorism."

Ava shook the agent's hand, realizing she'd seen her briefly in the hallways. "What's happened?" she repeated. Introductions were nice, but she needed to know why Ben had texted her three times.

"Ben was giving me a heads-up on the OSP captain's death at the coast when a little more information came in." Zander exchanged a look with Ben. "The victim was found with a Pinhead mask over his face."

Ava nodded, processing the odd detail. Images of a pale movie character with pins arranged in a grid across his face floated through her mind. "That's a new one."

"When I heard that I immediately thought of Vance Weldon," continued Zander.

"Our agent who committed suicide last week?" Ava asked. "I didn't know him. I only knew the name."

Zander looked grim. "He was found hanging in his garage wearing a Freddy Krueger mask. I already had Ben reach out to the OSP detective at the coast scene and let them know we might have a related case."

Ava stared at him for a long moment before looking to Ben and Mercy. She'd known the office had been shaken up about the man's suicide, but she hadn't heard details. A horror mask seemed like a detail that would have rocketed up the gossip chain. A dozen questions shot through her brain.

"You're familiar with Freddy Krueger?" Ben asked.

"From *A Nightmare on Elm Street*. He kills kids in their dreams." She paused. "But Vance was a suicide, right?" she slowly asked.

The three agents exchanged a grim look. "We're taking another look," said Ben.

Ava looked at Agent Kilpatrick. "I assume you know more about Vance's . . . suicide?"

"Correct," the domestic terrorism agent stated. "Special Agent Weldon was found hanging from the rafters of his garage last Monday by his wife," she said in an even voice. "The Vancouver Police Department got the call, and they handled the investigation, but I was assigned by our agency to work with the police and oversee our interests."

Ava nodded. She'd heard Vance Weldon worked in Domestic Terrorism. Besides the usual concerns for the agent's family's needs, this sort of incident would require interaction from the agency to rule out any foul play that might have been related to his job, and to make certain any sensitive intelligence was properly secured.

"What did you conclude?" Ava asked. She took a closer look at Mercy Kilpatrick. She had the long dark curls of a Kardashian but the intense presence of a highly experienced agent. Intelligence radiated from her gaze, and Ava wanted to know her better.

Mercy furrowed her brow. "I never saw or read anything in the reports to make me doubt it was a suicide. Even his wife said he'd been struggling with depression."

"Kids?"

"None."

"What about the horror mask? Surely that stood out in the case as something that shouldn't have been there."

Mercy shook her head. "Special Agent Weldon was a collector. He had a fascination with horror movies, especially Freddy Krueger. He actually had a little side business going where he sold Freddy Krueger gloves online."

"Gloves? Like the glove he wears in the movies with all the blades?" Ava asked. It was the character's primary weapon.

"Yes. His wife showed them to me. He makes them and they look straight from a movie set. Not sharp, though," she added quickly. "His wife couldn't say for certain that the mask was his, but she said it would be the type of thing he owned. He had a lot of horror movie memorabilia."

"Is there a Pinhead mask missing?" Ava asked.

"We're trying to find out," Ben said. "I've left a message for the wife to call me back."

"There's no way the captain's death at the coast could be a suicide," said Zander. "His neck was deeply slashed and there's no knife left behind. I've heard of people cutting their own necks, but hiding the weapon in time? Can't happen. And the only blood found was right with the body."

Ava nodded. Hiding the knife after cutting one's own neck would leave a large blood trail. From what she was hearing, everything indicated murder for the captain. "But two horror character masks on two dead law enforcement officers within a week is too big to ignore," she said flatly. "We need to be involved and take a closer look at our agent's death. If it wasn't suicide, it could be related to one of his terrorism cases."

"Agreed," said Ben. "I'm assigning it to you and Zander, but I want you to head to the coast death scene first because it's fresh. Do what you need to there, and then start looking into the Weldon case. Agent Kilpatrick will get you everything you need." He held up a hand as Ava opened her mouth. "I'm operating on the assumption Mason will soon be officially cleared of any involvement in his boss's death. If I recall, the two of you were in San Francisco at the beginning of last week, correct?"

Ava nodded.

"Then he wasn't involved in our agent's death. Right now that's good enough for me."

His logic was a bit weak, but Ava knew he didn't have anyone else to assign. She wasn't about to argue with him; she wanted the case.

She looked at Zander. "Ready for a trip to the coast?"

• • •

"Special Agent Vance Weldon was discovered hanging in his garage at six thirty A.M. by his wife last Monday morning," Zander summarized from the file on his lap. He'd been making calls and reading case details to Ava as she drove toward the ocean. "A stool in the garage had been kicked over and his hands weren't bound. His wife Sharon briefly tried to get him down, but realized he'd been dead for several hours and called 911."

"That's horrible," Ava murmured, envisioning herself trying to wrestle Mason down from the rafters and then realizing he was cold with death. "First on the scene was patrol from Vancouver?"

"Yes," said Zander. "This report says she begged them to cut him down, and the first two cops at the scene did it."

"Destroying evidence."

"Being human," countered Zander. "I'm not sure what determines if they have to try to resuscitate. I imagine it's hard to come across a hanging and make yourself leave the body up there, wondering if getting him down could have saved him."

Ava reluctantly agreed. It was easy to say from the comfort of a distance what the officers should have done; it was a completely different experience to be standing in their shoes next to a hysterical wife.

"What else does it say about the scene?"

"He was dressed in jeans and a T-shirt. His wife said it'd been the clothing he'd worn the day before."

"So he never made it to bed. She didn't notice until the next morning?"

"His wife said it wasn't unusual for her to go to bed before him." He studied his laptop screen. "The rope was turned in as evidence, but since it was ruled a suicide no testing was done. The wife couldn't say if the rope came from their house or not."

"Who did the autopsy?"

"Seth Rutledge."

"As the head medical examiner in the state, he runs a tight ship. I have a hard time believing he got one wrong," Ava said.

"We don't know he did," said Zander pointedly.

Ava pressed her lips together as she kept her focus on the highway. Zander was right. She was making assumptions. *Horror masks. Law enforcement.* How could one be suicide and one be murder?

Do they both have to be one or the other?

"It's bugging me, too," Zander said. She shot him a smile.

Zander Wells had developed into a good friend. Formerly with Cybercrimes, he'd managed to extend his temporary loan to the Violent Crimes Unit into a long stay. He'd told Ava that as much as he liked tapping on his keyboard all day, he liked the diversity of Violent Crimes better. Mason claimed the agent had wanted more than friendship from Ava, but she didn't quite believe him. Zander had never spoken of his feelings to her, but she'd always felt a vibe of admiration from him. She liked to believe it was a result of her work ethic. Not romantic interest.

Oddly, her close work relationship with Zander didn't bother Mason. If anyone was to be the jealous type, her slightly redneck, old-fashioned-values cowboy fiancé would be the man. But he liked Zander and wasn't threatened by his presence. Ava had eyes for no one but Mason.

I should set Zander up with Cheryl. Her neighbor was also her wedding planner. She could see the two of them as a good match.

Hmmmm.

"We could be on a wild goose chase," said Ava, putting matchmaking out of her head. "The masks could be pure coincidence. You ran a VICAP search with horror masks as one of the criteria?"

"I ran several using a blend of different key words. I didn't find any other crimes with horror masks and law enforcement in common."

"What about without the law enforcement terms?"

"Some oddball things turn up, but nothing that feels right."

"What's Weldon's history with depression? Has he tried to commit suicide before?" Ava asked.

"He has a few years of counseling and medication. His wife thought it was well under control. She says he had a pill swallowing incident in his late teens when he was away at college."

"He did?" Ava asked sharply, surprised he'd made it through the FBI's rigorous testing and background checks.

"She says he never told anyone, didn't go to the hospital, and the police weren't notified, so there's no record."

"It's just her word."

"His mother verified his wife's story. She knew about the pills and says her son admitted it to her about a year after it happened. He'd appeared to have turned his life and mental state around, so she chalked it up to a bad month."

"A bad month," Ava repeated, the words souring in her mouth. If only the rest of the world had her experience of living with someone with serious mental illness. She understood her twin was an extreme case, but it helped her see people living with lesser conditions in an understanding light.

"I know," said Zander. "But we don't know how Weldon behaved when he lived with her. From the outside he could have appeared symptom-free and never let her know what was going on. They might have had very normal lives."

She felt him studying her and stared straight over her steering wheel.

"How's Jayne?" he asked.

"She's good."

"How's she *really* doing?"

She glanced over at him. Nothing but concern showed on his face. She forced her apprehension at her sister's name to fade away. "I get an email from her once a week and I always write back."

"As you should."

"She's watched very closely. We were lucky to get her into such a good facility. I communicate regularly with her treatment coordinator, and she's optimistic for Jayne's health. Jayne even found a shop that was willing to show some of her paintings."

"Her watercolors? She had enough to show?"

Ava was pleased that Zander remembered Jayne's passion. They'd had a lot of discussions about her twin. "She made some new ones recently. I was impressed enough to buy one and another shopper bought one while I was there."

"Her art doesn't suck," stated Zander.

Ava grinned. "No, not at all."

"What's her doctors' plan for her future?"

She was silent for a long moment. "To slowly move her into independence. Keep her on medication and therapy schedules." It was nothing new to Ava. She'd dealt with the same plan for her twin a dozen times. Would it work this time?

"And your plan for you?" he asked softly.

"Keep my distance. Keep my eyes on my own life."

"Her suicide attempt nearly destroyed you."

Ava said nothing. Zander had witnessed part of her emotional collapse from the strain of Jayne's death wish. "Can we not talk about it right now?" she whispered.

"I'm sorry. It's none of my business. I just worry—" He stopped. She glanced at him, but his focus was directed out his window.

"I appreciate your concern. I really do," Ava said. "It's still very fresh." She felt horrible for shutting down the conversation, but her twin was difficult territory, and she knew Zander understood. He had his own demons he didn't like to talk about. She knew he'd been married and his wife had passed, but he'd never opened up about it.

Unlike her, who'd spilled her life history when he'd asked.

Maybe she needed to ask him questions about his wife. Her nature was to not pry into what someone didn't easily share, but it'd always felt right when Zander asked about Jayne. He never gave lip service.

"I'm glad you came back to work. I'd wondered if you would," Zander said.

Her heart warmed. "I wondered, too. It feels good to be back. It was the right decision for me."

"Turn left at that next road," he directed. Ava turned off the winding coastal highway. They'd been following the road for several miles, getting occasional gray glimpses of the ocean. The Oregon Coast was stunning on a sunny day, and even on the gray days it had a wild beauty, but Ava found it depressing after the warmth and energy of the Southern California coasts. The water was icy no matter the time of year.

"I hoped to see the bay," said Zander. "It's farther down the highway."

"We can drive down there when we're done."

She followed his directions for another ten minutes, heading east and away from the water. They went around a curve and Zander swore under his breath. News channel satellite trucks lined the road on both sides. Ava scowled at the intruders, wondering how Mason was handling the publicity. He hated press. Especially when it hit close to home.

A sheriff's deputy stepped into the road and held up his hand. Ava slowed to a stop.

"Our turn," said Zander.

5

Mason's heart jumped as Ava stepped out of her vehicle.

Every damn time. All he had to do was see her and his day brightened. She immediately spotted him in the crowd and smiled. Her familiar dark ponytail and warm smile made everything better. He suddenly needed to hear her speak, hear her low voice that always set his stomach aflutter.

Fluttering in a masculine way.

He was pleased to see Zander Wells climb out of the passenger's side. The agent's sharp brain never stopped processing, and he brought invaluable deductive skills that Mason wanted for this case.

Denny's body had just been taken away. Because of his position and the odd circumstances surrounding his death, he was being transported directly to the primary medical examiner's office in Portland instead of one of the closer morgues. Mason knew Ava and Zander would have preferred to see Denny still in the crime scene for their investigation, but they'd have to settle for photos. He was relieved the FBI had been brought in to assist on the case because it had resources that OSP and the county sheriff could only wish for.

He wanted the best for Denny.

And the worst for his killer.

"That must be the FBI," Nora said.

"It is. We're—I mean you are—lucky to have them," Mason pointed out.

"I agree," she stated.

"I'm surprised they sent Ava," added Ray. "You'd think—"

"Detective Lusco," Nora said sharply. "Don't tell me you have a problem with them sending a female agent."

Mason bit the inside of his cheek as Ray stuttered to explain. Before his partner could form a coherent answer, Ava and Zander reached them. Ava didn't stop but walked straight into Mason's arms, ignoring their standing rule of avoiding public displays of affection while on the job.

"Oh," Nora said in a surprised voice. "Sorry, Ray. Now I understand your reaction."

Mason wrapped his arms around Ava's shoulders and buried his face in her hair, feeling the stress of the last eight hours abruptly exhaust him. He wanted to find a quiet corner and simply hold her. Maybe that would make Denny's death exit his brain instead of constantly circling like a bird of prey, never slowing down. It was always present, always demanding his attention, never letting him relax.

"I'm so sorry, Mason," Ava whispered. "Are you okay?"

"I am now," he said gruffly, aware of several sets of eyes watching them. They could all go to hell. He needed a minute with her and he was going to take it. He heard Zander introduce himself to Nora Hawes.

Ava pulled back and looked him in the eyes, studying him closely. He must have appeared in control because she turned to Nora, holding out a hand.

"You're the OSP detective for this case? I'm Special Agent Ava McLane. I'm engaged to Mason, but my boss doesn't have a problem with me on this case. Do you?"

Detective Hawes automatically took Ava's hand, sizing her up. "It doesn't seem right to have an investigator intimately involved with a witness."

Mason held his tongue. The ball was in Ava's court, and she didn't need any help from him.

"You've been briefed on what we'd believed was Special Agent Weldon's suicide?" Ava asked.

"I have." Nora said, tipping her head toward Mason and Ray. "Everyone here has been."

They'd all been stunned by the connections involving the masks and law enforcement. Everyone felt that the probability that the two cases were unrelated was minuscule.

"Think of our role as more of observers looking over everyone's shoulders," Ava said seriously. "Special Agent Wells will be the FBI primary. We want to know if our agent was murdered, just as you want to find Denny Schefte's killer. We're here to make certain every rock is looked under twice."

Nora held her gaze. Ray and Zander both looked away from the tension between the two women.

"I'm sure that will be fine," agreed Nora. She gave a sincere smile. "I like your frankness, Special Agent McLane."

Ava nodded. Zander and Ray looked relieved, and Mason felt the air clear.

"The feeling is mutual, Detective Hawes." Ava glanced at the men. "Glad to know there was a calm head present this morning."

"You're telling me," said Nora. "I thought this group was about to go cowboy and start combing the woods for a killer when I got here."

"It's a beautiful location. Rugged, too," said Ava. She did a slow scan of the area, but Mason knew she wasn't admiring the scenery. She was getting a feel for the location.

Mason followed her gaze, trying to look at the area through fresh eyes. When he'd first arrived a few days ago, he'd appreciated the beauty. The deep red of the cabin against the dark firs. The mist at the tops of the trees in the early mornings. Tiny lavender petals among the tall grasses. After Denny's death, all he saw was a crime scene.

The property was tainted.

The crime scene techs moved in and out of the cabin. They'd already removed the evidence from behind the woodshed and enlisted all the responding officers for a grid search of the immediate wooded area, which hadn't turned up a speck of evidence. No footprints, no gum wrappers, no dropped trash.

How did the killer get Denny to leave the house?

Who did it?

A flash of dark yellow darted between the firs, and Mason spotted a shoulder and the back of a head rapidly moving away.

"Someone's running through the woods." He took off after the figure without waiting to see who'd follow, thankful he'd put on tennis shoes that morning instead of his usual cowboy boots.

Behind him he heard Detective Hawes shouting instructions to fan out through the woods and cut off the suspect. He ignored her. No one was between him and the runner, and he wasn't going to pause to listen to directions.

His heart pounded in his chest, his adrenaline spiking. He dashed between the trees and underbrush, pushing through limbs and leaves, painfully aware he wasn't armed. The figure vanished and he pressed forward, pumping his legs harder. Twice he tripped on the uneven ground but managed to stay upright.

A cracking sound came from ahead to his left and he changed course. He saw low branches move and he pushed harder. The shouts of officers behind him grew fainter and the figure came into view. It was a blond man in a dark-yellow sweatshirt.

"Oregon State Police! Stop!"

The man didn't stop, but Mason had gained ground. He estimated less than twenty yards between him and the suspect.

The blond man's arms flailed for a split second and he dropped out of sight. Mason heard him shout in pain.

Seconds later Mason stood over a man writhing in the dirt, clutching at his right arm. He'd fallen into a wide shallow ditch.

"On your stomach, arms out to your sides!"

"I fucking can't! I think it's broken!"

Mason stepped down into the ditch, rolled him to his stomach, put a knee on his back, and yanked his arms out to the sides as the man shrieked.

He didn't have cuffs or a gun, but the pain distracted the suspect from noticing. Mason knew he had a dozen officers with cuffs not far behind him. He pulled the man's left arm behind his back and awkwardly searched him for weapons with his other hand.

Footsteps crashed through the woods. "Over here!" Mason shouted. "He's down! Over here!"

A Lincoln County deputy burst through the brush. "I need your cuffs," Mason said. "Help me check him for weapons. He thinks he broke his arm."

"You take him down?" The deputy jumped into the ditch and handed Mason his cuffs. He ran his hands over the man's legs.

"Nah, he tripped."

"Uh-huh."

"Really. That's what happened. Hey, you tripped, right?" He poked the man in the back.

"Fuck you. *Watch the arm!*" he shrieked as Mason pulled on his right arm to cuff him.

"Here's another set." The deputy handed him a second pair to link to the first to give the man's arms more room. Three other officers, including Nora Hawes and Ray, stumbled into the area.

"Nice job, Callahan!" Ray slapped him on the back. Mason stood, breathing heavily as he looked around for Ava. The adrenaline felt like fire in his veins and he wanted to tear down the trees to find her. She showed up a second later and he relaxed.

"What were you doing in the woods?" he directed to the man on the ground.

"Not illegal to be in the woods," he snapped in reply. "You can't arrest me."

"Then why were you running?"

"Because you ran after me!"

Mason stepped to the side and knelt to get a good look at his face.

It was one of the guys from the bar incident.

"Did you enjoy the pitcher of beer I bought you?" Mason asked.

• • •

Ava listened to the suspect whine as he stood next to a deputy's vehicle while Nora made arrangements to have two deputies take him to the hospital. A wallet in his pocket had revealed the man's name was Tim Jessop and he lived in Depoe Bay. Mason's three detective friends stood nearby, arms crossed on their chests as they watched every movement the suspect made.

"I know this guy," muttered one of the local deputies. "I've arrested him and his buddies a half-dozen times for being stupid."

Ava grinned. She could easily imagine the types of things Jessop and his friends had done to draw the disdain of the police. Most probably involved alcohol. According to Mason, if he hadn't calmed down the group with a pitcher of beer last night, the idiot would probably be sitting in a jail cell still cooling off.

Maybe if they'd called the police Denny wouldn't be dead.

She shook her head, hoping Mason's brain hadn't followed the same train of logic. They had no evidence the men had anything to do with Denny's death. Yet.

The deputy knew the names of several of Jessop's friends. He pulled up their driver's license photos on his computer and the four OSP detectives immediately spotted the man who'd butted heads with Denny in the bar. Sam Gates.

"Sam didn't do nothin'," Jessop blurted. "Why are you lookin' for him?"

Nora stepped closer to the man. "How's the arm feeling?"

Jessop leaned away from her. "It's fucking broken. I'm gonna sue."

She looked over her shoulder at the four waiting OSP detectives, Ava, Zander, and the deputies. "What'd you say? The patrol car has engine trouble? But this man needs to get to the hospital."

Ava decided she needed to get to know Nora Hawes better.

"My car's outta gas," Detective Hunsinger said. "I can't help."

"Me, too," chimed three other voices.

"Screw all of you," said Jessop. "I want a lawyer." His voice was thin with pain.

And fear.

"We're trying to get you to the hospital," said Nora. "No one's under arrest. We just want to know what you did after you left Pete's Bar last night."

Jessop's gaze flicked to Mason. "Went home."

"You seem to recognize Detective Callahan. You do realize all five of the men your friend Sam harassed in the bar last night are detectives with the Oregon State Police?" Nora said sweetly.

"Sam didn't do nothin'. The one guy dented his truck. Sam wanted him to pay for it." His gaze bounced between the men. "I don't see that guy."

Ava stiffened. Jessop appeared unaware that Denny Schefte was dead. There was no guile on his angry face. The detectives shifted their feet as the same observation hit them.

"What did Sam do after you left Pete's Bar?" asked Nora.

"Ask him. I dropped him off at his house."

"What time?"

Jessop screwed up his face in thought. "Dunno. It was after last call. We shut the place down."

"Why were you in the woods?" Nora asked in a kinder voice.

He shrugged and looked away. "Just seein' what was goin' on. Everyone said cops were crawling all over this area. I don't live too far from here."

Ava glanced at one of the deputies, who looked at Jessop's license in his hand and nodded.

"You gonna get me to the hospital now?" Jessop pleaded.

"How's the engine coming?" Nora asked without looking back at the deputy.

"Better," he said. "Almost fixed."

Jessop wilted against the patrol car. "Why are you doin' this? We didn't touch no one. Last night," he added hastily.

"Have you talked today to any of your friends who were there last night?" Nora asked.

"Well, yeah. Sam and Josh were at the diner this morning. That's where we heard about the cops. They're probably still there. I said I'd go take a look since I lived close and knew a shortcut through the woods to this place."

"Did they seem nervous when they heard about the cops?" Ava asked.

Jessop looked her way. "Nah. Just wanted to know who'd gotten in trouble." His eyes struggled to focus on her and his face brightened as they finally did. "Hey. You from around here?"

Ava lifted a brow and said nothing. Next to her, Mason made an odd noise in the back of his throat. Ray coughed. Nora turned around and made eye contact, her green gaze dancing with mirth.

Can you believe what we put up with?

Ava had heard of guys asking out the female patrol officers who'd just arrested them, but this was a first for her.

"No, Special Agent McLane isn't from around here," said Zander in a steel voice. "We're from the Portland FBI office, and I *strongly* suggest you take this incident more seriously."

She'd never heard Zander use that tone, and struggled to keep a straight face.

"Yes, sir." Jessop straightened against the car.

Nora gestured for the officers to take him to the hospital. She pointed at two other deputies. "You know this Sam Gates?" They nodded. "Go see if he's at the diner. Politely ask him to sit in the back of your car." The two deputies immediately left.

"That shouldn't take more than five minutes," said Nora. "Either he's there or he's not."

"If Jessop knew Denny was murdered, he hid it really well," said Ava.

The other detectives gave a chorus of agreement. "I thought the same thing," said Nora. "And he doesn't strike me as the type of guy who can lie effectively." She shook her head slowly. "I don't think Denny would have stepped out of his cabin to meet with any of that group on his own."

"Maybe he went outside for a phone call," suggested Ava. She looked at the OSP detectives. "Would it have been disruptive to the rest of the cabin if he was on the phone in his room?"

The men exchanged glances. "I don't think it would have been disruptive, but I was in the bedroom directly above his. He probably thought I would hear," said Duff Morales. "I know I step outside sometimes when I just want some additional privacy."

"It's the most logical reason for no evidence of a struggle," added Ava. "It appears he willingly stepped out of the cabin, and I don't think it was in response to someone inviting him outside. Who does that at one in the morning? No cop I know."

"But it feels targeted," said Mason. "If he wasn't summoned outside, then it was a crime of chance. I can't believe that just yet."

"It's too early to draw any conclusions," Ava said. Her mind sped with questions.

Did someone draw Denny out?

Was he specifically targeted? Or would the killer have settled for Mason?

She fought to control the shiver that rocked through her body. Her morning phone call from her boss could have been much uglier.

Nora nodded at Zander and Ava. "If Sam Gates is at the diner, I want you two to talk to him with me, but the rest of you are witnesses and have no reason to be there."

A mix of grumbles came from the four OSP detectives.

Ava felt bad for the four men whose friend had been murdered, but Nora was right. She exchanged a look with Zander. Technically the FBI was part of the investigation at the request of OSP. Under the circumstances, he could take over completely. But she suspected he preferred to sit back and watch. So far Nora hadn't done anything they disagreed with.

"I'd like Detective Callahan to come along," said Zander. "He was in the bar and the first to find the body. I'd like to hear his opinion of what Sam Gates has to say."

Zander missed his calling as a diplomat. He'd made a polite request and hadn't been an ass about it. He'd left the option in Nora's hands to agree or disagree.

"Fine with me," Nora said. "You three can follow me to the diner."

6

Mason was happy to see Sam Gates glumly sitting in the back of the Lincoln County deputies' car. His dark head hung low, but as their group approached, he turned his face to the window and anger shot from his gaze.

"Any problems getting him to cooperate?" Zander asked the deputies.

"Not at all," said one. "We spotted him through the diner window as he was drinking his coffee. He barely looked at us when we went in. We walked over to his table and said we wanted to talk to him about a bar fight last night."

"He gave us some shit," said the other. "But he stepped outside. Seemed confident that he hadn't been involved in any fight."

"Know anything about him?" Zander asked.

Mason bit his lip as he stopped himself from simultaneously asking the same question. Taking a backseat wasn't his usual role, but he would stay quiet so he wasn't asked to leave. His presence had no purpose to the investigation.

But he was going to stick around as long as he could.

It was for Denny.

He thought back to his final conversation with his boss last night. It'd been uncomfortable. He'd never heard Denny ask for relationship advice, and relationships weren't something they talked about at work. He was a bit surprised Denny had approached him instead of Ray. Ray was the one who easily discussed feelings and therapy and flowers. Froufrou crap.

But Ray had never been divorced.

Maybe talking about froufrou crap makes a marriage last longer.

Mason had tried to joke with Denny at first, cracking a few ex-wife jokes, but Denny had stayed serious, so Mason listened carefully. The man was having a crisis of the heart, and Mason had been with Ava long enough to learn that everyone needs to talk at some point in their life. It doesn't kill a man to listen.

It was the first time he'd seen raw doubt in Denny's eyes when he asked Mason if he'd done the right thing by turning down his ex-wife's offer of reconciliation. It'd unnerved him. Why had he turned to Mason for advice?

"Geez, Denny," he'd said. "How long have you been divorced?"

"Nearly fifteen years. She married again, but he died two years ago."

"And she approached you? Have you guys been staying in touch that much?"

"We have two sons and three grandkids. We've always had some contact. She still lives in Portland."

Mason was silent for a moment. "What do you want to do?" He didn't know what else to say.

"I don't fucking know. I told her it wasn't a good idea, but now I'm having second thoughts." His eyes pleaded with Mason to give him an answer.

"Well," Mason said, trying to channel his inner Dr. Phil. "You haven't lived together in fifteen years. I doubt she's the same person she was fifteen years ago. I mean, are you the same?"

"Hell no."

"Then you can't just get back together." A burst of inspiration hit him. "You're gonna have to date her."

"Date my ex-wife?" Denny looked confused.

"Yeah. Get to know each other again. See if you're compatible now. Having kids and grandkids in common might not be enough. Take her out to dinner and go to a movie or Blazer game. You know . . . talk."

Denny stared at him for a few seconds. "Is that what you did with Ava?"

"Sort of. We worked together. It forced us to talk to each other and spend time in each other's company. When our case was over, I didn't want our time together to stop," he said gruffly, wondering if he'd shared too much information.

I'm way out of my comfort zone.

"Dating," Denny said as he rubbed at his chin, lost in thought. "I've dated quite a few women over the last decade. Never found one where I wanted our time to never stop. I was always finished at some point. You haven't hit that point yet?"

"Not going to happen," stated Mason. "We're in it for the long haul."

"Everyone says that at first."

"Yeah, but I *know*. I've got enough years under this belt to know it's true. I only say it when I mean it. I'm not swayed by mushy stuff."

Ava touched Mason's hand and startled him out of his musings.

"Hey," she said. "Where were you?" Her dark-blue eyes studied him, and he suddenly understood how she'd felt every time he'd analyzed her, looking for signs of stress over her sister. It was like a spotlight on his face. But a light that was aimed with concern and love.

"Thinking about last night. Denny and I had a long talk."

"A good one?" she asked.

"It was." His smile was genuine. "I realized how lucky I was to find you. Denny gave me a glimpse into what my life might have continued to be."

"All work and no play?"

"Exactly. And lots of doubts and what-ifs and concern for my future."

"What do you mean what-ifs?" Her brow furrowed.

He swallowed but plunged forward. They'd pledged not to keep secrets unless it was truly for the good of the other person. "I used to wonder how it would be if Robin and I got back together."

"Ah. I understand. That would be a normal train of thought. You have a son together and you've told me you liked being married."

Mason held her gaze. "Do you know how incredible you are? I just told you I'd thought about getting back together with my ex-wife and you didn't blink an eyelash."

"But that was before you met me. I don't care what you did or thought about before then. I only care about after." She paused. "Do you still think about what life with her would be now?"

His ex-wife had been remarried for several years. Mason had struggled when she first told him the news, but he'd seen it was a good situation for her and his son Jake. "Never," he stated. "That's the honest truth. Denny made me look at it for the first time last night, and it was hard for my brain to go there. I like where I'm at now."

She smiled. "Me, too."

He wanted to touch her but held back. They'd already broken their rule once that day and he wasn't about to do it with a suspect ten feet away. But he felt the invisible ribbons of affection that bound them together. Sometimes he wondered how other people couldn't see it.

"Dial it down, guys," Zander muttered.

Maybe they did.

• • •

From his expressions Ava could tell that Sam Gates was a professional at giving attitude. Right now "surly" and "defensive" were accurate descriptions of his mood. The deputies were very familiar with Sam Gates. They'd told the detectives that Sam was known for his temper and fists but not for any crimes involving a weapon.

"His mouth is his primary weapon," said one deputy. He'd glanced at Nora and Ava apologetically. "Just saying. Wanted you to be prepared."

Ava was amused. The deputy looked like a clean-cut kid straight from a farm and no doubt had been raised with good manners. "We're fine," she'd assured him.

Zander opened the back door to the patrol car and grabbed Sam's arm, forcibly hauling him out and to his feet.

So that's the role Zander's taking.

Ava hadn't seen Zander play the hard-ass very much. Nora started to step forward and then moved back, letting Zander take the lead, a look of understanding on her face.

He held Sam against the car and frisked him again, getting his face close to Sam's while not saying a word, his hands rough and fast as they sped through Sam's pockets and felt his limbs. Sam swallowed hard but was silent through the exam. He glanced at the two deputies, who'd taken up a position several feet away, clearly yielding the situation to the people Sam didn't know.

Zander finished and stood eighteen inches from Sam with his arms across his chest. Zander was tall and built like a long-distance runner. The attitude of barely restrained anger he'd adopted was having the expected effect of making Sam nervous as hell. Usually Zander had a calm manner that was comforting to witnesses.

"Where were you last night between nine P.M. and two A.M.?" Zander asked.

Ava could barely hear him, his voice was so low and rough.

Again Sam looked to the deputies, who'd intentionally turned away, and then glanced at Mason, Ava, and Nora. Ava met his gaze. *No friends to help you here.* He looked down at his feet.

"Pete's Bar," he muttered. "Why?"

"What time did you leave?"

Sam tried to look Zander in the eye but could do it for only two seconds. "Dunno. After last call. Tim drove me home."

Zander turned to the deputies. "Can you two find out when Pete's Bar closed last night? And who was tending bar?" The deputies gave him a casual salute and headed toward the bar two blocks down the street.

Zander turned his icy gaze back to Sam. "Want to guess at the time?"

Sam looked up at the gray sky, twisting his mouth in thought. "One-thirty? Two?"

"Remember any problems in the bar last night?"

Sam's gaze went directly to Mason. "No. I confronted a guy who'd dented my truck, but nothing happened. That guy there"—he tipped his head at Mason—"bought us a pitcher of beer."

"Who'd you confront about the truck?"

"Am I under arrest?"

"We're just having a chat." Zander showed him his teeth.

"Who are you? None of you dress like cops."

Zander reached into his jacket pocket and flipped open his ID. In unison Ava whipped out hers, along with Mason and Nora.

Sam's mouth dropped open. He stared at Zander's and then squinted at the other three IDs. "Holy shit! The FBI? Why? What happened? I heard someone was killed up in the hills, but no one said anything about the FBI!" His gaze grew eager and interested.

Ava's heart dropped. This wasn't the response of a killer. She glanced at Mason and saw he'd felt it, too. Either Sam was the biggest psychopath she'd ever met or he'd had nothing to do with Denny's death.

"The truck," Zander reminded him.

"Oh, yeah. That guy. Don't know his name. He's not local, but he's around here several times a year. Is that who was killed?"

The realization struck and Sam straightened his spine as his mouth dropped open. "Me? You think I killed him? Because I bitched about a dent? Jesus Christ! I wouldn't do anything like that!" He looked to Ava and Nora, his gaze pleading. "You got to believe me. I didn't hurt anyone."

Zander looked back at the women, too, his gaze questioning. Nora gave him a small nod. They all agreed: Sam Gates wasn't their killer.

The deputies returned. "Last call was at two," said the clean-cut farm boy. "The bartender from last night is there right now. He said Sam and his friends didn't leave until almost two thirty."

Zander moved toward the investigators and the deputies stepped to either side of Sam, each placing a hand on one of his arms. "Hey! Am I under arrest?" Sam shouted at Zander's back. "I didn't do anything."

"We're discussing that," Zander replied over his shoulder. In a quiet voice he asked their group, "Anyone have any thoughts? I think this is a dead end."

"Either he's the greatest liar in the world, or he's not involved," said Mason. "He doesn't strike me as being the greatest in the world at anything."

Nods all around.

"Could still be a local," said Nora. "Both he and Jessop said rumors were going around town. Either someone talked—"

"Or someone picked up on the squadron of police vehicles at Denny's this morning," said Ava. "In a town this size, news travels fast."

"I'll send some deputies to ask questions in the diner," said Nora. "And the same in the bar. I want to know who else was in the bar last night. It's not Sam, but it might be someone who was there."

"Looks like Zander and I need to move on to Special Agent Weldon's investigation," Ava stated, looking ahead to the next step.

"I'm meeting with his wife first thing tomorrow morning," said Zander. He looked at Nora. "We'll leave you to handle the questioning down here? All the evidence from Denny's scene is going through our lab. We can get it done faster than OSP."

"That's fine by me," said Nora. "The less I add to our lab's backlog the better. They're tired of hearing me say everything is a priority."

"Any other immediate leads?" Zander looked from one investigator to another.

The silence hurt.

"Then we'll follow where the evidence leads us," Zander said, looking at Mason. "We'll find this guy."

"I know we will," Mason stated.

Ava mentally crossed her fingers.

7

Zander straightened his notepad for the seventh time and glanced at the clock. He was early. Sharon Weldon wasn't expected for another four minutes. He was glad the widow of Special Agent Vance Weldon was willing to come to the Portland office to talk to him. Last evening he'd spent the long drive home reviewing interview questions and evidence points with Ava. Then he'd been up until two A.M. reviewing on his own. He'd studied every photo from Vance Weldon's death.

But his notepad was all he'd brought to the interview. No way in hell would he pull out crime scene photos in front of the widow. He didn't need to see them again because each one was stamped clearly in his brain. It was a special skill he'd discovered as a child, almost perfect recall. He had to concentrate when he committed something to memory, but once he did it was usually permanent.

Including the images he'd rather forget.

Ava entered the small interview room, a notepad and laptop in her arms. "Hey. How'd you sleep?" she asked politely. She set her things down on the table with a sigh and dropped into a chair. "Why did all that driving exhaust me? All I did was sit. I should feel rested today."

"It's the mental concentration. And we talked a lot about the two cases."

A faint scent of coconut drifted his way. A smell he always associated with her presence. It was probably shampoo, but each time he smelled it, he wished he were on a tropical beach with a drink with a little umbrella. And not by himself.

"Say." Ava kept her gaze down as she rooted through her purse. "My wedding planner is my neighbor. You knew that, right?"

Zander's defenses instinctively rose. "I think you mentioned it. You pick a location and date yet?"

She frowned. "Not yet. It's complicated." She turned a speculative look on him. "But she's really great and I'm surprised she's single."

"Oh," Zander forced out, his back growing rigid. "I don't think—"

"Don't say no. You haven't even heard what I have to say."

"But—"

"The only 'but' would be if you're seeing someone. You're not, are you?" Her blue gaze cornered him.

"No, but—"

"I've thought a lot about her and you, and I can see the two of you hitting it off. She's attractive and outgoing and I like her."

Zander was silent. *What's stopping me?*

"Do you have a reason to say no?"

He took a deep breath. "You like her? You're not just saying that?"

"She's great. I get along better with men than women, but she's an exception. She's about to kick my ass for not making decisions about my wedding and I like that about her."

He nodded. "She's not desperate or nuts, is she?"

"I don't see it. I think she's been single for about five years and if she's carrying baggage, I haven't heard about it. Her wedding planning business is very successful, but hectic at certain times of the year. She's the type who seems to thrive on that chaos and handles it efficiently."

The door opened again and an administrative assistant ushered in Sharon Weldon.

"We're not done here," Ava whispered. She stood and held out her hand to Sharon with a greeting and sincere words of condolence about her husband's death. Zander put Ava's suggestion out of his mind and mentally shifted gears back to the investigation.

Sharon Weldon could have been a blonde twin of the actress Melissa McCarthy, but she didn't project the mirth or smiles. Understandable. "I'm sorry for your loss," he said as he shook the woman's hand. She regarded him with unemotional eyes and thanked him. She looked drained as she took a seat.

"I appreciate you coming to the office and saving us a trip," Zander started.

"It was harder than I expected," Sharon answered. "I've been in the parking lot out front for the last fifteen minutes, trying to get up the nerve to come in. I think the guards at the security hut were about to come knock on my car window."

"Is this a bad time?" Ava asked kindly.

Sharon turned her empty gaze toward Ava. "This is as good a time as any. I don't expect there will be a good time within the next twelve months. But if there's a chance Vance was murdered, I want you guys on it immediately and this is the best way I can help. You'll understand if I'm a bit numb . . . it was bad enough that I believed he committed suicide. I never dreamed that someone killed him."

"We're still exploring the option," Zander said hastily. "We haven't made that determination."

"Was I wrong to assume he'd taken his own life?" she whispered, tearing up. "Am I a horrible person that I immediately believed he'd done the worst? What if he was murdered? What does he think of me now?" Her voice cracked and tears streamed. She sat motionless, holding Zander's gaze, silently begging him to make her feel better.

He couldn't speak.

She must feel like her husband has died twice.

Ava leaned forward, drawing Sharon's attention. "Vance knows your heart, Sharon. He would forgive you, but forgiveness isn't necessary. You were married for a decade and everyone has told me how happy the two of you were. If he was standing here today, would he be angry that you believed what you saw?"

Sharon silently shook her head, her gaze locked on Ava as if she held her lifeline.

"Of course not," Ava continued. "From what we've seen, all the evidence points at suicide. Even the medical examiner agreed. You weren't wrong to believe what you did! Vance loves you. He isn't disappointed in you." She paused. "I don't believe we can have negative emotions on the other side." She held Sharon's gaze.

"You don't?" Sharon whispered.

Zander internally cringed. He didn't get involved in conversations about the afterlife. It was touchy territory, along with politics and religion. If Ava was going to wade into a discussion about it, she was on her own.

"I don't," said Ava. "I've always felt it was a place of peace. There's no purpose for doubt or disappointment."

Holding his breath, Zander studied the woman across the table. She seemed to accept Ava's words and her tears had stopped.

"I dream about him. He's always smiling and telling me to not worry about him."

Ava nodded. "I'd focus on that. Let us investigate the details. Nothing changes, right?"

"No. He's still gone," Sharon whispered.

"Do you have someone to talk to?" Ava asked.

"The agency lined someone up for me."

Zander wondered if it was the same therapist Ava saw. If that therapist had been able to help Ava emotionally heal from her life-threatening injuries and Jayne's suicide attempt, she could help Sharon.

"I know Vance told you he'd tried suicide in the past," Ava said gently. "Were there other reasons you believed he took his own life?"

Sharon took a deep breath. "He'd struggled with depression for the last five years. He insisted we keep it quiet. He didn't want anyone at his job to know."

"So he was seeing a therapist?" Ava asked.

"No. His regular doctor prescribed something. At first Vance would be pleased with the results, but it seemed like after a few months the pills would stop working, so he'd go back and get his dose adjusted or try something else."

Ava nodded her head in understanding. "Some medications take consistent monitoring and adjusting."

If anyone had witnessed the ups and down of medications, Zander knew Ava had with her twin.

"Did he talk about hurting himself?" Zander asked.

Sharon shook her head emphatically. "Never."

"Did he discuss his domestic terrorism cases with you? Was he concerned about his safety?" Ava questioned.

"He's not supposed to talk much about his cases, but he did," Sharon said simply. "I guess he can't get into trouble for that now, so I don't see the point in protecting him, right?"

"It doesn't matter," said Zander. *Could Sharon be in danger because of something Vance told her about a case?*

He glanced at Ava, but she was focused on Sharon.

"If he was worried about his safety, he never told me," Sharon stated. "His latest case involved some of those sovereign citizens who live in Central Oregon. He didn't think they were dangerous. He thought they might do some stupid things, trying to protect their way of life, but he didn't believe this group would do more than their usual paper battle against the government. They just wanted to be left alone."

Zander knew the bare bones of the case. Vance had had a domestic terrorism watch list of Oregonians and part of his job had been to monitor their activity. Zander would need an update from Special Agent Kilpatrick to know if someone on the list could be a suspect.

"Did Vance know Denny Schefte? He's a detective with the Oregon State Police."

"He's the one that was murdered yesterday, right? The case you said had a mask?" Sharon asked. "I saw his picture on the local news, but his name and face weren't familiar to me. They didn't say anything on the news about a mask. I assume you're keeping that part quiet to eliminate the nutjobs that try to take the credit for the murder?"

"That's correct. We'll keep quiet about the same fact about Vance's death, too," said Ava. "Did you get a chance to see if there were any masks missing from Vance's collection?"

"I looked," Sharon said, shaking her head. "I can't tell you if anything is missing or not. I never paid much attention to his movie paraphernalia collection. You'd asked if he'd ever had a Pinhead mask, and I honestly don't know. There isn't one now, but he might have owned one."

Zander had already searched for cases Vance and Denny might both have worked on. He hadn't found any, but the men could have known each other outside of work. "Did Vance hunt or fish?"

"No. Outside of work he would play basketball at the gym with friends. He'd coach a few kids' club basketball teams each year. Those were his main interests."

Mason had told Zander that Denny was an outdoorsman and had no interest in sports.

"Did you know of any arguments he'd had? Any skirmishes with neighbors or even a stranger?" Zander asked. He was getting to the bottom of his list. After asking Sharon for possible connections between the men, he had to fish outside the pond and hope he'd catch a trout with a lucky question. Ava's shoulders slumped a tiny bit; she recognized his question as a Hail Mary pass.

"I've thought a lot about that," said Sharon slowly, shaking her head. "If something happened, he didn't tell me about it. Vance was one of the good guys. People liked him. It was his smile. He had a way of looking right at you and giving a smile that made you feel you were the most important person in the room at the moment. His personality was infectious. *Everyone* liked him."

It was similar to what Zander had heard from Vance's coworkers. No one liked to say bad things about the dead, but he had the impression that Vance had actually been the type of guy everyone had described.

"Bear with me a moment, Sharon," Ava started. "But I'd be remiss if I didn't bring this up."

Zander held his breath, thankful Ava had neatly taken over the next aspect of the interview. She'd developed an understanding with Sharon, and he hoped the woman wouldn't be offended by what she was about to ask.

"A lot of women love FBI agents and infectious personalities. It makes men prime targets for some females who are turned on by the badge," Ava said.

He watched Sharon closely. She'd started nodding as Ava spoke and knew exactly where the interview was going.

"You're asking if he had affairs."

"I'm asking if there could be any angry women. Women don't like to be shut down," Ava clarified.

Neatly done. Ava had placed all the focus on the women, not Vance, and implied that he'd refused any offers.

"You're right about women throwing themselves at agents. He called them badge bunnies. The agents I know often compared stories. I've heard of them being followed home from work and hit on by witnesses."

"That's true for both sexes," Ava commented with a half smile.

"If Vance was unfaithful, I'm unaware of it," stated Sharon. "We've had our ups and downs like any couple, but I've never found a reason to ask him if he's had an affair. There's never been a point in our marriage where I was driven to question it." She looked Zander in the eye. "He always came home to me, and I was happy. I firmly believe he was, too. I'm not saying we had a perfect marriage, but ours hadn't hit that roadblock yet."

"It sounds like you had something very solid," Ava said.

"We did," Sharon said thoughtfully. "There's a lot to be said for being content. We didn't need to travel to islands and party with friends every weekend. We were happy to just be home together. I hated anything to do with basketball, but we both liked to work in the yard and go camping. Doing things together was important to us." The tears started again, but she smiled through them. Ava brushed her eyes with the back of her hand and returned Sharon's smile, clearly understanding.

Zander felt alone in the room.

At one point in his life, he'd known that contentment. He missed it. He missed it desperately, but he'd done nothing about it.

It was safer not to risk the pain again.

• • •

Sitting in her car in the FBI parking garage after the interview, Ava reread the email from Jayne that Jayne's therapist had forwarded, searching for subtext. Each time she saw the therapist's email address appear in her inbox, she caught her breath and her heart stopped.

Every email made two thoughts race through her brain. *Is Jayne dead? Is Jayne hurt?* She couldn't stop her reaction. Logic told her that bad news would come via a phone call, not an email, but anxiety still raced through her veins at the sight of the email address.

Mason had suggested the therapist email him instead so he could tell Ava if the messages carried bad news. Ava had refused. It wasn't a matter of privacy; it was a matter of responsibility.

Jayne was Ava's baggage.

Mason had promised he would help her shoulder the load, and he had. He'd lifted a lot of Jayne pain and angst from Ava's mind and heart. After she read each email, she'd forward it to Mason and they'd discuss it. It was good therapy for her and an educational process for him. Mason learned to read the emails through Ava's eyes. What might seem inconsequential to him could be a sign to Ava that Jayne was struggling.

Ava knew Jayne chose every word with purpose; she wanted to affect Ava in a certain way. The sentences might be delivered in the most casual style possible, but they were deliberate and measured. Jayne could mention the purchase of a purse, and Ava would know it was an attempt to spark jealousy. An indication that Jayne needed to feel she could manipulate Ava's reactions. It was a grasp for power.

She didn't realize that Ava was no longer sixteen.

Jayne's social and emotional skills had frozen during high school. Or earlier.

The emails didn't make Ava jealous; they made her sad. It crushed her to see that her sister couldn't relax and simply enjoy her life. For Jayne, every moment of the day was about manipulating people to turn their focus to her. Everything in Jayne's life needed to circle back around to her. To the point where it had nearly cost her life. Today her email said she was going on a supervised outing to the mall with a few other residents, even though she had very little money to spend. Translation: you should feel sorry for me and send me money.

If you only knew how much I'm already paying.

Ava read the letter a third time. Two paragraphs. Nine sentences. Four of the sentences were about her watercolors. Two were about the shopping trip. Three were about another resident.

A man.

Ava's heart sank, and she read the personal note the therapist had included at the bottom of the email. She stated that she was encouraged by Jayne's enthusiasm for pursuing her watercolors. She assured Ava that the male resident Jayne had mentioned was just a friend. He was much younger than Jayne and married. The therapist claimed she was watching the relationship closely.

Ava knew better. A younger man? That meant that Jayne was emotionally closer in age to him. A positive in Jayne's brain. The fact that her sister had written about this man meant he was constantly in her thoughts, and that she had him in her sights. Ava knew this from long experience with Jayne and men. It was also an attempt to make Ava jealous.

No, thanks.

Nothing would stop her sister from pursuing her goal. That he was married didn't matter. An all-out assault of interest from Jayne McLane created men who left relationships bobbing in their wake. Solid relationships. Marriages.

They were all vulnerable.

Jayne knew how to get in men's heads and swing them her way.

Ava started to dial the therapist and froze.

What am I doing?

It's not my fight.

She clicked off her phone screen, hearing Mason's voice in her head. "It's not your responsibility. Let them do their job. That's why we pay them the big bucks."

The residential center cost a small fortune. Insurance had paid for some of it, but with Mason's blessing Ava had taken on the rest. Their other home remodeling projects could wait, he'd said. As long as they weren't putting themselves in debt, he'd agreed Ava could do as she wished.

Ava knew she wouldn't be as patient if Mason had a sibling who was a financial and emotional black hole.

Part of her wanted him to stop her from paying for Jayne's care. If he put his boot down and said hell no, it would be easier to bear.

But where would Jayne be then?

Jayne had good doctors. If they couldn't see what she was about to do with this young man, they would soon learn. It wasn't Ava's responsibility to point it out. If she called, they would pat her on the head, thank her, and ignore her advice.

Ava turned on her car. She needed a latte and a cookie.

8

The phone's ring jolted Mason out of a sound sleep.

Ava's phone.

A blurry glance at his clock showed it was two A.M. and he relaxed back into his pillow, listening to her fumble for her phone and answer. Her voice was thick with sleep, making him want to pull her close and absorb her heat.

"Are you sure?" she asked. There was a long pause. Mason heard someone speak but couldn't make out the words.

"Send me the address," she said. "It's not far from me. I'll be there in half an hour." She set her phone back on the nightstand with a sigh. "I need to go."

"What is it?" Mason yawned, wondering if he would be able to fall back to sleep or if he should get up and scramble some eggs.

"Another mask. Southeast Portland."

He sat up, fully awake. "Who is it?"

Ava swung her legs out of bed and sat on the edge, stretching her back. "An Oregon state trooper. Murdered in his home."

"Name?"

"Louis Samuelson. Know him?"

He thought hard. "I don't think so." He pushed the covers back and got out of bed. "I'm going with you."

She sat silent on the edge of the bed. Ava should say he couldn't accompany her to the scene, but she didn't.

"Okay, but I get the first shower," she said.

• • •

The narrow street in southeast Portland was brightly lit with flashing lights. Mason counted twenty patrol cars, both OSP and Portland police, and then stopped counting. His gut had overflowed with anger since Ava's call. Nothing infuriated him more than when someone targeted a cop.

OSP troopers put their lives on the line every day. When they pulled over a driver during a routine stop, they didn't know whom they'd encounter behind the wheel. Rarely was it someone happy to see them.

He followed Ava up the front walkway to the small bungalow. It was one of those older Portland homes that look like tiny cottages from the outside, but inside are sizable and made with high-quality craftsmanship that has lasted a century. Wooden floors, wooden arches, thick walls. A single-lane driveway led past the house to a small garage behind the home. Someone had hung a sheet over the large window at the front of the house.

The front yard had been converted to a Halloween graveyard. Mason read the names on the gravestones. DEE CAYED. WILL B. BACK. PAUL TERGEIST. Plastic bone arms and legs protruded from the grass. A headless stuffed body sat in a chair on the small front porch. Mason looked away from the decorations. The Halloween cheer was at odds with what he knew was indoors. Ava had learned more details as he drove them to the home, and he knew the scene inside would be difficult to stomach. He neatly printed his name in the scene log under Ava's, thankful the police officer had no reason to question the appearance of an OSP detective, and slipped on booties.

They stepped inside. Mason nodded at a few familiar faces in the foyer, unsurprised at the level of anger he felt in the home. None of the officers he recognized said a word; they simply nodded back. A few people he didn't know cast annoyed glances Ava's way. Sexism was rife in many police departments and some cops didn't want to see a female FBI agent when one of their own had been taken down. Mason returned the glares tenfold; Ava ignored them. She'd told him in the past she didn't care what people thought. She did her job and knew she did it well.

They turned a corner and found themselves in the living room at the front of the house. Ava froze and Mason nearly bumped into her back. He looked across the room and caught his breath. The trooper had been nailed to the wall with thick spikes through his wrists. A white contorted ghost mask covered the officer's face.

Mason wasn't a religious man, but he said a silent prayer for the man's soul and family. And then asked for the rapid capture of the person who'd committed such a sin. He saw Ava's shoulders rise and fall with her deep breaths. Her chin lifted and she moved into the room, crossing to where Zander stood with Nora Hawes.

Nora's eyes narrowed as she spotted Mason. "What are you doing here?" she asked as a greeting.

"I'm not here," he replied, shoving his hands in his pants pockets.

She held his gaze a moment longer and then gave a short nod. "As you wish. But if someone directly asks me . . ."

"I understand," he said. If asked, he knew she'd say he'd showed up and refused to leave. He could live with that and whatever consequences it brought.

This was about Denny. Screw anyone who tried to shut him out of this investigation.

"What do we know about him?" Ava asked.

"Louis Samuelson was a trooper with OSP for fifteen years." Nora looked at her notepad. "Forty-one, lives alone, divorced, no kids. He was spotted around one thirty this morning when a jogger ran by and saw him through the window."

"Wait," said Ava. "Who runs at one in the morning?"

"Our witness," said Zander. "He works a rotating schedule at Home Depot and runs when he can. He's outside with one of the patrol officers. We're going to talk to him more in depth in a few minutes. Needless to say, it scared the crap out of him when he decided to take a closer look through the window."

Mason glanced at the covered front room window. It was quite large and didn't have curtains or blinds. He hadn't noticed any large bushes or trees blocking the window from the street. The house sat up on a slight rise, but anyone on the sidewalk would have a clear view to the inside of the house. He wondered how long it'd taken the cops to hang something over the window.

Looking carefully, Ava stepped closer to the body, and Mason saw that most of its weight was supported on large metal spikes that'd been hammered into the wall under the victim's armpits. The same spikes had been put through the wrists, but Mason felt they were for shock value, not necessity.

He recognized the mask from a series of popular horror movies. The white mask's mouth was elongated and the eyes were a distorted jelly bean shape. "What movie is the mask from?"

"The *Scream* franchise," Zander said. "I just looked it up. It's never the same killer wearing the mask. It could be anyone in the films."

"Never saw them," said Nora. "Not my thing."

"Could we have more than one killer?" Ava murmured. "What are they trying to tell us?"

"It's almost Halloween," Mason pointed out. "It could simply be something handy for him."

"But his first victim worked with Freddy Krueger memorabilia," Nora said. "Assuming the Vance Weldon case is part of this. After tonight, I think the possibility is almost definite."

"Unless our killer heard about the mask used at Vance's suicide," said Ava. "Although that was kept quiet and out of the media as far as Zander and I could tell. But if the word got out, it could inspire someone."

"Either way, we've got a serial killer on our hands," Zander said. "We need to reach out to the Behavioral Analysis Unit for some input. This is a fucked-up case."

Mason didn't say anything. He considered the work done in the FBI's BAU to be partially witchcraft but admitted they'd been helpful in the past. They'd salivate over the file of a killer who used horror movie masks during the week of Halloween. Nora stepped forward and gently lifted the mask. The long mouth had covered Samuelson's neck, and they saw it had been sliced open like Denny's. Mason looked at the spikes through the wrists, noticing there was virtually no blood at the sites.

"He was dead before they hung him up," Mason said. "He would have bled more if he'd been alive when he put those spikes through his wrists." The other three investigators nodded. The neck of Samuelson's shirt was soaked with blood. He wore jeans and tennis shoes. Mason looked at the floor of the living room and noticed a smeared blood trail that led into another room. "He was killed in another room?"

Nora nodded. "In the kitchen. Follow me and watch your step."

They stepped carefully and followed Nora into a spacious kitchen. Here was the murder scene. A tech took photos as another set out numbered tags next to blood drops. A bloody kitchen dishrag lay on the floor along with a tipped-over water glass. Two large pools of blood were in the center of the gold linoleum, their centers still wet but their outside edges darkening and drying. Mason could see where Samuelson had been dragged out of the pools and into the living room. The heavy blood smears grew lighter along the path to the living room.

"Weapon?" asked Mason. "I assume it's a knife of some sort."

"Haven't found it. I've got men doing a canvass of the yards with flashlights, and we'll do it again once it's daylight."

"Samuelson's not that big of a guy," Zander commented. "I think one person could have managed this. We noticed a bunch of blood on that overturned chair in the living room. I suspect he used that to help him prop the body up while he lifted him to the spikes."

"I don't know," said Ava. "Two people would have made this task much easier."

"Easier, but not impossible for one guy."

Ava nodded in agreement, a thoughtful look on her face. "Someone took a big risk by doing it in clear view of the street. Maybe the lights were off for that part, and he turned them on before he left."

"That's possible. All lights on this level were on. Even the one in the powder room. Upstairs the master bedroom light was on," Nora stated.

"Was there a forced entry?"

"No," said Nora. "Both the front and back doors were unlocked."

"He's still in street clothes," said Zander. "Looks like he was caught before he got ready for bed." He glanced at his watch. "When will the medical examiner get here? I'd like to take the body down."

"He should be here any minute," said Nora. "Let's see if our jogger feels like talking now. He was too upset earlier to say much."

Mason hung back in the kitchen and took a long look at the dark puddles of blood, remembering how the blood had pooled around Denny. At least Denny's had merged with the soil, returning to nature. The blood on the old linoleum would be diluted and blended with soapy water in someone's cleaning bucket. A worker on hands and knees, who'd never known Samuelson, would clean up.

Mason hoped his own death wouldn't leave stains for a stranger to remove. He'd rather die under a fir tree, his blood soaking into the earth.

• • •

Ava recognized the athleticism in Brian Wasco. He had lean muscles and thin tendons that formed deep grooves down his neck. When it came to running, he said he didn't care about the time of day or whether it was pouring rain. Ice was the only thing that stopped him from his run.

The twenty-eight-year-old sat on the low rock fence that separated the sidewalk from the home, his elbows resting on his thighs. Someone had given him a bottle of water and he squeezed it like a stress toy while he spoke. Nora finally asked him to stop, the loud crunching noise getting on everyone's nerves.

"I got off work at midnight because I was filling stock after hours. By the time I got home it was almost one. I changed and ran out the door," he said, looking earnestly at the investigators. "I like running at night. It's quiet and you feel alone but sorta powerful because most of the city is sleeping. There's an element of mystery that makes it feel like you're doing something wrong." He gave a sheepish look. "Sometimes I've wondered if cops on the graveyard shift would think I was running away from something."

"Do you usually run this street?" Ava asked. Brian seemed direct and honest, but she hadn't made up her mind. Something about him seemed slightly off.

"About half the time. I try to mix it up, and I usually save this road for when I have to run in the dark because the roads and sidewalks don't have any root bumps to trip over."

"You said earlier that you don't always work the same shift," Zander added.

"That's right. Some days I work nights, some swing."

"What made you stop and look closer at this house?" asked Nora.

"I actually ran past two more houses and then came back," said Brian. "I assumed I'd seen a Halloween decoration out of the corner of my eye, but it was a bit odd that the house was all lit up. Usually every house on this street is dark when I run it at night." He took deep breath and squeezed his bottle. He shot an apologetic glance at Nora. "I came back because it'd felt too real. You know how you get that feeling when you're staring at something and your brain can't figure out what it's seeing? I stood over there at the beginning of the walkway and stared for a long time, expecting to see the guy walk through the room, setting up more decorations."

"The guy," Ava stated. "You say that like you know him."

Brian shrugged. "I've seen him working in the yard pretty often during the day. I've never seen a woman or kids here. Does he have a family?"

"No kids," said Ava. "Divorced."

"That's good. Well . . . not good. I'd worried that he had kids since there were so many Halloween decorations. I don't like the thought of kids seeing him like that." He shuddered.

Ava understood.

"So you stood at the end of the walkway," prompted Zander. "What made you move closer?"

Brian squeezed his bottle. "I don't know. It just didn't feel right. As I got closer, I could see the blood on his shirt and the spikes in his wrists, but I kept telling myself it was fake. It wasn't until I spotted the big tattoo on the inside of his forearm that I realized that was no mannequin." He looked nauseated.

"That must have been horrible for you," sympathized Ava. She'd been warned the body had been hung on the wall, but the sight had rattled her to the core. This was a scene that would be stored permanently in her memory banks.

"I can't get it out of my head," said Brian. "I banged on the window a few times and he didn't move. I rang the doorbell and called 911. I finally tried the doorknob. It was unlocked. I stepped in the house and yelled to see if anyone else was in the house."

"You didn't worry for your own safety?" Nora asked.

Brian stared at her. "That wasn't very smart of me, was it? I didn't even consider that the person who'd done it could still be inside until *right this minute*." He ran his hands over his face and bent over. "Holy shit. What the hell? I guess I'd assumed he'd done it himself." He looked up at the investigators. "But no one could drive those posts into their own wrists." He froze, leaped up, and then took large lunging steps toward a corner of the yard.

The investigators looked away at the sound of his retching. Ava picked up the bottle of water he'd dropped.

"Poor bastard," Mason said in sympathy.

Brian returned after a few moments and sheepishly took the bottle Ava handed him. "It happens to all of us," she told him as he rinsed his mouth and spit.

"Someone murdered him," Brian said with a shudder. "Deep down I *knew* someone murdered him, but it didn't hit home until just a minute ago."

"It was your brain trying to cope and protect you from what you'd seen," Zander pointed out. "You don't expect to see something like that every day. Or any day."

"Hell no," said Brian. "Do you know who did it?"

"Not yet," said Ava. "We'll find him. Someone doesn't create a scene like that without leaving a lot of evidence behind. Did you touch anything when you went in the house?"

He started to vehemently shake his head, but froze. "I was going to say no, but I did lift the mask because I was going to check for a pulse at his neck. Once I saw his neck had been slashed, I stopped. So my fingerprints are on the mask right at the bottom. Is that okay? *Shit*. I shouldn't have touched that."

"It's expected that you would try to check for signs of life," Nora said. "I'll have one of the techs take your prints for comparables. Did you touch anything else?"

"Just the doorbell and the door handle. I backed out of the room once I saw he was dead." He shook his head with a confused look on his face. "That mask is fucking creepy," stated Brian. "Who does shit like that? It's like a scene out of one of the *Scream* movies."

Ava exchanged a look with the other investigators. "About the mask, we're going to ask that you not share that detail with anyone . . . not your girlfriend or your mother or any reporter that contacts you. We'd like to keep that sort of unusual detail quiet to help weed out the liars who will call in trying to claim they did the murder." It wasn't the entire reason to keep it quiet, but it should be enough.

"You think reporters will contact me?" Brian asked, looking slightly stunned.

Ava was starting to think he wasn't the sharpest tool on the Home Depot sales floor. But it was the middle of the night and the discovery of a violent death had probably muddled his brain a bit. Hers felt muddled. "I'd say yes. You don't have to talk to them. It's up to you, but I think it rarely does any good. They can come to us for an official statement."

"I don't want to talk to them," said Brian. "I don't need to talk about this ever again. I want this shit out of my brain as quickly as possible."

"We'll have you come in and deliver an official statement tomorrow—today, I mean," said Nora. The sound of a car door slamming had them all turning to see who'd arrived.

"Seth Rutledge," murmured Mason next to her.

Ava nodded, pleased to see the chief medical examiner of the state had personally responded to their case.

9

"We've been busy tonight," Seth Rutledge said to the group of investigators. "Two drunk driving accidents and now this. As soon as I heard there was a trooper involved, I wanted to be here."

Mason had worked with the medical examiner more times than he cared to remember. The man was good at his job.

Seth frowned as he realized Ava and Zander were present as investigators. "What's pulled in the FBI?"

"You're aware of the OSP captain who was murdered at the coast?" Nora asked. At Seth's nod she went on. "He was found with a horror mask covering his face. This case also has a similar type of mask."

Seth didn't move. "Captain Schefte's autopsy was finished late yesterday afternoon. I got a quick briefing from one of my examiners, Dr. Trask. She didn't mention the mask. She primarily described the injury to the neck. I assume the mask is in her full report, which I'll receive tomorrow." He paused. "But we had another case last week where a horror mask was involved." His face was deadly serious. "He was an FBI agent."

"Vance Weldon," Nora said. "We're aware and have gone through your autopsy notes already. You were confident he was a suicide?"

"I'm glad you're aware of the case and have already reviewed it. Vance Weldon was a tough one, but I never assign a classification unless I'm comfortable with it."

"What made it tough?" Mason asked.

"We have to classify deaths as homicide, suicide, natural, or undetermined. Weldon clearly was not natural or undetermined—he died from strangulation by hanging. I went with suicide based on the position in which he was found, a statement from his wife about his past attempt, his medications, and how she described his recent state of mind. I didn't see anything that indicated murder. His wrists were clear of the abrasions I'd expect if someone had bound his hands to hang him. Maybe I rushed to judgment on that one, but it felt right at the time. I won't claim to be perfect. I've made classification errors before. Now I want to review it again."

"Based on what you knew, you made the right determination," stated Zander. "I've been through your notes and most of the investigator notes from the case, and it all points at suicide. The masks are the only thing making us take a look to see if he should be grouped with Denny Schefte and now Louis Samuelson."

"The second two are OSP," Seth pointed out. "Why include an FBI agent?"

"That's what we're hoping to find out," said Ava.

Seth looked at the house. "I'll get started right away. Let's nail the bastard who's doing this."

"Amen," muttered Mason.

They followed the medical examiner into the house. The crime scene techs were still working in the bloody kitchen. Nora told Seth they'd finished taking pictures of the body in its current position. Seth studied the body, looking at it from all angles. He moved one of the hands, peering at the spike in the right wrist. "That's a new one for me," he said softly. He pushed the shirt out of the way to get a clear view of one of the spikes under the armpit. "It was nailed in at a downward angle. Someone knew they'd have to do it that way to keep the body in place." He reached up and rapped across the wall with his knuckles. "The bugger even checked for the position of the stud in the wall. He knew driving the spikes into the drywall might not hold the man's weight."

"How hard would it be to drive a spike of that width into a stud?" asked Ava. "That doesn't sound like something I could do with a hammer."

"It'd take a lot of force," said Zander. "Probably a larger mallet of some sort and a lot of muscle and swing."

"A sledgehammer?" Ava suggested. "Or would that be overkill?" She grimaced at her poor choice of words.

"We'll run some tests to find out," said Nora grimly. "Someone thought through every aspect of this scene before they got here."

Premeditated.

Dr. Rutledge removed the mask, studied it, and dropped it into the paper bag that Nora held out. "Never watched those movies," he commented.

Mason was starting to wonder who had watched them. Maybe he simply didn't hang around with any horror movie watchers.

"Help me lift him down," Seth said. Mason and Zander stepped forward and each grabbed a shoulder and upper arm as Seth grabbed hold of the man's shirtfront. Mason held his breath as they lifted Samuelson off the spikes and laid him on the material Seth had spread out on the floor.

"Rigor is absent," the medical examiner commented. "You said he was discovered at one? I can still feel warmth in his torso. I'll say he was killed not long before that, but I'll run some tests for a more definite time."

"His socks are filthy with barkdust and dirt," commented Ava. "The floors of this house are pretty clean for a guy who lives alone . . . at least from what I've seen on this floor. It looks like he went outside wearing his socks and actually walked in the dirt."

"Possibly our killer drew him out of the house?" Mason asked.

"Who here would walk in barkdust in socks?" Ava asked. No one responded. "Right. No one walks in the dirt unless you're not thinking or don't have a choice. The kitchen sink and counters are clean. I glanced in the powder room, and it's very clean. I think he had no choice but to walk in the dirt or he was in a big hurry."

"Let's find the dirt," Mason said.

"Shit. I've got a search going on in both yards," said Nora. "They probably trampled all over the footprints."

"Not if they did it right," pointed out Zander.

The medical examiner crouched next to Louis Samuelson. He'd taken a good look at the socks when Ava spoke up and was now palpating the victim's skull. "He's got a serious dent on the back of the head," Seth said. He lifted his gloved hand from the skull and showed the sticky drying blood on his hand. "It cracked his skull. I'll know more after I x-ray it, but it's a wide one and would have been seriously debilitating. I assume no baseball bat or the like has turned up?"

"Denny had the same head injury," Mason pointed out.

"His hands are clean," observed Seth. "He didn't touch his head or his neck injury. The blow to the head definitely knocked him out. It might have been enough to kill him."

"I wonder if he was hit in the yard," Ava said. "There would be some sort of drag trail. I think we need to talk to the guys searching the backyard." Nora was already headed toward the back door, and Mason immediately followed.

They stepped through the door onto a small wooden deck with a huge barbecue and two deck chairs. The backyard of the home was enclosed by a high fence. Mason approved, liking the privacy. It wasn't one of those fences that gave glimpses into the neighbor's yard if you stood at the right angle. This one was a good foot higher than the standard fence and impossible to see through. Two large bright lights shone from the back of the house, lighting up the entire yard. Again Mason approved, and wondered if they were motion detectors. If anyone tried to sneak close to the house, there was no place to hide from the light.

Three patrol officers were at the far end of the yard, slowly sweeping the grass with their flashlights.

"Good. I told them to start at the far end so they haven't gotten very far," Nora said. "Hey, guys!" she yelled. "Hold up a moment. Stay in your positions, please."

The yard was 90 percent grass. No one had put any effort into fancy landscaping. It was a simple layout. Grass in the center, a wide strip of barkdust along the fences and around the wooden deck. Pulling out his tiny LED flashlight, Mason stepped to the edge of the deck and shone his light on the barkdust around the deck. The deck stood about two feet off the ground. There was no railing, but at the center of the farthest edge, a few wooden steps led to the grass.

"There's a large flattened area in the barkdust here," said Mason. "What's the weather been doing for the last five days?" He knew it'd been cloudy and damp at the coast, but the Willamette Valley weather was always different.

"We haven't had rain in over a week," said Ava.

"Things should be dry," said Nora. "No mud."

They stepped close and studied the impression from the deck. To Mason it looked about the size of a male torso, as if someone had lain in the dirt.

Samuelson's shirt had been clean of barkdust. Front and back.

Something or someone else had rested here. Had it been their killer as he waited for Louis?

Footprints dotted the area around the larger impression. Mason walked the edge of the deck, checking the rest of the barkdust area. Nothing jumped out at him.

"Scan this part of the barkdust carefully," Nora shouted at the cops who were waiting patiently at the end of the yard. "We're looking for footprints, a sharp weapon, and something solid and large that could be used to hit someone in the head. Keep your eye out for anything that could hold fingerprints." A chorus of acknowledgments came from the men.

A light came on in the backyard of a home two houses over. Mason could see the roofline of the home, but not the backyard or people. They were waking up the neighborhood. "You'll need a canvass of the neighborhood first thing in the morning," he said under his breath to Nora.

She nodded. "On my list."

Not wanting to step off the deck, Zander shone his flashlight at the barkdust along the fence. Mason noticed a tall gate where the fence met the house on the west side of the home. He walked to the other side of the deck and checked the east side of the home. No gate.

"I'll tell the techs to check the gate latch for prints," said Nora. "Let's check on the guys out front." The group followed her back through the house. The medical examiner was instructing the crime scene techs about additional photos of the body, and several cops stood around watching. "Outside, please, guys," Nora ordered. "Let's give him some respect."

The cops silently filed out the front door and joined two others who'd just finished the search of the front yard. One stepped up to Nora. "We didn't find anything in the yard that wasn't a Halloween decoration. There're tons of footprints everywhere, especially around the gravestones and other stuff, that I'd assume the victim made while he was placing them." Mason wasn't surprised.

"Did you see any large items that could be used as a weapon?" Nora asked. "Something to hit a guy in the head and take him down?"

The two cops exchanged a look. "Some of those gravestones are heavy," said one. "I'd assumed they were Styrofoam or a light plaster, but they're really solid. They'd kill a guy if you swung one at his head with enough force."

Death by gravestone?

That would be a new one for Mason.

"We need more light," said Nora. "We'll have to study them closer in the morning."

"Wonder if you'll find one with some real blood on it," said Mason. "Although I think this guy is a planner. He would have brought his own weapon, not relied on finding something handy."

Seth Rutledge stepped out the front door and joined the four investigators. "I'm going home to bed," he stated. "I don't know if I'll be able to sleep, but I want to shut my eyes for a while."

"No fair," muttered Ava jokingly.

Seth smiled at her, his eyes bloodshot. "Trust me. I get called out in the middle of the night a lot more than you do."

"You're the boss," said Mason. "I'd think you'd be able to pull rank and hand off the on-call night shifts."

"I do," said Seth. "But I've always felt I should cover a few nights here and there. Keeps my head in the game. My predecessor did it until he retired. I guess he had the same philosophy."

"Anything else we need to immediately know?" Zander asked.

The ME shook his head. "I'll have a report for you this evening."

10

"Howdy, neighbor."

Ava glanced over and saw Cheryl Noble standing by the border of short bushes that separated their properties. Ava had just slammed her car door, her mind occupied with horror movies and masks. Cheryl in her funky boots, jeans, and sparkly teal sweater was a feast for her eyes. She'd been studying too many crime scene photos. Having Cheryl as a neighbor was Ava's chance to escape into a girly world.

"Hey, Cheryl. Great sweater."

"It'd be perfect with your coloring," Cheryl returned. She was on a constant mission to get Ava to perk up her wardrobe. She'd already introduced some bright colors into Ava's closet. The items made Ava smile when she looked at them on their hangers, but they rarely made it onto her body. They didn't feel right for her job. But she was happy knowing the clothes were there if she and Mason went out to dinner.

"What'd you decide on the hotel ballroom?" Cheryl asked.

Ava's heart sank. She'd promised Cheryl an answer yesterday. "I'm sorry, I haven't even looked at it. I caught a heavy case."

Cheryl put her hands on her hips and tipped her head at Ava. "Seriously. I've never had a client like you. Usually women can't decide because they're in love with too many locations. You don't like anything and don't make any effort to find something you do like."

Cheryl's frankness was part of why Ava admired her. "I know. I'm making your job difficult."

"Do you *want* to get married?"

"Yes! That's why I hired you. I'm not good at planning."

"Or making decisions," Cheryl added. "You won't even pick a date."

"I'm trying to keep the date flexible in case the location isn't available."

"Well, we need to find this dream location. What's the holdup? You say you want to get married . . . what's keeping you from moving forward?"

Ava felt as if Cheryl's green eyes saw right into her brain. "I'm really sorry." She looked away from the penetrating gaze. "I've been up since two. Can I email you later?"

"You say that when you want to avoid conversations, Ava." Cheryl gave her a warm smile. "You don't fool me, but you do have me stumped. I've never had such a reluctant bride."

"I don't want to waste your time—"

"Stop it." The tall blonde held up her hand. "You're not. You're my friend and I *want* to do this. You need my help in the worst way. You're my special project, and I've made it my personal mission to create your perfect day."

Ava wanted to hug her. "You have more patience than I do, Cheryl."

"That's why we get along so well."

"Say . . . I work with a great guy—"

Cheryl cut her off. "Tell you what. I'll meet this *great guy* when you place a deposit on a venue."

She has a point.

"I think you two will hit it off," Ava said.

"If I had a dollar for every time I've heard that, I wouldn't have to work." Cheryl shook her head. "I swear each bride I've worked with has tried to hook me up with someone. Usually it's their divorced and lonely father. I've had to make a policy of not accepting dates with relatives of my clients."

"Zander is great. If I wasn't with Mason—" Ava stopped, abruptly aware that she hadn't been with Mason when she'd met Zander. There'd been no sparks. Instead she'd always regarded him with a brotherly affection. When she'd met Mason, she'd wanted to learn more about him even though it felt as if she'd known him forever; they'd been instantly comfortable in each other's presence.

"You should see the look on your face right now," Cheryl said. "You're thinking about your man and it's the reason I want to make your wedding perfect. You two are nuts about each other, and I'm so pea-green with envy, it's clashing with my sweater."

Ava had no answer for that.

"Go look at the hotel website I sent you and let me know *today*."

"I'll do it right now," Ava promised as she said good-bye.

Her neighbor was awesome. She was friendly, blunt, and outgoing. The third day after Mason and Ava had moved into the old Tudor home, Cheryl had brought over red wine, white wine, beer, vodka, and a big container of homemade white chocolate cookies. "I didn't know what the two of you liked, so I'll let you choose. I figured I was safe unless you're both alcoholics. In that case I'll put the alcohol in my own cupboard and you can keep the cookies."

She and Mason had reached for the red wine. "We'll take the cookies, too," Ava had stated. That evening the three of them finished the red wine, moved on to the white, and wiped out most of the cookies. Ava had promised herself she'd work to develop a relationship with the fun woman. She'd had several friendships fizzle away because she hadn't put forth the effort. Cheryl was worth keeping.

After a few months in their home, Mason had said Cheryl had made the move as worthwhile as the house had. Ava agreed.

Bingo did an "I need to go out" dance as she stepped in the door, his toenails skittering on the wood floors. Ava tossed her bag on a chair and rubbed his head. His dog door had broken, and Mason had ordered a replacement. Bingo had stood at the boarded-up door, stared at it, and turned sad doggy eyes at the two of them, wondering why they were torturing him. "It'll be here soon, boy," Ava had promised.

He danced at her heels as she moved through the kitchen to the back door. He bolted as she opened it. "Jeez, poor guy," she muttered as guilt flooded her. She watched him tear to the back fence and lower his nose to the ground, running back and forth along the fence behind the bushes and trees. The hair stood up on Ava's neck.

I've never seen him do that.

After a few more sniffing passes along the back of the yard, Bingo seemed satisfied and lifted his leg toward his favorite tree. He trotted about the yard, doing his usual curious inspection. Ava watched him closely, looking for any other new behaviors. The dog was a good alert system. Bingo found a tennis ball and galloped back to the door, his tail wagging. He dropped it at her feet with an expectant look.

She grabbed the ball thrower to scoop up the drooly ball and hurled it toward the back of the yard.

He probably saw a squirrel near the back fence while we were gone.

Images from the Samuelson crime scene filled her mind. The impressions in the soft barkdust. Her own backyard was nearly three times the size and fully fenced. Mason had a deck on his list of home improvements, but for now they had a small concrete patio. Bingo dropped the ball and Ava threw it again, stepping off the concrete onto the grass. She slowly moved to the back of the lot. Their home had a wide curving area of barkdust along the back fence, full of big bushes and trees.

Ava walked carefully, studying the grass. *I just left a crime scene and now I'm paranoid in my own home.* She stepped into the bark and started peering behind bushes, fully aware of the weight of the weapon still holstered at her side. She spotted three dingy tennis balls but no footprints. Bingo rushed past her and grabbed one of the balls. With him at her heels, she walked the length of the fence. At the far corner she stopped, staring at the ground. *Footprints?* Mason could have made them weeks ago.

She took a deep breath. *I'm being ridiculous.*

Was she? Last spring they'd had a break-in at Mason's old home. Her sister and Jayne's current boyfriend had been the guilty parties. She froze as she remembered that Jayne's "field trip" had been yesterday.

Déjà vu?

She marched back to the house and went from room to room, checking closets and drawers but discovering nothing disturbed. Their security system was the best. Mason had installed it before they'd even moved into the house, but that didn't mean someone hadn't wandered through their backyard and peeked in windows. Mason had turned off the outdoor motion detector lights a month ago after nightly disturbances by raccoons and neighborhood cats. "We can rely on Bingo," he'd said. "That dog acts like a horde of zombies is trying to break in when the UPS guy walks up the front steps."

"I'm losing my mind," Ava muttered. "No one has been in the house." She sat down at her desk off the kitchen and fired up her laptop. She opened her email and clicked the hotel link Cheryl had sent. Ava scrolled through the images, unenthused about the gorgeous ballroom and pictures of lavish weddings. It was lovely, but not the right place for them. She didn't even know how big a venue they needed. She and Mason had barely discussed a guest list, which, according to Cheryl, was one of the first things they needed to do.

She imagined a wedding ceremony with a few cops on one side and a few FBI agents on the other. It was a bit sad. Neither she nor Mason had much family to speak of. He had a brother on the other side of the state and a son away at college.

She had Jayne.

She couldn't see Jayne standing beside her. She imagined the part of the ceremony where the bride hands her bouquet to her maid of honor, but when Ava turned, no one was standing there.

Emptiness swept through her, and she missed her mother. It'd been five years since her mother's death. She would have loved Mason. He was smart, practical, egoless, and respectful. Everything she'd claimed Ava and Jayne's father had not been. Ava's father had never known they existed. He'd been married. After a short affair during which her mother discovered he wasn't single, she'd left town. And then discovered she was pregnant. Pride and embarrassment had kept her from returning. Ava had searched for him after her mother's death but come up empty. She suspected her mother had lied about his name to her and Jayne.

She focused on the pictures of the hotel ballroom. She listlessly flipped through them again. She tapped out a reply to Cheryl's email, telling her it wasn't the right venue for them, and that she and Mason would create a guest list by that weekend.

There. I put it in writing. Now I have to do it.

Another email flashed and Ava caught the name of Jayne's counselor. She opened it and quickly scanned. Jayne's trip to the mall and out to lunch yesterday had gone smoothly. Four residents and a counselor had gone on the three-hour trip and it had been considered a success.

Ava wondered what made a success. *No one got lost? No one had a meltdown?*

She suspected Jayne would have wanted a drink with lunch but knew the center wouldn't place the residents in temptation's way on their first outing. They'd probably eaten somewhere like McDonald's. What would Jayne have to say about the trip? Her sister knew how to behave so that her keepers would be happy and believe she was getting better.

Ava knew better. Jayne lied at all times. The best defense was to keep up her guard.

She closed the laptop with a sigh and headed for the coffeepot. She smiled as she turned on the shiny faucet at her new sink. At least the kitchen remodel was finished and gorgeous. The master bath's lavender sink, tub, and toilet could wait until Jayne was finished at the rehab center.

If she ever finishes.

She dumped old coffee into the sink and watched it disappear, wondering if her money for Jayne's treatment was doing the same thing.

11

Micah was in invisible mode.

Not really. But he knew how to vanish and keep people from noticing him. It was a skill he'd perfected in case it was needed to save his life one day. When he walked down a street, no one's gaze focused on him. If one did, it quickly bounced away as the person deemed him inconsequential. He liked it that way. Even his vehicle was nondescript, and he didn't tailgate or speed. He was noticed only when he wanted to be noticed.

He pulled his car over to the curb, watching the man exit his vehicle and enter the coffee shop. He'd followed him here countless times and knew he'd get a venti black coffee. He'd even stood in the coffee line behind him, invisible, wondering if today would be the day he ordered something new. He never varied.

Some people were like that. And it could kill them one day.

Change patterns. Vary routines. Be unpredictable.

Don't be the horror movie teenager who investigates the basement.

He loved horror movies. He studied them, rewriting them so the victims had a fighting chance. He also changed them so the villain always won in the end. The bad guy wouldn't die because a teen got lucky or suddenly had a good idea; Micah liked to revise them to be true battles of strengths and smarts. This made the movies more balanced. He appreciated a fair fight. Where was the fun if the sides were unevenly matched?

The man stepped out of the shop, a venti cup in his hand, and got in his car. He didn't even glance at his surroundings. Anyone could have stepped out and attacked him. He would have been helpless.

Micah shook his head as he took the time to scan his own surroundings. Rearview mirror. Side mirrors. Full turn of the head in every direction. He glanced in the backseat even though he'd checked before he got in the car and again when he'd pulled over near the coffee shop.

He couldn't help himself. His doctors had told him it was part of his OCD and they could medicate most of it away. But he liked being on his toes and staying sharp. It was important. The same way it was important to always have a backup plan or two.

What if the power grid went down? What if there was an earthquake? Terrorists, both domestic and foreign, would love to see a city crumble, its people panicking. He wouldn't panic; he had a plan.

He pulled away from the curb to follow the man's vehicle. Micah assumed he was heading to work, but kept his attention focused in case of any changes. Sometimes there were errands or appointments.

Stupid time wasters. Why did people spend time to find the right brand of clothing or worry that their kitchen looked out of date? People should focus on the important things: a stable food source, a solid roof over their heads, and trustworthy transportation. Nothing else mattered. The important thing about a vehicle wasn't its brand; it was its reliability. He always kept his gas tank above three-quarters. What if he had to leave town at a moment's notice? He wouldn't be slowed by something as mundane as filling his tank. If it was a widespread crisis, there could be long lines for gas or no gas available at all.

But it wouldn't affect him.

His long-term plan was to live without a vehicle. Fuel wouldn't last forever. He'd stashed a dirt bike to use less fuel and a regular bike for when it was appropriate. He'd briefly considered stealing a horse, but horses needed constant care. They couldn't be hidden indefinitely in a shed. Instead he studied horses and believed he could raise livestock if he found himself in a future without power.

It would happen one day.

He had no doubts.

His arms started to shake and his anxiety spiked as he imagined that future world. His brain cast about for something to occupy and calm his mind. He mentally reviewed how to build a hutch for chickens to protect them from predators. He felt his breathing slow and his shakes recede. It was important. He couldn't forget. Today the bombs could drop that would change their world forever. He wouldn't be caught with his pants down.

When he was younger he'd recite the multiplication table when the anxiety hit. As he got older he'd begun to choose useful mental projects to focus his brain. The chicken coop. How to lay out a leach field. How to make cheese.

Ahead the man signaled and turned into the parking lot at his office.

He continued past, relieved that his quarry had made it to work safely for another day. Not that his job wasn't without dangers. The man often came in contact with unsavory elements. It was how he'd met Micah.

He'd been grouped with the unsavory elements and been determined to prove to the man that he wasn't one of them.

The man had seen he was different and accepted him.

He'd never felt that level of acceptance before, and the man had become a hero in his eyes. Most people wanted to change him. Medicate him. Send him to new doctors. Talk about him.

He just needed to be left alone. He could take care of himself.

But this man needed someone to look out for him. He was too caught up in his own world to watch over his shoulder. So Micah did it for him. Twenty-four-seven.

It'd been enlightening. A glimpse into a very private life. He'd seen things he shouldn't have seen, learned secrets, and felt his power swell with the new knowledge. It'd fueled his desire to keep watching.

Some of his doctors would have told him the behavior was unhealthy. That he shouldn't fixate on other people. But he was help-ing, doing good, being the superhero. Everyone knows superheroes are misunderstood. They break the law only when it's for the good of the people. If he could protect this one important life, then it was all worth it.

He glanced at the time and knew where he'd find his friends.

Friends.

He knew they weren't true friends. They listened to him and allowed him to hang around only because he shared his pot and cigarettes. He considered it a small price to pay to tap into their knowledge. Street kids were skilled at hiding and seeing things regular people did not. Need bread? They know which bakery window has a broken lock. Need fuel? They know where extra tanks of every type of fuel are stored in the city. Need sex? Need drugs? Need a weapon? They had the connections to get it all.

He siphoned their knowledge and they pretended to listen to his warnings about the future. He knew when his message reached some of them. Usually the females. They didn't like the thought of an uncer-tain future and would latch on to whoever they thought would protect them. Some asked to see the place he'd prepared for an uncertain future, but he never took anyone there. People steal. People lie. People kill to get what they think they need. One look at his supplies and he'd be a marked man.

Several of the females had offered him sex in exchange for his pro-tection. He'd refused. He had no need for sex. Another curiosity his doctors liked to explore and offered to medicate. Why fix something that didn't bother him? To his horror they'd discussed it with his mother, along with his other treatments.

He'd raged when she'd brought it up.

She hadn't mentioned it again.

He parked at a MAX station and changed his shoes and coat, throwing the others in his trunk. He preferred to wear the Converse with the holes when he hung out with the street kids. He kept a ratty camouflage-print coat in his car. It was thick and warm but stank to high hell. They were articles he knew people from the street wouldn't try to steal from him.

Even if they did, he was prepared. He was never without a weapon handy.

It was important to dress and look like the other street kids. He'd studied them for a long time before making the subtle changes to fit in. In the end they'd approached him. He'd watched long enough to see what caught their interest. For several days he'd hung out near them with his cigarettes always handy, acting as if he didn't have anywhere else to go and ignoring their stares. Curiosity had driven them his way. Pot and cigarettes kept them coming back.

They wanted to know where he slept at night, but he never told them. He lied, saying that he slept on a friend's couch at night but had to be out of the apartment during the day. If they found out he went home to his mother's house, they'd never speak to him again. He was careful to maintain his façade. When he needed his bed, he took the light rail, hopping off and on at multiple MAX stops, watching for followers, but they never tried to follow him. When he finally got off at the stop where he'd parked his car, he'd cut through the lot and circle the block, watching to see if he was followed. He didn't go back to his car until he was positive he was alone.

Good habits.

He yanked a filthy cap onto his head and headed toward the MAX stop to wait for the train. The light rail system would speed him into the heart of the city, where he'd vanish for a few hours and hang with his *friends*. He'd be back in time to wait outside the man's office building and follow him home.

Maybe he'd watch through the windows for a bit.

The last week had been exhausting and he wondered if his quarry would have anywhere he had to be tonight. He hoped not. He was tired and ready for a break.

12

"What do we got?" Nora asked.

Mason leaned against the wall, trying to blend in with the paint. Nora hadn't looked in his direction, and he was determined to keep it that way. Zander, Ava, and Henry Becker, the detective who shared Nora's office, sat at the conference room table. Henry was also a new transfer from Salem whom Mason didn't know that well. He'd been added to the case that morning after OSP learned another of its officers had been murdered. Investigators from Vancouver, Lincoln County, Multnomah County, and the Portland Police Department also had joined. One from each location where a murder had been committed.

The task force had been formed within the last few hours, but across the country, officers had been feeling targeted. Several states had experienced sensationalized murders, and new ones were cropping up every month. This week it'd struck Portland. The nationwide hate and panic felt like an erupting volcano, impossible to stop or cool down.

The local media had been digging as hard as possible into Denny's murder and the Samuelson murder. National media correspondents had arrived and crawled through the small town of Depoe Bay like scavengers. Others had set up down the street from the Samuelson home, interviewing willing neighbors. So far the task force had kept Vance Weldon's case from being connected in the news. The investigators still weren't certain if it'd been suicide or murder. They'd all agreed the masks needed to be kept out of the news before the detail caught the imagination of every wannabe cop killer in the country.

The conference room was being transformed. A picture of each victim had been tacked to a bulletin board, along with crime scene photos, a timeline, and maps.

"We haven't found what was used to strike Samuelson in the back of the head. Careful inspection of the gravestones indicated they hadn't been moved for several days," said Ava.

"It looks like we were right that our killer brought a weapon with him. And took it when he left," said Zander. "What else appears to be missing from the scenes? What's been done to the bodies or scenes that we don't see the source of?"

"Good question," said Nora as she wrote, *What's missing?* on a whiteboard.

Mason thought back to the cabin at the coast and to today's early-morning scene. Then he mentally flipped through the crime scene photos from the FBI murder. "Two of the bodies were lifted. One was hung and the other was lifted to the wall. What did we miss that could have helped with that?" he asked.

The investigators exchanged looks. "In the Weldon hanging, I could see how a pulley could have been used and removed," said Henry Becker. "But there's no location for that in this morning's case. The body didn't have to be lifted that high and there was a chair nearby that we suspect he used."

"That's assuming Weldon wasn't a suicide," reminded Ava. "The medical examiner is reviewing the case again and we haven't found anything to indicate otherwise."

"The masks are the link," stated Henry. "I think we need to treat it as a murder for now."

"That's why the case is on the board with the other two," said Nora. "Let's keep a mental asterisk near all the evidence from that case. We'll view that evidence with a grain of salt until we have confirmation."

Mason's gut told him she'd have that confirmation soon.

"I had officers do a canvass of Samuelson's neighbors this morning," Nora said. "No one noticed anything unusual at the property yesterday. The owner directly behind Samuelson's mentioned that the backyard motion sensor lights go off and on several times a night because of small animals. He told us he refused to complain about it because there'd been a rash of burglaries in the neighborhood about six months ago, and he wanted everyone to do what they felt was needed to stay safe. He knew Samuelson was a state trooper. He liked having him in the neighborhood and wasn't about to cause problems with him over what he felt was a reasonable security precaution. Instead he invested in blackout shades for his bedroom and keeps them drawn at night. He couldn't say if the lights had been activated last night."

"Nothing else from the canvass? No strange cars parked on the road?" Zander asked.

"No," said Nora. "It's so damn clean, it's spooky. I want to live in this perfect neighborhood."

"What about home security systems? Did any of his neighbors have cameras running outdoors?"

"None," stated Nora.

"No one saw Brian Wasco jogging at night?" Ava asked.

"No one mentioned him," said Nora. "Some neighbors didn't even hear the police cars respond at one A.M. They woke up at their regular time and were surprised at the activity on their street."

"We found three sets of footprints in the backyard," said Zander. "One set was next to that larger indentation in the barkdust that we saw from the deck. The evidence guys say they look similar to what stocking feet would make."

"They can see prints in that choppy mess?" Ava asked.

"Samuelson's sprinklers are set to run twice a week. The ground was pretty soft right near the deck." Zander shook his head. "I could barely see them when they pointed them out, but our guys are used to looking for things like that. It was clear to them."

"So they think they're Samuelson's footprints from last night because he was wearing socks?" Henry asked.

"It's very possible," said Zander. "There's a bigger set in the same area but they're wearing shoes, and another set that indicates someone stood and looked in the kitchen window. Also in shoes."

"Those are different sizes?" asked Nora.

"They are."

"Two people wearing shoes in the backyard," murmured Nora. "No shoe prints in the house. Bloody or dirty. Did they take off their shoes?"

"One of the shoe prints in the backyard could be Samuelson's," argued Ava. "It's his yard and clearly he spent time outside. It's well manicured."

"Does he have a yard service?" Zander asked.

Silence.

"Putting it on the list," noted Henry. "I'll look into the burglaries from six months ago, too."

"If he has a service, ask about that large indentation by the deck," said Nora. "There might be an easy explanation for it. Maybe a barrel that they scoop leaves into."

"Our guys think it looks like someone laid down on their side," said Zander. "They pointed out where it's deeper where the shoulder and hip would have been. Once they showed me, I could see it."

Henry pulled up a photo of the indentation on his laptop. "I can't see it," he said. The investigators crowded around his desk. Mason quietly stepped forward and peered over shoulders. He didn't see it, either.

"You have to look at it from the right angle," said Zander. "This photo is from a different one."

"We know Samuelson wasn't lying there. At least not last night. His clothes were clean," said Ava.

"I would revise your statement to, 'He wasn't lying there while wearing the clothes he was killed in,'" said Zander.

Ava nodded in reluctant agreement. Mason felt her frustration. What'd seemed important at two this morning had been suddenly made irrelevant by logic.

"Have we found a connection between Samuelson and Denny Schefte?" Ava tried a new topic. "They're both OSP. Surely their paths have crossed."

"We're still looking," said Nora. "Nothing yet. I have a programmer running database searches of our records to try to put the names together in *some* way."

"If only there was a database to search for their personal activities," said Zander. "It's best to start with interviews of the people close to them. Who's close to Samuelson? Who does he hang around with?"

"We've reached out to his ex-wife," said Nora. "They were married for a few years about a decade ago. She lives in Idaho and said she hadn't heard from him in over a year."

"Denny's been single a long time. Almost fifteen years," said Mason, breaking his silence. "Maybe there's a connection with that? Maybe he and Samuelson were both members of a dating service or belonged to some singles clubs?"

"Weldon's married," said Henry.

"But his wife said they'd had their ups and downs like any couple," pointed out Ava. "I think we all know that people can find a lot of opportunities online if they want to have affairs or get a date."

Nora made a notation about dating on the whiteboard. "Bank records and credit card reports," she said. "That'll turn up a lot of leads. Who did Samuelson hang around with?"

"I asked his sergeant," said Henry. "He's promised me a list of coworker names."

"Can you set up the interviews with his associates and family?" Nora asked. Henry nodded.

"I'll handle the banking records, cell phone records, that sort of thing," said Zander.

"Did we get a complete autopsy report on Denny Schefte?" Ava asked.

"I saw it come in, but I only had time to glance at it," said Nora. "It's too early for some toxicology reports, but the bulk of it didn't reveal anything more than we already know." She glanced quickly at Mason.

He didn't look away. It was odd to know there was a document that described every aspect of Denny's dead body. Half the time Mason forgot he was dead. He expected him to walk through the door, or to hear him holler down the hall. Denny was one of those people who was too alive to be dead. His life force had constantly burst out of him.

It lingered in the building.

"His funeral is scheduled for tomorrow," Nora said slowly, meeting everyone's gaze. "We'll have cameras on all the attendees."

"I want to have this solved before that," Mason stated.

"You're not the only one," said Nora.

13

Ava rushed through the organic grocery store.

It wasn't her favorite place to shop, but its location by her home was convenient when she needed a few things. She preferred the big generic grocery store with its wide aisles and familiar brands. This store had narrow aisles, foods she'd never heard of, and a tiny bar where she could have a glass of wine or beer.

She liked the alcohol idea, but the brightly lit store was the last place she wanted to relax and enjoy wine. She noticed several men sitting at the small bar and wondered if they were passing time while their wives shopped. Or if they simply liked to hang out at the grocery store.

She shook her head and moved on, searching for crackers that Mason would eat. He liked familiar labels, too. He was highly suspicious of anything new. Especially if it claimed to be healthy. She spotted a type he'd reluctantly eaten in the past and pronounced edible. She'd stopped at the grocery store primarily to pick up olive oil, but she'd known they were low on a few other staples.

She grabbed the crackers, whirled around to dash to produce, and nearly knocked over an older man. She grabbed his arm to steady him. "I'm so sorry . . . oh . . . hello." She stared at his face, trying to place him.

He smiled back, "Ava, right?"

She nodded, her brain still spinning.

He saw her confusion. "We met the other day. You bought the art piece I wanted. I'm David."

"Oh! Of course." He clicked into place in her head. "I'm sorry, it's been a busy couple of days." She frowned. "Do you live in the neighborhood?"

A small suspicion niggled at the back of her brain.

"I'm staying nearby," he said. "Did you hang up that lovely piece of work yet? I've been trying to find out more about the artist. She's hard to hunt down. Maybe she paints under a pseudonym."

"No, that's her name," Ava said, and immediately wished she hadn't. "I believe it's the first time she's ever put her work up for sale."

"I'd love to find out if she has more available somewhere," he said.

Alarms sounded in her head.

"I don't know how to help you," she said. "You'll excuse me? I'm running very late." She turned and left before he could answer.

Twice in a few days? Both times with questions about Jayne? Her brain spun with scenarios. He could be a bill collector. No doubt Jayne owed *someone* money. But would a collection agency send someone to track Ava, hoping to reach her sister?

Maybe he was an enforcer for a drug lord Jayne had stolen from?

"David" was in his sixties. He didn't look like someone who would break Jayne's kneecaps, but to be effective all he needed was a gun. For a normal person, that would be a ridiculous scenario.

Jayne wasn't normal, and Ava knew the scenario was very plausible. *Oh, Jayne. What did you do?*

At least her sister was locked up and reasonably safe. If the man was following Ava and asking questions, it meant he didn't know where to find her sister. A good thing.

Is he dangerous?

She skipped the produce and went to pay for her olive oil and crackers, looking over her shoulder for David as she waited in the check-out line. She didn't see him. After paying she grabbed her items and went out the far door of the grocery store. She'd parked by the other door, but she knew there were a few trees and pillars at this end from which she could unobtrusively watch both entrances.

She stood behind the second pillar and watched. Nothing. His basket had held two items . . . both boxes of cookies. Things he could have picked up in the aisle where he'd finally approached her.

He hadn't been shopping; he'd been following her.

For how long?

She'd left the task force meeting in downtown Portland and then driven out to her office by the airport. After a few hours there, she'd gone straight to the grocery store . . . which wasn't anywhere near the small shop where she'd bought Jayne's painting. If David knew Ava was an FBI agent, he could have waited near her office building until he saw her leave and followed. Did he know where she lived?

Bingo's odd outdoor behavior popped into her head.

Had someone been in their backyard?

Dread crept up her spine. That would be very heavy-handed for a bill collection agency. It spoke of something much more important. Whom was Jayne mixed up with?

She had to talk to Mason. She'd forgotten to tell him about Bingo after the task force meeting.

Do I need to reach out to Jayne?

She wondered if Jayne's doctors would let her see her twin. Her stomach churned at the thought of facing and questioning her sister. Ava touched her left side below her ribs. She'd nearly died from a secondary infection after being shot that summer. She'd been mentally off her game, traumatized by Jayne's suicide attempt, which Jayne had made Ava believe was her fault. The months apart had been necessary for Ava to heal mentally and emotionally. She'd had to distance herself from her twin in every way.

Was she ready to bridge that gap?

Was Jayne ready? Her therapists felt the distance had been good for her.

"Dammit." Ava didn't know what to do.

She kept her gaze on both grocery store doors. People came and went, but not the man she was waiting for. He could have immediately left when she'd run off, realizing that she didn't believe their meeting was a coincidence.

He must have traced Jayne through the art show newspaper announcement, hoping she'd show up. Instead the second-best person had shown up: her twin. Is that when he'd started to follow Ava, hoping she'd lead him to Jayne?

She mentally ran through the information that would be available about Jayne on the Internet. It would primarily be newspaper articles on arrests. Jayne moved so frequently, she had to be next to impossible to track. Even Ava hadn't known where to find her half their lives.

But Ava had a more stable history. Any skilled skip tracer would figure out her home address through utility bills. "Fuck." Both she and Mason were very careful about keeping their private lives out of reach of the public, but professionals who searched for missing people knew how to find almost anyone.

What will he do next?

"Do I care?" she mumbled out loud. It was none of her business. If Jayne owed someone money, then she needed to pay. Of course she didn't have any money to pay with, but it wasn't Ava's responsibility to get her out of debt. "Not my monkeys." Jayne could dig her own way out of her problems. Ava had already paid for enough of them.

She stepped out from behind the pillar, feeling foolish for allowing Jayne's problems to get in her head. *I should know better. I do know better!*

The man chose that moment to exit the grocery store, two cloth bags of groceries in his hands.

Ava scowled and stepped back behind the pillar. He'd bought more groceries *and* brought his own bags?

Confused, she watched him walk through the parking lot. He didn't search the parking lot as if looking for her. He walked straight to his car, a small convertible Mercedes that she didn't understand why an Oregonian would own, due to the weather. The license plate was out of her view. She stepped out again, trying to position herself to catch a glimpse of the plate.

He backed out of the spot and immediately turned, effectively keeping his plate from her view. She hustled into the lot, no longer caring if he saw her or not. She was determined to find out who was following her. His car sped to the road and turned, vanishing before she could see the plate. She couldn't confirm it was an Oregon plate.

"Damn." She stood in the parking lot clutching her oil and crackers. *Should I go ask to see their camera footage?* She knew she could show her badge and probably get plenty of cooperation. But she had pride in her ethics.

And she'd like to keep her job.

Was he a skip tracer? The Mercedes had looked new. She didn't know how much money people in that profession made, but she bet the really good ones were in high demand. Or was his source of income from something dirtier? More dangerous?

She unlocked her car, mentally cursing her twin. For two months she'd been able to keep Jayne mostly out of her thoughts. She'd known exactly where Jayne was and trusted that her therapists would keep her safe and out of trouble. Now she'd taken over Ava's focus without lifting a finger.

What would Dr. Griffen say? Ava fought the urge to call the kind therapist who'd helped her ease Jayne's control of her brain. She took a few deep breaths and tried to look at the situation from a distance. *She'd tell me to move on. Let it roll off my back.*

But she would bring it up to Mason. If someone had spied on their home, he needed to know.

• • •

Mason stared at the ground in their backyard. It looked the same as all the other barkdust in the yard to him. Messy. Splintery. Brown.

"It appears to you that someone stood here?" he asked.

Beside him Ava put her hands on her hips. "I thought it did. I'm not so sure now." She looked at Bingo, who sat next to her, his tail slashing through the grass. He gave a doggy smile, unconcerned about their discussion.

"Show me exactly where Bingo sniffed," Mason directed. Ava walked along the back of their yard, pointing and explaining what Bingo had done. Mason agreed it was unusual behavior for the dog. Usually he picked the closest patch of grass when he was let out of the house. But he did have a fascination for squirrels, and Mason could understand the dog's behavior if he'd felt his territory had been trespassed on by a gray, furry rodent.

Mason didn't know what to think. Ava's story about the man at the grocery store bothered him. She wasn't the type to get overly concerned about nothing. She had good instincts. Even though she'd proved she was extremely capable of taking care of herself, he worried for her safety. He couldn't help it.

She was his other half.

Any hint of a threat to her filled him with concern.

"The security system is good," he said. "Bingo is an extra layer of protection. If someone comes remotely close to the house, the dog lets us know." He looked over at her as they both stood in the darkening yard. She was listening, hanging on his every word, and he could see she was worried.

He knew she wasn't worried for her safety; she was worried about the drama in their lives.

Mason was a no-drama person. Ava was, too. But her twin had always projected her excess drama into their lives, and Ava hated it.

"She's locked away and it still hasn't stopped," muttered Ava. "I thought it was over."

"We don't know this is about her," Mason pointed out.

"That man asked about her. Twice," said Ava. "He wants to find her, and he's going to use us to do it. I don't know if he's dangerous." She raised her arms in the air, tipping her head back. "Am I wasting brain power worrying about it? I feel like I've suddenly dropped four levels in my recovery." She lowered her arms, meeting his gaze. "It wasn't just a physical healing."

"I know." He did know. All too well. "Let's call her therapist right now and see if anyone's reached out to her or the recovery center looking for your sister."

Relief flowed over her face. Ava simply needed someone to share the burden of Jayne. They had agreed she'd tell Mason when she needed help; he *wanted* to help, but she was horrible about asking. He had to push and prod his way into her problems, and it went against his personal rule to mind his own business.

They were both stubborn and independent people.

They turned back to the house and he caught her hand, holding it as they walked. The sky had darkened with low gray clouds and the backyard was quiet and calm. He looked up at the back of the home they'd bought together. A few strings of outdoor lights dangled over the deck, adding a warm, homey glow. Pride and contentment washed over him. He'd never known this was what he wanted. He'd assumed he'd retire and move to a warm beach and become one of those unshaven guys who read books and sit at a bar for companion-ship all day.

It sounded lonely and empty. At one time it'd sounded relaxing and warm.

He'd never so looked forward to fall. The cooling temperatures had brought back the lush green Pacific Northwest colors after the long, dry summer. He even loved the sight of the fluorescent-colored thin jackets the runners wore along with their gloves and knit hats. He'd hauled in a big load of firewood and stacked it in his utility shed, excited to use their woodstove in the evenings. Wine, a fire, and his soon-to-be wife.

My wife. He squeezed her hand and she glanced at him and smiled, her eyes lighting up in the dim evening glow. He'd left the wedding plans up to her. She occasionally asked him for an opinion, but he'd told her to let him know what time to show up and what to wear. Cheryl had mentioned Ava was struggling to make decisions, but he figured that was normal for a bride. She'd have one wedding in her life; this was it for the both of them.

At least for him. She could do whatever she wanted once he was dead.

He was going to die first; he'd made her promise.

She'd looked at him as if he were crazy, but agreed. He'd suspected she thought he was simply making a joke, but he'd been deadly seri-ous. He didn't want to rebuild a life without her; he was done starting over.

He followed her up the deck stairs, and she pulled out her phone to call the therapist.

"Oh!" She halted before entering the house. "An email from Jayne." She frowned. "That's two this week. That's unusual."

Mason peered over her shoulder as she opened the email. It started with an explanation from Jayne's therapist that she was sending the extra email from Jayne because she thought it was beautifully written and showed a great improvement in Jayne's state of mind.

"Oh, brother," Ava muttered. She squared her shoulders as she scrolled down to the body of the email.

Mason wondered if Jayne had snowed the entire staff at the recovery center. He knew as well as Ava that someone like Jayne didn't make "great improvements" this rapidly. What Jayne did was adapt to situations and figure out how to use people to get what she wanted. Didn't her therapists see that?

> Dear Ava,
>
> I'm sorry. I'm so sorry. I'm sitting here in my room and I'm overwhelmed by the decades of hell I've dragged you through. I see it so distinctly now. You were always the stable and good one, while I ran wild and tried to stir up everyone around me. My brain and body craved both physical and mental stimulation, and it felt good when the people around me were upset. It gave me a rush of energy that I could make that happen. I understand now that I was sick. It's no excuse. I should have known what I was doing was wrong. Actually I did know it was wrong! I just didn't care to stop it. It felt too good. It gave me something I needed.
>
> How clear everything looks today. It scares me that I might not see it tomorrow. I know it's the medications that free my brain, take away the need for the constant stimulation. It scares me that my future is reliant on a pill bottle. What if they stop working? What if my

> body compensates for the chemicals and I go
> back to the way I was? Sometimes the future
> is scarier than my past.

Mason snorted. He'd seen what Jayne had done in the past to Ava.
It was amazing that Ava wasn't in a nuthouse.

Sheer force of will had kept Ava's head above water.

> I'm not asking you to forgive me. I realize
> that's a huge step. All I want you to know is
> that I can see it now. I see it all.

"No, you don't see it, Jayne," Ava muttered. "Forgiveness is the easy
part. I've had to forgive you over and over because if I don't then I can't
move on with my life."

> I won't hurt you again.
>
> Love,
>
> Jayne

Mason read it again, searching for the subtext that Ava had taught
him to look for. "Is she going to try suicide again?" he asked bluntly.
"Because that's the only way I know of that she won't hurt you again."

"I don't think so," Ava said. "That last line is a bit dramatic but not
in the usual Jayne way. I'm trying to figure out what's happened that
makes her feel the need to apologize."

"Has she ever said anything like this to you before?"

Ava was quiet for a few moments. "Not exactly. Usually this sort
of thing would spill out of her when she was drunk and regretting

something she'd done. I will say her ability to experience regret has diminished over the years. In high school she used to have huge bawling sessions where she moaned about the things she'd done and beg me to forgive her. Looking back, I suspect it was her way of reliving the event and reiterating that she'd managed to rip out a piece of my heart."

Ava's matter-of-fact tone told him she'd cut off her emotions to analyze the email. She'd developed the habit of learning from her sister's behavior instead of being engulfed by it. He hated that Jayne still pushed her into that mind-set.

"I suspect you're right," he admitted. "The therapist seems to think this is a big step. You don't agree?"

"No, not at all." She gave him a shaky smile. "Jayne will never recover. She will always be searching for the next way to exploit the people closest to her. I think she likes the praise this letter must have earned her from her doctors."

From any other person's mouth, those words would have made Mason raise an eyebrow, believing they were too pessimistic. But over the last ten months, he'd learned that Ava knew exactly what she was talking about when it came to her sister.

He wrapped his arms around his almost-wife and pulled her tightly to him. A small shudder went through her as she leaned her forehead against his shoulder.

"I'll call the therapist tomorrow," he said. "Consider that task removed from your plate. We still need to know if anyone has been looking for Jayne."

"Don't argue with the doctor."

"I won't. I'll tell her how we view the email and let her handle that information as she pleases. I suspect my words will later haunt her when Jayne lets her down."

"She will, won't she?" Ava whispered.

"Every time."

14

Bingo barked as if a dozen wolves were in the house.

Mason was out of bed and halfway down the hall before he'd fully awakened. He dashed into the kitchen, where Bingo leaped and snarled at the back door. His nails scratched the glass and paint as he threw himself at the door over and over. Seeing no one through the glass, Mason yanked open the door, and Bingo launched himself off their deck. The interior house lights still off, Mason watched as Bingo tore about the yard, barking at the top of his lungs.

Mason saw nothing to make his dog act insane. As he scanned the backyard, he felt Ava stop behind him.

"See anything?" she whispered.

"No."

"He's a good alarm. Do we need to call the police?"

His concentration was fixed on the dog, who'd stopped to sniff a patch of grass. "What do we tell them? Our dog is freaking out? Come drive through the neighborhood?"

Ava sighed. "I know. It sounds ridiculous."

"Bingo's calmed down. Whatever it was is gone."

"*Whoever* it was," Ava corrected. "He wouldn't do that over a squirrel."

"I thought he was going to break down the back door. He heard something he didn't like in the backyard."

"I hope he scared whoever enough to keep him out of our neighborhood."

"Now I'm having second thoughts about those prints you saw in the backyard," said Mason. "It's possible someone has been prowling around here."

"I wish the new dog door would get here."

Mason didn't say anything. He didn't know if he liked the idea of his dog in the backyard with someone who could hurt him. Anyone who saw Bingo would see a cute medium-size black-and-white dog. But anyone who heard him first would believe they were being chased by one of the hounds of hell.

"No one can fit through that dog door," Ava stated.

"I wasn't thinking about that," admitted Mason. "I don't like the idea of Bingo coming face-to-face with a prowler."

"Afraid we'll get sued? Because Bingo will kick his ass."

Mason smiled, knowing she was trying to make light of a situation that was bothering both of them. "It's twice in a few days . . . assuming someone recently made those prints you saw."

Ava called the dog back to the house. Bingo galloped across the lawn and took the few steps to the deck in a single leap. He slid to a halt at their feet, his ears forward and his tongue hanging to one side in eagerness. "He doesn't seem concerned," she said.

Mason closed the door and locked it. "If he's relaxed then I say we're safe to go back to bed."

"He's repaid you well for adopting him off the street."

"He's a good guard dog," Mason agreed. "But I'd say he adopted me, not the other way around."

"Smart dog." Ava kissed him and took his hand, leading him back to bed.

15

Mason sat and stared at the huge cross on the wall behind the speaker on stage. He estimated the cross to be thirty feet high and wondered how they'd secured it to the wall. If it fell, it'd be deadly. Guilt flooded him as he realized he'd tuned out the minister's words of comfort, and he ran a finger between his neck and collar. He hadn't worn a tie in months. What would Denny think of all the pomp in his honor?

He'd tell them to go drink a beer in his name instead.

Mason planned to do that, too.

He'd been stunned at Portland's turnout to grieve for his captain. Ava had insisted they hire a town car and driver to transport them to the memorial. Mason hadn't understood why until they'd headed toward the city on the freeway. Every overpass had been lined with people who'd come to watch the miles-long procession. Signs and banners hung from the rails. He'd known the news stations had broadcast the details of the memorial along with the procession's route, but he'd never imagined the overwhelming throngs of people. He'd gone weak at the sight of the first crowded overpass, overcome with emotion, and been thankful he wasn't driving. Ava had made a smart suggestion.

Patrol cars from every police department in the state filled the procession. He also spotted cars from Idaho, Montana, and Arizona. As they'd slowly driven down the street to the huge church, they'd passed beneath three sets of fire truck ladders that'd formed arches over the street, huge American flags hanging between them.

The flags had made his eyes water, and he hadn't believed anything else could rip his emotions that bare, but it happened again as they walked through the parking lot to the church. A band of rugged-looking motorcycle riders had lined the path for the attending police officers. The leather-and-denim-clad riders had alternated, half facing the walking officers and half standing with their backs to them, but not in disrespect; they'd been watching the crowds for threats.

With the national cop killings leaving police officers across the nation feeling like targets, the unrefined but proud-looking bikers silently made their point. A group of young men in high school football jerseys stepped up to the line and filled in the holes between the bikers, imitating their stance, their chins held high.

Mason's knees threatened to betray him. Ava gripped his hand, tears flowing freely down her cheeks. Inside they managed to get seats near the front, an amazing feat, as it appeared nearly a thousand people expected to sit indoors.

Now he stared at the cross, half listening as Denny's brother told a funny story from their childhood. He focused on the beautifully carved wood to keep from dissolving into a puddle. If he gave his full attention to Denny's service, he'd never be able to walk out on his own. On his left, Ray's wife gripped her husband's hand as he used a handkerchief with his other. Mason had spotted Duff, Steve, Nora, and Henry in the crowd. Anyone who'd ever worked with Denny had shown up.

His mind drifted to the burial. Denny's sons had requested a private service, keeping the details from the public and Denny's coworkers. Mason respected their wishes. He knew that after the publicity died down, Denny's sons would eventually reveal his resting place to those who'd been close to him. Mason imagined Denny with a hillside site.

Alone.

Most people buy a resting spot for two when their spouse dies. Denny had been alone for a long time. Would his sons buy plots close by for themselves and their spouses? Did children in their twenties think about that sort of thing? Mason didn't believe so. That meant Denny was alone, not waiting for anyone to eventually join him.

A year ago that would have been Mason.

Christ, I'm pathetic today.

He focused on Ava's hand in his, moving his fingers to touch the ring on her fourth finger. The promises it held.

I'm a fucking lucky man.

He'd had no idea the service would affect him this way. But Ava had known. She'd shown it in her insistence on the town car when he'd tried to talk her out of it. She knew him better than he knew himself, after only ten short months.

He tightened his grip on her hand and she glanced his way, concern in her eyes.

Yep. Lucky.

• • •

Micah had stood along the walkway with his back to the cops. Later, strangers had patted him on the shoulder, slapped him on the back in solidarity, and thanked him for his respect. It'd felt good. He'd liked the spotlight for that moment, but he was happy to blend back in and become invisible again. A few of the other volunteers had given him odd looks, not recognizing him, but he'd known that if he played the part no one would call him out. Something he'd learned from the people who lived on the street. *Show no fear. Act as though you belong.*

He'd heard about the email asking for volunteers and it'd been easy to get the right clothing.

The man he worshiped had walked right behind him, his attention on the police officers. He'd felt proud to be providing protection, and the public's acknowledgment made his chest swell. Then he'd seen the television cameras. He'd tugged his cap low over his eyes, fear swamping him. He hadn't minded the people with the cell phone cameras, but when the television logos started showing up, he'd fought the panic.

What if he later watched and spotted Micah?

He would question why he'd been there, dressed in clothing that didn't belong to him.

Chances are slim that he would spot me.

He'd stood his ground, but kept his eyes averted from the cameras, hoping none of them got a good shot of his face. He could probably explain away his behavior to the man, but he wasn't ready for his spy games to end.

He couldn't get inside the church, so he settled for watching the ceremony on a large outdoor screen. Hundreds of people had crowded around to watch, but he found it boring. He turned his attention to people watching, his favorite pastime. Many cried. The men were the most interesting: their expressions were stoic, but he saw tears form. They rapidly, almost angrily, brushed their cheeks, while the women didn't care who noticed their tears.

It was a powerful display of what one person could do to a community. One man's actions had rocked the city to its core and drawn the attention of national media.

Micah was proud.

The scrutiny was getting tighter. According to the media, the police believed the same person had killed the captain and the trooper from the day before. No mention had been made of the FBI agent and he wondered how long it would be before the media linked them. *Have the police not put it together?*

That was a good thing. It meant there was still time for him to keep moving in the shadows.

But there'd come a point when he might have to step forward. A small part of him yearned for the attention it'd bring.

Not yet.

He needed to see what happened next.

● ● ●

"Two more pitchers?" Ray asked. A chorus of agreement sent him to the bar.

Ava relaxed back in the booth and tried not to think about the investigation. The task force had paused for a few hours, knowing it needed to say good-bye. A small group of Mason's closest coworkers had picked the dim bar as a good place to reminisce about Denny Schefte. Duff Morales had set the tone by telling a story about the time he'd hidden an open can of tuna fish in one of Denny's desk drawers. For three days their boss hadn't noticed, although every person who'd stepped in his office had been assaulted by the odor. One of the custodians had finally taken it upon himself to hunt down the source of the smell. They'd later learned Denny had lost most of his sense of smell in his teens. He'd laughed long and hard when the fish had been exposed, considering the joke to have been on everyone but him.

More stories followed, the tone of the group fluctuating between all-out laughter and near tears. The men had taken turns buying pitchers of Coors Light, the only beer Denny would drink. For years they'd harassed their boss about his taste in beer when he lived in one of the craft beer capitals of the nation. Denny had never caved to their pressure and drank the weak beer with pride. Ava sipped at her glass, amused that today the other men were downing it with gusto.

Next to her, Ray's wife Jill downed her glass of beer. Ava had been slightly intimidated the first time she'd met Jill Lusco. Gorgeous, blonde, tall. And, according to Ray, a perfect mother. But she'd turned out to be fun and down-to-earth. Ava refilled her glass before Jill could ask for more.

"How are the wedding plans?" Jill asked, tapping her glass against Ava's in thanks for the refill. Her words were slightly slurred and Ava suspected her own words sounded the same. The first few pitchers of beer had gone down very easily.

Ava glanced at Mason, but he was deep in conversation with Duff. She snagged a piece of the baked pretzel and dipped it in the cheese sauce before answering.

"I can't pick a freaking location," Ava admitted. "Everything feels wrong. Too big, too small, too fancy, too plain."

Jill nodded in sympathy. "It's hard getting started."

"Where'd you and Ray get married?"

"It was different for us. I was only nineteen, so my parents' church was the logical choice."

"Nineteen?" Ava tried not to squeal the word. "You were a baby!"

"High school sweethearts. Corny, aren't we?"

Ava looked at Ray Lusco. The linebacker-size cop was a snappy dresser and wonderfully transparent about his feelings. Ava and he liked to discuss *Project Runway* episodes, nearly making Mason's eyes roll back in his head. She thought Jill was very lucky and told her so.

"You're good for Mason," Jill stated, leaning close. "I've tried for years to set him up. That old-fashioned silent type can be very appealing, but it only works with the right couple. I'm glad he found you. I didn't want him to be lonely anymore."

"Do you think he was lonely?" Ava asked.

Jill nodded emphatically. "Oh, yes. He just didn't know it."

Ava grinned.

"Where does Mason want to get married?" Jill asked.

"He says whatever I want is what he wants. That it's totally up to me."

"He's not helping at all?" Jill looked horrified.

"He's not Ray."

"But still, some input would be helpful. He thinks he's helping by staying out of the decisions, but that's making it harder for you."

"Maybe," Ava admitted. "But every time my wedding planner suggests a location, I try to picture the two of us in a ceremony there and I can't. It feels wrong."

"Perhaps you need to go to the county courthouse." Jill's sad eyes indicated that would be a tragedy. "Take the planning out of the equation."

"That doesn't feel right, either," Ava muttered.

"Do you want to get married?" Jill whispered confidentially, leaning inside Ava's comfort zone.

"Yes!" *Why does everyone ask me that?*

"Oh, good. You had me worried for a moment. I think you guys are a great match, but I know sometimes things aren't what they seem on the surface."

Ava reassured her that she and Mason were solidly on the same path, but doubt poked at her brain with its nasty red-hot spikes. What was her issue?

She looked deeper, asking the hard questions that she'd always avoided. *Is the age difference an issue?*

No. Twelve years was a drop in the bucket. And it would only get smaller as they got older.

Am I scared of this level of commitment?

No. She was done with all other men. He'd ruined her for anyone else.

"Mason doesn't want to have more kids, does he?" Jill asked, interrupting her deep thoughts. "How do you feel about that?"

Aha.

That one stung a bit. "I'm okay with that," she slowly replied. "I've never really had any maternal urges, and I can't imagine Mason raising a high school student when he's in his sixties."

Jill's gaze drilled all the way into Ava's brain; she didn't believe her. *Little frilly dresses. Minnie Mouse. Shiny black shoes. Disney princesses.*

Ava swallowed. "I don't want to discover that my sister's mental illness has been passed to my children."

Jill pulled back, understanding and sympathy washing over her gaze. "Oh, honey. I'd never thought of that."

Ava assumed Jill was well aware of Jayne's history. Ray and Mason were tight friends, and Ray had sat in a front-row seat for Jayne's destructive theatrics over the past year.

Jill wrapped an arm around Ava's shoulders, pulling her tight and pressing her temple against Ava's. "That's a hard reason to swallow. You're very brave to confront it."

Something inside cracked, and dammed tears leaked down her cheeks.

It felt final.

I've never been upset about it before.

Jill studied her face. "My motto is Never Say Never."

"Mine, too," Ava whispered, wiping at her cheeks. She glanced over at Mason, hoping he hadn't noticed her mini-breakdown. His attention was still on Duff. "There's no rational reason for us to have kids. It goes against everything we want. Everything we know."

"The heart wants what it wants," said Jill. "Mason will never deny you your heart."

I don't want to deny him, either.

No wonder she was in a state of confusion.

16

Mason answered his phone, seeing it was Jayne's therapist returning his call. It was nearly eight in the evening, and Ava had fallen asleep on the couch. Denny's memorial had made the day emotionally exhausting. Add in a lengthy drinking session at the bar afterward, and Ava was done for the day. She'd been quiet and slightly inebriated when they'd decided to head home. Mason had drunk more than usual, again thankful his fiancée had insisted on a car and driver for the day. He'd felt like a lazy lush as he'd gotten in the car, but he really hadn't cared. One of the perks of drinking. You don't give a shit about most things.

Probably why Ava's twin had addiction problems.

It felt good to not care about what the world thought.

Dr. Jolene Kersey was on the other end of the line. Mason had talked on the phone with her a few times and read her emails to Ava. Other psychologists worked with Jayne, but Dr. Kersey was primarily in charge of her case. He glanced at Ava. The phone hadn't woken her from her exhausted sleep. He got up and stepped into the backyard to continue the call.

"Dr. Kersey, thank you for returning my call."

TARGETED   123

"No problem, Mason. I noticed Ava hadn't replied to the email I forwarded her last night. Is it right for me to assume since I'm talking to you that it upset her in some way? That wasn't what I intended."

"She's got a lot on her plate at the moment," Mason said. "You know she tries to step back when she feels overwhelmed by her twin."

"As she should," Dr. Kersey replied.

"We're both concerned about that last email from Jayne," Mason said delicately. "We had a much different reaction than it sounds like her team of therapists had."

"Go on."

How could he explain without stepping on toes? He plunged forward. "We believe Jayne is manipulating the staff. Both Ava and I think there is no weight in her apology, and she's doing it to get some sort of attention or reward from you guys. In the end it's Ava who gets hurt, because she sees it coming but no one believes her when she tries to warn them about her sister. We both thought your staff would see Jayne's words for what they are: a bunch of bullshit."

"Oh." Dr. Kersey sucked in her breath.

"Excuse my language, Doctor, but that's what we believe is going on—hell, that's what we *know* is going on, and I hope you're taking appropriate steps. She's up to something. Don't let your guard down for a moment around Jayne. She's an expert at adapting to get what she wants. Has Jayne been offered something that would motivate her to pretend to change her behavior? A reward or privilege?"

"I wish you could see how much she's improved," Dr. Kersey said. "She's not the same person she was when she arrived."

"Of course she's not," argued Mason. "She wants out. She wants all of you to hop at her commands and give her praise. Any kind of praise. She's got to be bored out of her mind, so you're her current challenge. I don't think you should be keeping Ava apprised of what you believe is Jayne's improvement. Every time she gets an email, she picks it apart, searching for what it really means. Ava knows her sister better than any team of doctors, but she can't heal her mind. That's where we're hoping you can help." He fought to keep his voice level. What he wanted to do was reach through the line and shake the doctor until she listened to him.

"Well, Jayne has improved. We have standards here, and she's made lovely progress. She has earned a number of privileges, and I won't keep those from her. If she abuses a privilege, she loses it. We've found loss of privileges to be sufficient motivation to keep a lot of patients moving forward. Jayne also has therapy sessions three times a week and works in the kitchen. She's never missed a session or a work shift. She's learning responsibility."

Mason wanted to bang his head against a tree. Jayne lived where she worked. If she missed a shift, there was no excuse.

That wasn't the real world.

He knew Jayne was biding her time until she got out, and it put him between a rock and a hard place. He and Ava were paying for Jayne to stay there; it kept her out of their lives and hopefully gave her some mental help. But now he wasn't so certain about any mental improvements. It appeared her doctors had fallen under her spell.

Should they keep paying?

It's keeping her off the streets. And away from Ava.

To him that was worth its weight in gold. But was all the expensive therapy teaching her to act like a decent human being?

It was a futile question. He firmly believed Jayne couldn't improve until she decided she wanted to be a different person. Even then he had doubts about how long it would last. Commitments weren't Jayne's strong suit.

Ava had the same doubts.

"I'm glad she has a safe place to live," Mason said. "All we ask is that you don't trust her. Don't believe a single word out of her mouth. Keep working with her, but understand she has a brilliant part in her brain that knows how to manipulate people, and that includes all of her doctors."

"I understand, Mason. I'm sorry that's how you and Ava have come to view her sister."

"It's out of necessity and experience."

"We'll keep moving forward," said Dr. Kersey. "Should I continue the emails or not?"

He immediately wanted to say no, but knew the positives outweighed the negatives for Ava. "One a week," he said. "No more."

She agreed and ended the call.

"She didn't understand?" Ava asked from behind him. He turned around. She was barefoot, with Bingo beside her, one of her hands deep in his fur. She still wore her slim black skirt and silk blouse from the memorial. Her hair was mussed with sleep.

He would move mountains to protect her, but the biggest threat was from a small woman who shared Ava's genes. A woman who was nearly impossible to stop. She attacked with emotions that he was helpless to deflect, and made him feel powerless. "No," he said. "She didn't understand."

"We did what we could," said Ava. "They've been warned. I suspect they'll learn hindsight is twenty-twenty."

Drained, he shoved his hands in his pockets and simply looked at her. He didn't want to talk about Jayne. Or Denny. He was done being an adult for the day.

"Bedtime?" she asked.

"Please."

• • •

The next morning Ava entered the task force room and nodded at Nora Hawes as she looked up from her computer. Ava spotted the dark circles under Nora's eyes and knew hers were just as bad. Yesterday had been long and they'd all taken the day off for the funeral. The investigators had been torn about the time off. Should they continue their work or take a break to honor their friend? A unanimous vote had made their decision.

Mason had gone to his own desk that morning, aware he had work piling up and that Ava would keep him updated. His absence was palpable.

The other task force members were already present, and Ava slipped into a seat sat next to Zander. "Anything new?"

"Bits and pieces. No new deaths."

"Always a positive," Ava muttered.

Nora cleared her throat to gather everyone's attention. "What do we have from the memorial service yesterday?" She looked at Thad Chari, the detective from Multnomah County.

"We've got several hours of footage," Thad said. "The FBI has generously offered to run it through some of their facial recognition software. That database is limited, but I figure it can't hurt."

"Did you get the fight on camera?" Nora asked.

"What fight?" Ava whispered to Zander.

"It was outside during the service," he said quietly. "Some antipolice protesters decided to exchange words with the bikers who'd shown up to provide protection."

Disbelief swelled in Ava's chest.

"We did, Detective Hawes," Thad said. "Do you want to see what we got?"

"Did we get better angles than the news cameras? I saw the fight on two different stations last night, but they were far from the scuffle," said Nora.

"I think so." The detective brought his laptop to the front of the room and spent a moment connecting it to a projector aimed at the large screen on the wall. An image of a long line of bikers appeared. Ava's throat tightened.

"We tried to get all the faces of the people forming the lines," said Thad. "Even though it was a remarkable service they provided, sometimes the intent isn't the best, and we wanted a record of who'd been there."

"Good call," said Nora.

The camera neared the end of the line and a small group of people carrying signs moved into sight. They moved close to the bikers and yelled in their faces.

"Seriously? At a funeral?" Anger filled Ava's chest. "If you have a problem with the police, take it to the proper channels. No one will give you respect when you do that at a memorial."

"They wanted the shock value," said Zander. "They're picking arguments with people who aren't even part of the police force . . . playing it safe."

"I wouldn't get in the faces of some of those bikers," Ava stated.

"Watch," said Zander.

Immediately a burly biker stepped forward and punched a sign carrier in the mouth. The man collapsed and hit his head, and his friends rapidly stepped away, leaving him lying on the pavement. Two other bikers stepped out of the line and applied pressure to the bleeding head wound with a bandanna one pulled out of his pocket.

"His friends just left him there," Ava said in astonishment. "The cowards. Did we get their faces on camera?"

"Yes, we were able to pull some still shots from the video."

"Did anything else happen?" Ava asked.

"The general crowd took great offense at the protesters' tactics. Some more words were exchanged and the protesters left for good."

"Do you have those stills from the protesters?" Zander asked Thad. He nodded and pinned four faces to the bulletin board.

Ava moved closer to see.

"I already pulled the mug shots of three of them. We knew who they were. These three have arrest records in Portland," the Multnomah

County detective said. "The fourth is from Washington and doesn't seem to have been in trouble before. This is the one who caught the fist to the jaw." Thad tapped one glum face. The man looked forty, white, and angry.

"Do we know what made this particular group protest a cop's funeral?" Ava asked. "I mean, outside of the incidents that have been in the media across the nation." *Would that same anger drive him to kill a cop?*

"Haven't had time to look for a reasonable cause. Between the three protesters we have records for, we're talking pages of complaints and arrests to analyze to figure out what could have made these guys hate us."

"We could just ask them," Zander said quietly. "They seem to want to get a point across."

Ava grinned for the first time that day. "That's why they pay you the big bucks, Zander."

He made a wry face.

"Anything out of the tip line?" Nora asked Henry Becker.

"It's been going crazy since the press started talking about the funeral," said her partner. "We had to add another person to handle the volume of calls during the news hours last night. The sight of the procession really brings out the crazies. Four people called in to say Gary Ridgway did the killings."

"The Green River Killer? He's in prison," said Ava.

"That's what we told them. A few threw Ted Bundy under the bus for the murders, too."

"He's dead," muttered Zander. "Did you get any usable leads?"

"We're following up on each one," said Henry. "Nothing looks good yet. We're still sorting through the 'I'm pissed at my boyfriend, so I'll call his name in to the police' type of calls."

"Every freaking time," said Ava.

"The deaths have made every police officer look over their shoulders," said Nora. "We need to figure out who's doing this so people don't nervously pull triggers."

The room was silent. Officer training was vital for proper procedure in an escalating situation, but there'd been no escalation in the murders. The dead men had been flat-out assaulted and left on display. It was every cop's nightmare.

"I feel it's more personal," said Zander. "Several of the other cop deaths across the nation have been impulsive, and the murdered cop was simply in the wrong place at the wrong time. Someone *chose* our three men; deliberately hunted down these men. When we know the reason why, we'll be able to find him and prevent more."

A small shudder shot through Ava. *More deaths? More deliberate targets?* "How many people can one person target?"

Zander's smile was sad. "Depends on how much anger he carries and how many cops he believes wronged him."

"You've been talking to Euzent," she stated.

"Who?" asked Nora and several of the other detectives.

"Special Agent Euzent is with the Behavioral Analysis Unit at Quantico," Zander said. "I reached out to him last night. They'd already taken notice of the deaths."

Nora looked interested, but Ava saw the Multnomah County detective roll his eyes at the mention of the elite FBI unit. Not everyone was sold on its analytical skills and suggestions. Ava had imagined that the BAU office back East was full of nerds in bad ties who were short on social skills and stared at their computers all day long. Euzent had proved her wrong—the man loved to talk to people.

"What did he say?" asked Nora.

"He's the one who pointed out that the deaths appeared very targeted and well thought out—"

"We knew that," said Thad. "Why do these guys always point out the obvious and make it sound like some grand observation?"

Zander ignored him and went on. "He's very intrigued by the masks. Covering the face generally indicates that the killer knew the victim and it shows the tiniest bit of guilt as they try to preserve a small part of the victim's dignity or hide the victim's eyes from looking at the killer. But the fact that he deliberately brings horror masks to the crime scene for the sole purpose of covering the faces sort of goes against the first theory of covering the face. Euzent sees it as an indicator of pride and power. 'I did this. I've created you' type of mentality."

"So a serious ego problem?" asked Nora.

"Definitely. Along with anger," added Zander. "I sent Euzent everything we had on the three deaths. He'll get back to me in a day or two. Oh, he does agree that Vance Weldon needs to be treated as a murder victim."

"That's what we've been doing," Thad said under his breath. "What about common links between the three guys? Did anything turn up?" he asked louder.

"I've been going through their credit card statements," said Henry. "Denny and Samuelson belong to the same national gym. They're both automatically charged by the gym each month."

"Do they work out at the same location?" asked Ava.

"They did. So it's possible that they knew each other that way. I haven't gotten a chance to talk to Samuelson's coworkers and see if they believe the two of them knew each other, but everyone close to Denny says they weren't aware of Samuelson." He looked at his computer. "Special Agent Weldon and Denny used the same cell phone provider, primary bank, and mortgage company. Nothing surprising there. I have all the same, too."

"Outside activities?" asked Zander.

"Two have no church affiliation. Weldon attended the Methodist church down the street from his house. Denny and Samuelson both volunteered with a philanthropy group for kids."

"Did we find any cases that Samuelson and Schefte worked on at the same time?" Zander asked.

"We got a hit on the database search overnight," said Nora. "It was on my agenda for this meeting."

Ava and Zander sat up straighter. Why hadn't she said that first thing?

"The case is seven years old and I'm not sure what to think about it," Nora said. "Louis Samuelson was barely involved. His name is in the file because he provided some of the necessary legwork at the scene. He helped with the perimeter after a murder-suicide case out in rural Clackamas County. Schefte was one of the OSP investigators. A husband killed his wife and then himself in this case."

"That's a pretty weak connection," said Zander. "There must have been a couple dozen cops from several departments that helped with the perimeter. Any FBI involvement? Any other officers from that case that have died?"

"Those are the questions I wanted answered before I presented it here," said Nora. "I asked one of the IT guys to search for the answers a few hours ago and I just got a reply." She scanned her computer screen. "There was some very light FBI involvement. The brother of the husband was being watched for domestic terrorism in Central Oregon."

"That's Vance Weldon's department," Ava pointed out.

"But the husband had virtually no ties to his brother," Nora continued. "It appeared they were estranged. The FBI reviewed this case and moved on, classifying it as not relevant to any of their investigations. Vance didn't work out of the Portland office at that time."

"What was the outcome of the case?" asked Henry.

"It was exactly as appeared," said Nora. "Everything indicated the husband killed the wife and then shot himself. He was deep in debt and his home was about to be foreclosed on."

"We need to find out what the brother is doing right now," said Ava. "And find out what bank was foreclosing. This is a lead we can't set aside even if Weldon doesn't appear to have been involved."

"Any other deaths associated with the officers that worked that scene?" Zander asked.

"Two have died, but they'd also retired since that incident."

"They say cops often don't live long after retirement," Ava said quietly to Zander. She planned to make certain Mason lived a long and healthy life after his.

"Causes of death?" Zander asked.

"Working on it. It wasn't readily available, but out of the hundred or so names even remotely associated with the case—I'm talking evidence technicians and support staff, too—I don't see two deaths as unusual," stated Nora.

"Not two. There are *four* deaths counting Schefte and Samuelson," Ava pointed out. Nora nodded in agreement.

"Mason's name is associated with the case. It looks like he helped out at some point," Nora added.

Chills shot up Ava's back, and she sucked in a breath.

Mason worked a lot of cases with Denny Schefte. It doesn't mean anything.

All eyes in the room turned to her.

She didn't move and kept her gaze locked on Nora. "That doesn't surprise me," she said with a calm she didn't feel.

Nora nodded and sympathy flickered in her eyes. Being in a relationship with a cop meant you dealt with danger and the unknown every day. Ava understood. Both she and Mason did.

But it didn't mean she wasn't affected.

"We need to follow up on the protesters at the memorial and on the cause of death of those two officers," Nora stated. "Louis Samuelson's memorial hasn't been scheduled yet. According to his father, the immediate family didn't like how public Denny Schefte's memorial became and wants to do something privately."

"Can't blame them," said Henry. "That sort of publicity isn't for everyone."

"They don't want OSP to do *anything*," Nora said. "I realize it's not about us, but it can be helpful for other officers. We'll respect their wishes."

"Any new evidence out of either autopsy?" Zander asked.

Nora pulled out a sheet of paper. "According to the medical examiner, Denny didn't have any flesh under his nails or any defensive wounds on his arms."

"He didn't fight back," muttered Henry. "Or he never saw it coming."

"There was one long dark hair found on his shirt," Nora stated.

"DNA?" asked Ava.

"No follicle to remove it from."

Crap.

"It's a bit unusual," said Zander. "Obviously there were no women with them, but he could have picked it up from a previous guest in his cabin or even off a chair at the bar."

Nora nodded and gave a small grin. "They found one on Louis Samuelson's body, too," she said triumphantly.

A chorus of confusion sounded in the room.

Nora likes a little drama. Ava didn't know whether to admire her or shake her for making them wait for the information.

"Again, no follicle. But visually it's very similar to the one found on Denny."

"A woman?" Ava said slowly. She tried to imagine herself lifting Louis Samuelson onto the spikes on his living room wall and then driving more through his wrists.

"Holy shit," said Henry. "I can't see it."

"Could be a guy with long hair," said Zander. "I assume both hairs haven't been analyzed by trace yet?"

Nora nodded. "Correct. As soon as the second one was brought to my attention this morning, I requested a comparison."

Ava wondered how long it would take. "We don't have anything like that from the Weldon scene, right?"

Nora shook her head. "Dr. Rutledge did tell me he's taking another close look at what he has from Vance Weldon's autopsy. I don't think the presence of a long hair will turn up. He also told me the early tox screens on Denny and Louis didn't reveal anything interesting. We'll have more in-depth results in a few weeks."

"This can't go on for a few weeks," said Ava.

"Agreed," said Nora. "That's why we're going to find him. Or her."

17

Mason mindlessly shuffled papers at his desk. Across from him, Ray did the same. The detectives' corral was oddly empty, everyone out in the field except for the two of them.

And except for Nora and Henry upstairs in the task force room.

Mason's brain told his muscles to get up, head for the stairs, and listen in on their meeting. It took all his focus to stay seated and address his cases.

Ray appeared to have a hangover. Mason hadn't seen Ray hungover in two years. The last time had been after a bachelor party for . . . Mason paused. He couldn't remember the guy's name. All Mason could remember was that the guy had left OSP to join his new father-in-law's real estate company. Now he drove a Lexus.

The Realtor didn't feel the public wanted to shoot him in the back.

"Did you take some aspirin? And drink lots of water?" Mason asked.

"Yes, Dad," Ray answered, not looking up.

"I feel fine," Mason stated.

"Good for you."

"You should have stuck to beer."

"Morales was the one who ordered the tequila shots," Ray complained.

"Tequila gives you hangovers. Even I know that."

"I forgot."

Mason didn't answer that one. His desk phone rang.

"Detective Callahan? I'm Heidi Lain. I work with Dr. Kersey and help her treat Jayne McLane."

"I remember you, Heidi." He'd met the woman during one of his trips to the center with Ava. He couldn't remember what she did exactly, but he knew she wasn't a doctor. When Jayne had entered the center, she'd given written permission for all her medical records and medical discussions to be shared with both Mason and Ava.

"It's been recommended that phone calls go to you first instead of Ava, correct?"

"That's right. She gets emails only. She needs to have a filter between herself and anything to do with Jayne. That filter is me."

"During our team meeting this morning, Dr. Kersey shared the conversation she had with you yesterday."

"Does she think we're nuts?" Mason asked bluntly.

Heidi laughed politely. "She didn't say that. I will say the staff here is evenly divided on how much progress Jayne has made. Some of us share a more skeptical view. Dr. Kersey is fabulous, but sometimes sees the world through rose-colored glasses."

Mason wanted to cheer.

"You see Jayne for the liar that she is," he said.

Heidi paused. "That's one way of phrasing it. I prefer to say I don't take everything Jayne says at face value. I've learned that patients frequently tell you what they believe you want to hear. Oftentimes it's hard to tell the difference between truth and lies. Some of them are very skilled at it."

"Jayne's the best I've ever seen," Mason said. "And I've been a cop for over two decades."

"I agree."

"I appreciate you calling to tell me this," said Mason. "We were worried she'd fooled everyone out there."

"That's not the only reason I've called."

Uh-oh.

"I've been watching Jayne interact with another patient and I have concerns. I've brought my concerns to the staff and the other patient's family and now I'm taking them to you."

"Oh, crap." He gripped his phone tighter, and Ray looked up at his change in tone. "What's going on? Is it a man?"

"It is," Heidi answered.

Mason didn't vocalize the string of swear words that shot through his brain. Jayne had mentioned a man in one of her emails, and he knew Ava believed she was fixated on him.

"You need to separate them. Today," Mason said. Men and Jayne didn't mix well. She'd convinced one boyfriend to break into Mason's home, and she'd nearly died in a meth lab explosion because of the same man. According to Ava she latched on to a man, got what she wanted, and then went on her merry way, leaving bodies in her wake. The stories Ava told about Jayne and her past boyfriends made his hair curl.

He wasn't overreacting.

"I agree, but the center has rules in place and neither of them have broken any rules. They're only in each other's presence during some downtime in the common area. We have separate wings for the men and women but a shared public space."

"I remember," said Mason. He'd toured the center. It'd felt sterile and welcoming at the same time. The common area was the part that had felt like someone's home.

"They talk quietly nonstop," said Heidi. "Nothing else. But she's acting different. She smiles like she has secrets from everyone . . . not the type of smile that she's having a good day. It's a malicious smile—if that makes sense."

"It does." Mason had seen it. "What's the story with this guy?"

"I can't share much due to patient confidentiality laws, but he's quite young."

Vulnerable to a pushy older woman?

"What do you think she wants from him?" Mason asked. "If you were in her shoes, what is the appeal?"

"Attention. Admiration."

"That's pretty standard for Jayne, but I suspect there's more to it than that. She could get that from anyone. What makes this guy unique?"

"Well . . . he's from a very rich family."

"Bingo," said Mason. "Jayne can smell other people's money a mile away. You need to give this family a heads-up. If this guy has access to any accounts while he's in there, believe me, Jayne will figure out how to tap into them for her own benefit."

"But he's married," argued Heidi. "I've seen him with his wife. They're still in that newlywed phase. The whole reason he's here is to get cleaned up for her."

Mason wondered if Heidi had just crossed that patient confidentiality line. "Jayne doesn't see wedding rings. If she wants something, she plows through everything until she gets it. She doesn't care who she hurts. I'm sure your doctors have tested her and realize she's a narcissist, right?" In his own bits of research, he'd found Jayne to fit the textbook definition of the word.

Heidi was silent.

"You brought this to my attention because you know there's something wrong. I'm telling you that your instincts are right and this patient's family needs to take some precautions."

"It creates a bit of a delicate balance for us," Heidi said slowly. "These patients are here because the families want them in a safe place where they can focus on their healing. It's the reason you chose us for Jayne, correct?"

"Yes. You're saying that you don't want to warn his family that trouble might be coming from another patient? Because that would indicate your staff can't keep him safe," Mason said dryly. It was the same in all businesses: How do I cover my ass?

"He's not in harm's way," Heidi stated.

"Not physically, no," agreed Mason. "But I can assure you he'll be a shell of the man he is now if Jayne decides he has something she wants."

"I understand, Detective Callahan. I'll see what I can do on our end."

"Say, I forgot to ask Dr. Kersey last night, but do you know if anyone has called or come to the center asking for Jayne? Ava's had a couple of encounters with an older man who's shown an odd interest in finding Jayne. He claims it's because of her artwork, but Ava and I have our doubts."

"What do you think he wants?" Heidi asked.

"That's what we're wondering. It's very possible Jayne owes someone money, but that's just an educated guess."

"I'm not aware of any inquiries for Jayne. You know we'd never reveal if a patient is a resident during a phone call or to someone who walks in off the street. We have strict guidelines on patient privacy."

"I know you wouldn't. I'm primarily curious to know if this person has managed to track her."

"I'll check with our receptionist. All general calls go through her."

"Can you check right away? We'd like to know as soon as possible."

Heidi promised and wrapped up the phone call. Mason slowly replaced his receiver.

"Jayne strikes again?" Ray asked.

"Not yet. But I'm afraid she's up to something."

"Are you going to tell Ava?"

Mason didn't answer. He didn't know the answer.

"If you tell her," said Ray, "is there something she can do to help the situation?"

"That's just it. I don't think so. We're powerless on the outside. The only solution is for the staff to keep the two of them separated or else convince him or his family that he shouldn't be around her. I don't see either of those things happening."

"Will Ava be affected if Jayne messes with this other man's head?" Ray asked pointedly.

Mason understood his friend was trying to help him look at the problem logically. "Not really. She'll be disappointed in her sister, but that's nothing new."

The repercussions for Ava from Jayne's behavior couldn't be predicted.

How did you estimate the effect on a heart that'd been destroyed countless times?

• • •

Ava strode past the doors in the long hallway. The large office building stood in a nice area of southwest Portland with ample parking and quiet streets. Her assignment was to interview the director of the philanthropic organization that Denny and Louis Samuelson had both volunteered with. Mason had been on the organization's board for a good decade. It was similar to the Big Brothers Big Sisters programs. This one paired cops with at-risk youth, both boys and girls. Mason had volunteered for several years before his ex-wife pointed out that the program's children saw more of him than his own son did. Ava spotted the door that read COPS 4 KIDZ and pushed it open.

The office space was large and quite bare. She was pleased to see the nonprofit hadn't sunk its funds into designer furniture or fancy water features for the waiting room. Half of the furniture in the room was kid-size and appeared well used. Crayons, games, and books filled a large table in a corner. No signs of electronic entertainment.

Ava approved.

The receptionist greeted her and told her she'd let the director know she'd arrived. Ava had barely sat down when Scott Heuser entered the waiting room and held out his hand. She took it, slightly surprised at his youth. He looked like a fraternity pledge. Mason had spoken highly of Scott Heuser in the past, saying he'd infused the organization with fresh blood and optimism.

He introduced himself and invited her back to his office. The back area of the business was as bare as the front. No frills here. He ushered her into a small office and gestured for her to take a seat. "I've found what I can on those two officers." Candid brown eyes met hers. "You understand we try to keep track of who does what, but we have so many volunteer events it's nearly impossible to track everyone. People are supposed to sign in and they don't. Others promise to attend and then don't show up." He held up a hand as she opened her mouth. "I'm not criticizing. We're all very busy and either forget or overextend ourselves. Even I don't follow through on all my promises."

Scott flipped through a few sheets of paper on his desk. "Captain Schefte volunteered for almost twenty years. I'm impressed."

"I can see him doing that," Ava said. "He was very active outside of his job. What did he do for you?"

"He mostly coached our sports teams. Basketball for ages five through high school. Boys and girls. He also did one-on-one mentorships a few times. He hasn't done any for the past several years."

"That's where you pair a cop with a child who needs another adult influence, right?" Ava asked.

"Yes. Over two-thirds of the kids we work with come from single-parent homes . . . most of those are missing a father. The organization has more male volunteers than female, so it's worked well to pair up men with high-risk children over the decades."

"But what about proper training for these volunteers?" Ava asked. "They aren't experts in child psychology." She'd volunteered only at the big fund-raisers, which didn't have child involvement. She hadn't helped out on the true front lines.

"We have classes for the volunteers before we pair them up. We're very frank about some of the situations they might be walking into. A child might have an addict in the family or have been abused." Scott's face was stone-cold serious. "We tell them to use common sense and understand that most of the kids simply need positive attention. If they see signs of the child needing medical or psychological help, we have resources. The majority of our volunteers have been patrol cops at one point or another; they're already used to looking for the signs."

"Very true," said Ava. "They've learned on the job."

"It makes for an excellent pool of volunteers," said Scott. "Cops 4 Kidz wasn't originally intended to rely on police officer expertise; it was started because cops saw a need. Every day. Most police officers picked that profession because they want to help people. Our organization adds another opportunity to provide that help. Often on a more personal level."

"Most police officers?" Ava questioned.

Scott sighed. "You know as well as I do that some are more about their own egos. Once they realize that we don't pat them on the back for their service and that this can be heartbreaking work, they leave. We need people who have a deep desire to give and give."

"Are you saying some of them cause problems?"

"Oh, no. I didn't mean that at all. There's a level of quitting that we completely expect. We *know* it will happen. We try to screen our one-on-one volunteers very carefully so we don't let a child down when the volunteer decides this isn't the right fit for them. It's not for everyone." He looked at his papers again. "Captain Schefte was a very popular one-on-one volunteer. I wonder what made him step away?"

"How long ago did he quit doing that?"

"The last time he was paired up with a child was three years ago. I see he was assigned to fifteen different children over two decades. That's a lot of wonderful service."

"What about Louis Samuelson?" she asked.

Scott studied his second sheet. "Trooper Samuelson helped in one of the after-school homework clubs. Looks like he's good with middle school math."

"No, thank you," said Ava.

"Me neither," added Scott. "He also did mentoring. Looks like he was currently working with a fifteen-year-old boy." His mouth turned down. "I wonder if the boy has heard of his death yet. I think I better reach out to the mom and see what kind of support they need. Fifteen is a tough age for boys."

"Girls, too. All those teen years can really be difficult," Ava said. She was impressed with the director's level of personal involvement and hoped it was genuine. "You don't have Vance Weldon in your database as a volunteer?"

"I don't. That name doesn't come up anywhere. But it doesn't mean he hasn't helped out. There've been plenty of events where officers recruit their friends to come help. We don't care who shows up at the fund-raising events . . . the goal is to get out the word about our organization to struggling families. The more helpers the better. We keep precise records for the mentoring. We're very particular when we link an adult with a child."

"As you should be," Ava said. "I'll ask Vance's wife if he ever helped out. We're searching for a common thread between the three men, but this seems to only include two of them."

"I think over half the cops in the state have donated their time or money to us," said Scott. "I'm not surprised that there's a connection. Even you've helped out."

Ava nodded, mildly surprised he'd checked her out.

She stood and shook his hand. "Thank you for your time, Mr. Heuser. You have a good organization here."

"Only because of people like you." He smiled and Ava realized he'd make a good politician. She was glad he used his talent to help kids instead. She had a small flash of guilt that she gave too little of her time to his worthy cause. But everyone has a personal gift with which to help the world. Working with kids was not in her comfort zone. Her gift was the determination to stop a cop killer.

18

After leaving her interview with Scott Heuser, Ava headed southwest toward Oregon's "wine country." She'd promised to meet Mason and Cheryl at a winery in Yamhill County. Cheryl had twisted Ava's arm to convince her to drive the extra hour out to the venue. "It's perfect for you two. It's small and intimate and offers stunning views. And there's wine. Lots of wine." Cheryl had winked.

Ava wondered if Cheryl counted the number of wine bottles in their curbside glass recycling bin every other week. Or maybe she'd winked because Ava offered her a glass of wine every time she came over. Their backyard had been perfect for a quiet glass in the evenings this summer. She and Cheryl had spent many evenings sitting outside, enjoying the warm summer nights when Mason had to work late. Ava had been recovering from her injury and infection. Cheryl had proved herself to be a good listener. Other times she'd simply sat in companionable silence when Ava didn't want to talk.

Today the gray skies had burned off in the afternoon, and Ava put on her sunglasses as she sped through one of the smaller cities that dotted the highway out to the country. Suddenly golden fields and filbert orchards spread out on each side of the highway, and she relaxed for the first time in days.

It was stunning outside the metropolitan area. Rolling hills. Blue skies with fluffy clouds. Dozens of informational signs that directed visitors to wineries. If not for the fall nip in the air, she would have believed it was the middle of summer. She glanced at the clock on her dashboard and was pleased to see she'd be on time. The days were getting shorter. She would be driving back to the other side of Portland in the dark.

She took a few turns, following the directions of her GPS and enjoying the winding roads. The road straightened and she spotted a wooden sign with the name of the winery. She looked to her right and caught her breath at the Tuscan-style building at the top of the hill. She turned at the sign and drove between the fields of grapes. Butterflies danced in her stomach.

Cheryl might have found it.

At the top of the hill, she parked next to Mason's car and looked around, the butterflies growing stronger. Mason stepped out from the double doors of the winery, a big grin on his face. "What do you think?" He had a glass of red wine in his hand. Ava turned in a circle, taking in the views.

"It's stunning."

"And you're still in the parking lot. Come inside." He grabbed her hand and led her through the doors. Inside, Cheryl was talking to a man with a man-bun and neatly trimmed beard in a long room. The ceiling was lined with rustic beams, and huge windows looked to the west. Outside the windows was a patio with iron tables and chairs that begged her to sit and relax with a glass of wine. It looked out over the vineyards. In the distance the Coast Range separated the green fields from the blue sky.

"It's perfect," she mumbled to Mason. One of her eyes burned and she rubbed it. "It's perfectly perfect."

He pulled her tightly into his arms and held her. "I thought so, too."

Over Mason's shoulder she saw Cheryl hold up her glass of wine in a silent toast, her grin stating she knew she'd hit a home run.

Ava took a deep breath and moved out of Mason's bear hug. "It feels right. It's not pretentious. It's real and down-to-earth, and I could sit on that patio and stare at the mountains all day long," she told him, watching his eyes. He looked happy, and she realized it was the first time she'd seen him excited since he'd packed to go to fishing at the coast.

"But we have to do it on a sunny day," Ava said. "It wouldn't be the same if it was raining and we couldn't see ten feet past the patio."

His face fell, but he nodded. "I know. That crossed my mind. The wow factor won't be the same without the right weather."

She held his gaze. "Then we're talking about next summer. Can you wait that long? I wouldn't trust May for good weather. June is almost as iffy. July or August would be a safe bet."

"Is that what you want?"

I don't know.

Doubt must have shown on her face because worry filled his expression and he took her hands. "Do you want to wait that long?" he asked firmly.

"No," she whispered.

"But this is the right location?"

"Yes." She hated the dilemma she'd just brought to the table. "It feels right, doesn't it? And I *know* that I don't want to look at any more locations. I'm done. We found it."

"What about doing it at Christmastime?" Mason looked around the long but cozy room with its couches arranged in snug groups to facilitate conversations. It was charmingly decorated in a country Italian theme. "I'm sure it's gorgeous here at Christmas even if the weather isn't great."

Ava pressed her lips together. Nine times out of ten it rained on Christmas. She couldn't count on the weather's being clear. Snow was rarely in the holiday forecast, which was a good thing considering the winding roads and hills she'd traveled to get to the location. "I don't know. A lot of people aren't in town during Christmas."

She wanted sunshine. Blue skies and warmth. Views. Cheryl joined them and took a close look at Ava's expression. "You want it on a sunny day, don't you?"

Ava nodded, her frustration stealing her ability to speak. She wanted to marry Mason *soon*.

Cheryl patted her arm. "At least we made some progress."

• • •

Micah wondered where the man was going. He'd definitely broken his usual habits this afternoon by taking a long drive out of the city. Micah followed, a small ball of excitement growing in his stomach. The last few times the man had done something different, they'd been the most fascinating nights of Micah's life. He sat in his car and waited for the man to come out of the shop, fighting the urge to wander in and pretend to bump into him.

They hadn't talked for several months. Every now and then he got a polite email from the man, asking how things were going, but it felt forced and disinterested. Not like the caring and personal contact of the past. It'd been one of the reasons Micah had started his surveillance. Something had changed with the man and he wanted to know what.

Since he'd started following him, Micah had been stunned by the big changes in the man's life. His life had grown complicated. He'd always been dedicated and worked hard, but now he seemed preoccupied. He was more concerned with fixing something that Micah wasn't sure was broken.

He still didn't know why the man acted as he did. Watching every unusual move made Micah wonder if the man was heading for a breakdown. No one could continue as he had and not crack. He'd need someone there for him when that time came.

Micah stuck close, knowing the opportunity would come.

The man had helped him so much. He had a feeling his time to reciprocate was getting very close.

· · ·

Ava's phone rang as she followed Mason's vehicle back toward Portland. She hit the button on her steering wheel without taking her gaze from the road. Zander's voice greeted her.

"Can you come back to the office tonight?"

"Ours or the task force office?" she asked.

"Task force. We've got some things back from trace and Nora wants everyone to take a look. Euzent is also in town. He's spent the last twenty-four hours reading what I sent him and would like to meet."

Ava wanted to swear. She'd been looking forward to a quiet evening at home. Mason had bought a bottle of wine at the winery, and she wanted to sit on the sofa and figure out how to solve their wedding dilemma together.

"Yes, I can be there in half an hour."

"What did you think of the winery?" Zander asked.

"Cheryl nailed it. You should have come along. It would have been the perfect time to meet her."

"You found the right place? Did you reserve a date?"

"Lord, no. We've hit another wall as far as dates go. The problem is that this place is only perfect on a beautiful sunny day."

"Not many of those in the forecast for the next six months," said Zander.

"Probably longer," she admitted. Zander's voice sounded odd. "What's up with the evidence? Something big?" *Is he holding out until I get there?*

"Nothing that can't wait."

Maybe I shouldn't have mentioned Cheryl.

She ended the call and dialed Mason to let him know she was headed back to work instead of home. "Don't you think Cheryl would get along well with Zander?" she asked him.

"Are you playing matchmaker?"

"Maybe."

"They don't seem like the same type."

"They aren't, but maybe that's why it would work. She's outgoing and he's reserved. Sometimes reserved people appreciate being around people who bring them out."

"Or they find them annoying as hell."

"I still think it's worth an introduction."

"Zander doesn't seem to be the type who's looking for a girlfriend. He's all about work," Mason pointed out.

"He needs something in his life besides his work," Ava argued. "If anyone knows that, it's you. I don't know how his wife died—do you?"

"No, he's never brought it up. I wouldn't have known he was previously married if you hadn't said something."

"He goes silent and I can feel his defenses shoot up when he thinks our conversation is going in that direction," Ava said slowly. "It must have been very hard on him. I don't know who he has to talk to about it. I think he talks to me more than anyone else at work."

"You're lucky I'm not the jealous type."

"You're totally the jealous type," Ava stated. "You practically growl if someone talks to me in a bar."

"But I'm not worried about Zander. I know he'll respect what we have."

Ava frowned. Mason had told her he believed Zander had feelings for her, but she'd never seen him as anything but a friend. "Of course he will." Her phone did a double beep through the car's speakers. Zander was calling back.

"Zander's calling again. I'll let you know what he says." She ended their call and switched over.

"It looks like we've got another mask murder," Zander said as she answered. "It just happened. We've got an eyewitness on the scene. Put this into your GPS." Ava pulled over to the shoulder of the road and tapped in the address as he rattled it off. "I'll see you there in fifteen minutes." He ended the call.

Heart racing, Ava pulled a U-turn and headed toward an on-ramp.

19

Ava drove through the Gresham neighborhood on the edge of Portland. City of Gresham police cars lined the streets, and uniforms held back the growing crowds of gawkers. She passed two local news vans and wondered how they'd managed to get to the scene before her. During the drive she'd found out the victim was a patrol officer with the West Linn Police Department from the other side of the Willamette River. She parked where directed and got out of her vehicle. Anger and pain lined the faces of the cops she walked past.

Straight ahead a midsize Craftsman-style home waited for her. Looking around, she noticed that every home on the street was similar. The homes were too close together for her taste, but she understood the appeal of the neighborhood. Especially to young families who wanted a good-size home in a development with like-minded neighbors. Sidewalks to easily push strollers on. A small park at the entrance to the development. Neighborhood watch signs. A feeling of community and safety.

She knew a neighbor had called in suspicious activity. Maybe the neighborhood watch program did work. She moved up the walkway, nodding at the officers who waited. She had her ID and badge handy, showing them when requested. This home was decorated for Halloween, reminding her of Louis Samuelson's home, but the decor was child-friendly. Ghosts with smiles and kittens with witch hats. Not realistic blood and heavy tombstones.

Did this officer have small kids?

Her heart clenched for a brief second.

Was he a father?

She signed the log, pulled on her shoe covers, and slipped on the gloves a polite patrol officer handed her. He didn't say anything and she didn't ask questions. His expression told her that what she'd find inside was bad. Low voices sounded indoors, and she set out to find them.

She passed a formal living room, noticing a strong odor of smoke—not cigarette smoke; more like burned-dinner smoke—and headed to the back of the house, where she found an open-plan family room and kitchen. Zander and Nora stood outside the kitchen speaking with a crime scene technician who held a large camera. The dead officer was on the floor, a mask clenched in his hand. High-velocity blood spatter covered some of the lower kitchen cabinets.

Ava froze as she spotted the blood. "He was shot?" she asked.

"Nice to see you, too," said Zander. "Yes, he was shot in the chest. We definitely have a different type of scene here compared to the others." He looked at his notebook. "A call was made to 911 at six P.M. A neighbor had heard a gunshot. She stepped onto her front porch while still on the phone with the operator and saw a man running toward the entrance of the subdivision, trying to keep to the shadows of the homes."

"He ran across their lawns?" Ava asked.

"Yes, trying to avoid the streetlights."

"Where's the neighbor?"

"I have an officer sitting with her in her home," said Nora. "I told her we'd take a look at the scene and then talk with her. She has a sleeping infant in the house."

"Who is he?" Ava asked, studying the man on the wooden kitchen floor.

"Lucien Fujioka. Forty-five. Married, no kids. He's been with the West Linn Police Department for nine years. Was with the Vancouver PD before that."

"Where's the wife?"

"Sacramento," said Nora. "She travels for her job. I have an officer trying to track her down and get someone from a local department to notify her in person. This isn't the type of news you break with a phone call."

"No," agreed Ava. She squatted next to the victim and looked at the mask. "This one is from *Friday the 13th*, right?"

"Yes. The character is Jason Voorhees."

"A hockey mask?" asked Ava.

"In the films it is," said Nora. "This one is made for someone to dress up as the character. It's not an *actual* hockey mask. I compared it to images online already."

"He pulled it off," Ava commented. "Or did it never get put on?"

"Look here how the high-velocity blood spray fans over it." Zander crouched next to her and pointed with a pencil. "He wasn't wearing it when he got shot. It was in his hand. The spray pattern is consistent from the hand to the mask."

"But it looks like he exhaled blood, too," said Ava. "Which makes sense if he was shot in the chest. Could some of that spray be from him expirating blood?"

Nora stepped close and shone her flashlight on the blood, looking closely. "He expired onto his shoulder over here."

Ava stared. It all looked like high-velocity blood spatter to her. "How can you tell?"

"Someone explained the difference to me during a previous case," Nora said. "When you look closely, the tails of the blood drops are blunt and the pattern is chaotic and random. That's not what high-velocity blood spatter does. Over here on the mask you can see the sharply narrowed spines of the drops pointing in the same direction—that's what it looks like. I can also see mucus strands in the expired blood on his shoulder."

Ava leaned closer and saw the patterns Nora described. "Fascinating." She filed the new information away in her brain. She took a closer look at his hands. "He fought back!" she exclaimed. The victim had scrapes and abrasions on his knuckles. She squinted at his fingers, trying to see if he'd scratched the assailant and caught some skin under his nails.

"Yes," said Nora. "Another difference in this case besides the gunshot. He saw him coming and put up a fight."

"But the attacker was prepared with a gun. I wonder if he had a gun with him at the other murders."

"He messed up here," said Ava. "Somehow Officer Fujioka knew he was in trouble and forced the attacker to shoot. In the other attacks, they were subdued with a blow to the head and killed, and then the masks placed over their faces. Is there any evidence that the killer tried to subdue him first? Rope? A struggle somewhere?"

"The rest of the home is very neat," said the female evidence technician with the camera. "I've taken shots in every room, and I didn't see any sign of a struggle. I was about to move outside and shoot in the backyard, but I did a preliminary walk when I got here, nothing out there caught my eye. I've spent most of my time in this room."

Nora nodded. "I noticed the same lack of struggle elsewhere. I think everything happened right here. Front door was unlocked so the attacker could have walked in or been let in. There was a pizza burning in the oven when we got here, so he was making something to eat. I turned off the oven."

That explained the odor.

Their victim was barefoot, wearing jeans and an Oregon State sweatshirt. He'd been shot in the chest. Even on the dark wooden floor, the sight of the large pool of blood was overwhelming.

"A bullet hole leads into that lower cabinet," said Zander. "It looks like he was leaning his back against it when he was shot. And then he slid down to the floor."

"Cowering from someone?" Ava asked quietly. The change in the MO bothered her. Why had this one been handled so differently? Had their unsub been surprised when he entered the home, and panicked and shot? She wondered if they'd find a blow to the back of the officer's head. That would explain his low position. But why the gun?

"Why did he use a gun?" Zander echoed her thought. "He had to know someone would hear."

"Either he had no choice or it was what he wanted," said Nora.

"He wanted the police to arrive at the scene sooner?" Ava asked.

"According to the neighbor, the wife isn't due back for three days. There's a good chance no one would have found him until then," stated Nora. "He could have been here for days."

"But why get us here early?" Ava's brain tried to compute. "Did he want to watch *us* for some reason?"

An electric bolt struck her.

"What?" Zander asked sharply.

"Is someone filming the crowds out front?" she whispered.

"Yes," said Nora. "Two people. One is filming and the other is taking stills."

"I need to see them as soon as possible," Ava said, as nausea threatened to bring up her wine. Nora headed to the front door.

"What is it?" Zander asked in a low voice.

"Twice I've run into a guy who's asked me about Jayne," Ava said. "He has to be following me somehow."

"How can that be related to this?" Zander asked slowly. "You think he's doing these murders?"

The error of her premise hit her. She covered her eyes. "I'm so stupid. No, there's no way he's done these crimes. When I wondered if someone was trying to manipulate us to a location so he could watch us, I was swamped by the thought of this guy. He seems to know where to find me."

"You're saying you have a stalker." Zander eyed her seriously. "Have you reported this? Does Mason know? How often have you seen him?"

"Twice. But each time he's asked for Jayne. He's looking for her, not me." She felt like a fool for bringing it up in the middle of a crime scene. "Forget I even mentioned it."

Nora reappeared with a tech and a large camera. "Show her what you've filmed so far," she ordered, with a gesture toward Ava.

"It's not necessary," Ava said as the tech placed her camera in Ava's hands with video rolling on the large display. Ava watched as it slowly panned across the faces. The camera automatically adjusted for areas of poor lighting. "Nora, I'm sorry. I overreacted. This has nothing to do with these—"

She froze. "How do I pause this?"

The tech pressed a button. "Need me to back it up a bit?"

"Please." Ava's nerves twanged as if someone had plucked them. *I saw him. I know it was him.*

The video moved forward and Ava's finger hovered over the PAUSE button. *There.*

She stopped the video and expanded the screen with two fingers, looking at the face of the man she knew as David.

"That's him," she said quietly. "That's the guy who's approached me twice about Jayne."

Zander took the camera and studied the screen with Nora. "Stay here," he ordered Ava. "Nora and I will go take a look." They headed toward the front door, taking the camera and leaving Ava alone with the two technicians.

"Umm . . . do I need to wait, too?" asked the tech who'd been filming outside. "I have other stuff to do."

"No," Ava said, feeling exhausted. "Go get it done." The woman
paused, exchanged a glance with the other crime scene tech, and
then left.

"Hello?" a female voice called from the front of the house. A dark-
haired woman strode in carrying a black satchel. She smiled at Ava and
the crime scene tech, and took a good look at the body on the floor.
"Looks like I'm in the right place." She held out a hand to Ava. "I'm
Gianna Trask with the medical examiner's office."

Her smile was a little too sunny for Ava. "Special Agent Ava
McLane." Her vision tunneled as she looked at the medical examiner.

The smile faltered. "Maybe you should sit down, Agent McLane."
The doctor grabbed one of her arms while the tech grabbed the other,
and they guided her into a dining room chair.

Ava lowered her head between her legs, anger flooding her. *Dammit.
Get a hold of yourself.* She sucked in deep breaths.

The medical examiner squatted beside her. "Is it the blood?"

Ava choked out a laugh and lifted her head, looking into the woman's concerned brown eyes. "No, the blood doesn't bother me at all. It's
something not related to this."

Gianna nodded, but she didn't appear convinced. Ava's vision
finally seemed normal, so she stood, testing her legs. She noticed the
medical examiner taking an assessing glance at her stomach.

"Not pregnant," Ava said dryly.

The medical examiner grinned. "If it's not a dead body, then pregnancy is usually my second guess."

Her head felt like it was about to crack open, and she fought to
keep her thoughts on the crime at hand. They had another murder to
solve and her personal problems had no business getting in the way. She
exhaled and turned to Dr. Trask. "I'm better. I believe we're done taking
pictures if you want to get started."

Dr. Trask nodded and turned her attention to Lucien Fujioka, but Ava noticed she positioned herself to keep Ava in her peripheral vision. *She thinks I might get light-headed again.*

Ava was determined not to repeat the experience. She watched the medical examiner palpate Fujioka's skull. "Is there a blow to the head?" Ava asked.

"Yes. I can feel it on the left side."

"I think he realized he was about to be attacked and turned," Ava commented. "Two of the others were hit squarely in the back of the head."

"I assisted on Vance Weldon's autopsy," Dr. Trask said as she ran her hands down Lucien's arms. "I went back and reviewed all our notes when I heard it might be tied to those other officers' cases. I didn't see anything to indicate it wasn't a suicide."

"He didn't have the blow to the back of the head, right?" asked Ava.

"Correct. If it wasn't suicide, I don't know how he was subdued enough to be hanged." Dr. Trask shook her head in frustration, and Ava felt bad for the medical examiner.

"Dr. Rutledge says sometimes mistakes are made in classifications."

"They are. Doesn't mean it won't drive me batty and make me second-guess everything I saw."

Ava studied Fujioka's neck, the smooth cords of tendons and muscles, and mentally compared it with the slashed necks of two of the other cops. Weldon's neck had also looked relatively intact. *How did he get Weldon to cooperate?* "Would a stun gun have left behind some evidence if it had been used on Weldon?" asked Ava.

"Pressed directly against his flesh? Depends on the type of weapon used. I've seen a few stun guns leave small bruises and some leave nothing."

"I thought it left two little red marks."

"A Taser definitely would. Those prongs can bite into the skin. Stun guns vary widely. I didn't see any marks on Weldon that could be from a stun gun. But it doesn't mean one wasn't used."

That's not much help.

Ava looked back at the body. "This officer might have got in some blows on the suspect before he was shot," said Ava. "Please be careful bagging his hands. Our killer's DNA might be under his nails. No one else managed to lay a hand on their attacker, which might be why he was shot."

"I'm always careful," Dr. Trask said with a smile, and Ava felt a touch of embarrassment about telling her how to do her job.

Nora and Zander reappeared, their cheeks pinked from the chill of the night air. "We didn't see him," Nora said. "We both walked the crowd and didn't see anyone who could remotely look like this guy." She handed the camera to the tech who'd helped Ava sit down. "We showed it to a few of the officers holding the perimeter and no one said they'd seen him."

"Well, he's not a figment of my imagination," stated Ava. "We have him on-screen."

"Right," said Zander. "But he decided to split. I bet he became aware of the filming when the tech was asked to come inside. What's he hiding from?"

"I don't know," said Ava. "It makes no sense. I really think he's trying to find Jayne. My best guess is that she owes someone money."

"You don't believe he's related to this?" Nora pointed at the officer on the floor. "Because if not, we need to get to work."

"I really don't," Ava stated as doubt crept up her spine. Nora held her gaze for a second and then introduced herself to the medical examiner. She and Zander started a discussion about the death with the ME.

Ava half listened, wondering how "David" could be related to the mask murders.

"A hanging, two cut necks after a blow to the head, and now a gunshot with a blow to the head," Zander said. "I'm a bit surprised by the variety of murder methods."

"Has someone tried to see if the methods relate to that particular mask and movie?" Ava asked. "Does the villain in each movie prefer a method? Maybe our killer is using movies for his inspiration."

"I looked into that after hearing the Weldon case involved a mask. I couldn't find a correlation," Nora said. "Good thought, though. Let's go talk to our witness next door. Maybe that will shine some light on these cases."

20

Zander thought Audrey Kerth looked too young to have a baby. A quick request to see her driver's license showed him she was twenty-seven. At first he thought she looked young because he was getting older, but after Nora asked him her age in a whisper, he knew it wasn't just him. Audrey sat in a living room chair, her legs crossed at the ankles and her hands twisted in her lap. The home smelled like baby shampoo.

"Mr. Fujioka was the nicest guy," she said tearfully. "I thought it was cool living next door to a police officer. It always felt safer, you know?"

Her manner of speaking made her sound young, too.

"His wife Jeanine bought the cutest outfit for Molly when she was born." She wiped her nose with the back of her hand. "Did you get a hold of her yet? Does she know that her husband's been . . ." Fresh tears streamed.

"I haven't heard," said Nora. "I asked the local Sacramento Police Department to go to her hotel and notify her."

Beside him Ava sat very still as she watched and listened to the young mother. Zander's train of thought kept wavering from the crime at hand to Ava's possible stalker. *A definite stalker.* The man had shown up three times at Ava's location and vanished out front the moment he'd thought someone had spotted him.

Zander wasn't surprised to hear Jayne's name associated with the stalker. Anything disruptive in Ava's life traced its origins to her twin.

"Then I heard a gunshot," Audrey said. "I waited a few seconds to see if there'd be another. That's when I crept into Molly's room and took her out of her crib. I wasn't going to let her out of my sight if someone was shooting."

"There was only one shot?" Nora asked.

"I only heard one. I thought it'd come from the direction of the Fujioka house, so I peeked through Molly's blinds. I could see someone moving in the kitchen."

"Show us," said Nora. She, Ava, Zander, and the female officer who'd been waiting with Audrey followed the mother down the hallway. Audrey stopped outside a bedroom door that was open a few inches.

"Please be quiet," she whispered. "Molly's asleep." She pushed open the door. Inside she reached over the diaper changing table and twisted the rod to open the blinds. She had a perfect view through the window over the Fujioka side yard and into the kitchen. The distance appeared to be about twenty feet.

Zander could see Dr. Trask talking to one of the techs.

"What did you see?" Nora whispered. Audrey motioned for them to leave the baby's room. Zander stood back to let the women leave first. Ava paused and looked into the crib. She reached out as if to touch the baby but pulled her hand back at the last second. She glanced up and looked Zander's way, but he couldn't see her expression in the shadows. She gazed in his direction for a long moment and then followed the other women.

Huh.

He didn't know what to think of her behavior. Women loved babies, right? It was in their genes to touch soft baby hair and cheeks. But he'd never heard Ava say a maternal word in her life.

But she's getting married. Married can mean babies.

He couldn't see Mason Callahan going the kid route again. His son was in college, and he seemed content to blissfully move on, just he and Ava.

Is that how she feels, too?

He put it out of his head. The same way he'd earlier dismissed the images of a winery wedding. He was good at mentally filing away things he didn't want to think about.

"I saw a man leaving the kitchen," Audrey said as Zander entered the living room. "His back was to me, so I never saw his face."

"You knew he'd fired the gun?"

"No," said Audrey. "But he wasn't someone I'd seen over there before." She looked down and blushed slightly. "I don't spy. But sometimes when I'm changing Molly, I look over there. It's hard not to."

"So he was a stranger to you." Ava paused. "But you didn't see his face. How do you know he was a stranger?" She smiled at the young woman to take the sting out of her direct question.

Audrey's brows furrowed. "I don't know. You're right, though. I guess it's just my instinct telling me I didn't know him. I saw him again when I went outside."

"You went outside with your daughter? After a gunshot in the neighborhood?" Zander asked.

"Looking back, that was rather stupid," Audrey admitted. "But I was holding her. Your baby feels safe when she's in your arms, you know?" She raised her brows and looked at Ava for agreement. Ava gave a stiff nod.

"I had my phone in my pocket when I stepped out on the front porch. I wasn't worried about the man I'd seen next door, because I didn't realize that the gunshot had hurt someone. I thought it was an accident . . . that maybe one of Mr. Fujioka's guns had gone off while he was cleaning it or something. But then I saw someone dash across the street and I could see the gun in that man's hand. That's when I called 911."

"He had his back to you at that time, too?" Ava asked. They moved through Audrey's front door and out onto her porch. Two Adirondack chairs with a small table between them filled the welcoming space. An autumn bouquet in Halloween colors graced the table, and a happy stuffed scarecrow sat in one chair. The number of people on the sidewalk across the street had thinned a bit, but the spectators turned in the direction of Audrey's home.

Audrey stepped backward as the impact of their nosy stares hit her. "Oh, my," she muttered. "He ran across the street right where that second patrol car is." She pointed and moved her arm as she traced a route. "Then he ran up close to the Pearsons' garage, and I thought he was going to go in their house, but instead he stood in the shadow at the front. I don't know if he saw me or not, it was too dark to see, but it felt like he looked right at me and that's when he decided to run. He sprinted across their lawn, keeping close to the house and into the next yard. He did that all the way around the corner." She pointed to where the street arced to the left and went out of sight. "He was trying to stay out of the streetlights. Those homes didn't have their outside lights on."

They had them on now, Zander noticed. Every street on the house was lit up, and faces often looked out the windows.

"I never saw his face," Audrey said slowly, "But I saw his profile . . . in bad light. It's more like I have an impression of what he looks like instead of an actual view of his face."

"You told the operator he had dark hair," said Nora. "And that it was a medium length. He wore a dark long-sleeved jacket or shirt and dark pants. You couldn't guess his age and you said he wasn't heavy or super skinny, but very average build."

Audrey nodded. "I couldn't guess at his height, either. I had nothing to compare him to."

Zander pointed at the garage across the street, ignoring the gawkers. "You said he stood over there. Do you remember where the top of his head was in relation to the panels on the garage door?"

Audrey scowled as she looked. Her shoulders lifted as she took a deep breath and tilted her head, concentrating. "But he wasn't standing up straight," she said. "He was hunched over, like he was trying to hide."

"Good point." Zander let the question go. "I know you said you couldn't tell his age, but would you say he ran like someone young or old? Or perhaps like someone who didn't run very often?"

"He moved smoothly," Audrey said. "It didn't look difficult at all. He didn't hold himself like someone older, either. He bent over deliberately, not because he needed to."

"What can you tell me about the weapon?" he asked.

She shook her head. "Not much. It was small. A handgun. Not a rifle or shotgun."

Zander figured they'd be able to find the bullet below the kitchen. He hadn't opened the cupboard door with the bullet hole in it, because the body was in the way, but he knew there was a chance the bullet had gone all the way through the flooring. He was glad he wouldn't be the one scrambling through the crawl space under the home.

"Will they want to talk to me?" Audrey asked quietly, looking at the news cameras setting up across the street from the Fujioka home.

"They will ask," Ava said. "By the look on your face, I'd guess that's the last thing you want to do. Can Officer Layden take you somewhere?" she asked with a gesture at the female officer.

"I think I better go to my sister's," Audrey said, moving back into the house. "I don't want to be a part of this."

"We have your number," Nora said. "We might need to talk with you again."

"That's fine." Audrey started to pace in the living room, wringing her hands again. "I need to pack up all Molly's things. Her bottles, her toys, enough diapers. Who knows how long we'll be gone." She grabbed a big diaper bag off a chair and dashed down the hall, disappearing into the baby's room.

Zander looked at Nora and Ava. "So we have a description of our suspect. A man. A man who is extremely average in every way."

"Should make our job easy," said Nora.

He wondered where the long hair on the previous two victims had come from.

• • •

The next morning Ava glanced at the clock in the hallway of the morgue. It was seven A.M. and she felt as if she'd barely slept. Probably because she hadn't gotten home until two A.M. They'd waited at the Fujioka murder scene until Dr. Trask had finished her exam. The doctor hadn't seen any other obvious evidence on the victim. "I suspect I'll discover he was hit in the head and then shot," she'd told the investigators. "He'll be my first patient in the morning and I'll know more then."

Zander had told her and the evidence techs to keep an eye out for any long dark hair.

She and Nora were waiting for Zander before they joined Dr. Trask for the autopsy. "I think the victims have to know our suspect," said Ava as she put money in a machine to buy herself a cup of questionable coffee. She needed caffeine. There was no sign that she'd be able to catch up on sleep anytime soon. "There's no forced entry in any of the homes. Although Denny Schefte was lured outside somehow. I wish we knew what'd made him go outside, I have to imagine he got a call or text on his phone that made him step out."

Nora shook her head. "We heard back from his wireless provider. He hadn't had any calls or texts within his last few hours. And all the calls and texts from earlier that day were from the guys he was with."

"Dammit. So why'd the killer take his phone, if not to slow down our investigation?"

"Maybe to sell it?"

"Mason said it was old. I doubt it was worth anything. And this guy is good . . . he's got us scrambling to find him. I don't see him grabbing a phone because he might make a buck off of it."

"Then it was probably for a trophy."

Ava nodded grimly. That answer made sense. "What was the evidence Zander called me about before the murder last night?" she asked. "I kept meaning to ask you yesterday."

"We found the same fingerprint on two of the masks that doesn't belong to any of the responders or family members," said Nora.

"It's on two masks?" Ava's attention perked up fifty points. "Which ones?"

"On Weldon's and Samuelson's."

"Yes! I *knew* Weldon belonged to the group." Ava grinned. "It's that final confirmation we needed. No leads on the print, though?"

"It hasn't turned up in any of the databases we've searched," said Nora. "We're combing through some others."

Ava could tell there was something she hadn't shared. "Just one print? A one-fingered killer?" she joked.

"We're wondering if it was planted on the masks," Nora said.

"Why is that?"

"Have you ever listened to the fingerprint guys talk when they find an unusual print?" Nora asked.

"Yes." Ava nodded. "They turn into a bunch of science geeks. Totally excited and talking in jargon that I don't understand. I think an interesting find after looking at boring fingerprints all day shoots them over the top."

"This print made the whole evidence department have nerdgasms," said Nora.

Ava snorted.

Nora pulled out her phone and opened up an image, holding it out to Ava. Ava studied the enlarged fingerprint. She knew very little about prints, and she glanced at Nora in confusion. "Am I seeing a happy face?"

Nora nodded, and Ava looked at the print again. The whirls and swirls of the print formed two eyes and a perfectly symmetrical smile. Apparently this was heaven to fingerprint technicians. "It's very unusual. Is that why you think it might be planted?"

"This was the sole print inside of each mask." Nora stated. "It's such a rare print, it made us wonder if they're having a bit of fun with us."

"If we find a suspect with this print, that'd be some pretty incriminating evidence," said Ava. "If everything else makes sense."

"If the suspect doesn't have it, does that mean he didn't do it?" Nora countered.

"No, of course not," Ava admitted. "But it wasn't on Schefte's mask?"

"No. But we'll check the mask from the scene last night."

Ava studied the smile on the phone. Was someone messing with them? "Are they sure it's real? Could someone have created it?"

"It's real. They were positive. A print like that isn't unheard of, but it is quite rare."

"Pretty cool, isn't it?" Zander asked, looking over her shoulder.

"You would like this sort of thing." She turned to look at him. "You're the biggest science geek—" She stopped, stunned by the dark circles under his red eyes. "You okay?"

Zander looked away. "Yeah. Didn't sleep."

Ava bit the inside of her cheek. She'd worked with Zander on cases where no one got sleep, but she'd never seen him look this bad. He looked as if he'd finished a fifth of tequila and not slept in days. "It was a disturbing scene last night," she agreed, watching him closely.

"Bad one."

Bullshit. Louis Samuelson spiked to a wall in his living room had been ten times worse than their murder scene last night. Whatever was bugging Zander, he clearly wasn't going to share it at the moment. Either he didn't want to talk or it was nothing and he was coming down with the flu.

Or he was just being Zander. Silent man who never shared what bugged him.

Probably that last option.

"You up for this?" she asked, tipping her head toward the door to the autopsy suite.

"Not a problem," he stated.

"Is Henry joining us this morning?" she asked Nora.

"Henry doesn't do autopsies," said Nora with a smile. "He gets to skip them because I'm afraid he'll crack his skull open when he hits the floor, and he refuses to wear the protective brain bucket I suggested."

"He's fainted?" Zander asked.

"Three times. I let it go after that. It's easier to hold the weakness over his head and demand favors."

The three of them stepped into the autopsy suite and Ava felt the temperature dip ten degrees. She'd expected it and had worn two layers under her sweater. They donned long-sleeved ankle-length gowns and shoe covers and picked up face shields, planning to get up close to Dr. Trask's work. Ava was curious to see how the petite doctor worked with death. She'd found her to be down-to-earth and amusing while she did her once-over of Lucien Fujioka last night. Most pathologists Ava had met had pretty good senses of humor. She figured it was necessary to face their job day after day.

The doctor was already at work in what reminded Ava of a big industrial kitchen. Stainless steel tables and gurneys, long hoses, scalloped knives that looked like bread knives, and the large colanders at the sinks perpetuated the kitchen impression. The body on the table with the long Y incision did not.

Neither did the heavy-duty hedge shears in Dr. Trask's hands. She moved onto a step stool to get a better angle over the body, and glanced over as the three of them neared the table. "Good morning," she said cheerfully. Her dark eyes and long dark ponytail were all Ava could see of her under her protective gear. An eighties band played a rock ballad in the background, and Ava noticed the assistant silently moved her hips with the rhythm.

Ava steeled herself for the crack of the ribs between the blades of the shears and looked away. The sound belonged in a horror movie. She looked back in time to see Dr. Trask and her assistant lift out a bony section of chest. Ava had watched the violent cutting and prying open once before; it'd been enough.

The doctor deftly removed the major organs for her assistant to weigh and log. Ava knew a small sample would be removed from each one for study and preservation, and then the organs would be returned to the body. But not in the perfect positions they'd held during his life; they'd be dumped back in rather unceremoniously. "I've already done a thorough exam of the exterior," Dr. Trask said. "I was right about the blow to the side of the head. I didn't find any other trauma except the shot to the chest." She tipped her head to the bony section her assistant had set aside. "I followed the path of the bullet. It went directly between two ribs, through his left ventricle, and out his back in a downward trajectory. I took several pictures so you can see the angle. Since the bullet hole in the cabinet door followed a similar trajectory, it's logical that Mr. Fujioka was leaning against the cabinet door and was shot by someone standing in front of him."

"They'll look for the bullet today," said Zander.

"It'll be a big one," said Dr. Trask. "He has a wide entrance wound and it traveled very straight. Lots of power behind it."

"Any gunpowder or stippling on him?" Ava asked.

"Very light. The killer wasn't holding the gun very close to his victim."

"But the victim was definitely shot while he was sitting on the floor," clarified Nora.

"Yes. Unless your shooter is eleven feet tall," said Dr. Trask with a smile. "I suspect your eyewitness might have mentioned that odd fact."

"Nope. He was average-size. Too average," said Ava. "Did you find anything unusual?" she asked as the doctor prepared to finish her work.

"I didn't find any long hairs that Agent Wells asked me to look for, and there wasn't any tissue under his nails. From the films of his skull, he was hit once with a blunt object that could have been a baseball bat or something of a similar size and width."

Ava looked at Nora and Zander. "Audrey didn't mention seeing our suspect carry anything like that. Even though it was dark, I would think she'd spot that."

"No one reported anything like that inside or outside of the house. How could we have missed something that large?" asked Nora. "I'll have Henry call Audrey and ask if she remembers him carrying a bat."

"I'm not positive it's a bat," Dr. Trask said quickly.

"Understood," said Nora. "But it sounds like we missed something at the scene." Her phone rang. "Perfect timing. It's Henry. Excuse me a minute." She stepped out of the autopsy suite to take his call.

"We have a mutual friend," Dr. Trask said to Ava in the silence that followed.

"Who's that?" Ava had heard the medical examiner was new to the state.

"Michael Brody. The newspaper reporter? He's my boyfriend's brother." She stumbled over the word "boyfriend," and Ava understood. It'd been awkward for her to use the teenage term to describe Mason. It'd been a relief when she could start saying "fiancé."

"Yes, I've met Michael a few times. My fiancé has known him for quite a while. They seem to have a love/hate type of relationship."

"That's how Chris described it, too."

The autopsy suite doors swung open and Nora strode back in. "We've got a guy who claims he killed all four cops," she exclaimed. "And he knows about the masks."

21

"We have a subject who wants to confess." Mason heard the excitement in Ava's voice over the phone. "He walked into the Portland police's North Precinct and asked to speak to a detective about the murders. They're transporting him to your building downtown and thought I'd give you a heads-up. I'm leaving as soon as I wrap up some paperwork at the medical examiner's office, but Zander and Nora should be there by now."

Mason glanced around the detectives' room. No one else was present. Duff Morales and Steve Hunsinger hadn't returned to work yet after Denny's death. The other Major Crimes detectives were out on calls. He'd have to go up a floor to find Nora Hawes. "Got it," he told Ava. "I'll figure out where they're bringing him. He hasn't confessed yet?"

"Once the detective realized that this person knew what he was talking about, he halted the interview and reached out to Detective Hawes, thinking the task force needed to handle the interview. Nora said he brought up the masks."

"Good move."

"I'll be there as soon as I can. Nora said she'd wait for me before starting the interview." Amusement entered her tone. "She said it very deliberately. I think she was trying to hint that you shouldn't be there."

"Too bad. I'll watch through the mirror. She can't complain about that."

"Sure she can."

"She won't." *I hope.* He ended the call, telling her to drive safely, and jogged down the hallway to the stairs. He took them two at a time and hit the fire door from the stairwell a bit too hard, announcing his entry to everyone who worked on that floor. He knew Nora was using the room directly over his. They'd joked about running a cup-and-string system out the window for communication. Nora stepped out of a room, a file tucked under her arm.

"I see you've heard," she stated. She cut him off as he started to plead his case. "You'll stay in the observation room and you won't say a word."

"Agreed."

They moved down the hall together, and she looked at him out of the corner of her eye. "Don't think I'm a pushover."

"I don't." He matched his stride to hers.

"I might expect the same courtesy one day."

"I hope I never have to extend it to you," he said sincerely.

"I'm doing this for two reasons," she said firmly. "One: I want all the eyes and ears possible on this case. You were at the scene and might pick up on something I or the FBI might miss. And two: you and Denny go way back."

"I appreciate it."

"I could be risking my position."

"I'll go to bat for you. I can be very persuasive and everything's feeling disorganized in the office with Denny gone. I don't think anyone will come down on us for coloring outside the lines a bit."

"There's talk that you're being considered as Denny's replacement."

Mason tripped. "What? No. That can't be right." *I'm not supervisor material.*

"I've heard it from two people. It hasn't reached you?"

"Lord, no. I'd turn it down anyway."

"Why?" Green eyes turned his way.

"I'm not a boss. I don't want the headaches that come with supervising people, and I'm crappy at telling people what to do."

"From what I've seen you're a natural leader."

"You haven't seen much. Sure, I can manage a scene in the field. But sit behind a desk and listen to everyone's complaints? Berate a detective for breaking a rule that I probably would have broken, too? That's not for me."

"Huh."

He glanced at her. "You like doing that stuff?"

"I like people. I've had supervisory positions in the past. I've been told I do it well."

"If they come to me, I'll suggest you."

She snorted. "That'll go over well. I've been in this office for two weeks and am the only female in Major Crimes. Is this your way of getting me to go back to Salem?"

"The guys around here could use some shaking up. If you're fair, they'll be fair." *I think.*

She lifted an eyebrow, giving him a "You're bullshitting me" expression.

"Maybe not," he admitted.

They worked their way to the interview rooms and found Zander waiting outside one. They stepped inside the adjacent observation room to get a look at the confessor.

"He's young!" Mason exclaimed. "There's no way . . ." He let the sentence fall away. Age didn't matter these days. Teenagers filled the headlines with their brutal crimes. Even some preteens.

"The masks might make more sense if he's our guy," said Zander. "I kept feeling there was a younger element to those choices."

"How old is he?" asked Nora.

"He's twenty," supplied Zander. "Name's Micah Zuch."

Mason studied the slouching young man at the table. He had dyed his unruly hair an impenetrable black and wore black skinny jeans, a ripped black shirt, and a black jacket. He was thin to the point that Mason wanted to order him a Big Mac. Two of them.

"Street kid?" he asked.

Zander shook his head. "I have a home address from southeast Portland. His mother lives there. No father in the picture."

"He's twenty and lives at home?" Mason asked. Although his son Jake was nearly twenty, and he still lived at home when he wasn't in school. Micah didn't look like a college student.

"I think it's more common these days than when we were twenty," said Zander. "It's cheaper to live at home. Cost of living is higher now."

Only because kids today believe the cost of living includes an iPhone, a new car, and a big-screen TV.

"At first he told us he was homeless," Nora said. "He told the detective he lived on the streets with some of the other homeless kids but eventually admitted he went home to sleep. Sounds like he spends a lot of his time on the streets, though."

"A street kid wannabe," Mason murmured. "What type of person wants to pass himself off as one of them?"

"They're edgy. Independent," said Zander.

"They're also hard up to find a place to shower and sleep. Many of them resort to crime to fund their drug habits or meals."

"There's got to be a misguided admiration on his part," suggested Zander. "Why don't kids look up to real leaders?"

"Beats me," said Mason.

"He knew about the masks," said Nora, pulling them back on topic. "He told the detective which masks were at each scene. We've kept that completely to ourselves."

Mason shot her a sharp look. "Did he include Vance Weldon? Even the press isn't aware of that case."

Nora looked at her notepad. "He said the first guy wore a Freddy Krueger mask." She exchanged a look with Zander and Mason. "I'd say he knows a lot about our cases."

"You're assuming he's telling the truth," said Zander. "We've had a half-dozen people call to claim they killed Denny Schefte. Up until now it's been easy to eliminate them." He looked at Micah. "I have the feeling this isn't our guy—no matter what he knows. He's a toothpick. Do you really think he had the arm strength to lift Samuelson up on that wall in his living room?"

"Maybe he wasn't alone," said Nora. "But he claims he acted alone."

Someone rapped on the observation room door and Ava stuck her head in before anyone could move. "Sorry I'm late." She stepped inside and looked through the window. "He's so young!"

Mason felt justified. It wasn't *his* age that'd made him see Micah Zuch as young; Ava was twelve years younger than he. Nora brought her up to date.

"I'd like to go in first," said Zander. "I don't see the point in easing our way into his good graces. I want to know if we're wasting our time. That shouldn't be too hard to figure out."

Nora agreed, and Zander stepped out of the observation room.

Mason bit his tongue, remembering his promise to stay silent.

Zander appeared in the interview area and placed a notepad on the table as he sat across from Micah. "I'm Special Agent Zander Wells. I understand you have information on some murders." He clicked his pen, positioned it over the notepad, and looked at Micah expectantly.

Micah stared back. "Special agent? Like as in the FBI?"

"Yes." Zander offered no more explanation.

"Can I see some ID?" Micah hadn't moved from his slouch.

Zander silently held out his identification. The young man looked at it and nodded. "Why is the FBI here? Isn't this a Portland police building?"

"I'll ask the questions. Do you have something to share with us or not?" Zander glanced at his watch.

Micah straightened in his chair and lifted his chin. "I killed those cops."

"Which ones?"

"The guy at the coast. The one in southeast. The one last night and the one up in Vancouver."

Zander didn't write down anything. "What are their names?"

He recited four names, which Zander listed across the top of his pad.

Mason didn't get excited. All that information could have been found online. Except the information about Vance Weldon.

"How did you kill Special Agent Weldon?" Zander emphasized his title.

"I hung him," he said simply.

Zander wrote something under Vance's name and looked hard at Micah. "Vance was a big guy. How'd you do that?"

The young man snorted. "Don't you know anything about engineering? Ever hear of a pulley?"

"There wasn't a pulley at the scene."

"I took it with me."

"What was Special Agent Weldon wearing?"

Micah described the man's clothing perfectly, including his shoes and the type of mask he'd had on.

Optimism swept through Mason. Had their killer walked in off the street?

"Why'd you kill Special Agent Weldon?" Zander asked as he wrote down the articles of clothing under Vance's name.

"No reason."

Zander looked at him for several seconds.

No reason? Mason exchanged a look with Ava and Nora.

"How did you kill Captain Denny Schefte?" Zander moved on as if Micah's answer didn't matter. Mason knew he wouldn't feed the man's ego. An answer like "No reason" was a clear request for more questions about his motive. Zander neatly stepped on it by setting the question aside as if it held no consequence.

"I cut his neck. But first I hit him on the head."

"What did you hit him with?"

"A baseball bat."

"Where did this take place?"

"A cabin outside of Depoe Bay." He went on to perfectly describe what Denny had been wearing that night.

Mason listened, seeing the clothing in his mind's eye. He was disturbed by the monotonous delivery of Micah's answers. The man sounded like a robot. He sat perfectly still in his chair, having moved only when he'd first realized the FBI was interviewing him. That appeared to be the one element he hadn't been prepared for. He'd had ready answers for every question and didn't hold back. Except when questioned about motive.

Again he answered, "No reason," when Zander asked why he'd killed the captain.

"He could have gotten all this information from photographs or police reports," Ava whispered. "Could we have a leak somewhere?"

"But that still doesn't explain why he's confessing," Nora said.

"It could take a team of psychiatrists to answer that," said Ava. "I don't like his behavior. It's unnatural. He doesn't move, there's no inflections in his voice." She rubbed at the back of her neck as she frowned. "It's like he's been programmed. Is someone pulling his history?"

"Yes. I have a staff member digging right now," said Nora.

Zander continued with identical questions about Louis Samuelson and Lucien Fujioka. Micah answered perfectly.

Zander stood, thanked him, and started to leave.

"Wait!" said Micah, looking startled. "Now what?"

The three investigators in the side room leaned closer to the window.

Zander frowned. "You just confessed to four murders of cops. You go to prison."

Nora snorted as Mason and Ava grinned at Zander's exaggeration.

"But . . . what about a trial and stuff?"

"Don't *you know anything* about crimes?" Zander asked, throwing Micah's earlier words back in his face. "You just confessed. Prison." He scowled at the man. "Or are you changing your story now?"

Mason couldn't read the young man's face. He seemed torn. Whatever he'd expected would happen after he'd confessed hadn't happened.

"Don't you need to take my fingerprints? My DNA? And compare it to your evidence?"

Zander waved a hand. "Later. They'll take all that when they process you at the prison. Your confession is solid. You got all the facts right. Only someone who'd killed these men could have told me everything you just did."

"I did kill them!" he said earnestly.

"Did I say you didn't?" asked Zander. "I just wrote down your confession. We're good with this. I don't think I have any more questions." He moved toward the door. "I'll send in an officer."

Micah stood. "Wait a minute. This can't be all!"

"Oh, shit," muttered Mason. "This isn't right. Why's he trying to convince us?"

"He may have not killed them, but he was there, or else he has access to the facts of these cases," said Nora.

"I think he's glory-seeking," said Ava. "He wants to be questioned more. He's not a killer."

The door to the observation room opened and a female officer stepped in with a file. Zander entered right behind her. She handed the file to Nora and excused herself. Zander waited until the door closed and then looked at the three of them. "I don't know what to think about that kid," he stated. "Yes, he knows everything, but he's not acting right. He's involved somehow, but I don't believe I was sitting across from a cop killer. It felt as if I was interviewing someone who plays a lot of video games and has never caused real violence." He shook his head. "Something is off with him."

"He wanted you to question him more," Ava said. "Why would he do that?"

"I have no idea." Zander turned to look at Micah through the glass. "What do we know about him?" Micah now paced back and forth in the interview room, a fixed scowl on his face, waves of frustration rolling off him.

Nora frowned as she scanned the file. "Oh brother."

"What is it?" Mason asked.

"His background is a mess and I'm only looking at two years of it. This report started when he turned eighteen, and I suspect there's more from when he was younger. He was expelled from high school his senior year after planting a fake bomb and calling in a threat. Portland police responded, and the bomb was a mishmash of harmless pipes and powder. Before that he'd been kicked out of *another* school for bringing two knives and an unloaded gun to school."

"All that since he turned eighteen?" Ava asked.

"Yes. Looks like he was eighteen before he started his senior year . . . a bit older than the other students. He's been busy. There's a statement from a teacher that says she'd seen a disturbing pattern of overreaction to situations and it made her very nervous to be around him. The slightest thing would set him off in the classroom. He'd take offense if someone looked at him wrong or said something rude. She thinks that's why he brought the knives and gun—on the same day—to the school. He felt he had something to prove."

"What about his home life?" asked Zander.

"Doesn't say. It lists the same address he gave earlier. Oh, wait. Here's a report. His mother filed a report with local police that twice someone had left a dead cat on her porch. The responding officers questioned her son and Micah confessed that he'd done it."

"What? That's disgusting," said Ava, wrinkling her nose. "Then what happened?"

"I can't tell. That was pretty recent. I imagine he has a court date coming up. This report says the mother tried to stop the officers from pressing charges, saying that she didn't want her son arrested, but it was out of her control by then. If he admitted to it, he's going to be charged."

"If my kid was killing cats, I'd want the police involved," Ava said slowly. "I don't think I'd try to protect him. Clearly he needs some sort of mental help."

"It's hard when it's your kid," Mason stated. "I'd murder Jake if I caught him doing that. But would I want him thrown in jail? I think I'd drag him to a shrink first."

"What if he confessed to the cats like he just confessed to the murders?" Ava asked. "What do they call that, when someone continually confesses to things they didn't do?"

"It's called needing a kick in their ass," muttered Mason. Ava poked him in the ribs.

"I wonder if he's seen a psychiatrist," Nora asked. "I'd like his doctor's opinion on this. Do you think Micah would tell us if he's had mental health treatment?"

"Can't hurt to ask," said Zander. "Even though he knows a lot of facts from those murders, I don't think he did it. I do think he knows who committed them."

"Could he want to impress some street kids?" murmured Ava. "Maybe he's stepped forward to steal their thunder or protect some of them."

"These weren't sloppy murders," Zander pointed out. "Not something I'd expect a group of street kids to do. He's confessing for a reason, but we don't know what it is yet."

"No one here thinks he's our killer?" asked Nora. Silence met her question.

"Dammit."

22

Nora Hawes had given him the stink-eye a few times, but Mason ignored it. He was going to push every boundary he could until she explicitly told him to get lost. Until then he wasn't going anywhere. He read the computer screen over Henry Becker's shoulder as the detective went through Officer Fujioka's history. Henry had checked Fujioka's name against the crimes on which Schefte and Samuelson had crossed paths, and had come up empty. Zander had supplied some of Vance Weldon's FBI case history, but Mason knew it was incomplete. The FBI wouldn't blindly hand over information on its domestic terrorism cases. Zander had taken Fujioka's information and gone back to the FBI office to work with Special Agent Mercy Kilpatrick in the privacy of their own computers and databases. He'd promised to return to the task force by that evening.

"Officer Fujioka volunteered with three different philanthropy programs," said Ava, stepping into the room. "I don't know how he had time to go to work. He also attended the HealthNut fitness center that the other two men belonged to." Frustration crossed her face. "We need to find a narrower connection."

"The connection might be pretty old," said Mason. "Remember the Bridge Killer?" He was referring to a past case in which the adult murder victims had been friends as teenagers.

"I can't forget," Ava muttered. "And now I'm thinking about the women who were murdered last summer because they were all in law enforcement."

Her face had paled a bit. That case had nearly pushed her over the edge, and she'd considered leaving the FBI. "How long are we going to let Micah Zuch sit in that room?" she asked.

"He's fine," said Mason. "He's got McDonald's and a soda. That keeps every kid that age satisfied for a while."

"He's not a kid. He's twenty."

"He's a kid," asserted Mason. "He's no man." He'd been disgusted with the whining behavior Micah had displayed after Zander's interview. Displeased with the brevity of the interview, Micah had asked to talk to Zander's boss. Nora had mollified him with promises of "I'll see what I can do." The fast food had kept him quiet for an hour, and Mason suspected a video game system would keep the kid silent for the next twenty-four hours.

"Special Agent Euzent is upstairs," said Ava. "He's watching the video of Zander's interview with Micah. I peeked in and saw him shake his head over and over."

"He knows the kid is lying."

"Now to get Micah to tell us who really did it," Ava said. "He has to know."

"I wonder if Euzent would be useful in that interview. With all his hocus-pocus, witchy reading of people, I bet he can get the kid to beg to tell the *real* truth."

"Profiling isn't hocus-pocus." She gave him a stern look.

He knew that, but at least he'd distracted Ava from thinking about last summer's near-death experience. "I have the utmost respect for your profiler. You know that. He's been a big help in the past. Let's go see if

Micah's ready to talk to us." He followed Ava up to the next floor and into the small conference room. Six other members of the task force were already present, including Nora and Henry.

Nora stepped to the front of the room and held up her hand to capture everyone's attention. "Before Special Agent Euzent gives us his thoughts on our unsub, I just heard from the evidence team. We've got a fingerprint from last night's mask. It matches the unusual print on Samuelson and Weldon, and we checked Micah Zuch's fingerprints. He doesn't have the smiley face."

Ava had told Mason about the smiley face fingerprint. He wasn't surprised to learn it didn't belong to Micah Zuch. It'd bugged him that it hadn't been present at Denny's murder scene, and now it'd turned up at the fourth death. Why not at Denny's?

"Is there anything else that's different from the Schefte scene?" Henry asked, voicing Mason's train of thought. "One case without that marker seems odd."

"I agree," said Nora. "And the fingerprint has been in the exact same spot on each mask. It's on the inside of the forehead area." She looked at Special Agent Bryan Euzent. "Your thoughts? Are we wrong to include Denny Schefte's murder?"

No! Mason clamped his lips together to keep from speaking out. Denny was part of this. He could feel it.

"Everything but that fingerprint indicates Denny was killed by the same person," said Euzent. "I'd speculate that he forgot to leave that signature behind or it was eliminated during the actual murder . . . or the during the evidence collection."

Nora's chin shot up, but she stayed silent. Mistakes happened. They all knew it. "The press has reported that we have a suspect in custody," she said. "I've asked public relations to issue a statement to set them straight, clarifying that someone has come forward with information."

"I think you knew Micah Zuch wasn't your suspect before you fingerprinted him," said Euzent. "I want to know how he got his information. Let him stew in that room for a few more hours and then go in strong to find out how he knows so many facts."

"What would make someone confess to murder?" asked Henry. "Especially four murders?"

Euzent gave a pleased smile that made Mason's stomach clench. The clean-cut FBI agent enjoyed talking about psychopaths a little too much. Over the past year, Mason had learned that the more twisted the mind, the more fascinated Special Agent Euzent became. A twenty-year-old kid who'd confessed to four murders he hadn't committed must have made Euzent's day. Or year.

"Keep in mind that all I've seen is the interview," said Euzent. "Although I did read his file. I *know* there has to be a juvenile record on him. In it I suspect we'd find more acting out and childlike crimes of impulsiveness. The adolescent brain feels fearless and has no appreciation for consequences."

"But he's twenty. He should know better," said Ava.

"Exactly. His brain hasn't caught up yet. Maybe it never will. It doesn't matter what he's been told by his mother—and I'm sure at some point he was taught that murder is wrong and punishable—what matters to him is what *he believes* within his frame of reality. It appears to me that he expected something else would happen when he confessed. It's pretty clear on that video that the interview didn't proceed the way he wanted.

"The brains in this room are fully developed, right?" Euzent raised an eyebrow as he scanned his small audience. "We take consequences into account before we act. For some reason Micah doesn't do that." He tapped the file on the table in front of him. "And from what I've read in his file, he never has. I see a lot of behaviors of concern here and the file is only two years old. There's lying, blaming others, animal abuse, a strong interest in weapons, and evidence of intense resentment where he blames others for his issues. I don't know if you read the statement by his teacher, but she said he'd blamed her for his test failures and therefore for his poor GPA and his failure to be admitted to college."

"He could go to community college," Mason muttered.

Euzent pointed at him, amusement in his eyes. "Aha. A rational brain sees another path. But in Micah's brain, it's all his teacher's fault. His college hopes are over and *none* of it was his fault. Therefore he has the right to be angry and cause problems for others because his own hopes have been destroyed. The kids who display this sort of behavior won't take the blame for anything. It's always someone else's fault that their life isn't what it was supposed to be."

"But he's taking blame for four murders. You just said he won't take blame for anything," Mason pointed out.

"I'm curious to find out what's pushed him to take that step," said Euzent. "One possibility is the status of the murder victims. A policeman is a symbol of power and public respect. When you murder or commit an act of violence against someone, you briefly take their power. What better crime for him to claim if he wants to gain respect from his peers?"

"His peers are a bunch of homeless kids," said Ava. "He doesn't have a job; he doesn't attend school. As far as we can tell, he hangs out in Pioneer Courthouse Square all day."

"Why shouldn't he try to impress those people? Every type of society assigns status to its members' actions. He views those kids' opinions as very important; they *are* his reality. A group of street kids may not seem like a society to us, but I suspect it's a big part of his world. Another possibility for his reason for lying is a simple grab for fame without considering the consequences. What better shortcut to being featured on the news than admitting you committed a crime the public is desperate to solve?"

"But—" Ava started.

"You're thinking like a normal person," Euzent said, cutting her off. "Think like someone who can't see the consequences."

She sat back in her chair, nodding in understanding.

"All that excitement and fame and press sounds pretty good, now doesn't it?" he asked.

"Not to me," she stated.

"Or he could be delusional," Euzent said simply. "He could truly believe he committed those crimes."

Mason raised a brow. The delusional people he'd encountered had usually smoked or popped something first. Micah Zuch looked perfectly aware of where he was and what he'd said.

"Not many people are truly delusional, but they're out there," said Euzent. "The chance is slim that Micah is one of them."

"So what can you tell us about the guy we're looking for?" asked Nora. "It's clearly not the goth kid in the other room. I don't want to waste time talking about him if no one thinks he did it. Although any suggestions you have to pull more information out of him will be appreciated."

Euzent pulled out his notepad and flipped through several pages. Mason noticed his handwriting was atrocious. Similar to Ray's chicken scratch. It surprised him; he'd expected the agent's notes to be picture-perfect. Like his own. "I've been reading everything you've sent me. Granted, I've only been able to skim the reports of what happened last night, but I feel well informed on Special Agent Weldon's case, Captain Schefte's, and Officer Samuelson's death.

"The best I can offer right now is a brief overview of some elements you'll find in your killer. Hopefully they'll help you narrow your field of suspects and give you a guide when guys like Micah Zuch try to take the credit. Some of this is pretty general. Any good investigator will already be aware of the obvious elements, but bear with me, okay?" He quickly scanned the group, his gaze frank behind his glasses.

Mason nodded. Sometimes it helped to have someone state the obvious.

"You've got a smart guy here. He's organized and intelligent. He leaves a very clean scene. I suspect he was aware of everything he left

behind . . . including that happy fingerprint." He shook his head, giving
a half smile. "I admit I haven't seen one of those before. The scene last
night feels less organized . . . the change in his method of killing . . . the
mask in the hand of the victim. I need more time to look at the evidence
from that scene.

"Our killer brought everything he needed to each scene and took
the tools with him when he left. I think Micah might be right that
some sort of pulley was used to hang Vance Weldon, but there's nothing
like that in Weldon's garage. The other victims were hit in the head to
disable them, and we can't find the weapon that made the blows. He
purposefully brought a mask and knife. Apparently he carried a gun as
backup and needed it last night. He traveled all the way to the coast to
silently kill Denny Schefte. Clearly he is a planner."

Henry Becker's hand shot up. "Why do you think he chose that
coastal location? Our other three officers were murdered in their homes."

"Good question. My theory is that he did it because of the presence
of the other police officers in the cabin."

Murmurs filled the room, and Mason felt sick to his stomach.
Denny was murdered because his friends were there?

"You think he was thumbing his nose at the profession," Henry stated.

"I do. Killers like to see the feathers ruffled, but there was no publicity for Weldon's death, no big hunt for a killer. He could have found
Weldon's death anticlimactic and decided to try something different.
He wasn't brave enough to target Denny in his work environment, but
to target five detectives in a cabin in the woods? That's ego-building
and it created tons of press. He could have killed Denny at home, but
I think he found out about that trip and decided to use it."

"But was Denny the target? Would our killer have settled for one of
the other detectives?" asked a voice in the back of the room.

Mason felt everyone's gaze drill into his back.

"I'm almost positive Denny was the target."

Beside Mason, Ava exhaled and set down her pen. Her fingertips were white where she'd clenched it.

"So it's personal?" Mason asked. "It's not police in general?"

"I think each one of these killings was extremely personal. He did his research. He went to their homes, he picked a time when they'd be alone, he knew how to approach them in a way that didn't raise an alarm with the victim—although it appears last night's case didn't go the way he expected. He was able to smoothly approach the first three victims. Yes, he hit them in the head, but he was already in their immediate presence. Either he moves like a silent ninja or his presence was expected or not a surprise. Who would Louis Samuelson not be surprised to see at his home late at night?"

"The killer could have been there for hours," Ava pointed out. "And hit him in the head after socializing for a period of time. We don't know that he knocked on his door late at night—it might have been at dinnertime."

"Good!" Euzent's eyes lit up. "I think it's very possible your victims knew their killer. Your suggestion doesn't disprove that. Denny Schefte was outdoors, so I think our killer had a different tack to draw him out. So my question is *why* would Denny go outdoors at night?"

"His cell phone records show he wasn't contacted," Nora pointed out.

"So he heard something outside? What kind of noise would a seasoned cop comfortably check out in the middle of the night?"

"He knew what it was," said Mason.

"*And* he didn't feel the need to alert anyone else," Euzent finished. He held Mason's gaze. "Who or what would have drawn you outdoors at night by yourself?"

Mason shifted in his chair. "My son. Ava. My dog. Not much else. I would have alerted one of the other guys if it'd been a voice I didn't recognize or someone who sounded like they needed help. Or"—he paused—"the killer got lucky because Denny stepped outside to make a phone call or take a walk."

"But that would mean it wasn't personal. It could have been any one of you who stepped outside," said Euzent. "I admit I'm not one hundred percent convinced Denny's attack was personal, but the killer left the rest of you alone, so I will continue to give weight to that theory.

"If each case was personal, our killer has a lot of specific cops on his hit list. Why is that?"

"They did him wrong at some point in time," suggested Henry. "He's taken offense and wants to pay them back."

Euzent nodded. "What else? Has he been arrested numerous times? Special Agent Weldon shakes things up a bit here. His background is totally different than the other victims, so I think we should focus on the regular law enforcement officers for the moment. Possibly he's managed to have negative experiences with all these officers . . . perhaps he wasn't arrested but had a bad time somewhere else."

Mason felt lost. It seemed Euzent raised more questions than he answered. "What do the masks mean?" he asked, deciding to throw one of his own questions into the mix.

Euzent twisted his lips. "I have a couple of ideas on the masks. It could be a number of things. Halloween is right around the corner. Maybe he's leading up to something big that night."

Mutters filled the room and Mason felt everyone's stress level rise. They didn't want more deaths or a buildup to a climax of some sort.

"Do we need to prepare for something to happen on Halloween?" Nora sounded stunned. "Kids and families are out everywhere . . . there are events downtown . . . free candy everywhere." She ran a hand over her forehead. "Christ. What could happen?"

Euzent held up his hands. "Slow down. I'm not saying there will be a domestic terrorism event on Halloween. His behavior doesn't lead me to believe that at all. He's focused on law enforcement. He's chosen a very narrow field of targets. We don't need to set the city on alert . . . outside of the usual 'Check your candy' and 'Trick-or-treat where you know your neighbors' warnings given every year. But there's a possibility Halloween means something to him along with the focus on law enforcement."

Nora relaxed a fraction.

"The masks could be symbolic for him in some way. I suspect they make him feel powerful," continued Euzent. "Or they could be a way for him to try to mislead us . . . they're childish. Is he trying to appear younger than he seems?"

"Like Micah Zuch's age?" asked Ava.

"He's of the age I'd expect to be interested in those masks," said Mason. "Not an adult."

"Plenty of adults love those movies," countered Henry. "Perhaps the movies were hot when they were growing up or the movie symbolizes the first time they went to a horror movie and felt independent. Their parents probably hated the movies . . . even more reason to idolize them."

"Or they enjoyed the acts of violence on-screen?" Ava asked. "Acts a person might secretly crave to act out?"

"That's the key," said Euzent. "It's not a crime to have deranged fantasies. Making the choice to act upon them to the harm of others is what makes the crime."

"So they're nuts," said a voice from the back.

"Not nuts," corrected Euzent. "This person clearly understands right and wrong. He is going to great pains to avoid getting caught and cleaning up every shred of evidence to keep us from finding them."

"*Trying* to clean up," clarified Mason.

"Yes. He'll trip up somewhere," said Euzent. "It may have happened last night. That killing didn't go as planned and someone saw him for the first time. We might find our case-breaking lead in last night's scene once all the evidence has been studied."

Mason shifted in his chair. Evidence analysis could take forever.

The killer had to be stopped before he targeted his next cop.

23

Nora pulled Ava aside after Euzent's briefing. "Micah Zuch's mother is here."

"Shoot. We still need to find out how he knows so many facts about these murders," said Ava. "What's his mother say?"

"She wants her baby out of jail."

"He's not in jail," countered Ava. "He's had a cheeseburger, four packages of cookies, and enough soda to float a boat. I'm out of change from keeping him full of sugar."

Nora grinned. "I know. I told her we're still interviewing him and put her in a room with a fresh cup of coffee and a good-looking officer to chat with. She seems content for now."

"Does she know why Micah is here?"

"Doesn't seem to and didn't really ask. She came in ranting like she was Norma Rae or Erin Brockovich, but she didn't know what to complain about other than her baby was in the big bad police station. She comes across as a bit scatterbrained."

"Let's go talk to her," said Ava. "Maybe she knows why Micah has information only our killer should have."

"When's Zander coming back?" asked Nora as they headed downstairs.

Ava glanced at the time on her phone and frowned. Zander had promised to return after reviewing records back at the FBI office. "Let me call him. I'm surprised he's not here yet."

Her call went to voice mail and she left a message. She didn't think she'd ever left Zander a message before; he'd always answered her calls. She shot off a text asking for his ETA.

Nora stopped outside an interview room, and Ava glanced through the door's window at the woman preening before the officer. And sighed.

"What's her name?"

"Regina."

"Of course it is."

"Is there a problem, Special Agent McLane?" Nora asked, amusement dancing in her voice.

"I'm pretty certain she's the clique leader from the *Mean Girls* movie, but twenty years older." Guilt flashed through Ava for her instant stereotyping of Regina Zuch. But now she knew why Nora had put a good-looking officer in the room with Micah's mother. She opened the door and followed Nora inside.

The officer popped up from his seat, excused himself with a quick good-bye to Regina, and darted out as if the room were on fire. Ava spotted the gold wedding band on his left hand and figured she knew why. Regina's appreciative gaze followed his backside as he left, and Ava struggled not to roll her eyes.

"Ms. Zuch, this is Special Agent McLane from the FBI. She's helping us with the case that Micah has volunteered information for," said Nora.

Ava bit her lip at Nora's description of Micah's role and shook the woman's hand. Regina analyzed her and sharp defenses rose in the woman's eyes. She considered Ava a threat.

For what? There's no one else in the room.

Unless we're competing for Nora.

She choked back a laugh and gave the woman a big cheery smile. She'd learned long ago not to be sucked into emotional competition.

Ava couldn't pinpoint Regina Zuch's age. Her heavy but perfect eye makeup and trendy clothing indicated she was quite young. But hands don't lie. Regina had an older woman's lined hands and her neck had the softness and beginnings of folds that occur later in life. Her blonde hair looked freshly platinumed. She smiled, and Ava was blinded by her perfect teeth. She was the contrast to Micah's dark, depressing colors and mood, and Ava wondered if he tried to counterbalance his mother.

Her competitive energy made Ava tired, and she hadn't even spoken yet.

"That officer was such a nice man," said Regina with a coy smile. "He did a good job keeping me company."

"That's nice," said Nora noncommittally. She and Ava pulled out chairs and sat across from Regina. "Is there anything else you need?" she asked pleasantly. "I'm not certain when Micah will be ready to go home. He's being very helpful in our investigation."

"I could use some more coffee," said Regina. "When Micah called me, he said he was under arrest and going to jail. That's not true?" She blinked wide eyes.

There's no way those lashes are real.

"Not exactly," said Ava. "This is sort of an odd question, but can you tell me if Micah has some learning difficulties or perception troubles that would distort some of the information he's giving us?" She winced at her word choices, but she didn't want to make the woman any more defensive.

"Ohhh." Regina's face fell. "Did you catch him lying to you? He's had problems in the past with telling the truth. He's a good boy, but he's fallen in with the wrong crowd."

"I take it you've experienced this yourself? What have you had problems with?" Ava wasn't ready to tell Regina that her *good boy* had confessed to four murders.

"Well, you know. School. He never could sit still and listen. He struggles with some OCD and the doctors gave him some medication for it. A typical boy." She leaned forward and lowered her voice. "They claimed he brought weapons to school. I don't know why they would try to pin that on him. Everyone at that school was against him. He didn't do anything."

Euzent's words about Micah's failure to accept responsibility rang in Ava's head. *Looks like he learned it from Mom.*

"How is he at home?" asked Nora.

"He likes to keep to himself. He enjoys video games and movies."

"Does he work anywhere?"

"We've tried to find a job that fits his personality," Regina said earnestly. "But he's a tough fit. Working with the public isn't good for him. His patience level is rather low. It's his father's fault."

Ava wondered if Regina had ever suggested Micah take responsibility for his actions.

"His father?" prodded Nora.

"Oh yes. He left us when Micah was four. Never communicates with Micah except to send him a birthday card. What kind of man does that to a child? It's really affected him over the years."

"Did you get counseling for Micah?" asked Ava. "I know the loss of a parental figure can have devastating effects. The child feels abandoned." She mentally stomped on the memory of her mother explaining that her and Jayne's father simply couldn't handle raising a family.

"I couldn't afford counseling." Regina waved her hand airily. "I made certain to give him lots of attention and find other men to have strong roles in his life."

Ava was scared to ask where she found these men.

"Ms. Zuch," Nora started. "Micah came in because he had information on the recent murders of four law enforcement officers. Has he talked to you about this?" Nora leaned forward, her elbows on the table, her expression open and honest.

Regina's jaw dropped. She stared at Nora and then Ava, look-ing for an indication that Nora was telling the truth. Her mouth closed and opened as she tried to speak. "Murder? Four of them?" she squeaked.

"Yes," Nora said simply. She and Ava waited, wanting the mother to fill the silence. Regina's surprise felt genuine.

Regina slumped back in her chair, her bangle bracelets jingling. "He didn't say a word to me," she said. "He saw these men killed?"

"We believe so."

"But four? All at once?" she asked.

"No, three happened recently, but Vance Weldon was killed over a week ago."

Regina sat up straight, alarm on her face. "Vance Weldon?" she gasped.

"You know him?" Ava asked sharply. The woman had paled under her makeup.

"Yes, yes, I know—I knew Vance. Oh, my God." She pressed her hands against her forehead and peered at the investigators. "Vance worked for the FBI. Is that who you're talking about?"

"Yes," said Ava as dread grew in the back of her throat. "How did you know him?"

I don't know if I want to hear her answer.

Regina looked away, her palms still covering part of her face. "I can't believe this," she muttered, and Ava saw tears run down her cheeks.

"How did you know Special Agent Weldon?" Ava asked in a firmer voice.

Bloodshot eyes met hers. "He was a good friend." She held Ava's gaze.

"You had an affair with him," Ava stated. If Regina wouldn't say it out loud, she would.

Regina looked away. "It was a long time ago." She seemed to wilt into her chair.

"How long ago?" Nora asked.

"Three years? Four? I haven't heard from him since then." Her gaze stayed on the floor, more tears running. "He was a good man."

"Did you know Denny Schefte, Louis Samuelson, or Lucien Fujioka?" Ava asked. *Is she a black widow? But her son kills the lovers instead?*

Regina shook her head, not looking up. "Never heard of them."

Ava exhaled. *I watch too many movies.*

"Ms. Zuch." Nora paused. "Micah came in and confessed to killing these men, do you—"

"He what?" The lashes nearly touched her eyebrows.

"Do you believe Micah could kill Vance Weldon?" Nora asked. Her voice was steady, her eye contact deadly serious.

"No, no, of course not! Micah wouldn't hurt a fly."

Ava saw doubt flash in Regina's eyes, but she instantly controlled it.

"My boy wouldn't hurt anyone! He's a good boy!" Regina's voice shot up an octave.

"Regina," Ava said in a lower voice. "We don't believe Micah killed these men, but we're concerned because he knows so much information about the deaths. He knows facts that only someone who was there could know."

Regina held her gaze, her chest rising and falling with her rapid breaths. "You don't believe he killed them? You're not lying to me, right? Are you trying to trick me into saying something?"

"No. Can you tell us why he'd try to make us think he did it?" Ava asked kindly. The grown-up mean girl had vanished and in her place sat a terrified mother.

"I don't understand," she whispered. "Who confesses to something like that? I need to see him." She half rose out of her chair. "Take me to him."

"Now, Ms. Zuch, we—"

"Take me to him!" she shouted, anxiety shaking her voice. "You're holding my boy!"

"Ms. Zuch, Micah is an adult. He's here of his own choosing," said Ava, standing to look Regina in the eye. "You understand that when someone admits he killed someone, we need to know the whole story. We have four families whose loved ones have been murdered. Micah is our first solid lead. We're going to get every ounce of information we can out of him, so we can find out who did this."

Regina was silent, studying Ava's face, searching for lies.

"Is he going to be okay?" she whispered.

"We want him to tell us how he knows facts about the murders," said Ava. "Can you convince him to tell us?"

Regina sat down in her chair, defeat in her face. "No, he hates me. He doesn't listen to a word I tell him. I can't even get him to put his dishes in the dishwasher. He seems to take pride in never doing what I ask. It's like a game for him."

"I'm very sorry," Ava said. Inside she was shaking her head. This was a case of a kid who'd needed some tough love long ago. "Can you tell me how you met Vance Weldon? Did Micah know him very well?"

"I think Micah only met him once or twice. He couldn't have known we were having an affair."

You'd be surprised what your kids know. The face of Vance's widow, Sharon Weldon, flashed in Ava's mind and she remembered Sharon had said during their interview that if Vance had had affairs, she hadn't known about it. That was different from claiming her husband had never had affairs. A subtle choice of words. Looking back, Ava believed Sharon had suspicions. Did Sharon know Regina Zuch? Did she know Micah?

"I met Vance at one of those basketball fund-raisers. The type where professional players play against amateurs to raise money for one cause or another."

"Did you ever meet his wife Sharon?"

"No." Regina looked away. "Our relationship didn't last very long. He told me it was a mistake."

No kidding.

24

Mason was ready to pull out Micah Zuch's fingernails. The kid knew who'd killed Denny; Mason could feel it. But the punk sat there like King Shit of Turd Island and brushed aside every question asked of him. He'd wanted more attention, so they were giving it to him, and now he was reveling in it.

"Calm down," Ava said in a whisper. She'd joined Mason in the viewing room to watch Euzent and Nora Hawes question Micah. "He'll eventually tell us how he knows everything."

"He's wasting our time," stated Mason. "This investigation could be wrapped up and finished if he'd just tell us what he knows. He's having fun, drawing it out. He doesn't care that someone else could be killed!"

She took his hand and squeezed, keeping her gaze on the conversation in the next room. Her touch made him take a deep breath and relax his shoulders.

"Where's Zander?" Mason asked, wanting the agent's level head in the room. "Twice Micah has asked where the other FBI agent is. I think he'd talk to him. He must have formed some sort of rapport with the guy even though Zander told him he was going to jail."

"He must still be going through Vance Weldon's files back at our office," Ava said. "I hope he and Mercy are finding something useful."

Mason hoped so, too.

"Micah," Mason heard Special Agent Euzent say through the speaker. "I don't think you killed these men."

Micah looked at the wall.

"I do believe you were there," added Euzent.

The boy was silent.

"Who are you protecting?" asked Nora. "It must be someone very special to you. I know I wouldn't confess to murder for anyone. Not even to cover for my mother."

Micah glanced at her and looked away.

"His mother?" whispered Ava. "No way. Regina's not the type."

"Never say never," said Mason.

"Did you know your mother had been involved with one of the men who was killed?" Nora asked.

Micah's gaze flew to the detective's and his body stiffened.

"Surprise," said Mason. Satisfaction rolled through him that they'd finally gotten a reaction out of the kid.

"You're lying," said Micah in an adamant tone.

"No, we're not," Nora assured him. "Your mother is downstairs. I already talked to her. She's very upset about Vance Weldon's death."

Confusion crossed his face.

Euzent watched Micah like a hawk, hanging on every word, tone, and facial expression. Mason wondered what was going on in his brain. "Did you know the victims, Micah?" he asked in a casual voice.

"No."

"We still don't understand why you killed them."

"You don't need to know. I did it. That's what's important." He leaned back and crossed his arms. "I'm hungry."

Ava shook her head. "No way. He's eaten more than I eat in an entire day."

"It's the age," said Mason.

"I see you've caused problems at school," said Euzent. "You tried to scare everyone with an obviously fake bomb. You brought an unloaded gun to school. I'd say you aren't very good at being threatening."

"That'll poke at his pride," muttered Mason.

Micah was silent, but anger flushed his face.

Euzent continued, "I bet you've had to sit through a lot of sessions with psychiatrists and doctors. Anyone else try to help you?" The agent made air quotes as he said the word "help."

"All the fucking time," snapped Micah. "Stupid people telling me how wrong I am."

"Who else?" asked Euzent.

"Everyone."

"Is there a possibility they're honestly trying to help?"

"No. They're only doing it to make themselves look good. They think if they can act like they're helping me, they'll earn points from other people."

"Earn points from what people?"

Micah shrugged. "My mom. Their boss."

"Men try to look good to your mom by being nice to you?" Nora asked.

"All the time. Especially when I was younger. They were so fucking obvious. They'd come over under the pretense of being my buddy . . . trying to provide me with a *positive male role model*, but they only wanted to get close to my mom." Disdain dripped from his words.

Mason stared. *A positive male role model?*

"Holy shit," Mason said. "Can you text Nora?"

"Yes." Ava pulled out her phone.

"Tell her to ask if Micah was in the Cops 4 Kidz program."

Mason watched as Nora checked her phone. She showed her screen to Euzent, who nodded.

"Were some of those men who befriended you from the Cops 4 Kidz program?" Euzent asked.

Micah didn't answer and shuffled his feet under the table.

"Who'd you meet through that program?" Euzent leaned forward, his gaze locked on Micah's face. "You said you didn't know any of the victims. Do you want to change your answer on that?"

"I didn't know those guys," he said firmly.

"None of them?"

"Never heard of them before I killed them."

"Did they mentor him?" Ava said excitedly. "And he thinks we can't verify that?"

"Check with Henry. He's babysitting Regina downstairs, right? Have him ask her if Micah was in the program."

"She told us she met Vance Weldon at a fund-raiser. We never asked who was hosting the fund-raiser," muttered Ava as she tapped out another text.

Mason thought back to the dozens of Cops 4 Kidz events he'd attended. Basketball games, auctions, formal parties. He'd been proud to volunteer for the organization; it did good work in the community and produced results. He still kept in touch with some of the boys— now men—he'd mentored when there'd been no father figure in their lives.

The young men weren't on the streets, and they weren't in prison. Some of the kids he'd seen go through the program had had an amazing number of strikes against them and no amount of mentoring could help, but Mason still strove to give what he could. Being on the board of the organization wasn't quite as rewarding, but he felt as if he helped.

"Henry says Micah was in the mentoring program. But Regina says he wasn't mentored by the cops who were killed," said Ava. "Dammit. Why isn't this adding up?"

Her phone buzzed again. "He says Regina can't remember the names of the men who *did* mentor Micah. I'll call the director and find out who worked with him," said Ava.

We're onto something here.

But Mason couldn't connect the dots.

• • •

A half hour later Ava still hadn't heard back from the director of Cops 4 Kidz. Mason paced the task force room as Ava took a turn questioning Micah Zuch. Mason wondered if he should go knock on Scott Heuser's front door.

His phone rang. "Callahan," he snapped.

"Detective Callahan, this is Jolene Kersey."

Mason abruptly refocused at the voice of Jayne's doctor and all thoughts of Micah Zuch shot out of his head. "What happened? What'd she do?"

"Is Ava with you?" the doctor asked hesitantly.

"Not at the minute. Do I need to get her?"

"No, not yet." She paused, and Mason's heart rate tripled.

"What happened to Jayne?" he asked, holding his breath. His knuckles blanched as he clenched his phone, and he was glad he was the only person in the room.

"We don't know," said Dr. Kersey. "She's missing."

"What?" Relief and concern simultaneously swamped him. Every day he expected a phone call stating that Ava's twin had committed suicide. Or burned down the rehab center. He knew Ava waited for the same call and had been waiting for most of her life.

A call that stated Jayne was simply missing was a relief.

"We just did the evening check. The residents are to be in their rooms by now. Jayne is nowhere to be found. We've searched all the buildings."

"Did you check the other residents' rooms to see if she was hiding?" Suspicion grew in his stomach.

"Yes." Dr. Kersey's tone sounded slightly guilty.

"Is there another resident missing?"

Dr. Kersey sighed. "Yes, we have a male resident missing, too. I just got off the phone with his family."

I knew it. His brain spun. Should he tell Ava now? Or wait for the rehab center to look some more?

"I'm sorry, Detective Callahan. I don't know how this happened."

Mason knew.

"Is the other missing resident the one Jayne referred to in her last letter to Ava? The one I talked to you about?" he asked.

"Yes," the doctor said reluctantly. "We've been watching them. Some of the other employees had voiced your same concerns about Jayne and Brady."

"Brady?"

"His name is Brady Shurr. We've notified the police that they're missing."

"They're both adults. I doubt the police were very interested."

"That's true. But we have a policy to follow and notifying the police after a thorough search is the first step. Calling family is second."

Mason wanted to tell her to pull the stick out of her ass. If Dr. Kersey had listened when he and the other therapist had warned her about Jayne and her new obsession, she wouldn't be filing reports due to their *policy*.

"Shurr," he repeated. "As in Shurr car dealerships?"

"Yes, that's his family."

He remembered that Heidi Lain had told him the man came from a family with money. She hadn't been exaggerating. The Shurr dealerships had dominated the Portland metropolitan area for decades.

Jayne knew how to sniff out money.

"Brady Shurr is married, right?"

"Yes," the doctor said in a disappointed tone.

Mason wondered how much of the man would be left once Jayne had used him up and tossed him aside. If Brady's wife had half a brain, she was already filing for divorce.

Will Jayne contact Ava?

Mason blew out a breath as he remembered he'd activated his home's security system before he'd left that morning. If Jayne and her new boyfriend decided to break in, they were in for a deafening alarm. Assuming Jayne knew where they lived. As far as he knew, Ava had never told her twin that they'd moved. For good reason.

"I hope this doesn't influence how you feel about the work we do here, Detective. We work very—"

"Are you kidding me?" Mason bit back harsh words. "You let a patient out! Two patients. Two people who have no business wandering around in public right now. I don't know Brady Shurr's situation, but if Jayne managed to manipulate him, he's emotionally unstable, and the worst part is *I warned you!* Your staff warned you!"

"Brady Shurr's family would appreciate—"

He laughed. Dr. Kersey had just lost the last shred of respect he'd had for her. Her priority was her rich patient. He wondered if the Shurr family paid more for Brady's treatment than Ava paid for Jayne's. Wasn't Ava's money just as green?

"Feeling a little heat from the Shurrs?" Mason prodded, his anger growing. "I imagine staying in their good graces is rather important. I've heard they produce quite the line of drug addicts. They've probably helped keep you in business for years. What are their thoughts on this mishap?"

"They know it was no fault of ours that Jayne—"

"Why am I not surprised that you placed all the blame on Jayne?"

Isn't it all Jayne's fault?

He pushed on. "Jayne has no financial resources at the moment. They'll need somewhere to go. Who out of that couple do you think has access to money? Because I know it's not Jayne." Guilt poked at him. He *knew* Jayne had orchestrated at least 90 percent of the escape; it was exactly the type of move she'd pull. But Dr. Kersey was pissing him off with her attitude. "I have a good buddy who's an investigative reporter at the *Oregonian*. You can bet you'll be getting some phone calls from him regarding your record at the treatment center. Has anyone else escaped over the years? Do some clients pay more than others?"

Did I just call Michael Brody a good buddy? He caught his breath and tried to shake the red aura that'd clouded his vision. *Jayne's affecting me and she's not even here.*

He counted to ten. "What are you doing to find them?" he asked in a calmer voice.

"Our policy is to contact family and police," snapped Dr. Kersey. "We aren't required to do anything beyond that. Yes, we are very concerned for their safety, but we can't afford to hire a private security force to hunt for people who don't want to be found."

"So you sit and wait."

"Exactly. Like you said, they're adults."

"Adults who were entrusted to your care, Doctor."

"I'm sorry we let you down, Detective. I hope you'll relay my regrets to Ava. Hopefully Jayne and Brady will appear soon." She ended the call.

Mason stared out the window and down at the streetlights. *Now what?*

What will this do to Ava?

25

Ava studied Mason's face.

Jayne is missing?

She looked deep inside herself, searching, waiting for the alarm. And realized she didn't care.

She's my sister.

Worry and concern shone from Mason's eyes, and she wondered what he saw on her face.

He'd pulled her aside after her useless interview with Micah Zuch, led her into a quiet room, and blurted the news from Jayne's doctor.

Missing. Another man. Police notified.

The words spun in her head. Jayne wasn't dead. Her death might be the only thing that would wrench emotion out of Ava over her twin. She'd formed thick scabs and scars to protect her heart from Jayne's next event. And here it was. Her defenses had protected her and she felt . . . nothing. "Do you remember if we set the alarm when we left the house this morning?" she whispered.

Amusement crossed his face. "First thing I thought about, too. Yes, I set it."

"She's okay," Ava stated, still shocked by the calm in her chest.

"That's right," he reassured her. "No one's reported anything. She ran off with someone with a lot of money, so I imagine she has a solid roof over her head tonight. Possibly a nicer one than ours."

"About time she met someone with *real* money."

Mason blinked and then coughed out a laugh. "I wasn't going to say it."

"Am I a horrible person that I don't care?" Ava asked. Her lack of emotional reaction disturbed her. *Am I broken? Did I kill the part of me that gives a shit?*

"Lord, no. She's stomped all over you. She's not in any immediate danger that we know of, so I think your reaction is normal."

He didn't appear to be patronizing her; he looked as if he believed what he'd said.

She took a deep breath, nodding, trying to convince herself that she hadn't evolved into a sociopath with no conscience. *Now what?* She switched her brain to investigator mode. "Should we reach out to Brady Shurr's family?"

"That's up to you. Do you think they'll want to hear from you?"

"Good question. On one hand, we're in law enforcement and that might be of comfort to them. On the other hand, I don't think they'll be happy to hear that Brady was the next in a long line of men that Jayne used for her own amusement."

"I'm afraid they'll expect us to find them."

Ava shook her head. "I have no idea where they'd go. We don't have time to waste on a couple of grown adults who made their own stupid decision. We need to focus on the case at hand."

Aren't I the least bit concerned about Jayne?

No.

"She knows how to take care of herself," Ava said, for her own benefit as well as Mason's. "She gets into trouble, but she's managed to survive this long."

"Barely."

He watched her carefully, and she fought back an urge to assure him she wasn't about to crack. Far from it. She was pissed and it felt good.

"I hope she doesn't make more bad decisions," Ava muttered.

Mason raised a brow at her. "Aren't bad decisions a given with her?"

"You're right. They are. When her hole gets too deep, she'll turn up, needing something from me."

Please stay away from drugs, Jayne. I can't help you there.

Her phone rang. Ava didn't recognize the number.

"I'm going to check in with Nora," said Mason as she looked at her phone. "I'll be back in a minute." He strode out of the room.

"Special Agent McLane."

"This is Mercy Kilpatrick, Zander suggested I call you."

Relief swept over Ava. "Of course, Mercy. What did you the two of you find out about Vance Weldon?" She held back the information about Regina Zuch, wanting to hear Special Agent Kilpatrick's information first.

"I took a close look at who Weldon had crossed paths with in his domestic terrorism cases and to see if any of the other officers who'd been murdered had been involved in the investigations in some way. I haven't been able to find anything. Most of Weldon's work involved suspects in Central and Eastern Oregon, and our outside support came from officers in those regions."

"Did you find *anything* that might be useful in our case?" Ava asked, getting to the heart of their conversation.

"Not really." Mercy sighed. "Vance hadn't reported any issues with suspects or been worried about his safety in any way."

Ava told her about Regina Zuch's affair with Weldon.

"Well now. Isn't that interesting?" Ava heard her tap on computer keys in the background. "Let me see what we have on her."

"Micah Zuch still hasn't told us how he knows all this accurate information. We're guessing that he's protecting someone. We considered his mother, but I can't see it," Ava said, hoping she wasn't wrong. She let her brain travel down that path again. *Could Regina be involved and her son is trying to keep her out of jail?*

The long hair found on two of the bodies.

The hair was dark, but Regina clearly colored her hair a bright blonde.

"I don't have anything on Regina Zuch," Mercy said in a disappointed voice. "Her name doesn't come up in any of Vance's cases or otherwise."

"Ask what Zander thinks of her affair with Weldon," suggested Ava.

"He's not here."

"Oh. I thought he told you to call."

"He did when he asked me to dig into Vance Weldon's cases. He wanted you to immediately have any information I found. I'm sorry I haven't—"

"Wait." Ava froze. "He isn't with you? I thought the two of you were working together this evening."

"No, I haven't seen Zander since this afternoon. I've left messages for him to call me, but I assumed he was tied up with the task force."

Ava's brain spun in confusion. "I'll go to his house. It's five minutes away. Maybe he's working on something from there, and I misunderstood where he'd said he'd be."

"This doesn't sound like him."

"I agree. But he looked exhausted this morning. He said he didn't sleep last night," Ava said. "I wouldn't be surprised if he's simply crashed."

"I'll meet you there," said Mercy. "The two of you are working a case where cops are being murdered. I'm sure Zander is fine, but you shouldn't go alone. I'll leave in two minutes."

Ava ended the call with the concerned agent and glanced at the time. She could get over to Zander's home and back in less than fifteen minutes at this time of night. No one would even notice she'd left.

• • •

Ava parked at the curb and looked at the dark house. Zander's car was in the driveway, and she let out a relieved sigh. *I was right. He's just exhausted.* She fumed a bit because he hadn't checked in with her or Mercy, but she knew that Mason could sleep eighteen hours straight when he'd worn himself out on a case. A fire alarm wouldn't disturb him, let alone the ringing of his phone.

She'd told Mason and Nora that she was dropping by Zander's home. Mason had offered to come with her, but she'd refused. "I'll be back soon and Mercy Kilpatrick will be there, too."

She waited a few minutes for Mercy, but impatience got the best of her and she decided to knock on the door. She walked carefully up the dark path to his front door. No Halloween decorations. Unlike at all the other homes on his street, whose residents seemed to view decor as a competition. The neighborhood was flat and easy to walk, and the homes were close together. It probably swarmed with kids during Halloween. It was an ideal trick-or-treating neighborhood because a lot of houses could be covered in a short time. Prime real estate for a large candy haul, every kid's priority on Halloween. When she was a kid, it was exactly what she'd have wanted when she chose a neighborhood for trick-or-treating. She'd always lived in an apartment with her mother and sister, so they'd gone to subdivisions to trick-or-treat. Ava had memorized which ones were the best. No hills, no long stairs to the front doors, and tons of kids.

Zander's neighborhood rated a high score in her book. She wondered if he was the only single guy on the street.

Does he turn off his porch light on Halloween? Warning kids not to knock?

She hoped not. Those houses contained lonely, cranky people.

Noticing it was eleven P.M., she cringed as she pushed the doorbell.

Listening closely for any sounds of movement inside, she waited.

She pushed it again, blowing out a breath and watching it float away in the cool night air.

And waited.

She turned around and looked down the street, hoping to see the headlights from Mercy's car. It was silent.

What if Zander is a victim?

Her adrenaline spiking, she touched the weapon at her side and stepped to the side of the door.

A footstep sounded inside. "Zander?" she called.

A curse sounded through the door. Recognizing his voice, she blew out a breath and was relieved she hadn't drawn her gun.

"Zander? You didn't return my texts. I just wanted to check on you."

Clicking sounded as he flipped the locks, and she exhaled. Finally.

He opened the door, and she gasped as alcohol fumes filled the air. She waved a hand in front of her face. "Jesus Christ! What are you doing?"

He wore baggy pajama bottoms and a sleeveless shirt. She couldn't see his face.

"Turn on the light," she said sharply.

"Ava . . ."

"Turn it on." She reached in the house, around the doorjamb, and felt for a switch. "Oh, my God."

He turned away at the rush of light but not before she'd caught a glimpse of red puffy eyes and nose.

"Are you sick?" she asked, knowing that wasn't the case. No one bathes in vodka when they're sick.

She stepped into the house, forcing him to retreat, and turned on more lights. "What's going on? Why haven't you returned my calls? Mercy said you haven't returned hers, either. I thought you were working with her today?"

He wouldn't look her in the eye. He turned and stalked away. She followed as he headed into his kitchen. She'd been to his home at other times to pick him up, but she'd never been farther than the doorway. It was as neat as she'd expected but very plain. The kitchen was the pale oak that'd been so popular decades before, but seemed organized and clean. Except for the empty fifth of vodka on the counter and the empty knocked-over carton of orange juice.

Ava stared. Vodka and OJ was one of Jayne's favorites. The familiar sight sent anxiety shooting through her brain.

"Why are you drinking?" she asked.

He didn't answer as he twisted the lid on a new bottle of vodka. A loud crack sounded as the seal broke, and his hand shook as he poured the liquid in a glass.

"Can I get you some ice?" Ava offered.

He ignored her snark and opened his freezer, digging in the ice with a bare hand and dropping a handful into his glass. Vodka sloshed over the side. He picked it up and held her gaze over the rim as he drank.

"Out of orange juice?"

"Don't need it," he muttered.

"Why didn't you call me back?"

"Why are you in my house?"

She bit her lip and lowered her voice. "I was worried about you. Several people are worried. It's not like you to not return calls."

He took another drink, still staring at her with reddened eyes. She gazed back. *He's hurting.*

"I shouldn't have come."

"That's right."

He wants me to get pissed at him. "What is going on, Zander? I came here because I give a crap about you."

He looked away.

"Did you know it crossed my mind that I might find you staked to your *goddamned wall*?"

His gaze flew back to hers.

Now I have his attention.

"That's right. You went dark when officers are dying. What was I supposed to think?"

"I'm sorry. I didn't think," he mumbled. He set the glass down on the counter with a loud clank and wiped the back of his hand across his nose.

"No, you didn't think." She grabbed his hand and pulled him to the table in the dining nook. "Sit. Tell me what happened." She pushed him into a chair and took the one next to him, giving him her full attention.

"Nothing happened."

"Yes, something happened. This isn't you. You don't get smashed and avoid your coworkers. *What happened today?*"

"It's the date . . . it's my date." He stared at his hands on the table.

Tomorrow was Halloween. October thirtieth meant nothing to her. "I don't know what you mean," she said slowly. "What happens on October thirtieth?"

He slowly raised his gaze to meet hers, his eyes red and moist. "My wife died on October thirtieth. Our baby, too. This is the one day a year I let myself fucking fall apart. I can get through the rest of the year if I know I have permission to crumble on October thirtieth. But today I wanted to push through it just this once so I could work the case. I didn't make it."

Ava wanted to cry. His anguish had ripped holes in the air in the room.

I yelled at him.

She put her hands over his on the table. "You never talk about it. I didn't know." Her voice cracked. She'd known his wife was dead, but she hadn't known about a baby. "I didn't know you had a baby."

"We didn't. She was pregnant when she died. Later they told me it'd been a girl."

Her heart broke. "You never told me."

"You never asked."

"I was trying to respect your privacy. I figured if you wanted to tell me, you would." Her shoulders sagged. He was her friend and she'd let him down.

"I'm being unfair," he said. "You're right. I didn't want to talk about it. I avoid thinking about it at all costs."

"What was your wife's name?" she asked softly, watching his face. "I've never heard you say it."

"Faith. Faith Alexandra Wells." He stared at her hands on his.

"Do you want to tell me about it?"

He swayed slightly in his seat, and she wondered if she should just put him in bed.

"We tried for years to get pregnant," he said. "It finally happened, but they found the cancer early during her pregnancy. They suggested we abort the baby so they could treat it more aggressively."

"Oh, Zander." She hadn't thought her heart could break any more. "How horrible for the two of you."

"I told her to do it." He looked at Ava, his eyes hard. "She refused."

"No one should ever have to make that decision."

"You've got that fucking right." He looked back at the kitchen and his glass on the counter. "I need my drink."

"In a minute," said Ava. "What happened?"

"She refused to have an abortion and she died."

"She would have survived if she'd given up the baby?"

He seemed to shrink. "Probably not. Her cancer had invaded several organs by the time they found it. Stage four. They said treatment might extend her life a little longer."

"And that wasn't good enough for her," Ava said, understanding the horrible decision his wife had made. "She was going to die no matter what."

"We could have had more time," Zander said urgently. "Maybe a new treatment could have been found in those extra months, maybe we could have gone somewhere else, where the drugs didn't have to go through the trials and approvals." His words slurred, and his chin dropped to his chest.

"I'm so sorry, Zander." She'd never seen him so defeated. He'd always been the quiet rock. Dependable. Steadfast. Driven. When she needed something, she never hesitated to ask. He always came through for her.

"She never knew it was a girl," he whispered.

"Oh, *she knows*, Zander. She knows."

"We'd agreed on the name Zachery for a boy and Fiona for a girl. I think about my daughter every day. Would she have looked like Faith?" His eyes begged for her to agree.

"No doubt."

"I have to pull out Faith's pictures to remember what she looked like when she was healthy. Those last few weeks at the hospital, she didn't look like herself, and those images are burned into my brain. She was swollen everywhere, a horrible caricature of the beautiful woman she'd been." He covered his eyes. "My memory of her is fading. Sometimes when I'm at work, I'll try to remember the exact color of her hair and I can't. I hate myself for it . . . I'm forgetting her and she doesn't deserve that. Yesterday I couldn't remember what the color of her eyes looked like."

"How long has it been?"

"Eight years."

"I would expect the memories to have faded a bit, Zander. But as long as you have her photos, you don't have to rely on your memory."

"But I remember everything! Why can't I recall the woman she was instead of that horrible sick body she was at the end?"

Ava fumbled for an answer. "I don't know." Guilt swept through her. "I'm sorry I kept pressuring you to accept dates, Zander. I didn't know you weren't ready."

He waved an unsteady hand in the air. "I've dated."

"Oh." Ava frowned. "You seemed so reluctant. I always assumed it was because of Faith."

"I know she didn't want me to be alone. She told me that. She knew she was going to die, Ava. She made me promise to look for someone who made me feel alive." He looked away sheepishly. "I've turned down all your suggestions because . . . well . . . because they came from you," he finished quietly.

She pulled back, stung. "You don't think I'm a good judge of character? I wouldn't set you up—"

"It's not that," he stated, meeting her gaze. "It's because I wanted it to be you."

She froze, feeling her heart pound in her chest. A tiny part of her had known, but for him to state it out in the open when it was clearly too late . . .

He gripped her hands. "Don't run away."

"I'm not."

"Yes, you are. I can feel you pulling back. I just fucked everything up, didn't I?"

"No. Nothing has changed."

"You're lying to me."

Blood pulsated in her ears. "I'm not. I knew . . . sorta, I think. I think I chose to ignore it. Even Mason knew . . . he was okay with it."

"*What?*"

"Mason likes you. He knew you wouldn't make a move on me because you'd respect his friendship."

Zander looked away. "He's right."

"You're still my friend, Zander . . . oh, my God. Was it the talk of the wedding venue the other day that was bugging you?" He still had a firm hold on her hands. She tugged, but he didn't let go.

"Yes," he said simply. "It's getting closer. Before there was always a chance that the two of you wouldn't last. But now I can see you're meant for him. Not for me."

"That's right," she said softly. "I love him like nothing I've ever experienced before. He's part of me. I suspect you know the feeling I'm talking about."

"I do." He gazed at the table.

"Can you live with this relationship?"

"I have no choice."

"Do you want off our case? Would that make it easier?"

He looked back up at her, holding her gaze for a long time. "No and no. I don't want to lose what we have."

"Me neither."

His doorbell jangled.

"That's Mercy Kilpatrick."

He rubbed the back of his neck. "Christ. How many other people are coming?"

"Just her. We were both worried about you. You're lucky I didn't send over a squad of patrol cars first. I probably should have."

He pushed back his chair. "Send her home. I'm going to bed." He eyed the freshly opened bottle of vodka. "I'm done with that. Take it with you, would you? And I'll be at work in the morning. Good as new."

"Thank you for telling me about Faith and Fiona, Zander."

The doorbell rang again.

"Can you handle Mercy? I don't want to see anyone else tonight."
He headed for his stairs.

The slump of his shoulders worried her, and she decided to shock
him out of it. "Isn't Mercy single?" she nudged.

He stopped and turned to stare at her, his jaw dropping. Then
he spotted her small grin and swore under his breath. "Screw you,
McLane." He continued his unsteady trek toward his stairs.

She watched him go, satisfied she'd gotten a reaction out of him
but ready to rush forward if he couldn't manage the staircase. He carefully stepped his way to the top, and she went to answer the door. At
least she'd seen him smile when he realized she was joking about the
other agent.

But she'd never forget the soul-deep pain in his eyes when he'd said
his daughter's name.

26

He scrolled down through the local news station's website, looking for new information on the murders of the cops. The other night had been a close one; he'd fucked up. He hadn't expected Lucien Fujioka to fight back.

He'd incapacitated each man before he'd known what was happening.

Luckily he'd been armed. He'd been armed for the other encounters, but he'd never had to actually fire the gun. Fujioka had nearly gotten the upper hand.

He'd placed the mask on the kitchen floor when Fujioka was out of the room. Confused, Fujioka had picked up the mask when he returned. The floor creaked as he stepped into his swing with the bat. Fujioka heard it and turned. The bat didn't fully connect and Fujioka lunged at him. They'd fought. He'd knocked the slightly dazed cop down and fired.

The sound had been deafening.

He'd fled, leaving the mask still in Fujioka's hand.

An ad blasted from the news station's website and he turned off the volume. He wouldn't screw up like that again.

His list had one more name.

The last person who'd torn out her heart.

As he scrolled, a familiar name jumped off the screen. Micah Zuch. He caught his breath and rapidly read the article. And then read it again.

Why is that punk a person of interest in the case?

He knew Micah. He knew Micah *very* well.

Over and over he'd seen echoes of himself in the boy. Their lives had too many similarities and parallels. He'd tried to ease the boy's way, make up for what he was lacking. Protect him from what he knew was coming.

He read the article a third time, looking for subtext. It stated the police didn't consider Micah a suspect—which they shouldn't—but that the information he'd brought to the police had made them focus their efforts in a different direction.

What direction?

How could Micah know *anything* about those deaths?

He pulled out his phone and called a friend. "Hey, Steve. I just read about the young guy they're holding for the cop murders. You guys must be relieved they caught someone."

The cop predictably set him straight that they didn't believe Micah Zuch was the killer.

"I must have misunderstood. Then why are they holding him?" he prodded.

The cop's next few sentences chilled him to the bone.

"Well, I hope he's a good lead and you guys nail the bastard." He ended the call and sat still, staring at his computer screen.

Why did Micah confess to the murders? How could he have known exactly what the victims were wearing?

His train of thought shot in a million directions. "Maybe he knows someone who had access to the crime scene documentation," he muttered out loud. But different law enforcement departments had handled the evidence collection in each case. He could understand Micah having a friend in one department, but not in four of them.

That left one option.

Micah had followed him.

He slammed his laptop shut and pushed out of his chair, stalking about his dining room. He'd thought he'd been so careful. Fury raked through him.

"That little sneaky asshole! This is what I get for trying to help him?" He turned and slammed his fist into the wall, leaving an impression in the drywall. "Fuck!" He hit with his other fist and the drywall broke. He yanked his hand out of the wall, staring at the blood that immediately welled in the scratches on the back of his hand. The pain cleared his head.

How long did he have before Micah told them the truth?

Why had he kept it a secret this long?

He had a mission to finish and he wasn't going to let that goth loser screw it up. There were twenty-four hours left in his personal timeline. He would finish.

He wouldn't let his mother down.

• • •

Twenty years ago.

She sobbed as she sat cross-legged on the floor next to the Christmas tree. Their tree was scraggly, decorated with strings of popcorn, a few lights, and some of his little old toys, which his mother had hung with ribbons. "I love these old toys," she'd told him. "They remind me that you're no longer a little boy."

He didn't think toys from McDonald's Happy Meals deserved to hang on their tree.

His friend Jason's mother had decorated their tree with a million strings of white lights and dozens of glass ornaments that were all the exact same shade of blue. She'd bought matching strings of shiny blue beads. Jason said a blue tree was dumb, but he thought it was the most beautiful tree he'd ever seen. It made their popcorn and toys seem cheap and lame.

His heart broke as he watched his mother cry. Lately it seemed all she did was cry. They were poor. He understood that and knew better than to ask to go see the movie Scream *with his friends. Movies at the theater were not in their budget. He also knew he wouldn't get the videotapes of the* Evil Dead *movies that he'd put on his Christmas list.*

His mother believed horror movies would warp his mind.

Her hatred of them increased his desire to see them.

He knew what had crushed her this time. It was that man. It was always a man. Why did they choose his mother to abuse? This last one had started off so good. He'd been kind and helpful, and appeared genuinely interested in helping him with his math homework. He'd taken him to a Winterhawks hockey game.

He'd never been to the ice arena downtown. It was loud and cold and huge and packed with people excited to cheer for their team. Best of all, he'd seen a fight. They'd been sitting in the right place when it'd happened. Two players had slammed into the side of the rink, making the plexiglass shake. The people in the rows in front of him had leaped out of their seats and beaten their hands on the glass, shouting, "Fight, fight, fight!" One player held the other in a headlock and swung his fist at his face over and over.

Blood had dripped on the ice.

All his fifth grade friends had been impressed when he'd told them the next day.

The man had come to their house every week, sometimes eating dinner with them, sometimes showing him how to throw a football in the backyard.

But then the man had pulled back, only offering to pick him up and take him to McDonald's, saying his spare time was tight.

He'd known the man lied.

It'd happened a few times before. The men would use him to get close to his mother. He didn't mind that much. He wanted his mother to find someone who'd bring her flowers and make her happy. Each time a man started coming to the house, she'd get excited. She'd invite him to dinner, bake her special apple pies, and spend an hour choosing her clothes and putting on her makeup. He knew his mother was delighted when it took her a long time to get ready for a simple dinner at home.

But the men never came around for long. This time the man had called and said he couldn't take him to the video arcade until late in January. He claimed he was swamped at work.

He knew a brush-off when he heard one. His mother did, too.

He'd thought this man might be the one. He'd stayed very late one night last week, drinking wine and laughing with his mother. She'd made an incredible dinner. A pot roast with gravy, and mashed potatoes with lots of butter. There were even store-bought rolls. She never bought rolls, saying they were too expensive and not good for him. Dessert was a cheesecake, and he'd had two pieces. She'd smiled as she dished up his second piece, and he'd hoped they would eat like that every night from now on. When he'd gone to bed, the man and his mother had been sitting on the couch, two empty bottles of wine on the table beside them, leaning close as they talked. He'd been happy when he crawled in bed, enjoying the sound of his mother's laughter from the other room. She didn't laugh very often. Maybe their luck was turning.

The sound of the man's car had woken him at four A.M. when it backed out of their driveway. He'd smiled as he watched the taillights move down their street. He must really have liked his mother to stay so late.

Within the next week he'd realized the man wasn't coming back.

"Why do they do this to me?" she sobbed from beside the tree.

There were three presents under the tree. He knew one of them had been for the latest man. Would he ever come back to get it? He knew she'd spent too much on the man's present because she'd had little money left for his gifts. He suspected that one of them was new pajamas. His current ones stopped halfway down his calves. New pajamas weren't anything to brag to his friends about. He'd have to lie when they all shared what they'd gotten for Christmas. His mom had promised to make it up to him for his birthday in June.

Anger flowed through him. How could these men do this to his mother over and over?

Other men had come in the past. They took him to movies and once his mother started inviting them to stay for dinner, they'd leave the two of them in the dust.

It must be him. He wasn't clever enough or engaging enough or talented in sports. The men found him boring and unworthy of their time. His mother probably knew this but was too polite to place the blame on his shoulders where it belonged.

She wiped her eyes and smiled at him. "It'll be a good Christmas tomorrow, you'll see. Let's plan to make cookies. We can watch TV all day long, just you and me. It'll be fabulous."

He forced a smile and nodded eagerly at her.

One day the men would pay for the pain they'd caused his mother.

27

Once a week Ava allowed herself a whole milk, sugary, syrupy coffee drink. Every other day she stuck with black coffee. As she pushed open the door from her usual coffee shop, she took a sip of her pumpkin spice latte and every nerve receptor in her mouth sighed in happiness. Now today felt like Halloween.

The employees had dressed up for the holiday. Iron Man had taken her order and a sexy nurse had made her latte. Somehow it'd made her drink taste even better, and she'd needed the jolt of sugar and caffeine after her late night. Mason had stayed up with her, talking about Zander. Ava had held back tears as she told him about his wife and baby.

"I knew something horrible had happened to his wife," Mason had said. "But a baby, too? I can't imagine."

"I wonder if he'll want more children," Ava speculated. "I don't think he's forty yet."

Mason shook his head. "That's a hard one to answer. I'm glad I'm done."

Her heart had cracked at his answer. It was a subject they'd touched a few times, and she'd been positive that kids weren't for her.

But now she wondered if she was misleading him.

Am I?

She still didn't know.

Lost in thought, she glanced up as two men blocked her path. She froze as she recognized her stalker, David.

She dropped her coffee and reached for the weapon in her bag. "Don't move," she ordered, stepping backward. A dozen scenarios flashed in her head as she realized she'd never get her gun out in time. *Foot to his crotch. Elbow to his throat. Run!*

"Ava, wait! I didn't mean to startle you," David pleaded.

"Special Agent McLane," stated the other man, pulling out a wallet. "I'm a private investigator in the state of Oregon."

She froze, eyeing the second man. He was shorter than David and dark-skinned, with graying hair. Something about his body language said *cop* in her head.

"Who are you?" she asked sharply. "Both of you?"

The shorter man held out his identification. "My license is right there. My name's Glen Raney and I retired from the Gresham Police Department ten years ago. David Dressler is my client."

She glanced at his license. It meant nothing to her; she didn't know what a PI's license looked like and really didn't care. She studied the way the PI held himself and believed he'd been in law enforcement. She looked at David, whose eyes pleaded with her not to run.

David Dressler. I don't know you from Adam.

"Why are you following me?" she demanded.

David's shoulders slumped. "I shouldn't have approached you so often. I couldn't help myself."

"You're not helping your situation. Start talking."

David looked at the PI, who shrugged. "This is what you wanted, right?" Glen said to David. "Here's your chance." He bent over and picked up the coffee cup Ava had dropped and tossed the dripping mess in the garbage.

"We're looking for Jayne," David began.

"I knew it. She owes you money, doesn't she?" Anger burned through her. "She doesn't have any money and you're barking up the wrong tree if you think you're going to get anything from me. I barely know who she is."

David's face fell, and she was pleased. He could go to hell for unnerving her. "Anyone who loans her money needs their head examined," she told the men. "Trust me. I've been there."

David looked at her, and she saw the pain radiating from his gaze. "What did she do to you?" she whispered.

If he got his heart broken . . .

Jeez, Jayne. Disgust rolled through her. Nothing stopped her sister when she had a conquest in sight. Age. Marriage.

"You look like your mother," David said softly.

Ava's world tilted and her knees shook. "You knew my mother?"

"Very well." He held her gaze.

Jayne's eyes looked back at her. Her own eyes.

No.

She blinked several times and the resemblance faded. But it didn't disappear.

"Who are you?" she whispered.

"I'm pretty sure I'm your father."

"No." She shook her head. "That's not possible. No," she repeated. "What do you want from me? Just because I work for the FBI doesn't mean I can help you with something." Her brain shot ahead in leaps and bounds as her tongue formed words she had no control over. "Our father left before we were born. He didn't want anything to do with us or our mother."

His mouth turned down, and Ava caught her breath at its resemblance to Jayne's.

She looked at the PI, wanting him to tell her David Dressler was full of crap. Glen Raney nodded at her. "My client is willing to take whatever test you want to verify he's your and your twin's father. I've seen the letters your mother sent him before she left. I tracked down your birth certificates—you know she changed her name after she broke it off with my client, right?"

"No." *I don't believe him.* "We're not who you're looking for," she said to Glen, unable to look at David again. "My mother was born McLane. If you think she changed her name, then you're wasting your time talking to me." Relief swept through her. *He's got the wrong people.*

"I lived on McLane Street when I knew your mother," said David. "I think that she selected it to be your new last name says a lot."

"She's always been McLane," Ava repeated.

"No, it was originally Ryder."

Colleen Ryder? Ava shook her head. "You're wrong. She had no reason to change her name."

"What did she tell you girls about her own parents?" Glen asked gently. "That they'd died before you were born?"

Ava couldn't feel her hands or feet. "Yes."

"Did you ever look for records of them or your mother?" Glen asked. "I know you have access to a lot of databanks."

"I never felt the need," she whispered. How many times had she started to look and stopped?

"Let's sit down," Glen suggested. Ava blindly followed him and David to an outdoor table under the eaves.

What is happening?

Glen handed her a business card, and she stared at it without comprehension. "David hired me last summer. He'd been in Portland and seen your face in the local newspaper after you were . . . injured. You look a lot like your mother, you know."

Ava nodded silently. She'd known there'd been media coverage of her near-deadly encounter with the mastermind of the mass shootings in the Portland area last summer. But she'd been too ill to care.

"He hired me to find out if you were his daughter. All he had for me to start with was your mother's original name, your name from the paper, and a guess of when she'd given birth."

Ava looked at David. "She told us you didn't want anything to do with us." Glen's part of the story sounded plausible, but she didn't believe David.

"I was married. I'm not proud of it." His eye contact was strong, his face solemn. "Your mother called it quits and let me know two weeks later that she was pregnant. She said she didn't need anything from me but wanted to let me know. I think it was her way of twisting the knife a little bit. I hadn't told her I was married when we started seeing each other."

"You were a cheating asshole," Ava snapped.

"I was." He took a deep breath. "Then she vanished. She left town within days and never contacted me again. I always wondered if she'd lied about the pregnancy. I searched for her a time or two but never found anything."

"Where do you live?" Ava asked.

"San Diego. Glen managed to track her to Northern California once I gave him your name."

"You initiated a search based on seeing me in the paper?"

He gave a half smile. "A one in a million chance, wasn't it? It was easy to find out more information about you. But then Glen stumbled over the fact that Colleen gave birth to twin girls. Your sister has been harder to track down."

"Her records on the Internet and in various databanks are much different than yours," Glen said delicately.

"That's because she's a drug addict," Ava said shortly.

"I gathered that," answered Glen. "But I couldn't find a current residence. I just found out about the treatment center yesterday. Before that, the most current mention I'd found was an announcement about an art show. I passed that on to David, assuming she'd show up."

"Instead I met you." David smiled, a pleased look in his eyes.

"Wait a minute." Ava placed her hands on the table and stood. She wanted to slap the smile off David's face. "This isn't a happy family reunion. *I don't know you* and I don't plan to get to know you. My mother left you behind and it sounds like she had a good reason. I don't need to know my roots," she lied. "You creeped me the fuck out by showing up everywhere I went, and why the hell were you at a *murder scene*?" She'd planted her hands on the table to hide their shaking, but every muscle quivered under her skin.

"That was on me," said Glen. "I keep my finger on what's going on with my old department. When I found out the FBI had an interest in the case and you were one of the assigned agents, I let David know. I didn't know he'd actually go to the scene." He glared at David. "I just thought he'd like to know what sort of work you did."

"I'm done here," Ava said, adjusting the strap of her purse on her shoulder. "Stay away from me and my sister. Even if you are our father, we don't need this sort of fucked-up-ness in our lives right now."

She pushed in her chair and turned away, her feet shaking in her boots. She spotted the brown puddle from her latte and debated buying another.

What I really want is wine.

"Ava," called David's voice from behind her. "Glen tracked where Jayne went when she left the treatment center."

• • •

"Callahan."

Mason knew by the tone of Nora's voice that some shit had hit the fan. He halted in the hallway outside the detectives' corral and waited for her to catch up. Her face was grim.

"What happened?" he asked. *Who ratted me out?*

"I just spent a few pleasant moments with the assistant chief."

Aw crap. "No moments with him are pleasant."

"No they're not. He got a call from a reporter who wanted to know why a witness was working on the task force to solve these murders. They'd seen you at the Fujioka scene. I just lied through my teeth, saying that you'd simply accompanied the FBI agents because they'd been interviewing you when the call came in."

"Shit. I don't think he knows anything about my personal life, right?"

"If you mean does he know you're engaged to the investigating FBI agent, no." She put her hands on her hips, staring him down. "This might come back to bite me in the ass. My career is over if he finds out that I let you prance all around this investigation."

She's not kidding.

"I know. I appreciate it and I owe you a big one."

"I'm calling in that favor right now. You're to stay away from all aspects of this case from now on. I've got no one to blame but myself for letting you poke your nose around, but I just stared into my commander's eyes and lied. So I'm done. I'm not doing that again."

Mason stared at her, feeling his access to Denny's killer slip out of his hands. "Wait—"

"No *wait*! There's nothing else to be discussed. I shouldn't have let you in and you know it. Your only role in this case is as a witness. *Nothing else.*" She gave him a penetrating stare. "And if you think you're going to use Ava to get close to this case I'll get her replaced."

He started to reply and closed his mouth. He'd pushed too far. He'd taken advantage of Nora Hawes and he didn't have any right to continue. "I'm fully aware what you did for me, Nora. I won't forget it."

"If I need a couch to sleep on because I've lost my job, you'll be the first person I call."

"I'll loan you my own pillow. It's a Tempur-Pedic."

She wrinkled her nose. "What am I? An old woman? I don't need one of those concrete pillows."

"Yet."

"Go back to your desk and stay away from my cases," ordered Nora. "If I find out anything new, you'll hear."

"Have you heard back from Scott Heuser yet? He was supposed to tell us who mentored Micah Zuch."

"Did we *not* just have a conversation about how you're off this case?" She looked ready to knock his head against the wall.

"You just said you'd let me know if you found out anything new. Did the director of Cops 4 Kidz get us the *new* information?"

"No. We haven't heard from him."

Mason considered his next words very carefully. "I missed the last Cops 4 Kidz board meeting. I should go pick up my copy of the minutes."

"They don't email those?" Nora asked with heavy sarcasm.

"I heard their email was malfunctioning."

"Uh-huh." She chewed on her lower lip, studying him.

He wanted to squirm. "Don't look at me like that," he muttered.

"Then stay out of my sight."

"I'm going." He turned and headed for the exit.

• • •

"Scott called in sick yesterday and left a message that he's still sick today," said the receptionist, looking rather harried as she spoke to Mason. "He's the type of person that doesn't stay home unless he's very ill. If he hasn't returned your messages, it's because he can't."

A stubborn look swept across her face. "He's an excellent director. I've worked with three of them over the last decade, you know. I wouldn't hold this against him. I'm sure he'll call when he's feeling better."

"I wasn't thinking badly of him," Mason assured her. "Did he tell you he'd been contacted by the FBI? They wanted some information about the cops who'd participated in the mentoring program."

"No, he didn't say anything. I met the female FBI agent the other day when she came to talk to him. She needs more information?"

"Yes. I believe she's reached out to him twice about it."

"This is in relation to the deaths of those cops?" She whispered even though no one else was in the office.

Mason folded his arms on the high reception counter and leaned in. "Yes. It's been very upsetting that they've all volunteered with our organization at one point or another."

"Well, eighty percent of the local police departments have worked with us," she said. "We're very proud of the number of people that give of their time." She paused. "But I'm not saying anything that you don't already know, Detective Callahan. What was the information she needed?"

Mason kept his excitement under wraps. "They needed to know who mentored Micah Zuch a few years back."

Her face fell. "Only Scott has access to those records. That isn't something I can look up for you."

A brick wall rose in front of him and he deflated.

"Ah, crap."

"I'm sorry, Detective Callahan, because the kids are minors, we keep a tight lid on the information, but if I hear from Scott before you, I'll remind him that your task force is waiting on this information."

Mason nodded and thanked her for her time.

Outside the building he pulled his collar snug around his neck against the chill of the October air. The temperature had dropped a good ten degrees since the cloud cover had blown away.

Now what?

Ava had been worried that something had happened to Zander when he didn't return calls. All the cops in the city were watching out for one another, wondering if there'd be another death. A visit to Hauser's home to see if he was okay and to ask him to open those records would be worth his time.

Finding Scott Hauser's home address shouldn't be a problem.

Nora didn't need to know he was poking around.

28

"I'm listening," said Ava.

She'd stopped in her tracks at David's claim that his private investigator knew where to find Jayne. She turned back to the two men, who'd stood up from the outdoor table as she'd stalked away. Looking for deception in their faces, she stared from one man to the other.

She didn't see it.

"They got on a plane at three A.M. this morning," David said as Glen nodded in agreement. "I'll tell you where they were headed as soon as you hear me out. I have more I need to say."

Ava's heart raced, and she gripped the strap of her bag, taking a hesitant step toward the men. "What do you need to say?"

"You need to hear my side of the story."

Anger ripped through her. "No, I don't. You've already admitted you were a deceptive asshole to my mother."

"I was, and I understood it as soon as she left. I'm not looking for pity or an instant daughter. I'm looking for a little bit of grace for the wrongs I did to you girls and your mother. That's all I want." His eyes pleaded with her.

Curiosity got the better of her. "Make it fast. I want to know where Jayne went." She sat back down in her chair, her spine stiff. The men exchanged a glance and took their seats. David looked relieved.

"I met your mother when she was waitressing in a bar in San Diego."

Ava nodded. That much her mother had told her and Jayne. She'd said it'd been a brief relationship, and they'd gone their separate ways.

"When did you tell her you were married?" Ava asked.

He looked down at the table. "Not soon enough. My wife and I were separated at the time, and I was living in my own apartment. I didn't know if we were going to be able to work it out. Not that it makes any difference now."

You were on a break.

She kept her lips closed, glaring at him, remnants of a previous nasty breakup jolting through her mind. Her ex had also believed taking a pause to reevaluate a relationship was permission to sleep around.

"My kids were three and five."

She blinked. *I have siblings? Half siblings?*

He gave a small smile. "I have a son and a daughter. You remind me of Kacey. She has the same low voice that makes me think of a singer in a smoky blues lounge."

Her mother had always encouraged her to embrace her voice. It was one of the few distinctions between her and Jayne. When they were kids, Jayne would imitate it to pass herself off as Ava.

Ava had been in her midtwenties before she'd accepted her unique sound.

Is it possible that gene came from this man?

Watching him carefully, she relaxed her spine an inch. "Where are your kids now?"

"Both still live in San Diego. I have four grandkids."

"Do they know about us?" she whispered.

"They do. They're the ones who encouraged me to start looking. They're curious about the two of you." He paused. "My wife died a few years ago and I never told her about the affair. But a year ago I was having issues with depression and started to drink. I couldn't get your mother's last words to me out of my mind, and I finally confessed to my children. After some initial anger, they forgave me and said they were glad their mother never knew. Then they tried to help me find the two of you."

"How's the depression?" she asked. Is this where Jayne's mental illness came from?

"Better. Some therapy and some meds and having a goal in life brought me around." He frowned. "I take it your sister has long struggled with mental health issues?"

"Most of her life. I hang on by my fingertips most of the time. I swear the goal of not becoming my twin is what keeps me from falling over the edge." She clamped her mouth shut, uncomfortable with the private fact she'd just shared. Pity filled his eyes and she looked away.

"I'm sorry about your mother," he said softly. "Cancer took my wife, too."

"It's a brutal disease."

"Absolutely."

"Do you have any paperwork that proves you're related to us?" Ava asked, knowing it was a pointless question; she'd doubt anything he produced.

His shoulders sank. "I have nothing. Not even pictures. I got rid of the few I had of us together."

Because you were married.

"My mother never showed us any photos of you," Ava stated. Part of her wanted to make this man hurt. "She said you passed through her life too fast." He winced, and she had a spark of satisfaction.

"It was brief," he agreed.

"The place for the father's name on our birth certificates is blank."

"I saw that. I have copies."

"We were poor all our lives," Ava said, twisting the knife she'd plunged in his chest. "My mother worked her butt off waiting tables and was promoted to restaurant manager to provide for us. Some days she didn't eat so that we could."

He closed his eyes. "I would have helped had I known."

"Would you?" she said sharply.

"I would. We always had plenty."

She exhaled, hating the thought of this man living the high life in San Diego. Probably in a big home with a pool. She could envision a young boy and girl playing in the water with him and his wife. One big happy family.

I never wanted for love. Mom always gave plenty of that.

"I had to get an after-school job as soon as I was old enough. We needed the money."

He met her gaze. "I'm truly sorry."

She swallowed and looked away. "You might be wrong. This could all be a mistake."

"It could be, but I don't think it is. I have something to show you." He pulled out his cell phone and touched the screen. "This is a picture of Kacey." He held out the phone.

Ava eyed the phone. From her angle she could see a picture of a woman with dark hair. She was terrified to look closer and squeezed her hands in a death hold under the table. He moved the phone closer to her.

"Take it," he directed.

She wrenched her hands apart and took the phone. Kacey had her eyes. Hers and Jayne's. Her face was more oval, and her nose and mouth were different, but the eyes were the same dark blue with dense lashes. Ava blinked and enlarged the image, searching for differences.

There was no denying the eyes. Or, according to David, the voice.

"Do you understand why you caught my attention on the news? And why I had to find out more?"

She nodded. "What does your son look like?" she asked softly. He reached over and swiped the screen. A blond man with two toddlers appeared. He was the spitting image of David. Ava understood how her mother must have been swayed if David had been as good-looking as his son when he was younger.

"Now tell me where Jayne went." She was exhausted and still craved a large glass of wine. She handed back the phone.

David looked at Glen and gave a small nod. "She and Brady Shurr flew to Costa Rica," said Glen.

"Costa Rica? Seriously?" Anger surged through her and she wanted to hit something. She was working a huge serial killer case and trying not to worry about her missing twin only to discover she'd taken a vacation with her new married boyfriend? "I'm going to kill her," she muttered. She pressed the heels of her hands into her eyes until she saw white spots. "Why am I not surprised?"

"Not surprised?" asked David.

"Nope. Jayne has always done whatever strikes her fancy without thinking twice about how it affects anyone else."

"Surely her taking a trip doesn't affect you," said Glen.

"In all your *investigating*, did you find out the cost of that treatment center she'd been in? Who do you think was paying for that? I wanted her to *get well!*" Her voice rose an octave. "You bet it affects me. Every stupid thing she does affects me because I have to pick up the pieces. I've distanced myself as far away from her as possible, but then she pulls a stunt like this?" She stood, more than done with the conversation and the haunting image of the woman who resembled her.

The past should stay in the past.

"I have a bunch of dead police officers on my hands. I'm not going to waste my time thinking about my twin as she lays on a sunny beach in Central America." She held back the expletives she wanted to call her sister. "You'll understand if I don't care to see either of you again? Sorry about that, *Dad.*" Red anger blurred her vision as she pushed out of her chair and headed toward her car.

Screw Jayne.

Screw David claiming to be my father.

In her car she paused long enough to send a very brief email to Jayne.

What the fuck did you do?

She put her phone away, started her car, and threw it in reverse. Sweat had cropped up under her arms, and she cursed as she realized she had on a silk blouse. She counted to ten and focused on the road.

She had a killer to find.

29

"Oh, honey. I'm so sorry, but I'm not feeling well today."

His mother rested her head in her hands at the breakfast table. He'd known she wouldn't be able to make it to his basketball game, but he'd asked anyway. Hoping . . .

"I understand. Maybe next time."

"Of course, darling. I love to watch you play. You're sooo good! But as you can see, my eyes are swollen and I look like a mess today. I shouldn't go out in public."

"You look great, Mom. You always look great."

She beamed at him.

He gave a weak smile. It made no sense to him that she needed to hear his eighth grade opinion on her looks, but it always cheered her up. He'd noticed she'd been very down since the last man hadn't fulfilled his six-month agreement. He'd stopped hoping for one of the mentors to last longer than the six months they signed up for. Over and over the men had proved that they were unreliable. Maybe it was part of their profession.

Deep down he'd prayed one of them would fill a need for his mother. But they had all left. Some after the first week or two. Clearly they didn't know how to fulfill a commitment. His mother needed someone stronger than the losers who'd been assigned to him.

Last week he'd told his mother that a friend's father was interested in meeting her. She'd asked what he did for work and then refused when she found out he worked at Macy's department store. "Boring," she'd said. "Retail sales, really?"

"Maybe he can get you a discount?" he'd suggested.

She'd looked interested for a brief second and then refused again.

For some reason she was drawn to cops.

He thought cops were cool, too. When he asked, they'd always show him their weapons. One had let him hold an empty gun after showing him how to remove all the ammunition. Most of them said they'd never had to fire their weapon. One of them had said his words and his voice were his best weapons.

That was stupid.

If he was a cop he'd pull out his weapon all the time to get people to behave. Who wants to argue with people?

"I'm going to take a shower and see if it clears up my sinuses," she told him. "Clean up your dishes, okay?" She stood and strolled out of the room, leaving her own dishes on the table.

He put hers and his in the dishwasher and then wiped up the crumbs she'd left by the toaster. He studied the kitchen, an inspection to spot anything else she could get upset about. It looked perfect. It was the least he could do for her since she was so sad.

"Honey?" she called from her bathroom.

He hooked his backpack onto one shoulder as he headed down the hallway, knowing he needed to be out the door and on his way to the bus stop in a minute. He stopped outside her bathroom door. "What?"

"I can't reach the buttons on the back of this shirt. Can you help me real quick?"

"Sure." He waited for her to open the door a crack so he could slide an arm through. The door opened wide and she stood with her back to him.

She'd already removed her sweatpants and underwear. He stared and then yanked his gaze up to her back. With shaking hands he undid her buttons. Her bra was black, with lace.

He grabbed the door handle, stepped backward, and slammed it shut. Holy cow.

Sweat bloomed under his arms. He'd never seen his mother naked before. She opened the door three inches, peering at him with her wide blue eyes. "I'm sorry. Did I surprise you?"

"Uh . . . no." His voice shook.

"It's okay, honey. I'm your mother. No big deal."

He didn't know what to say.

"Go to school. I'll see you tonight after your game."

He turned and left.

• • •

They lost the game. The other school had crushed his team and twice his coach had yelled for him to get his head in the game. He'd ridden the late activity bus and he slowly plodded up the street to his house. He didn't want to go home.

In his mind he kept seeing his mother in the bathroom that morning. He felt dirty, like when he'd looked at the naked layouts in his friend's magazine. Those women were whores, posing for men to stare at. His mother wasn't like that. His mother had never let anyone see her naked in her whole life.

Except for him.

Another explicit image from that morning shot through his brain. He hadn't told any of the guys what he'd seen. It was cool to brag when you saw a naked girl or got a hold of a dirty magazine, but he was positive that gloating that he'd seen his mother's naked ass wouldn't score him any points with his friends.

She didn't bring it up that evening. He loaded the dishwasher in silence as she watched TV in the living room, and he hoped she'd forgotten the incident. Maybe it was nothing. Maybe it was a bigger deal in his head than it should be. She was his mother; she knew what was right and wrong.

But it felt wrong.

Later he brushed his teeth and kissed her good night on the cheek like he'd done all his life. She'd already crawled in bed and was reading a book. He turned to leave.

"Before you go, can you scratch a spot in the center of my back?" she asked. "It's been itching for the last ten minutes and I can't reach it."

He swallowed hard. "Sure, Mom."

She presented her back to him and lifted the back hem of her pajama top. "Right in the center, sort of up high."

He reached out and scratched on top of the fabric up by her neck.

"No, silly. Lower than that. And under my shirt, please."

He grasped the hem of her top and lifted. She wasn't wearing a bra, but he doubted they were worn under pajamas. Black lace from her underwear showed above the waistband of her pajama bottoms. He looked away and scratched.

"Ahhh. Don't stop." She leaned back into his hand. "Press harder."

He scratched faster, trying to hide the tremor in his hand. His gut gave an odd twist and warmth flowed from it out to his limbs. She glanced at him over her shoulder and smiled. "That's perfect."

He yanked his hand away as if he'd been burned. Her shirt fluttered back into place.

"While you're right there, can you massage my right shoulder? I don't know what I did to it, but it's aching like crazy tonight."

Not lifting her shirt, he rubbed through the material, massaging as hard as he could.

"Who needs a man around when I have you?" she said, looking back at him with a smile. "We don't need anyone else."

He didn't say anything.

"*That last jerk didn't hurt me,*" she said. "*He just used me. That's what they all do, you know. As soon as they see a beautiful single woman, they think they can pretend to be kind to her for a little while and then just move on. I cooked him that nice dinner and pie, and then he backed out of his mentoring agreement.*"

Why were these men so mean to his mother? Over and over. For years they had done this to her. It was completely unfair. She was a good woman. They must find him unbearable to be around. Or they discovered he was too big a loser for them to help.

"*One of these days they'll regret not being kinder to me,*" she said.

"*Yes, they will,*" he agreed.

30

Ava checked the address on the house against the one on her phone. This was the right place. Nora had called after Ava left David and Glen at the coffee shop and asked her to talk to Lucien Fujioka's wife, Jeanine. She'd flown home a few hours after her husband had been found but had spent the last twenty-four at her parents' house, avoiding the media. She wanted to talk to the police but had requested time to pull herself together.

Ava knocked on the door and it was instantly opened by a sweet-looking, smiling older woman with white hair. "Are you the FBI agent?" she asked. She looked like a movie-perfect grandmother. Curly hair, translucent skin, kind blue eyes.

Ava held out her identification. "Special Agent Ava McLane. How is Jeanine doing this morning?"

Sorrow transformed the woman's face, and Ava wanted to hug her.

"You can call me Hildie. Jeanine is doing as well as can be expected after finding out her husband of fifteen years has been murdered."

"I'm so sorry for your loss," Ava said as she stepped into the home. The phrase was automatic, but her heart was truly behind it.

"Thank you. Lucien was a dear and very good to our Jeanine. We'll miss him terribly." She blotted her eyes with a handkerchief from her robe pocket.

"Good morning."

A tall woman spoke as she stepped into the formal living room. Jeanine Fujioka was incredibly thin, with her mother's fair skin. Ava knew she'd been a fashion model twenty years ago. Her eyes were bloodshot.

Ava introduced herself and shook Jeanine's hand. It felt like ice.

"I'm so sorry for your loss," she said again. The woman briefly closed her eyes and nodded.

"Let's sit in the kitchen," Hildie suggested. "Would you like some coffee, Agent McLane?"

An image of her dropped latte crossed her mind. "Yes, please. And call me Ava." The three of them filed into the kitchen, and Ava gawked at the pale-pink stove and matching fridge. *Antiques!* The room was homey and warm and smelled strongly of fresh-brewed coffee. She sat at a dinette set of metal and pink vinyl as Hildie poured her a cup of coffee in a tiny floral china cup with a matching saucer.

"Cream or sugar?"

"Black. And thank you so much." She took a sip of the coffee and could barely taste it. She'd been drinking brew made from burned beans for too long. Hildie poured coffee in an identical cup for Jeanine and set a small matching pitcher of cream next to it. She excused herself and vanished down the hallway.

The women sat in silence for a moment, sipping their coffee.

"Do they know who killed Lucien?" Jeanine asked. Her gaze said she had no expectations. Exhaustion flowed out of her, and she seemed wrung out and eerily calm. The past hours must have been a tidal wave of emotion and now she was drained. Ava understood.

"Not yet. I assume you know we believe he's connected to three other deaths of law enforcement officers?"

"Yes, Detective Hawes updated me on the phone yesterday. She said Lucien fought back . . . and that you hadn't seen that with the other officers."

"That's correct," said Ava. "We believe the other officers were incapacitated with the blow of a baseball bat or something similar. It appears the blow to your husband wasn't as strong. I suspect he spotted or heard the killer and managed to deflect the full impact."

"Which is why he was shot and the others weren't."

"Correct."

"I don't understand why he was holding a Halloween mask," Jeanine said. "We didn't have anything like that . . . unless he'd just bought it while I was gone."

"We're confused on that, too," Ava lied, hating to mislead the woman, but the masks needed to be kept out of the media. She knew only the real killer could explain them.

"Why these men?" Jeanine whispered, her eyes filling. "What did they do?"

"We're still searching for the link between them," Ava told her. "We have noticed that they all worked with Cops 4 Kidz."

"All the guys Lucien worked with volunteered in some way."

"Right. Even I have. But most of the murdered men were part of the mentoring program. How long had Lucien been doing that?"

Jeanine leaned back in her chair and gazed to the side as she thought. "He was doing that before we married. We've been married for fifteen years. He loved it. He said he felt like he was making a difference in kids' lives."

"You don't have children." It wasn't a question; Ava knew they did not.

"No. We decided long ago it wasn't for us, but Lucien still enjoyed helping other kids. He said volunteering once a week was enough kid time for him."

"Do you know if he ever mentored a boy named Micah Zuch?"

Jeanine tipped her head in thought. "I don't remember that name, but that doesn't mean he didn't. He's probably worked with a dozen kids over the years. I can't recall names . . . I know his latest was Brennan—I never knew the last name. And I remember a Nathan, Rory, Jason . . . um . . . Kyle. I'm sorry, but I rarely bothered to learn the last names. Lucien didn't bring them to the house. He believed in keeping them separate from his home life. He took them to sporting events, movies, shopping, or just hung out with them."

"Why didn't he bring them by his home?" Ava asked. She believed she knew, but wanted to hear Jeanine's explanation.

The woman looked slightly embarrassed. "It makes sense. We didn't know these kids, and we didn't know the types of homes they came from. Lucien saw the best in everyone, but that didn't mean he wanted these kids to know his home address. Every now and then he would work with a kid who really attached himself to Lucien and wanted to see his house. It broke his heart to not invite them into his home, but he knew it was the right thing to do."

"How did the kids react?" Ava was curious.

"Some told him that they felt like they were just part of his job. That he didn't really *care* about them . . . that he walked away from them each night, back to his happy house, and forgot about them until the next week. Others shrugged and acted like it didn't matter. But Lucien *knew* it hurt them. It's a good program," Jeanine said fiercely. "But this is the only way it can work."

"I agree." Ava paused. "Were there any other parts of the program Lucien felt were difficult?"

Jeanine rolled her eyes. "Oh, my goodness. Some of the mothers."

"Explain."

"So many of them were such overboard badge bunnies that Lucien wondered if they enrolled their kids in the program just to get close to the cops."

"I can see that," agreed Ava. Regina Zuch came to mind.

"It comes with the job," said Jeanine. "Women constantly hit on him. He was pretty good at ignoring it, but I know some cops who enjoyed the attention."

"I'm engaged to a detective," Ava admitted. "I've heard the stories."

"Some of the mothers who put their kids in Cops 4 Kidz were the worst."

"Give me an example."

"Lucien requested to be removed from a mentorship because the mother pursued him so hard. Then she went batshit crazy on him. She came down to his precinct and proceeded to scream that he'd used her son to get close to her and then dumped her. Lucien wasn't even in the building that day, but she kept coming back, waiting for him outside, or trying to follow him home."

"Why wasn't she arrested?"

"She managed to just keep it legal. She knew what lines not to cross. This was when he worked in Vancouver. He finally applied for a position with the West Linn Police Department."

"Just to get away from her?"

"Not completely. He wanted to work closer to home, but she sped up the process."

"That's horrible. She didn't show up anymore?"

"His department told her he quit and she backed off. I suspect she continued to watch the building for a while and finally realized he'd left."

"No other problems from her over the years?"

"No, thank goodness. Lucien and I have never opened social media accounts, primarily because of what he does for a living, but I know in the back of his mind he never wanted her to be able to find him. She was nuts. Although I imagine she simply moved her focus to whoever next mentored her son."

"Lucien didn't report her to the organization? Keep someone else from going through the same thing?"

"We talked about it several times. I wanted him to, but he thought it was important that her son have a male figure in his life. He said the kid was one of the needier ones he'd worked with and didn't want to take away any opportunities the boy might get through the program."

"He was a good man," Ava said. "Other people wouldn't be so forgiving."

"That was Lucien," Jeanine said simply.

"Do you remember the names of that mother and son?" Ava asked.

"Sonja. Sonja Parish. Her son was Jesse," she replied without hesitation. "I'll never forget her name."

Ava made a note, wondering if the boy had been assigned to another cop or if his mother had given up on the program.

"I know you've heard the description of the man who was seen in your home at the time of your husband's death," Ava said. "Does that sound like someone you know?"

"An average-size man with dark hair. I probably encounter twenty a day," Jeanine stated. "I've thought long and hard, wondering if I knew the person who did this to him, and I can honestly say I can't come up with anything. Lucien was a kind man—ask anyone—he didn't make enemies . . . outside of the people he had to arrest, but that happens with every cop. I can't think of anyone that we know who would do this."

Ava nodded. The task force had heard the same things from Lucien's coworkers. *Impossible to get mad at. All-around good guy. Thinks of others before himself.* "Were there any work incidents that worried him? Any encounters he told you about that concerned him?"

Jeanine shook her head. "I know this will sound awful, but he didn't talk about work that much, and I didn't ask. He liked to leave it behind when he came home. Early on I used to ask him about his day, but he finally requested I stop. We came to an agreement that he'd initiate any conversations work-related. He knew I was there to listen if there was something he needed to get off his chest."

Ava knew several cops who operated this way. Whatever worked. She and Mason enjoyed discussing their respective cases.

"What was the purpose of your business trip?" she asked, switching gears. Jeanine shifted slightly on her chair and took another sip of her coffee before answering.

"It's a yearly convention for us. I buy holiday-themed outdoor lighting and electronics for an online retailer. Mainly it showcases the merchandise that will be available next year. I'm always looking for the next big thing."

"Before the holiday season has even arrived?"

Jeanine gave a smile. "Our current season's planning was done months and months ago. Stores placed their orders late last winter for this season. That's retail."

"Does your company do any Halloween costumes?"

She shook her head. "No clothing, either. It's primarily a home-furnishings-type retailer."

Ava remembered the simple decor outside the Fujioka home. "You don't decorate your home with the items you pick out for your company?"

"By the time I've seen it all and placed our orders for the following season, I don't want to have anything to do with it. Lucien does a bit of holiday decor. I wash my hands of the whole thing and tell him to have at it." Her face fell. "I *told* him to," she corrected. She took a deep breath and crumpled in her chair, covering her face with her hands. "I'm trying so hard to be strong," she whispered. "But it keeps hitting me like a blow to the face at unexpected times. Each time it's just as powerful. It's not easing up." She moved her hands and looked at Ava with begging eyes. "When does it get better?"

Ava scooted her chair around the table and hugged the woman, feeling her lean into her shoulder. "It takes a long time," Ava admitted, thinking of her mother's death. "Just when you think you're finally healed, you'll discover something that triggers a powerful memory and your knees will go weak again."

Jeanine trembled.

"The pain doesn't go away for a long time. You simply have to make room for it. It's a price we pay to love someone."

Fifteen minutes later she drove away from the home. A block later she pulled over and leaned her forehead against the steering wheel, her chest moving in silent heaves. She hadn't wanted Jeanine to see how much the conversation had affected her. Jeanine's despair over her husband's death, and the kindness of her mother, had made Ava ache for her own mother. Twice in one day her mother had been thrust into her thoughts.

There'd been four months between the diagnosis and when her mother passed. To Ava it'd felt like hell, and when she heard of people who'd fought for eighteen months, she knew she'd been lucky. But to have a loved one vanish without ever having the chance to say good-bye would be a million times worse.

She and Mason told each other "I love you" when they parted. Always. They both went to work with a weapon at their side. Any day could be their last.

Jeanine Fujioka had experienced Ava's greatest nightmare. The pain and emptiness in her eyes had nearly been too much for Ava to bear.

Her phone rang and she scowled at the unfamiliar phone number that appeared on the screen on her car's dashboard. She took one more shuddering breath and pushed the ANSWER button.

"Ava McLane."

"Ava?"

Jayne. She sat ramrod-straight, her heart hitting a staccato rhythm. "Jayne? *What were you thinking?*"

"I'm okay."

"That's not what I asked. *Why did you leave the rehab center?*"

"Does it really matter?" her sister snapped. "I'm safe, I'm happy, and everything is going to be okay. I only called so you wouldn't worry."

Since when does Jayne care if I worry or not?

"Is Brady Shull with you?"

Jayne was silent for a moment. "Yes, he is. It's not what you think."

Anger swept through her. "Let me tell you exactly what I'm thinking. You ran off with a married man from a facility that I was paying a lot of money for and now you're drinking a margarita on a beach. Now tell me again that *it's not what I think.*"

"Yes, that is all true, but—"

"No *buts*, Jayne. You've screwed me over again. Don't expect me to ever contribute to your recovery again. I know I've said that before, but I've always caved and paid, hoping that this time would be different, but seriously, Jayne, I'm really over it."

"Listen to me!" her twin screeched.

"I'm *listening*." Ava was a split second away from ending the call.

"Brady understands me."

Dear Lord, give me strength.

"I was frustrated with the people there. It felt like the doctors were always judging me and looking down on me. Whatever I did was never good enough."

Ava recalled Mason's last conversation with Jayne's primary doctor; he hadn't been impressed.

"I made great strides in there, Ava, I really did. But I didn't feel like they could help me anymore. I needed someone who would be more supportive. Brady was struggling with the same problem and his family refused to listen to his concerns. Then he read about a facility in Costa Rica. It sounded so wonderful, Ava. I knew the warmth and sun would help me get stronger."

Ava blinked. "You went to a different treatment center?"

"Yes. The minute I stepped in the door here, I knew it was the right place. It's what I need right now. The people are warm and attentive, and I don't feel like they're just waiting for me to stop talking so they can get to the next patient. Brady feels it, too."

Ava couldn't speak for a long second. She'd gone to another facility? "What kind of place is this, Jayne?"

"It's a recovery center, Ava. It's not a luxury resort, and it's going to be more hard work, but they get great results. I needed a change."

Of course you did. A fresh start. "What's your relationship with Brady? His family is worried sick about him."

"Well . . ."

Some parts of Jayne will never change. "Is he paying for this?"

"Yes, but we're supporting each other. His wife doesn't understand what he's going through. I do. You don't know how important it is to be around people who are experiencing the same struggle as you."

Ava was silent.

"I love him, Ava," Jayne whispered. "I've never felt like this about anyone."

What do I say to that?

"Can you be happy for me?" she asked in a small voice.

"What will you do when he leaves, Jayne? You're ten years older than him! Are you going to fall apart and start abusing again? Are you going to slash your wrists?" She spoke cruelly. Her sister was blindly skipping down a familiar path. "Do you know how many times I've heard this sort of story from you? I'm *worried* for you. You get caught up in a man and when he leaves you in the dust, I have to pick up the pieces."

"I know how many times I've done that to you, Ava, and I'm sorry for every time. I ask myself every day what I will do if I'm suddenly alone. And do you know what? *I'm good with it.* I can stand on my own two feet now. I want to get better, Ava. Not for him or even for you, but for me. I don't need someone else to prop me up. I'm choosing to be with Brady and if it ends, it ends. It's not the end of my life."

Shock kept Ava speechless. She'd never heard her sister speak with such self-confidence. She sounded healthy and balanced. She almost believed her . . . almost.

"Don't forget that, Jayne."

"I won't. I'm not going to improve if I'm constantly looking for someone to lean on. That's one thing I did learn in that center. I learned I have to rely on myself for my own happiness, not others."

Ava stared at the phone number on her dash as if it would explain who'd taken over her sister's brain.

"I'm glad you know that now, Jayne," she stammered.

"I need to go. Just understand that I'm in a good spot and I'll make certain Brady reaches out to his family. It's over between him and his wife. He knew that before he went into therapy."

"Be careful, Jayne. That's his problem, not yours."

"I know. He's doing what he needs to do for himself, just as I am."

"Are you still painting?" she asked.

"Oh, yes. I'm going to get set up down here and keep going. I love it."

"Your paintings are beautiful, Jayne. I was so proud of you when I saw your pictures." Thoughts of David and his revelations invaded her brain. *I can't tell her about him yet. What if it's not true?*

She needed proof before she told Jayne that their father had found them.

"Thank you," Jayne whispered. "I love you, Ava."

"Love you, too."

"I need to go. I'll email you."

The call ended.

What just happened? She'd never heard such logical words from her sister. *Is she truly on the right path?*

She did know that Jayne's health was out of her hands, and she was at peace with that. She silently wished her sister the best. Brady or no Brady, it sounded as if Jayne might be doing something right for herself for once.

Ava could only hope.

31

Mason turned into the long gravel driveway. Scott Heuser lived in an old house on a few acres set way back from the narrow country road. Tall firs lined part of the drive, and he passed small pastures that needed a horse or two.

I've been here before. He thought hard, trying to remember when he would have visited the home. Maybe it only felt like a place he'd visited before. Or had work brought him here?

He'd visited the immediate area several times. The property he'd driven past before Scott's was the huge farm where he used to bring Jake to pick out his pumpkin. The agri-tainment farm offered a corn maze, hayrides through a haunted forest, pumpkin launchers, a snack bar, and a petting zoo. He'd passed the large gravel parking lot packed with minivans and SUVs as families did their Halloween duty. Popular opinion stated that parents were to give kids every possible experience; it was nearly a competition. Mason had been sucked into it as he and Robin raised Jake. They had dragged their son to every holiday event. Santa's lap, Easter Bunny, Fourth of July parades, state

and county fairs. Picking out a Christmas tree or a pumpkin had to
be an *adventure.*

Mason had found all of it exhausting. He'd eagerly gone the first
time or two but had become burned out on the lines and crowds. And
cost. Robin loved it. She continued to take Jake on her own as Mason
begged off most years, blaming work or lack of energy. He simply didn't
want to go.

Did that make me a bad parent?

Ava would never know the highs and lows of raising kids. He felt
bad about that, but part of him knew she would miss out on a lot of
heartache. It'd been her decision.

Or had it?

He frowned as he parked his car in front of the white farmhouse.
He and Ava had briefly touched on the subject of kids a few times. He'd
always said he was done. And she'd said—he concentrated to remember
her exact words, but he couldn't recall them. He knew she'd always
smiled, nodded, and agreed.

*Would she want to take a child on the hayride through the haunted
woods?*

He could visualize it.

The first time he'd taken Jake on the hayride at the adjacent farm
had been a disaster. The ride wasn't recommended for kids under
the age of ten, but nine-year-old Jake had begged and begged to go.
Mason had relented. The night had been clear and cold. He could see
Jake's breath as he'd panted with excitement, sitting close to Mason
on a bale of hay in the back of the wagon. The high school's drama
department had supplied the actors and makeup for the roaming
zombie horde, and terrifying dead people crawled out of holes in the
graveyard. Random body parts were scattered along the dirt road and
hanging from the trees.

Jake had screamed and hidden his eyes in Mason's coat as the first
zombie reached through the slats of the wagon to touch his foot. He'd

crawled into Mason's lap and refused to look for the rest of the ride. Mason hadn't allowed his son to go back until he was twelve.

He grinned at the memory. Jake had had nightmares for months, and Robin wouldn't let Mason forget he'd overruled her opinion that their son was too young for the terrifying ride. By the time Jake went again, he'd mastered the disdainful junior high attitude and claimed the ride was "for babies." But Mason saw the pulse in his neck speed up at the sight of the new and improved zombie horde that rushed their wagon.

He stepped out and slammed his vehicle door. The house was a traditional-looking white farmhouse and it surprised him that a man as young as Scott lived here. He'd pictured Scott in an urban loft in northwest Portland where he shouldered his bike up and down the stairs for his green commute. This house was nearly twenty miles out of the city. It needed a family with lots of kids who rescued stray cats and retired greyhounds.

The walkway was brick and its pavers looked fresh and clean. He took the half-dozen stairs up to the wide wraparound porch, noticing that the paint looked immaculate though the house had to be nearly a hundred years old. He knocked heavily on the wooden door, hoping that Scott could hear him inside the big home. An antique glass inset in the door reminded him of looking through a kaleidoscope as a kid. He admired the dozens of intricate glass pieces, wondering if anyone still spent the time to create that quality of work, and abruptly remembered the last time he'd stood in front of this door.

•   •   •

Ava grabbed a sandwich from the deli tray at the back of the room. The task force room was empty, but she could tell several people had been there. Only ham sandwiches were left and all the bags of chips were gone except for two bags of Sun Chips.

That was fine with her. She opened a bag and shoved a few chips into her sandwich. She was crunching noisily when Zander and Nora walked in. Zander gave no sign that he'd been nearly incapacitated twelve hours before until he looked at her sandwich and glanced away.

Apparently his stomach was not fully recovered.

"How was your conversation with Jeanine Fujioka?" Nora asked.

"Good," said Ava through a mouthful of sandwich. She swallowed. "She has a solid support system in her mother, and I think she'll get through it. Eventually."

"She have any insights?" Zander asked.

"She couldn't think of anyone who was angry enough with Lucien to murder him. She did talk about his time with Cops 4 Kidz and that got me thinking a little bit."

Nora raised her brows. "What'd she tell you?"

"She thinks some of the mothers who enrolled their kids in the program might have ulterior motives."

"Getting close to a cop," suggested Zander, looking resigned.

"Exactly," said Ava. "I can see you're not surprised."

"Not one bit."

"Her husband encountered some crazies?" Nora asked.

"Definitely. One was nuts enough to make him stop mentoring her son and go work in another city."

"Christ. That's extreme," Zander said.

"I plugged her and her son's names into our computers. Neither have records and they both show current residences in Louisiana and it looks like they moved six years ago. I wonder if Lucien was aware of that. If I'd had a stalker I would have kept tabs on where they lived, but Jeanine seemed to be under the impression that Lucien hadn't received any information about the woman since he left the Vancouver department." If Ava had been his wife, she would have occasionally asked if he knew what the woman was up to. But Jeanine had said Lucien liked to avoid work conversation. Perhaps, in her mind, this fell into that category.

Had Lucien and Jeanine assumed that it could never turn violent? Had the fact that the stalker was female made them assume she'd go away?

"Have we given enough thought to our female killer theory?" Ava asked, thinking of Sonja Parish. "We have those long hairs and we're pretty sure a bat was used to incapacitate three of them, I think that opens it up to either sex."

"Euzent seemed convinced we're dealing with a man," Nora said slowly. "The brutality of the deaths and the fact that it had to take some muscle to maneuver the bodies of Weldon and Samuelson. Since there was exactly one long hair on the bodies, I felt as if it was deliberately placed there . . . maybe to mislead us."

"Audrey Kerth saw a man leave the Fujioka scene," added Ava.

"We have one eyewitness to that scene. Eyewitnesses make mistakes," Zander said. "Perhaps she didn't see everyone who was present. Someone else could have left in another direction."

"We haven't found a hair in the evidence from that scene, right?" asked Ava. "Maybe he didn't plant it in the confusion. I think we're right about that murder not going as he expected. I do think a woman could still have been involved . . . either alone or as a partner."

"Even Micah brought up that someone with the right equipment could have hung Weldon on their own. That applies to the Samuelson case, too. With enough planning, a woman—"

"Or she had someone with her to help with the heavy lifting," suggested Zander.

"Are you saying there's an angry mom out there that wanted to exact revenge? Revenge for what?" asked Nora.

"A woman scorned," said Ava. "Jeanine Fujioka described Sonja Parish as a seriously unbalanced woman who'd stalked her husband. Who knows what she was capable of? Jeanine said she and her husband wondered if this woman would show up again in their lives."

"Maybe she did," said Zander.

"Well, if she did, she's been behaving herself for the last decade," said Ava. "I have a hard time believing she flew here from Louisiana to get even."

The three of them were silent for a moment, weighing the possibility. Ava tried to picture a woman carrying out the murders. She couldn't see it, but she knew they couldn't rule it out.

"Our smiley face fingerprint showed up on the Fujioka mask," Nora stated. "But your fingerprint lab has burst our bubble of excitement on its origins."

"Explain," said Ava.

"It's fake. Well, at one time it was on a real person. Turns out this print is available for purchase online. You know those latex gloves with fake fingerprints they sell?"

Ava nodded. She'd read about them. Marketed as novelty items to "impress your friends," the mass-produced gloves were designed to screw with investigations. They weren't illegal to sell and the prints were flagged in databanks around the country. She'd never heard of a case in which they'd shown up. Until now. "Someone sells happy-faced gloves?"

"Yes," said Nora. "The lab figured it out this morning. Someone wanted to mess with us."

"Are we looking into who sells it?" asked Ava.

"I assigned it to Henry."

"Dammit. I'd really hoped that'd lead somewhere." Someone was having a good laugh at their expense.

"Did you get the children's names from the mentoring program yet?" Nora asked.

"No," said Ava as she finished the last bite of her sandwich. "Scott Heuser has been out of the office and hasn't returned any of my voice mails. The receptionist says those records are password-protected and that Scott hasn't gotten back to her, either. I'm about ready to go down there and take their server."

"What about Micah's mother?" asked Zander with a thoughtful look on his face. "Are we ignoring her as a possible suspect? Remember how she flew off the handle when she first got here? She clearly has a thing for cops and we already know Micah was in the program. That's three things we just talked about in a suspect."

"Are you suggesting that's how Micah knows so much about the murders? Because he was there helping his mother?" Nora sounded skeptical. "He's still sitting in a holding cell downstairs. I'm having a DA figure out what else to charge him with so we can hold him longer."

"Do we need to have Regina come back?" asked Zander. "We were so focused on Micah, maybe we need to take a closer look at Regina."

"It can't be Regina," said Ava. "Jeanine Fujioka said her husband didn't mentor Micah Zuch."

"Just because Lucien didn't mentor Micah doesn't mean he didn't encounter his mother," argued Zander. "Maybe Regina attended some of the organization's public events. She could have met Lucien there, or possibly she knows other mothers who crossed the line when it came to the mentors. It could be someone in her peer group."

"I don't think women discuss their cop conquests." Ava rubbed her eyes. "Or do they? Oh, what if it's like a private little club where they pass around the names of the cops who are willing to step over the ethical lines?"

"Seriously?" asked Nora. "I think that's following a very weak tangent. This isn't a soap opera. Women don't do that."

"You haven't met my sister," muttered Ava as Zander deliberately nodded.

Nora stared at them. "You're both cracked. The chance that we're dealing with a scorned woman who's planned revenge on every cop who refused to sleep with her is minuscule."

"I want to talk to Regina again," said Zander. "I want her to get a look at her son in a pair of jail coveralls, too."

"He's not in coveralls," said Nora.

"Find him some and tell him to put them on. I think it'll be a good image for his mother to see."

"There's no way Micah is the muscle to go with his mother's murdering rampage," said Ava. "It doesn't fit. Regina is the type who uses her tongue as a weapon, not a blade to the neck."

"Maybe that's how she *wants* you to view her," said Zander.

"Quit messing with my head." Ava glared at him as she silently questioned her perception of Micah's mother. Had the woman completely fooled her? "You think she'd let her son sit in jail, possibly taking blame for the crimes she committed?"

"I'm not ruling it out."

"Let's get Regina Zuch back here," said Nora, making a decision. "Zander and I will talk to her." She looked at Ava. "Get a warrant for the Cops 4 Kidz server. Take a computer tech with you so the equipment is removed appropriately."

"I filed a request for the warrant an hour ago," Ava said, smiling. "It should be ready any minute."

Nora's eyes lit up. "Nice."

What if we're wasting too much time on Cops 4 Kidz?

Her face must have shown the direction of her thoughts because Nora immediately spoke up. "I've got Henry following up on a domestic terrorism suspect that Vance Weldon argued with and the other guys are digging through records, searching for another common connection

between these men. I'm also expecting forensic results on footprints at
the Schefte and Samuelson scenes."

"All of the prints from both scenes indicated a male," added Ava.

Nora held up a foot. "See this boat at the end of my leg? Not all
women have tiny cat feet like yours. Any woman with half a brain will
try to mislead us if she knows she might leave footprints behind, right?
My point is we aren't just focused on this mentoring organization. I've
got a lot of irons in the fire. We're going to get lucky very soon. I can
feel it. Now go get that computer equipment."

Ava went.

32

The FBI computer specialist who rode with Ava to Cops 4 Kidz talked nonstop. She'd grabbed one of the techs from the FBI Northwest Regional Computer Forensics Lab near Portland's convention center. Keith looked as if he should be riding a Harley or directing a construction crew instead of playing with computers. She wondered if he didn't have anyone to talk to at work. His floor in the lab had been silent except for the nonstop hum of fans and computer equipment in the huge workstations. She'd spotted a bookshelf full of ancient computer hardware she'd seen only in movies from the seventies and eighties, and wished Zander could see it.

She listened to Keith's banter. Small talk was never high on her priority list and today it was even lower than usual. Luckily he carried 90 percent of the conversation on his own, and the Cops 4 Kidz office building was only a fifteen-minute drive in the early-afternoon traffic.

With a firm shove, she pushed open the door to the familiar waiting room. The receptionist looked up with a stunned look. "Hello again, Agent McLane." Her forehead wrinkled in confusion and her black cat ears shifted on her head. She'd drawn a cat nose and whiskers on her face to go with her black furry sweater and rhinestone collar. Ava wondered if she had a tail.

A few minutes ago, Ava had called her to see if Scott had contacted his office yet. The receptionist had grown snippy on the phone, and repeated that when she'd heard from her boss she'd let Ava know. Ava hadn't warned her to expect a momentary visit. She didn't want the woman hiding any equipment they might need to remove.

"Why didn't you tell me you were stopping by?" the woman asked.

Ava handed her the warrant. "We have a warrant to remove computer hardware. We're very concerned that your boss is not returning calls—I'm worried for his safety in light of the recent murders," she exaggerated. She didn't need to expand, as her mention of the murders immediately caught the woman's attention. Her whiskers stretched as her mouth opened in shock, and she automatically accepted the paper.

"Surely you don't think something has happened to Scott?"

"I don't know what to think about his silence. I do know we need the information in your databases and you've told me you can't get to it." She paused and lifted a brow. "Is that still the case?"

The woman had turned her gaze to the warrant, but it jumped back to Ava. "Oh, yes. I can't get into the files you've asked me for." She looked back at the paper. "I don't know who I need to call about this. Without Scott here, I guess I should contact one of the board members to see if I can do this."

Ava smiled sweetly. "There's no point in asking anyone for permission. That paper allows me to get exactly what's listed on there. It's not a request."

"But I can't let you take our equipment," the woman said earnestly. "I need it to get my work done."

Ava turned to Keith, who'd been listening quietly and standing at her side like a bodyguard. She pointed over the reception counter to a hallway in the rear of the office. "It's the first door on the right."

Keith nodded and opened the door between the waiting room and the office business area. The receptionist stood up but stayed quiet as Ava silenced her with a pointed look.

Her tail was black.

"I need you to stay off your computer until we're done," Ava told her as she followed Keith to Scott Heuser's office and stood at the door. She kept one eye on the receptionist as Keith took a seat at the desk.

"Do you want me to take a quick look first?" Keith asked. "Or you can wait until I get it back to the office and hook it up to my equipment." His fingers flew over the keys.

"If you can get in, let's look now. We can remove it afterward."

She glanced back at the receptionist, who'd sat down in her chair and was tapping rapidly on her cell phone. Ava strode back to the woman's desk and looked over her shoulder. The name at the top of the messaging screen was MOM.

"I'd like you to refrain from using your cell phone while we're here, too," Ava said.

The receptionist laid her phone on her desk, facedown. "Anything else I can't do?" she muttered. Her mouth turned down. *Grumpy cat.*

"Maybe you should go get a soda from the machine down the hall." *Or milk.*

She stood and reached for her phone.

"Your phone will be safe left on the desk," Ava stated. The woman marched out of the office without looking back. Her chin was up, but her tail swayed awkwardly behind her, destroying any sense of dignity. Highly amused, Ava checked on Keith.

"What exactly are you looking for again?" Keith asked. "The mentoring program?"

"Yes." Ava went around the desk to look over his shoulder. Lists and lists of files covered the screen. "How did you get in?"

"It's a private server." Keith glanced around the small office. "It's got to be close by. It has a wireless connection and Scott set it up to connect automatically with this computer. I didn't even need to enter a password." He shook his head. "It's pretty lazy on Scott's part and not secure at all. I bet the receptionist's computer isn't set up that way. If you tried to log in from hers, it'll probably ask you for a password. The files are organized by type and date. He really should have someone build him a database so that he—"

"Can you search by names?"

"Not from this point. That's why I'd started to say he should have his information placed in a database so it's easy to search. Right now I need to be in the specific file to search for a name. What year do you want to look at?"

She wrote down the names of the four murdered men and handed them to Keith. "Start with last year and give me the name of every child they were paired with."

"How many years do you want me to go back?"

Captain Schefte volunteered for almost twenty years. She remembered the smile on Scott Heuser's face as he made that statement two days ago in this very office.

"Twenty years," she said.

"This server only has seven years of data."

"Are you sure? Is it stored in a different way?"

Keith made a dozen clicks. "I don't see anything older than seven years. Even his payroll and accounting files only go back until then. I suspect they weren't computerized until then."

"So there should be paper records somewhere."

"Somewhere."

"I'll ask the receptionist. Maybe she knows where they're stored."

"Be nice," Keith suggested.

"Can you search for those names while I grab her?"

"Sheesh. I'll need a spreadsheet." Keith clicked on the Excel application and created a blank chart. "Beats pencil and paper every time."

"Uh . . . should you be using that?"

Keith looked over his shoulder at her. "Really? You're worried about me using his Excel program to make a tiny chart when we're authorized to take all the hardware?"

It wouldn't be the end of the world if Keith built a little spreadsheet. "Add Micah Zuch to your spreadsheet. I want to know who's worked with him."

They were onto something. She could feel it.

33

Her arms loaded with two file folder boxes, Ava shouldered open the door to the task force room. She felt a pull in her left side where her gunshot wound had been stitched back together. It wasn't painful; it was simply uncomfortable enough to remind her that she was human. Behind her, Keith carried two more boxes. The receptionist had led them to a small storage room where they'd found the dusty boxes. By the fresh fingerprints in the thick dust, Ava could tell they'd been recently disturbed, and she asked the receptionist about it.

"Scott went through them before your visit the other day," she'd said, looking down her cat nose at Ava. "It took him an hour to dig up the information you asked for. I assume all that work didn't help you in your investigation?"

"It helped. Now we need more," Ava had replied. The warrant had been worded loosely enough that Ava was comfortable removing the hard copies of the records. Keith located the private server and removed that along with two computer towers.

Now they had to search through the paper files and see whom their victims had mentored. Keith's electronic search of the last seven years had found three children's names associated with Denny Schefte, two with Louis Samuelson, and two with Lucien Fujioka.

None of them were the same.

Ava had stared at Keith's mini-spreadsheet, a sinking feeling in her stomach, and wondered if they were on a wild goose chase. She'd hoped there would be a common name among the men. "We need to dig through the older records," she'd stated.

At the police department, Zander and Nora stared as she dropped her boxes on the conference table. Keith set his down gently next to hers.

"What did you find?" Nora asked, skeptically eyeing the big boxes.

Ava gave her a quick rundown. "Are there any spare eyes to help us go through this?" She glanced at Keith, who was inching backward toward the door. "Where are you going?"

"I need to get back to the computer lab."

"I still need your help," she said, planning to use him to sift through the paperwork.

He grimaced. "I'm better with a screen and keyboard."

"Give me two hours. Please." She gestured at the nearly empty room. "We need help."

Zander pulled the lid off a box and lifted out an old accounting notebook. He flipped through it. "Shit. This is going to take forever."

"Where's Mason?" Ava asked. "We could use him on this."

"I sent him away," said Nora. "I had to answer to the assistant chief about why a witness was hanging around our investigation. I managed to explain away his appearance at the Fujioka murder, but I'm not about to get called in again. He needs to not be seen with us."

"He didn't say anything to me," Ava said as disappointment flowed through her. She wasn't surprised that someone had questioned his role, but she missed having him around to share ideas with.

"I assume he has his own caseload to work on," answered Nora. "Sorry about that," she added in a sincere voice.

"You let it slide by for a long time," said Ava. "More than you should have."

"I told him the two of you will have a roommate if I lose my job over it."

Ava grinned at Nora's matter-of-fact tone. "Find anything?" she asked Zander.

"They appear to be organized by program. There's the mentoring program, fund-raising events, school programs, and community outreach." He set aside a small stack. "This is all mentoring from 2005 to 2010. The older years must be in one of the other boxes."

Ava removed the lid of another box and sifted through the ledgers as Nora and Keith did the same with the remaining boxes.

"Did you talk to Regina Zuch again?" Ava asked.

Nora and Zander exchanged a look as smiles crossed their faces. Ava's curiosity was piqued. "What happened?"

"Regina didn't want to come back to the department, so we surprised her with a visit to her home."

"And?"

"We met her current boyfriend." Nora grinned. "They were still in pajamas." She wrinkled her nose. "The house smelled like sex and cigarettes."

"Oh, Lord." Ava's stomach did a mild spin; she knew that odor. It'd hung around her sister.

"Regina sent him home once she realized we weren't leaving. I guess having her son locked up gave her a bit of freedom that she doesn't usually get."

"Did she even ask about Micah?" Ava quickly scanned a notebook and set it in the "nope" pile.

"She did when I first called," said Zander. "At first she wanted to know when he was being released, and I thought she was concerned for him, but I think she was trying to figure out when to kick out her guest."

"That's horrible."

"I agree," said Nora. "Although it has to be hard with your adult son living in your house. He should be on his own."

"I don't see Regina encouraging that," said Ava. "In our first interview, she seemed desperate to keep him close to her. She let him do whatever he pleased to keep him happy. I think she likes having him around."

"I think she uses him as a substitute for a man in her life," said Zander in a serious tone. "There's something really unhealthy there. The way she talked about him gave me the creeps. She tries to keep him dependent on her, and she wants him to need her even though he's a grown-up. I don't think she knows how to have a healthy relationship with a man her own age. She treated the guy that was there like a piece of dirt. I hate to say it, but it was like he was there to scratch an itch for her and once he'd done his role she wanted him gone."

Dread filled Ava's chest. "You don't think she's . . . um . . . being inappropriate with her son, do you?" The thought made her ill.

"I don't think so," said Nora. "I'll wager she brings in an occasional man for that part."

None of them speculated out loud about whether she'd snared any cops in her web.

"Did you ask her about other women with kids in the program?" Ava asked.

"We did," Nora said. "We focused on Vance Weldon since she'd had a relationship with him. She claimed she wasn't aware of any other women he'd been involved with."

"Vance's wife said she didn't know about other women, either," said Ava. "I think she tried to look the other way when she suspected something was going on."

Ava had learned the hard way how to find out if her ex was cheating. Asking directly had triggered lies. She'd resorted to following him.

It hadn't felt good, but it'd gotten results, and she'd taken immediate action. *What would I do if I ever suspected Mason was cheating?*

If I asked, he'd tell me.

It'd be a sign that something had gone seriously off track.

"Regina gave us the name of two women who 'rubbed her the wrong way' at events." Nora made air quotes with her fingers. "She couldn't explain what she meant by that term, but Regina seems very narcissistic. I suspect these are women who steal her thunder when they're in a room together."

"Let's see if their kids' names are associated with our murdered cops." Ava suspected Nora was right. "Did you get anything else from her? Did she have any new thoughts on why Micah confessed?"

"I told her we believed he was protecting someone," said Zander. "She seemed surprised and claimed she had no idea who that person could be. I believed her. If she's a liar, she's a really good one."

"Here's some mentoring records from the late 1990s." Keith held up a small stack of notebooks. "Do you want me to start reading them?"

"Yes." Ava wrote the four men's names and those of Micah Zuch and Jesse Parish at the top of an empty whiteboard, and added the children's names Keith had found in the office computer. "The director said Vance Weldon didn't participate in this part of the program, but keep an eye out for his name in case he was wrong. Jesse Parish should turn up under Lucien Fujioka's name at some point, but I want to know who else mentored him and may have dealt with his crazy mom."

"Read slowly," Nora instructed. "Don't skim. You'll miss something."

"When you find the cops' names, list the child's name and parent and year assigned underneath it," Ava added. "I'll keep digging through the boxes for the rest of the years."

Zander and Nora each grabbed a few ledgers and took a seat. Ava quickly sorted out the rest of the notebooks and the room grew quiet. An hour ticked by as they read, and each of them occasionally added a new name to the whiteboard. Ava made herself read every line.

Mason Callahan.

She smiled at the sight of his name in a record from fifteen years ago. He was proud of the work he'd done for the organization. "Did Mason know we pulled the computer records when you talked to him this morning, Nora?"

"No. I saw him before that."

Ava pressed her lips together, wondering what he'd think of the way they were digging through the company's history. He'd approve. He'd asked a few times if she'd heard back from the director. She spotted Denny's name a few pages after Mason's and checked the board to see if that child had been listed under any of the other cops yet.

Dammit. She went to the board and wrote *Scott Nickle* under Denny's name. He now had six names listed.

Are we going down a dead end?

She glanced around the room, wondering who else was thinking the same thing, questioning if they were wasting precious time reading through old logs.

Zander finished his stack and grabbed one of Ava's books, determination on his face.

If Zander hasn't given up on this lead, then it's still a good one.

"Got a shared name," Zander announced. "Finally." He went to the board and pointed at *Scott Nickle*. "Samuelson mentored him the year after Denny." He added the name and year under Louis Samuelson's name.

Elation filled Ava. *Now we're getting somewhere.*

"I'll see what I can find on Scott Nickle and his parents," said Zander. "These two records are nearly fifteen years old. Keep looking." Zander moved to one of the computer stations in the room.

Ava noticed Keith looked enviously at Zander at the computer but turned his attention back to the written record in front of him. She did the same, hoping to find Scott Nickle's name linked with Lucien Fujioka. Or anyone else. The fact that today was Halloween and their killer seemed preoccupied with horror movies weighed heavily on her mind. *Will we have another murder tonight?*

How could their killer let the popular, horror-filled holiday pass by?

I wish Halloween were another week away.

As she moved on to the records of another year, Ava spotted Mason's name again. She continued reading down the page and froze, the letters jumbling together. Her gaze went back up to Mason's name and checked the name of the child. She looked at the board, not seeing that child listed anywhere. She grabbed the ledger she'd just set aside and flipped pages until she found her first sighting of Mason's name and read the name of the child from that year.

Scott Nickle.

"Has anyone heard from Mason since he left this morning?" She fought to keep a quaver out of her voice.

Zander looked sharply at her over his computer screen. "What's wrong?"

She swallowed, a sense of unease settling in her bones. "Mason mentored Scott Nickle the year before Denny." She leaned over and dug in her bag for her cell phone.

"Who?" Keith asked.

"Her fiancé," Nora supplied. She spun in her seat to face Zander in the back of the room. "Zander, have you found anything on Scott Nickle?"

Ava listened to the ringing of Mason's phone. *Pick up, pick up, pick up.*

I'm jumping to conclusions.

He's fine.

Voice mail. She left a message for him to call her and then searched her contacts for Ray's number.

He answered immediately. "Lusco."

"It's Ava. Have you heard from Mason today?"

"Not lately. I've been trying to stay off his back, knowing he was helping you guys."

"Nora told him to keep away from the case this morning. He didn't tell you?"

"No." Ray's tone grew concerned. "What's wrong?"

"I haven't heard from him all day. Do you know where he might be?"

"I don't. I've barely talked to him since Denny's funeral."

"Ava," said Nora. "Mason told me he was going over to Cops 4 Kidz this morning."

She stared at the detective. "Why didn't you say that earlier?"

"I forgot until right now. He was very vague, saying he hadn't received his minutes from the last meeting and was going to go pick them up in person."

"What's going on?" Ray said forcibly in her ear.

Ava turned her attention back to her call. "I don't know. His name has come up in some research we're doing on the mask cases and now I'm concerned because I can't reach him."

"Shit," said Ray. "Let me ask around a bit." He ended their call.

Ava set down her phone. "Zander?"

He looked up from his computer and shook his head. "I'm still looking. It's like Scott Nickle doesn't exist. I've estimated his current age, based on fifteen-year-old records, to be anywhere between twenty and thirty-five, but I can't find anyone with that name and in the right age range that lives in Oregon or Washington."

"Add Idaho and California," suggested Ava. "Everyone look and see if you can find a parent name somewhere. Maybe there're mentions in the other ledgers that aren't about the mentoring program?"

Nora picked up a notebook, flipped through it, and gave a small moan. "This is going to take forever."

"Nothing when I add the two states," stated Zander.

"Try females in the age range of forty and sixty-five with that last name," said Ava. "Let's see if we can find his mother. Start with just

Oregon and the Vancouver area." She held her breath and watched Zander's expression.

"Shit. I get seventeen names just in our state. I'll look at it by county." He glared at the screen.

Mason, where are you? She dialed again. Voice mail. She punched in a text. CALL ME.

Keith moved to look over Zander's shoulder. "I'll see what I can find on the three names in Washington County. You take the four from Multnomah. Then we can look at Clackamas and Clark County." He sat at the computer terminal next to Zander and tapped on the keys.

Ava went back to her ledger. The names and dates blurred on the pages.

I can't just sit here.

She focused on the pages and made herself search for Nickle.

34

The pain radiating through his body felt like a baseball bat blow to his funny bone that had been multiplied ten thousand times.

Mason's head hit the porch as he fell, and his nose crunched on impact.

His body no longer worked, his brain unable to send commands to his muscles. But out of the corner of his eye, he recognized a face.

Scott Heuser knelt beside him, his stun gun still pressed to the back of Mason's neck.

Agonizing bites of electrical pain reverberated through his muscles and bones. Heuser removed the stun gun, but Mason's body continued to rebel, and he fought to breathe through the blood clogging his nose. One thought echoed through his mind.

I'm in deep shit.

35

"Heidi Nickle," stated Zander. "Age fifty-six. Unmarried. Lives in unincorporated Washington County. I can't find any employment history on her in the last five years, but there are utility records in her name that go back twenty years."

Ava studied the woman's driver's license picture. "Her driver's license has been out of date for two years."

"I noticed that," said Zander.

"Then why do you like her?"

"Because I've got an old newspaper article that quotes her and her son as they enjoyed the Rose Festival twelve years ago." He clicked and pulled up the record.

Standing next to Ava, Nora leaned closer and read the account on the screen. "They refer to her son as a high school student," Nora said. "But they don't use his name. Why would they leave it out?"

"Either the reporter was lazy or he was asked not to use it," said Ava.

"I've got a Desiree Nickle in Clark County who's a year younger and lives a quarter mile from Vance Weldon's home," said Keith. "I don't know if she has kids."

Crap. "Those are both pretty good leads," said Ava. "But why can't we find Scott Nickle?"

"He may have changed his name. Or moved to another state." Nora rubbed her temples. "Is this a wild goose chase?"

"Anyone have any other leads to immediately follow?" asked Ava. Silence.

"I think we need to go to both of these homes and talk to these women," said Nora, looking from Zander to Ava. "You two want to choose who goes where?"

"Washington County," said Ava immediately. She raised an eyebrow at Zander, who shrugged.

"I'll take the home near Vance Weldon's place," he replied.

"Go," ordered Nora. "I'm going to see what's taking so long on our boot print analysis. Keith, thank you for your help. You can head back to the lab now."

Ava grabbed her purse and followed Zander out of the building.

"Why'd you pick the first one?" Zander asked her.

"Because of the fact that she had a son."

Her phone vibrated in her bag. Disappointment struck as she saw Ray's name instead of Mason's on the screen. "Mason told Duff Morales that he was working on the Molalla River park case today," Ray said. "If he went to the state park, I know the cell service is spotty out there. That could be why he's not returning calls."

"But aren't you working that case together?" asked Ava. "Wouldn't he have told you?"

"Yeah, he would," Ray admitted. "Dammit. I don't know where he could be."

"I have to follow up on a lead. Can you check the park?" she asked. "And keep trying to reach him?"

"It's going to take me nearly an hour to get to the park at this time of day," Ray said. "I'll request a trooper to check the park and look for his vehicle. There's probably one within a few miles." He ended the call.

"No Mason?" Zander asked.

"I'm sure he's fine," said Ava. "Seeing his name along with Denny's and the other victims in those records made it hit too close to home for a few minutes."

"Don't get worked up until you know something's wrong. His phone could be in a dead spot or he's too tied up to answer."

"I'm trying to not think about it." She yanked open her car door.

"Hey," said Zander. "Relax. Mason can take care of himself."

I bet Denny Schefte felt the same about himself.

She smiled at Zander, pretending her gut wasn't full of acid, and told him good-bye. She started her car and carefully backed out of her space.

• • •

His head hurt like a son of a bitch.

Mason moaned as he turned his face to the side, feeling the roughness of dirt and rocks against his cheek. He couldn't breathe through his nose, and the taste of iron and dust filled his mouth. He spit and it dribbled down the side of his face to the ground.

His hands were bound behind his back and his feet were tied together. He rolled onto his side and pulled his knees toward his stomach, trying not to scream in pain. It felt as if he'd been hit by a large truck.

Scott Heuser.

He killed Denny.

Scott had hit Mason in the head while he'd been incapacitated on the front porch. He faintly remembered the first two head blows. The third must have finally knocked him out. His stomach felt as if he'd been kicked a dozen times with pointy-toed cowboy boots. Nausea rocked through him and he closed his eyes, willing the contents of his stomach to stay in place. He breathed deep and fought to stay conscious as pain ripped through his left side and lungs.

Broken ribs.

Someone had continued to batter him after beating him unconscious. He hurt everywhere.

Why Scott?

The intricate mosaic of glass on the front door had triggered his memory. The home had belonged to one of the kids he'd been assigned to mentor. He remembered the first time he'd knocked on the door.

The woman was stunning. Liquid brown eyes and a body to die for. She smiled and held eye contact for too long. Mason had to look away. "Are you Heidi Nickle? Scott's mom?"

"I am. Come in." She stepped back into the home, holding the door open wider, inviting him in with her body language and direct eye contact. Seduction oozed from her. It was in her gaze, her movements, and her smile. Her words dripped with innuendo.

Shit.

Mason removed his hat and stepped into her lair, hoping he was misinterpreting her stares. But he'd been a cop long enough to recognize when a woman had the hots for an officer. He was there to meet her son for the first time and figure out a schedule that'd work for both of them.

"Can I take your hat?" She said it as if she'd just rolled out of bed after a marathon sexual encounter.

He dug his nails into the hat, not wanting to let it go. He already felt naked with his head uncovered. Handing it over would be losing the shield in front of his stomach.

He couldn't let it go. "No, thank you. I can't stay long. Is Scott around?"

Fire briefly flashed in her dark eyes.

This isn't going to work.

"He's in his room. I thought I should meet the man who's going to be helping my son. He misses his last mentor. I swear they never last long. Are you going to have staying power?" She slowly raised one sculpted eyebrow.

The double entendre slapped him in the face.

"I always fulfill my commitments. I'll be here for the full six months."

Her face lit up. "Good."

Steps sounded on the stairs to her right and Mason looked up to see her son studying him. Scott was fourteen. His hair was freshly combed, and his gaze was eager but nervous. He politely held out his hand to Mason, introducing himself.

Mason took his hand, impressed with the young man's confidence. Scott looked to his mother, seeking approval, and she gave it with a regal nod. The boy lifted his chin and brought his gaze back to Mason's. Heidi put her arm around her son's shoulders and kissed him on the cheek. Scott didn't push her away or look embarrassed as most teens would.

"I'll get dinner started while the two of you talk," said Heidi. "I have some steaks and I'm going to make twice-baked potatoes. Mason, can you stay for dinner?"

His mouth watered. But his wife and four-year-old were waiting at home for him.

"I'm sorry, but my wife's already planned our dinner tonight."

Fire flashed in her eyes again, but it was immediately quenched by her smile. "Maybe next time."

"Maybe."

He turned to see disappointment in Scott's eyes. "You should stay for dinner," he stated, his expression serious.

"Sorry, Scott. Like I said, my wife already has things planned. This is my day off, so I try to be home in time to eat."

The boy simply blinked, holding Mason's gaze.

Mason knew he couldn't last six months.

Scott Heuser had been the boy. He'd changed his last name.

Mason took shallow breaths and opened his eyes. It was dark and he was in some sort of outdoor shed. He could faintly taste the fertilizer and old mechanical grease that hung heavily in the air. Two high, narrow windows showed him a dark sky and a far-off source of light.

He remembered he'd given a month of his time to the boy before asking to be reassigned. Scott's mother had thrown herself at him every time he met with Scott.

Scott had grown up to become the director of Cops 4 Kidz. Mason had sat in a half-dozen board meetings with him and never recognized him as that fourteen-year-old. Now he saw the resemblance. He remembered the boy had been obsessively neat and driven about his schoolwork. Scott Heuser was still like that.

Did Scott murder Denny and the other men?

What'd gone wrong with him?

The faint laughter of children sounded off in the distance. The pumpkin farm.

He tried to yell and pain ripped through his neck and head. He'd been kicked in the throat, which had effectively destroyed 95 percent of any sound he could make.

But I'm still alive.

How long had Scott kept the other victims alive?

Blackness started at the back of his brain and slowly crept forward; he fought to stay conscious but it rushed through him like a tsunami, and he was swallowed by its depths.

36

Scott darted between the rows of corn, ignoring the strong odor of gasoline.

He knew the layout of the farm next door like the back of his hand. He'd explored the property since he was in grade school. His farm was three boring flat acres, but the farm next door was huge, with a large grove of firs and acres and acres of different crops. A river cut through the southwest corner. It'd been heaven for a boy with a wild imagination.

He'd spend entire days during the summer climbing the trees, spying on the workers, and hiding in the barns. Occasionally he'd find a small treasure . . . a tool left behind . . . a dropped thermos . . . a sharp knife.

His collection of weapons had started with the discovery of a simple pocketknife. A rich prize for a ten-year-old boy. He'd carried it with him everywhere, showing it off to the other boys at school. At night he'd hide it, worried the owners would come knocking on his mother's front door, demanding that he return what he'd stolen.

Finders keepers.

No one ever came.

He continued to comb the farm, searching for more treasures. He didn't notice when the crops started to take up less and less space. His mother mentioned that their neighbors were struggling to make a living off the farm, that times were hard. He knew he and she were poor, but he'd always considered the farmers next door to be wealthy. Surely someone who had all that land and a half-dozen huge tractors must be rich?

Eventually the neighbors opened the farm store, putting a big sign out at the road and selling local produce to passersby. Then they added pumpkins at Halloween and trees at Christmas. More people stopped as they expanded their seasonal entertainments for children.

Scott had been in high school when they started the Halloween haunted forest. The first year he'd stayed at the periphery, watching as actors lurched out of the woods to scare the customers. Soon he joined, buying his own fake blood and costume pieces, and blended in with the staff. They never questioned his presence, in fact they often complimented his makeup.

Hiding and scaring the crap out of families was a mind-blowing rush.

The productions got bigger and better. Corpses hanging from trees, dead bodies in shallow graves, an insane asylum in the north barn. Scott loved it. Every year he watched and spied as his neighbors prepared for that season's scary scenes.

He dreamed of doing more.

Real blood. Real bodies. Shocking the spectators.

His anger had been fueled by the men who used his mother and left her crushed. Mason Callahan had been typical. His mother told him how he'd call her or take her out to lunch while he was at school. Mason swore he'd leave his wife and son and make their family his new one. His mother had been over the moon with anticipation.

Scott was convinced she'd found the right man.

Until the day Mason had told him he wasn't coming back.

He held his cowboy hat in both hands, twisting it in front of him, and Scott instinctively knew the cop had something bad to tell him. He'd picked him up without coming in the house as usual. His mother had told him to ask Mason to stay for dinner. "He keeps promising he will," she'd said. "He needs to make good on that promise."

The man had taken him to a local arcade, bought him a soda, and asked him to sit down to talk.

Scott knew it was serious.

"I'm leaving the Cops 4 Kidz organization," he said. "I'm going to continue to help out at the main office, but I'm not going to go to kids' homes anymore." Mason looked him in the eye, and Scott knew he was lying.

"You don't want to visit us anymore," Scott said.

"That's not it. I have a family and my wife feels she never sees me and she's right. I work twelve-hour days and then spend my days off still doing things for my job. I need to make a change."

"You said you'd stay the full six months."

"I did and it kills me to go back on my word, but my wife is going to divorce me if I don't spend more time at home." There was a forced lightness in his tone. He lied. Scott knew he'd told his mother he wanted to leave his family to live with the two of them. He must have chickened out.

Or maybe he didn't like Scott.

His mom would be crushed. She'd already talked to Scott about how the three of them would go camping together, and how they could plan a wedding at the beach.

How dare he do this to his mother?

Mason was just like the rest of them. He looked away when Mason dropped him back at home. He wouldn't let the asshole cop see him cry.

He didn't see Mason again until Scott's first Cops 4 Kidz board meeting. He'd nearly vomited as they'd shaken hands, but Mason didn't recognize him after all those years. Scott had changed his last name after college, wanting to distance himself from a father he'd never known.

He'd studied marketing and management in college. When he saw the opening for a director at the volunteer organization, he jumped on it. The appeal of the position that put him in a superior position over tons of cops was strong. The group had been a source of frustration for his mother and him for years. The salary was laughable, but he didn't care.

One board meeting, when he'd listened to two of the other members jokingly harass Mason Callahan about the new woman in his life, Scott had gathered the relationship was serious. Callahan had looked relaxed and happy instead of being his usual no-nonsense self.

Scott needed to crush that happiness. Callahan didn't deserve it.

Neither did any of the other men who'd played with his mother's mental and emotional health. They weren't entitled to joy.

A plan had formed in the back of his mind.

He'd encountered names and faces from his past in his new position. And he had their addresses . . . he knew their profiles.

They were primed for him to avenge the pain they'd caused his mother.

He created a goal and sketched out a timeline. He knew from his business classes that every goal needed a plan of action and then a deadline to measure success. He picked Halloween for his deadline, liking the tie-in with his passion for horror.

His first attempt had flopped.

It'd been strangely anticlimactic after his months of preparation and the intense rush of excitement that had started when he'd pressed his stun gun against Vance Weldon's neck. The rush had stuck with him until the next day, when he watched the news and there was no mention of the grisly suicide of an FBI agent. He'd combed the Internet looking for affirmation. Instead he'd been left wanting. As if it had never happened. Looking back, he realized he'd done it too perfectly. He'd staged a suicide and everyone had believed it. The cops, the EMTs, and the medical examiner. No newspapers, no television, no mention anywhere.

He corrected that the second time.

Tonight was to be his finale. The last man on his list would be checked off.

And he would do it in a style that would keep people talking for years.

His mother could rest in peace.

37

"Wake up!"

"Wake up!"

A twisting, burning sensation in Mason's upper arm made his eyes jerk open as his body spasmed in pain. He tried to focus on Scott's face floating above him. The man was dressed in black, including a black hoodie that he'd pulled over his hair. His face was the only pale thing in the room. He stepped back for a fraction of a second and Mason glimpsed the knife in his hand, blood dripping from the tip.

That's what I felt in my arm.

A boot connected with Mason's ribs, and a red haze swamped his vision as he fought to stay conscious through the pain.

A hand yanked on his damaged arm. "Get up!"

Mason's legs fumbled to get underneath him as Scott pulled, and he realized his feet had been untied. His muscles refused to keep him upright and he lurched to one side, landing on an elbow.

His eyes squeezed closed at the pain.

"For fuck's sake! Get up!" Scott hauled on his arm again. Mason shakily stood, not trusting his legs and biting his lips to keep down the vomit that pushed up in the back of his throat.

"Barely walk," he croaked between clenched lips. "Legs not working."

"We're not going far," Scott said. He pressed his knife into Mason's ribs. "Just in case you're shitting me."

"Not," muttered Mason.

Scott pulled him to the door of the little shed and let go of his arm to open the door. Mason struggled to stay on his feet. He looked away as Scott's hand multiplied into four hands as he pushed open the door. The multi-vision made his stomach clench.

Running away was out of the question.

He stumbled through the dark as Scott steered him with a hand on the back of his arm. Mason lost track of their direction. They moved between fir trees and tripped through a field of pumpkin vines. Voices grew louder. Children's voices and the occasional speech of an adult. Scott stopped and tied a gag around his mouth. Mason concentrated on breathing around the foul-tasting cloth. Blood ran from his nose into his mouth and he struggled to spit it out. Instead a constant thread of drool oozed down his chin.

"Get down," Scott hissed in a hushed voice as he dropped to the ground and yanked Mason down with him. Mason twisted, landing on one shoulder, protecting his face somewhat. He panted as he tried to catch his breath, momentarily pleased that he was no longer upright. The loud chug of a tractor moved in their direction and the laughter of people grew louder.

The haunted hayride.

He turned his head, trying to see the tractor he knew was pulling a big trailer lined with hay. The forest was dark, the tractor's lights off to enhance the Halloween mood.

"Make a noise, and I'll start shooting. Kids first," Scott whispered in his ear.

Mason didn't doubt him, but he was incapable of making a sound. The vibrations from the big engine shook the ground. He simply lay still and listened as the ride passed twenty yards away from their dark hiding spot, leaving them in the silent black woods again, and he remembered the dark ride with his son. A few minutes later Mason heard shrieks and screams and knew the ride had driven into a zombie horde or the interactive graveyard.

He put the thought of his son out of his head.

Ava. She'll figure out Scott Heuser is our man.

But would it be before or after he became Scott's next work of art? Scott released his arm. "Don't fucking move."

I don't have much choice.

He heard Scott dash away, leaves and twigs crunching under his feet. A raspy sound of plastic scraping against plastic came from his direction.

Mason listened, straining his eyes to see in the dim light. Scott cursed as something made an abrupt cracking and splashing noise.

An odd taste floated through the air and touched his lips. Mason blew through his nose, trying to clear the bloody blockage. Wet clumps flew out and splattered on the ground.

He carefully inhaled through his nose.

Gasoline.

• • •

Over the past month, Scott had stayed busy. He'd stashed his supplies in hidden caches on the farm next door. He'd watched the staff set up for the Halloween season, preparing its gory props and ramshackle buildings. The corn maze had been planted earlier in the year, and he'd memorized every twist and turn. He'd spent hours building his own devices, studying online tutorials, and downloading instruction manuals.

He was ready.

It would be a Halloween to remember.

Now to move his final piece into position.

Earlier in the week he'd tried to enter Mason's home, only to be screwed over by the presence of a dog. A really loud dog.

He'd had to regroup, but he always had a backup plan.

His backup plan had saved his ass at Lucien's home, but as soon as he'd fired he'd known he had to leave.

It'd felt incomplete.

When the FBI had asked him for help in its investigation, his stress had increased along with his determination to finish his plan. He had to stay one step ahead.

He was so close.

He'd lost his breath when he saw Mason get out of his vehicle in front of his farmhouse. He'd given up on getting to the man before Halloween, and then he'd knocked on Scott's front door like a trick-or-treater.

Did Mason remember the last time he'd knocked on that door?

It'd been pitifully easy to walk up behind him with the stun gun. The sense of satisfaction as he saw the man drop to the ground had been beyond comparison.

Now the last symbol of his mother's pain was trussed at his feet. He'd originally planned for Lucien Fujioka to be the finale, but clearly Mason was meant to be. He'd been hand-delivered to his home, next door to the location where he'd dreamed to create the final spectacle.

Someone was watching out for him.

The haunted hayride chugged out of the forest, headed back to the farm store and main area to pick up its next load of children. He had a good fifteen minutes before it looped by again.

Would anyone on the next ride notice the addition to the scenery?

He hauled the detective to his feet. "This way." Mason stumbled and caught his balance. He turned his head, coughing and spitting.

"Shut the fuck up," he hissed.

Mason muttered something behind the gag.

The two of them floundered through the dark. He knew every path and gave a wide berth to the small shed where the group of zombies reconnoitered after every pass of the hayride. His goal was the gallows, a good fifty yards from the zombie village and past the graveyard.

The gallows were a couple of flimsy stands with a half-dozen hanging bodies. More bodies hung from the surrounding trees. He'd spent a few days reinforcing the second set of gallows. No one had noticed the added boards, nails, or rope.

Now it was capable of bearing the weight of a real body.

When will they notice?

The thought of the body hanging there for days put a spring in his step.

He'd set up enough distractions to confuse the owners, attendees, and investigators for a while.

Who'll be the lucky fellow to come across my big secret?

A laugh burst out of him and he struggled to be quiet. Next to him Mason tripped over a tree root and fell to his knees. The detective groaned as Scott jerked up his arm to get him moving again. Their timeline was tight.

Another hundred feet to the gallows.

38

Ava turned into the long driveway in rural Washington County. The drive had taken much longer than she'd expected. An accident had clogged the freeway, and she'd sat for what felt like hours in the traffic, slowly inching forward. She'd nearly missed the driveway. A couple of tiny reflectors marked its position along the dark, narrow road.

Ahead, a vehicle was parked in front of the big white home. Bright outdoor lights lit up the grounds. Ava stopped her car, staring at the familiar back of the vehicle. She read the license plate three times and then picked up her phone and dialed Mason's phone number. Voice mail.

She called another number.

Nora Hawes answered.

"Mason's car is here at the Heidi Nickle residence," Ava blurted. "The house looks dark inside, and I still can't reach him on his cell phone."

Nora sucked in a breath. "I'm sending backup. Wait for it."

Ava ended the call. She'd stopped her car just outside the umbrella of light cast by the outdoor lamps, but her headlights pointed directly at the home. She turned off her car, stopping the beams streaming in the house's front windows, and waited.

Check his car.

She drew her weapon, keeping one eye on the home fifty feet away and another on Mason's car. She darted out of the shadows and directly into the stream of light and peeked in the windows of his car.

Empty.

She tried the door, found it unlocked, and hit the trunk release. With two long steps and a racing heart, she peeked into the trunk.

All clear.

She closed the trunk and car door and made tracks back to her vehicle.

Where are you?

What was the connection to Heidi Nickle? Somehow Mason had figured it out before all of them and decided to pay a visit.

Damn you, Mason!

She swore at Nora, too, for telling him to keep his distance. If he'd been included, he would have told them about the lead he was following.

The inside of her car was too quiet. She left the door open a few inches, hoping to hear her backup coming at any moment. She froze. *Was that laughter?*

Huge fir trees rose behind and to the right of the house. She stood and looked over the roof of her car, her gaze trained in that direction.

More laughter. Some screams. But happy screams.

The woods lit up with an orange glow a split second before the sounds of the explosions reached her ears.

She dialed 911 and raced toward the burning woods, her phone at her ear.

• • •

His energy was gone, but Mason fought back.

One look at the gallows told him what Scott had in mind.

No fucking way would he dance at the end of a noose.

Scott would have to kill him, haul him up the steps, and then hang his dead body.

Maybe that's acceptable in Scott's book.

It wasn't in Mason's.

He thrashed and broke out of Scott's grip on his arm. He took three reeling steps away from the gallows and Scott grabbed the collar of his coat. His head jerked backward as Scott yanked him to a stop. Twice Mason lurched his body weight forward to break the grip, but it was no use. Seeing no other option, Mason dropped to the ground and curled up in a ball the best he could with his hands still tied behind his back. He waited for more kicks to his broken ribs.

Lightning flashed behind his eyes as Scott pressed the stun gun into his flesh. His legs shot out in spasms.

"Don't fuck with me again," Scott said. "I can drag your ass just fine."

He grabbed Mason's shoulders and dragged him the last twenty feet to the gallows.

• • •

Four days ago Scott had attached a pulley to the top of the gallows. It'd seemed easier than rigging a ramp. He'd known no victim would willingly move up the ladder to the gallows. Even with a gun in his back. He'd recognized he would need to use his stun gun and pulley. Again.

He'd stashed a small harness underneath, accepting that it wouldn't be easy to haul a body up to the platform. Once the body was on the platform, the rest would be simple. There was no trapdoor. The guilty would be pushed off the platform and the fall would be enough to break his neck. If he didn't die from the jerk of the rope, then he would slowly strangle to death.

He'd wanted to repeat Vince Weldon's death. To get it right this time. It'd been the most satisfying killing, standing and watching the man slowly die, even though there'd been little fanfare afterward. He'd been too cautious, too smooth, too good at setting the stage. He'd researched the marks his stun gun would leave on a body. If he was careful, at the most two small bruises *might* show up hours after death. He'd set aside his stun gun for the more visible baseball bat head blows for the other three men. No doubt that had caught the attention of the police and medical examiner.

How long will it take for someone to spot the real body among the fakes?

Mason flopped onto the platform and Scott wiped his forehead. Even with the pulley and harness, it'd been a bitch to get the man to the top. Most of the stun gun's effects had worn off, and he was starting to fight again. He'd lost his gag in the struggle up the ladder, but Scott was glad he'd tied his feet again before using the pulley to haul him up the gallows. He had to get this done and get back home. If he moved Mason's car to the farm among all the other cars, they couldn't connect him to the man's death.

His goal would be achieved.

"This place is going to be crawling with cops any minute," Mason croaked.

"Yes, it will be. But not for the reason you think. They have no idea it's me." Scott knelt on the man's back and roughly looped the noose around his neck. Mason froze at the yank of the rope and then thrashed again, knocking Scott off his back. The cop scooted toward the edge of the platform, searching for a way down.

"Go ahead and jump off. You'll speed up my process," Scott said in amusement. Mason's eyes grew wide as he judged the distance to the ground. "Having second thoughts?"

Scott checked the time. He still had ten minutes before his distractions were set in motion. But the hayride should be along soon. He sat back, leaning against a pole on the gallows, taking a moment to relish the man's fear.

Mason met his gaze. "Why me?"

Scott frowned. "You don't remember?"

"I remember you. I put it together once I stood on your porch. I'd been assigned as your mentor but had to cut it short."

"You abandoned my mother. You made all sorts of promises to her. You were going to leave your wife and help us start a new life. But once you got what you needed from her, you ran." Scott sneered. "Was the sex worth it, Callahan? Was it worth destroying our lives?"

Mason stared at him. "I didn't make any promises to your mother. I was married."

"I know. But you led her to believe your marriage meant nothing to you."

"Bullshit! I never said anything of the sort and I never *fucked your mother*. She came on so strong at our first meeting I knew I couldn't stay in that situation. That's why I left. She fucking threw herself at me."

"She did not!" Fury raged through him. *How dare he impugn my mother that way.*

"She did! Is that why you targeted those other cops? Because your mother sent them scrambling? After she lied to you and told you they were the answer to your prayers?"

"They had it coming! They all used her. Every single man led her on and made her promises and then abandoned us!" *I have every right to do this!*

Mason shook his head. "I hate to break it to you, but your mother was a liar. That may have happened with another cop or two, but I sure didn't do it. I didn't give her the chance. I was out of there the minute I saw what she was about. She used *you*—she kept you in the mentoring program to get close to cops."

"You don't know what you're fucking talking about!" Scott shrieked at the lying cop. *Liars! Every last one of them. How dare he blame my mother!* "You did this!"

"We have a name for women like your mother—badge bunnies." Mason smirked.

Scott scrambled to his feet, ready to throw the man over the edge. Anger focused his vision. "You—"

Explosions cut off his words and the forest lit up like a fireworks display.

39

Ava didn't wait for her backup. She'd counted four explosions coming from the woods. Fire licked the trees and the happy shouts had turned into screams of fear. After reporting the fire to 911, she dashed through a garden plot and between shrubs and trees, keeping one eye on the flickering flames that lit up the sky ahead of her. She entered the dense forest and the light from the flames was nearly blocked out. She turned on her camera's flashlight and pointed it at the ground as she ran.

Who is screaming?

A figure dashed across her path, and she gasped at the sight of his bloody face.

A zombie costume. The man stopped and she saw a dozen more similarly made-up people catch up with him. "What happened?" she shouted.

"Is this part of it?" he asked her. "Did they add explosions?" The other zombies shouted similar questions. "Where's the hayride?" one asked. They physically shook, looking over their shoulders, their attention going in a hundred directions.

Understanding hit her. She'd stumbled into some sort of Halloween-themed party.

"I don't think that was supposed to happen," said the first zombie, panting heavily.

"Is anyone hurt?" Ava hollered, waving her arms for their attention.

"No," said several zombies. Several of them pointed at the growing fire in the distance. "We can't go back that way."

Ava gestured behind her. "Head that way. There's a white farmhouse and the police should be there any minute. Fire trucks, too."

"What about the graveyard crew?" asked one.

"The what?" Ava asked.

"The graveyard. There're another dozen actors over there waiting to scare the hayride."

"Which way?"

All the zombies pointed toward the fire. It'd diminished after the initial explosions, but grown again as it caught hold of the dry firs. She estimated it was a good hundred yards away.

"I'll go," she said. "Tell the police where I am."

The actors took off in the direction she'd come from. The first zombie paused. "You don't know the way. I know this set inside and out."

She agreed. "Let's go."

He turned and started to jog. "Follow the hayride tracks." Ava followed and realized she no longer needed her phone light to see between the trees. The fires lit up the sky and filtered down between the branches. She was too far away to feel the heat, but the smell of the smoke was almost nauseating.

The tracks led to a clearing in the woods, and she stumbled as she spotted a body hanging from a tree. "Jesus Christ."

Her zombie partner didn't even glance at the body, and she noticed there were a half-dozen more in the trees ahead.

She jogged on, shaking her head. As a kid she'd hated haunted houses and they still held no appeal. This setup would give her nightmares for months. She took a close look at a body as she ran by. The creator had perfectly imitated the gray skin and slack facial expression of death.

A shudder ran up her spine, and she ran into her zombie partner, who'd stopped on the path.

"What the hell?" he said.

She looked past him. Two fake gallows lined the hayride's tracks. On top of one, two men struggled. Scott Heuser kicked the other man in the gut.

Scott Nickle.

Heidi Nickle's son is Scott Heuser.

Her legs shook as she made the connection. The task force had been so close.

Scott Heuser had killed the cops.

The other man up there had a noose around his neck and was about to be shoved off the platform.

Mason?

• • •

Mason blindly kicked with his feet, not caring where they landed on Scott's body. Satisfaction rolled through him as he saw the stun gun skitter off the edge of the platform. After a long pause, he heard it hit the ground with a thump. *It's a far drop.*

He kicked and kicked, scooting himself to the safety of the center of the platform. He dug his chin into his chest, trying to get it under the noose, but Heuser had looped it tightly about his neck. Without the use of his hands, it wasn't coming off.

Scott swore at him and scrambled to his feet.

Get him over the edge.

Mason attacked with his legs, feeling splinters from the platform slide into his shirt and pants. His upper arm throbbed where Scott had buried the point of his knife. The knife reappeared in Scott's hand, triggering another round of two-legged kicks from Mason. Sweat ran down his face and his energy dropped to running on fumes. Scott launched himself and leaped over Mason's legs. From the other side, he threw himself at Mason's back and shoved.

Mason shot across the platform, unable to stop Scott's momentum. His head dangled over the edge and he stared down at dirt and pine needles. One more shove sent his body flying off the platform.

He swore he heard Ava scream.

• • •

Her heart stopped as he fell.

Screams filled the forest. Her screams.

She sprinted past the zombie and launched herself at Mason, grabbing his waist and lifting with all her strength to keep the pressure off his neck. "Help me!" she shrieked at the zombie. Mason dangled at the end of the rope, but Ava noticed that his boots kicked the loose dirt. Blood covered the lower half of his face, and his gaze held hers. His mouth moved but no sound came out. The zombie imitated her grab and lift. He was a foot taller than she and, thankfully, strong.

"Do you have something to cut the rope with?" she gasped.

"In my back pocket," said the zombie. "Hurry."

She let him take Mason's weight and dug in his pocket, finding a multipurpose knife. She flicked it open and sawed at the rope above Mason's head. The rope was new and fresh. She stared into Mason's eyes as she sawed at the fraying rope. "Hang on, dammit!" His eyes were bloodshot, his face turning a deep red.

But he held eye contact.

The rope broke and Mason slumped into the arms of the zombie, who gently lowered him to the ground on his side. Ava knelt beside the two of them, her fingers shaking as she struggled to get the noose over his head. "Are you okay?" she shrieked. *"Are you okay?"*

His jaw opened but no sound came out. She wiped the crusted blood on his nose and he arched his back in pain. "Fuuuuck!" he moaned.

A broken nose.

Tears of relief streamed down her cheeks. "Is it just your nose? Are you hurt anywhere else?"

"Ribs," he choked out. He met her gaze. "It was Scott. Stop him."

"I know. I just figured it out, but I'm not leaving you. Not right now." She wiped more of the blood off his face, avoiding his nose, as the zombie worked to cut the ropes on Mason's hands.

"I'm fine," he said hoarsely. "Get Scott." His gaze moved behind her, his eyes widening.

She looked. Scott Heuser stepped off the last rung of the ladder and sprinted into the woods.

Mason looked at her again. *"Get him!"*

She drew her gun from the holster at her side. The zombie's hands froze on Mason's bindings, his gaze on her weapon. "I'm a federal agent," she told him. "Can you get him out of here?"

"Yes. Here." He pulled a flashlight out of his cargo pants. "He headed in the direction of the corn maze."

She took the flashlight and gently kissed Mason on his bloody lips. "I'll be back." She brushed tears off her cheeks.

"I know."

She ran after Scott.

40

Scott zigged and zagged through the woods, swearing under his breath. He'd managed to launch Mason off the platform but the rope had been too long. The cop's feet had hit the ground. He might have slowly strangled if those people hadn't shown up and immediately cut him down.

Ava McLane. A few days ago the FBI agent had sat in his office and calmly interviewed him. At that moment he'd known the noose was starting to tighten, but he'd believed he'd have time to finish. Now she'd shown up and ruined everything.

Not everything. To his right and ahead fires raged through the dry forest and started on the corn maze. He could hear the shouts of people struggling to find their way out of the maze as the flames drew closer. He'd watched as the owners had planned and planted the maze, trimming it to create a challenge.

He knew every inch.

The pounding of running footsteps sounded behind him and he glanced back. A bobbing flashlight bounced in the dark behind him, gaining ground.

The FBI agent?

He ducked into the maze. *Try to find your way out of this one.*

• • •

Ahead she saw Scott dart down a dark path between the tall stalks of corn.

Noooo.

She stopped at the edge of the corn. People shouted from inside and fire burned aggressively in one quadrant of the field.

Let him go. It's too dangerous.

Close by, a woman screamed in pain. Ava dashed into the corn and encountered the woman clutching her arm, two teenagers behind her, one of them carrying a flashlight.

"He stabbed me!" she shrieked at Ava. Ava paused to look at the dripping wound; it was long but shallow.

"Get your mom to the fire trucks. Don't go back in the corn maze," she told the two teens. Their faces were white with terror. "She's going to be okay."

"What's going on?" the girl whispered, holding her brother's arm. "What started the fire?"

"Something exploded," said the boy, one arm supporting his mother.

"Stay together," directed Ava. "Just keep moving away from the fires."

A man's angry shout came from the corn maze, and she heard the wail of a terrified small child. Ava pointed her flashlight down the dark path.

I can't leave.

"Go," she told the family. "I'm going to get more people out."

The family moved on, and she jogged down the packed dirt path. The corn towered over her head. It wasn't the fresh green cornstalks that she'd seen from the freeway as she'd driven by cornfields in the summer. This was browning, rotting, rust-smelling, claustro-phobia-inducing cornstalks. The stalks hadn't looked tall from the forest. Now they seemed twice her height. She followed the cries of the child.

Turning a sharp corner, she found Scott Heuser face-to-face with a bulldog of a father who had a five-year-old cowering a few feet behind him. The father had his fists up, challenging Scott, who crouched in the path with his knife. The father took a step and rounded a heavily booted kick at Scott's knife hand. Scott leaped backward. He was between Ava and the father and child; she didn't have a safe shot.

"Drop the knife!" she shouted. Her feet were planted and her weapon ready, but she kept it pointed away from the three. She shone her flashlight directly at the back of Scott's head.

Scott glanced behind him, blinking in the bright light. He grinned and darted sideways, directly into the stalks of corn. She followed, using her flashlight hand to push the dense stalks out of the way. Rotting leaves slapped her in the face and dirt worked its way into her mouth, leaving grit between her teeth. Her flashlight was useless as she fought to find places for her feet. She could hear Scott a few feet ahead of her, cursing and tripping his way through the corn. He let out a gasp and his footsteps sped up as she heard him break out of the corn and onto a maze path. Ava pushed harder and broke out from the corn a second later. Smoke filled the path and the sky glowed intensely to her right. Flames flickered in the rotting corn. The screams and shouts had dwindled, and she prayed it was because people had found their way out of the maze.

She looked to her right and left, not seeing Scott. She slowly followed the path to the left, assuming he'd move away from the fire. She clutched the flashlight in her left hand and her weapon in her right as she waved the light over the cornstalks beside her. Fire engine sirens sounded over the screams of scared children, and she welcomed them.

Mason?

She put him firmly out of her thoughts, confident he was in capable hands and that his wounds hadn't appeared to be life-threatening. The zombie would get a big thank-you from the both of them.

Her boots made no noise as the sirens multiplied. She coughed from the smoke and wished she had an extra hand to hold her shirt collar over her nose and mouth. The smoke grew thicker.

I need to get out. Let Scott go for now.

Every fiber of her body struggled to accept the decision, but she didn't want to let him go.

I'm so close.

She stopped in the path, straining to hear past the sirens, listening for footsteps or breaking stalks or rustling leaves.

Nothing.

A cloud of smoke engulfed her path and alarm shot through her. *Which way is out?* She pushed on, her internal compass stating that she was moving toward the edge of the maze and away from the fires. New far-off shouts reached her ears, but they were commands and orders. Firemen.

She bent over, seeking cleaner air, and sucked in deep breaths. A fit of coughing took over as her lungs protested against the amount of crap she'd breathed. She paused and crouched down for a moment where the air was better.

Gun or flashlight? One had to be put away so she could cover her nose. She reluctantly holstered her gun, unwilling to walk blindly in the dark. She pulled the neck of her shirt up over the lower half of her face and moved forward through a break in the smoke. Her eyes burned from the ash.

An arm roughly circled her neck and jerked her backward against a male body, her head smacking against his chest. Her flashlight skittered across the dirt and stopped, shining in her eyes.

Scott.

A knife flashed in front of her face, an arcing glint of metal in the dark, and she didn't pause to think. Her training took over and her body reacted.

In one rapid movement, she twisted to the side and shot her elbow into his windpipe and her heel into his kneecap. A muted crack sounded as her elbow connected. His arm loosened and he took several stumbling steps backward, bending over as he fought through his pain in his throat.

She faced him, her gun drawn and pointed at center mass. "Do. Not. Move." Her heart raced as she stared down the man who'd killed cops and nearly hanged Mason, her dropped flashlight and the smoke casting odd shadows across his face. Hate raged through her, but she kept her trigger finger in control. One of his hands dug at this throat as if he could tear away the pain she'd inflicted.

"Fuck you." He met her eyes and launched himself at her, his knife hand leading.

She fired. And kept firing.

Surprise lit up his face but the shots didn't stop him. He plunged forward as she shuffled back, her finger pulling her trigger over and over.

He stopped, swaying in the smoke, and for a split second she believed he was immortal.

How is he still alive?

He fell.

Ava stood in the smoke, her gun still trained on his immobile body, expecting him to leap up, his face transformed to that of a creature of the undead. She couldn't move. Her panting echoed off the cornstalks and she wondered if her body would be found next to Scott's, dead of smoke inhalation. She holstered her weapon, wanting to simply sit in the dirt and wait to be found.

Voices drew closer, shouting orders.

Her legs gave way and she sat.

• • •

Shots sounded over the fire engine sirens and Mason's heart stopped.

Mason pushed away the hands of the EMT. He was capable of holding his own oxygen mask. His voice was gone and his throat felt as if it was swelling by the minute, but his airway was clear. The trauma seemed contained to his voice box and the left side of his mandible. The EMT had cleaned up his bloody face and bandaged the stab wound in his arm, and then ordered Mason to alert him the second he had trouble breathing. Mason had grimaced, imagining the EMT cutting open a new airway through his neck.

The zombie had dragged him out of the woods and back to Scott Heuser's driveway, where fire trucks and police cars had arrived. He suspected he had a broken a foot in his fall but he didn't care. Right now he wanted to see Ava come out of the forest. A bleeding woman with two teens had emerged from the woods, saying a crazy guy with a knife in the corn maze had slashed her arm and he'd been followed by a woman with a gun.

Every cell inside Mason commanded him to run in and find her.

Instead he sat and sucked on oxygen, knowing he could barely walk and worried that his airway would close off.

The helpful zombie had given the Washington County deputies a description of Scott Heuser and told them Ava had been in the woods, headed toward the corn maze. They'd proceeded cautiously, knowing a fellow officer was inside.

Somewhere.

Did Ava fire the shots?

He didn't think Scott had a weapon other than the knife. If he'd had a gun, he would have used it on Mason.

Mason stared at the dark trees of the woods. Smoke billowed around them; the light from the fires toward the back cast an orange glow from within. Assorted zombies and actors with fake traumatic injuries milled around the driveway. It was a set for a horror movie. He crumpled his fear for Ava into a ball and gripped it tight, forbidding it to take over his thoughts. She was tough. She was experienced.

She would come back.

Two firemen moved in the shadows at the edge of the woods, a small zombie between them.

His zombie.

He got to his feet, dropping his mask, and the EMT immediately tried to settle him back down. Mason gestured and batted at his hands, pushing him away, and took off. Pain shot from his feet with every step and he was reduced to hobbling. She spotted him and ran forward, shock growing on her face as she focused on his neck.

"Oh, my God," she started. "Look at—"

He grabbed her and pulled her close, muffling her voice in his shirt. He tried to ask if she was okay, but only grunts came from his mouth. He stepped back, his hands gripping her shoulders as he studied her from head to toe. Dusty ash covered her dark hair and blood dripped from a thin slash on her cheek.

Concern filled her face as she reached to touch his neck, then stopped, fear in her eyes. "You look like . . . like I don't know what. Someone who's been strangled and punched in the nose, I guess."

He chortled, a saliva-filled sound that made her rapidly blink.

"Are you okay?" she asked hesitantly.

He nodded, longing to vocalize his happiness that she was unharmed.

"Can you speak?"

He shook his head as relief overwhelmed him.

"Scott is dead," she said in a flat voice. "He stabbed a woman and tried to stab me." Her gaze dropped and he pulled her close again, wishing he could comfort her with words, but knowing she would read his feelings in his touch. He settled for stroking her hair and back.

The world could continue to burn. He no longer cared.

41

Five days later

His neighbor across the street was putting up Christmas lights, fake deer, and an inflatable Santa. Mason watched through his front window and felt a subtle tug to keep up with the Joneses. Lights could wait. Hell, maybe he'd hire someone to do it this year. The thought of climbing a ladder with a broken bone in his foot held no appeal. He'd gotten by with a splint and a pair of crutches that he'd refused to use after the first two hours—they pushed on his broken ribs. His nose and throat had turned all sorts of vibrant colors, with impressive levels of swelling the first few days. Now his tissues were primarily yellow and brown, the swelling almost gone.

He wondered if his voice would ever sound the same. It was rough and raspy. The doctor had told him it could take months to return to normal. Or never return to normal at all.

Ava joked that their matching voices were a sign that they were meant to be together, but Mason didn't agree. Her low voice was sexy and bluesy; his was horror movie villain material.

A car pulled into his driveway and Zander Wells stepped out. Ava's footsteps sounded on the wooden staircase behind him and Bingo's nails announced he was right beside her.

Good homey sounds.

Last Christmas Ava had been in a hospital room, her shoulder permanently damaged by a gunshot. This Christmas would be drama-free—he hoped. Jayne appeared to be settled in her new rehab facility in Costa Rica. Ava was cautiously optimistic. He saw it on her face and heard it in her tone. He hoped three thousand miles was enough distance to keep Jayne's drama at a minimum. New drama had appeared in the form of someone claiming to be Ava's father. For now Ava was content to keep him at a distance. David had pressed for a DNA test; Ava wasn't in a hurry. She still hadn't accepted that she might have two half siblings.

Mason wasn't going to push her.

Knowing the truth wouldn't change who she was.

Bingo pressed against his leg and Ava's hand slipped into his as she watched Zander come up the walk. "He said he had more news about Scott Heuser."

Mason didn't care to ever hear the director's name again. "I can't believe I admired that guy."

Ava said nothing. They'd talked the subject of Scott into the ground. Murderer. Psychopath. Son of a crazy mother. Good program director. It added up to a profile that'd made Special Agent Euzent stay in town for two extra days to dissect the killer's background.

Halloween night haunted Mason's dreams. The sensation of falling. The rope around his neck. His hands useless behind him. Ava's scream. Scott's eyes.

Sometimes it was fourteen-year-old Scott who pushed him off the platform.

Sometimes his feet never hit the ground.

Sometimes Ava found him hanging hours later.

He squeezed her hand, feeling his palms start to sweat, and hobbled to the front door before Zander could ring the bell.

A wave of brisk outdoor air entered with the FBI agent, and he looked run-down from a grueling week of investigation and cleanup. Ava had taken the week off as her shooting was reviewed, but ASAC Duncan had privately assured her of a positive result. The victim who'd been stabbed in the minutes before she shot Scott had provided clear testimony about the threat Scott posed.

Ava got Zander a cup of coffee and they took seats next to the woodstove. Bingo laid his head on Zander's knee, staring at the agent until he received a head rub.

"We found Heidi Nickle," Zander said with a grim look. "I didn't tell you about the initial discovery two days ago because I wanted confirmation from the medical examiner."

"He killed her," Ava said flatly.

"We found remains buried in a shed near the home. One of the investigators had questioned some odd pavers that'd been laid in a rectangle in the corner of the shed. They seemed to serve no purpose, and we brought in a cadaver dog to see if there was a point in digging beneath them. Euzent had theorized that Scott had killed her and buried her body somewhere close to the property, because we couldn't find any recent records of her. It was like she'd vanished."

"Did the shed have two narrow high windows? And the rest of the floor was dirt?" asked Mason.

"Yes. We also found a couple of baseball bats with blood on them in there. We're having them analyzed."

I shared a room with a corpse?

"She was in a shallow grave under the pavers. We covered the rest of the property with the dog, but didn't find anything else."

I could have ended up under the pavers, too.

"What did the ME say?" asked Ava.

"Based on dental records, it's her. She had one huge fracture from a bash to her skull and her hyoid was broken. Dr. Rutledge suspects the blow to the head came first and then Scott strangled her."

"And continued to live in her home as if nothing had happened," added Mason.

Sick.

"One of the bedroom closets was full of her clothing. And the attached bathroom still had a woman's hygiene products."

"I wonder when he killed her." Ava gave a deep sigh. "He seemed so normal. I genuinely liked him when I interviewed him."

"That's the general consensus. He was a master at hiding his other side."

"What pushed him to target the cops?" asked Ava. "Why now?"

"Euzent theorizes that Regina Zuch might have triggered some anger in him."

"Micah's mother?"

"Yes, Scott mentored Micah for an entire year, and Regina admits she pursued him pretty hard. I guess his position as the director appealed to her as much as a uniform."

"She's at least ten or fifteen years older than him," stuttered Ava.

Mason elbowed her.

"We're different," she argued.

Mason straightened. "Scott didn't believe that his mother pursued me. He said I crushed her with my lies and behavior. Maybe he didn't want to believe his mother had been like Regina."

"What's Micah doing now?" asked Ava.

"We released him to his mother. He confessed he'd been stalking Scott Heuser for a long time, even following him to the coast when Scott targeted Denny Schefte. He was a bit obsessed with the director. Regina says he's supposed to take medication for OCD, but she suspects he throws it away. I think this shook her up enough to reevaluate how much help her son needs."

"It's over now," said Zander. "We'll probably never know what went on in his brain, but Euzent will do his best to figure it out."

Mason didn't doubt it.

"We also found more horror masks and a silicone finger with the happy face fingerprint at Scott's place. All he had to do was touch his nose with it to pick up some oils and press it where he wanted to leave the fingerprint."

"Did he plan for more victims?" Ava asked.

"Good question. No other mentors had worked with him, but he killed Vance Weldon for some reason. I suspect his mother hooked up with Weldon through a different element of Cops 4 Kidz and Weldon's wife didn't know about it." Zander met Mason's gaze. "You were lucky that rope was an inch too long."

"Tell me about it."

"It was a brand-new rope. Somewhere I read that the experienced hangmen would use an old, well-conditioned rope because it doesn't stretch. New ropes stretch."

Mason shuddered. He hadn't meant for Zander to *literally* tell him about it.

"Can you come for Thanksgiving dinner?" Ava changed the subject. "I'm excited to cook in my new kitchen and we'd love to have you."

A small smile crossed the agent's face. "I'd be honored."

"Good. My neighbor Cheryl is coming, too." She paused. "I'm not trying to set you up. You both happen to be two of our favorite people. No pressure."

The smile faded a bit. "None taken. I'm looking forward to meeting her." Zander stood. "I need to be going."

• • •

Ava watched Zander's car back out of their driveway and wondered if she'd pushed too hard. "Did I scare him?" she asked.

"He needs a little shaking up," said Mason. "He's too set in his ways."

She gave him a side eye.

"I'm proof," Mason stated. "Shaking up is good. You just don't appreciate it until it's over."

"I'm glad you appreciate it now," she stated.

"I do. I'm stunned at how dense I was. I'd sat back in my easy chair and was content to let life stream past me. You came along and yanked me into the rushing water." He took her hands and made her face him. "Now. When are we holding this wedding?"

She swallowed hard, blinking under the intensity of his brown gaze. "I don't know."

"Why don't you know?"

"You choose," she countered, unable to answer his question.

He was silent a moment, his gaze searching hers. "There's something between us that's stopping you. Is it the age difference?"

"No! I've told you a dozen times that I don't care about our ages." *Truth.*

"Then what is it?"

"Do you want kids?" she blurted. Her lips pressed into a tight line. She'd said it. The one little anomalous piece that couldn't find its proper position in the puzzle of their lives was now out in the open. It hung between them, heavy and dense. A turning point.

Mason took a half step back. "Do you?" His brows furrowed.

She felt raw and exposed under his scrutiny.

"I don't know," she whispered as her brain shot into fifth gear and her fears tumbled from her tongue. "You've said you're done with kids, and I'm scared that Jayne's weaknesses will be passed to my child, and I don't know if I'm cut out to be a mother, and what if one of us dies on the job and—"

He yanked her close, wrapping his arms around her and pressing his face into her hair. "I want whatever you want. Forget what I've said in the past. All that matters is that we move forward together. We've got a lifetime to figure it out."

I almost lost you.

She burrowed into his chest. "But I don't *know* what I want and it's not fair to you—"

"I know what's fair," he said. "I'd love to share a child that's a blend of me and you, but I also believe we can be happy if it's just the two of us. We don't have to decide right this minute. It's something for us to explore together."

She pulled back, studying his brown eyes for honesty.

Pure truth stared back at her.

"After we're married." He raised a brow at her.

She owed him a wedding decision.

Decisions on children could wait; they'd find the answer together.

The silent burden lifted from her shoulders, and her doubts vanished. Her vision filled with a crystal-clear picture of the two of them exchanging vows. "I want a summer wedding at the winery." She couldn't speak fast enough. "I know it's farther away, but I want to see blue sky and smell fresh flowers . . . and for the sun to shine on us as we say our vows."

His face lit up. "Done. It sounds perfect."

Contentment filled her heart.

She couldn't wait.

ACKNOWLEDGMENTS

It felt good to return to Mason and Ava. I'd taken a break to write a new Bone Secrets book, and during that time readers contacted me, hoping *Spiraled* wasn't the last book for this couple. Readers also begged me to take it easier on Ava. One asked me to get her pregnant and simply let her enjoy her new kitchen. I love to hear how readers have connected to the characters. I'd never planned for *Spiraled* to be the final book, and I don't plan for *Targeted* to be, either, but there will be another break while I write a few books in a new series, starting with *A Merciful Death*. You'll find a few familiar faces in the new series, and a new couple in the spotlight.

Thank you to my Montlake team, which gives me amazing support to write my books: Anh, Jessica, Marlene, Kimberly, and Hai-Yen. A high five to my agent Meg Ruley; I smile when I see that New York area code pop up on my phone. A gigantic thank-you to Charlotte Herscher, the only person I allow to see my work in its unedited state. I don't use beta readers or critique partners before my publisher sees my books; I only have room for one other voice in my head when I'm writing, and it is Charlotte's.

My girls are my cheerleaders and always want to know what's going on with my books. This week my youngest pointed out that she hadn't seen me writing lately. I explained that I was between books, which in turn made it clear why there'd been fewer frozen pizzas for dinner. My husband is fantastic about clearing my path so I can focus on writing. Everyone knows he's zombie- and horror-obsessed, so this book is for him.

READ ON FOR A SNEAK PEEK
OF KENDRA ELLIOT'S NEXT
BOOK, *A MERCIFUL DEATH*.

*This is an uncorrected excerpt and may not
reflect the finished book.*

Mercy Kilpatrick wondered who she'd ticked off at the Portland FBI office.

She stepped out of the car and walked past the Deschutes County Sheriff's Department cruisers and two SUVs to study the property around the silent, lonely home in the woods in the eastside foothills of the Cascade Mountains. Rain plunked on Mercy's hood, and her breath hung in the air. She tucked the ends of her long, dark curls inside her coat, noting the large amount of debris in the home's yard. What appeared to be a series of overgrown hedges and casual piles of junk to anyone else, she immediately identified as a carefully planned funneling system.

"What a mess," said Special Agent Eddie Peterson, who'd been temporarily assigned along with her to the rural setting from their Portland office. "Looks like a hoarder lives here."

"Not a mess." She gestured at the thorny hedge and a huge, rusted pile of scrap metal. "What direction do those items make you want to go?"

"Not that way," stated Eddie.

"Exactly. The owner deliberately piled all his crap to guide visitors to that open area in front of the house, stopping them from wandering around to the sides and back. Now look up." She pointed at a boarded-up window on the second story with a narrow opening cut into its center. "His junk positions strangers right where he can see them."

Eddie nodded, surprise crossing his face.

Ned Fahey's home had been hard to find. The dirt and gravel roads weren't labeled, and they'd had to follow precise mileage-based directions from the county sheriff to find the house hidden deep in the forest. The tired-looking cabin was far from any neighbors but close to a natural spring.

Mercy approved.

She'd smelled a light odor of decay in the yard. As she climbed the steps of the porch to the house, it slapped her full in the face. *He's been dead several days.* A stone-faced Deschutes County deputy held out a log for her and Eddie to sign. Mercy eyed the deputy's simple wedding ring. When he got home with corpse scent clinging to his clothes, his wife would not be happy.

Next to her Eddie breathed heavily through his mouth. "Don't puke," she ordered under her breath, as she slipped disposable booties over her rubber rain boots.

He shook his head. She liked Eddie. He was a sharp agent with a positive attitude, but he was a young city boy and looked the role out here in the boonies, with his hipster haircut and nerdy glasses. His expensive leather shoes with the heavy treads would never be the same from the mud in Ned Fahey's yard.

But they looked good.

Had looked good.

Inside the home she stopped to examine the front door. Custom-made with heavy, dense wood, the door had four hinges and three deadbolts; the additional bolts were positioned near the top and bottom of the door.

Fahey had built an excellent defense. He'd done everything right, but someone had managed to break through his barriers.

That shouldn't happen.

Mercy heard voices upstairs and followed. Two crime scene techs directed her and Eddie down the hall to a bedroom at the back of the house. An increasingly loud buzzing sound made Mercy's stomach turn over—it was a sound she'd been told about but never heard for herself. Eddie swore under his breath as they turned into Fahey's bedroom and the medical examiner glanced up from her inspection of the bloated body on the bed.

Mercy had been right about the source of the noise. The room vibrated with the low roar of flies that'd discovered the corpse's orifices. She tried not to look too closely at the distended belly that strained the buttons of his clothing. The face was the worst. Unrecognizable behind the black screen of flies.

The medical examiner nodded at the agents as Mercy introduced herself and Eddie.

Dr. Natasha Lockhart peeled off her gloves and laid them on the body. "I understand this was a *friend* of yours," she said, lifting a brow.

"He's on the no-fly list," Mercy said. The FBI relied on the list for their domestic and international terrorism persons to watch. Mercy guessed the medical examiner wasn't much older than she was. She was tiny and trim, making Mercy feel abnormally tall. The corpse on the bed had a history of brushes with the federal government. His preferred company was sovereign citizens and right-wing militia types. From the reports Mercy had read on the long drive up the gorge from Portland, she gathered that Fahey talked the talk but couldn't walk the walk. He'd been arrested several times for minor destruction of federal property, but someone else was always the ringleader. Fahey's criminal charges seemed to slide off him as if he were coated in Teflon.

"Well, someone decided they no longer needed Mr. Fahey around," said Dr. Lockhart. "He must have been a sound sleeper to not hear our killer enter his house and place a weapon against his forehead."

"Against?" Mercy asked.

"Yep. I can see the tattooing of the gunpowder in the skin around the entry hole. One nice hole in and one out. Through and through. Lots of power behind the round for it to go through that cleanly." Dr. Lockhart grinned at Eddie, who slightly swayed as he stood by Mercy. "The flies brush away easily enough. For a moment."

"Caliber?" Eddie asked in a strangled voice.

Dr. Lockhart shrugged. "Big. Not a puny twenty-two. I'm sure you'll find the bullet burrowed in something below."

Mercy stepped forward and squatted next to the bed, shining a flashlight underneath, intending to see if the round had gone into the floor. The space under the bed was crammed with plastic storage containers. *Of course it is.*

She glanced around the room, noticing the heavy-duty trunks in neat stacks in each corner. She knew exactly what the closets would look like. Floor to ceiling storage neatly labeled and organized. Fahey lived alone, but Mercy knew they'd uncover enough supplies to last a small family through the next decade.

Fahey wasn't a hoarder; he was a prepper.

And he was the third Deschutes County prepper to be murdered in his own home in the last two months.

"Did you handle the first two deaths, Dr. Lockhart?" she asked.

"Call me Natasha," she said. "You mean the other two prepper murders? I responded to the first, and an associate went to the second. I can tell you the first death wasn't nice and neat like this. He fought for his life. Think they're connected?"

Mercy gave a smile that said nothing. "That's what we're here to find out."

"Dr. Lockhart's damned right about that first death," said a new voice in the room.

Mercy and Eddie turned to find a tall, angular man with a sheriff's star studying both of them. His gaze grew puzzled as it lingered on Eddie's thick, black glasses. No doubt the residents of Deschutes County didn't see a lot of hip, fifties-era throwbacks. Mercy made introductions. Sheriff Ward Rhodes appeared to be in his sixties. Decades of sun exposure had created deep lines and rough patches on his face, but his eyes were clear and keen and probing.

"This room looks like a tea party compared to the scene at the Biggses' place. That place had a dozen bullet holes in the walls, and old man Biggs had fought back with a knife."

Mercy knew Jefferson Biggs had been sixty-five and wondered how he'd earned the title of *old man* from this sheriff who shared his age group.

Probably an indication of Biggs's get-off-my-lawn attitude more than his age.

"But none of the homes—including this one—showed forced entry, correct?" asked Eddie politely.

Sheriff Rhodes nodded. "That's right." He scowled at Eddie. "Anyone ever tell you that you look like James Dean? With glasses?"

"I get that a lot." Eddie smiled.

Mercy bit her lip. Eddie claimed to be surprised by the comparison, but she knew he liked it. "But if there's no forced entry here and Ned Fahey was asleep, then someone knew how to get inside the house or was also sleeping in the house."

"He's wearing pajamas," agreed Dr. Lockhart. "I don't know the time of death yet. The putrefaction is very progressed. I'll know more after lab tests."

"We examined the house," said Sheriff Rhodes. "There's no sign that anyone was sleeping here or of any forced entry. This is the only room with a bed, and the sofa downstairs doesn't have any pillows or

blankets to indicate that someone else was here." He paused. "Front
door was wide open when we got here."

"I take it Ned Fahey was the type to keep his doors locked tight?"
Mercy asked, half in jest. The short walk through the home had shown
her a man who took home defense very seriously. "Who reported his
death?"

"Toby Cox. Young teen who gives Ned a hand around here. Was
supposed to help Ned move some wood this morning. He said the door
was open and when he saw the situation he called us. I sent him home
a few hours ago. The boy's not quite right in the head and this shook
him up something fierce."

"You know most of the residents?" Mercy asked.

The sheriff shrugged. "I know most. But who can know everyone?
I know the people I know," he said simply. "This home is far from any
city limits, so whenever Ned had an issue, he called us at the county."

"Issue? Who'd Ned have problems with?" Mercy asked. She understood the politics and social behaviors of small towns and rural com-
munities. She'd spent the first eighteen years of her life in one. The
residents tried to make everyone's business their own. Now she lived
in a large urban condo complex where she knew two of her neighbors'
names. First names.

She liked it that way.

"Someone broke into a couple of Ned's outbuildings one time.
Stole his quad and a bunch of fuel. He was pretty steamed about that.
We never did find it. Other calls have been complaints of people hunt-
ing or trespassing on his property. He's got a good ten acres here and
the borders aren't marked very well. Ned's posted some 'Keep Out'
signs, but you can cover only so much ground with those. He used to
fire a shotgun to scare people off. After that happened a few times, we
asked him to call us first. Scared the crap out of a backpacking family
one time."

"No dogs?"

"I told him to get a few. He said they eat too much."

Mercy nodded. *Fewer mouths to feed.*

"Income?" she asked.

"Social Security." Sheriff Rhodes twisted his lips.

Mercy understood. It was common for the antigovernment types to raise hell about paying their taxes or buying licenses, but don't you *dare* touch their social security.

"Anything missing?" asked Eddie. "Is there anyone who would even know what's missing?"

"As far as I know, Toby Cox was the only person to step foot in this house in the last ten years. We can ask him, but I'll warn you he's not the most observant type." Rhodes cleared his throat. "We've come across one storage unit outside that's been broken into. Follow me."

Mercy sucked in deep breaths of fresh air as she followed the sheriff down the stairs from the porch of the house. He led them through the junk-lined funnel and fifty feet down the dirt road before veering off on a path. She smugly noted her toes were dry in her cheery rain boots. She'd warned Eddie to dress appropriately when told their destination, but he'd brushed it off. This wasn't rain on concrete sidewalks in downtown Portland; this was autumn in the Cascades. Mud, heavy brush, wandering streams, and more mud. She glanced back and saw Eddie brush the rain off his forehead, and he gave a wry smile with a pointed look at his mud-caked shoes.

Yep.

They ducked under a yellow ribbon of police tape that surrounded a small shed. "The crime scene techs have already processed the scene," Sheriff Rhodes advised. "But try to watch where you step."

Mercy studied the mess of crisscrossing boot prints and didn't see a clear place to step. The sheriff simply walked through, so she followed. The shed was about fifteen by twenty feet in size and was hidden by tall rhododendrons. From the outside, it looked as if a strong wind would flatten the tiny outbuilding, but inside Mercy noticed the walls had been heavily reinforced and the room was lined with sandbags along the dirt floor.

"Chain on the door was cut. I should say all *three* chains on the door were cut," the sheriff corrected. He gestured toward a big hole near the back wall of the shed. The lid to an ancient deep freezer opened out of the hole.

Bodies?

Mercy peered into the buried freezer. Empty. She sniffed the air, catching the minty odor of a weapon lubricant she knew some gun enthusiasts swore by and a hint of a faint musty gunpowder smell. Ned had packed an arsenal in the ground.

"Weapons," she stated flatly. Fahey had three registered guns. He wouldn't have worked this hard to hide three guns. More sand bags were packed between the freezer's walls and the dirt pit. Mercy wondered how Ned had controlled the humidity for the guns. As far as weapons storage went, this wasn't ideal.

"There was one of those little cordless humidifiers in there," Rhodes stated, as if he'd read her mind. "But someone had to know where to dig to find the freezer." He gestured at the piles of fresh dirt around the shed. "I wonder how well camouflaged the freezer was. This isn't a place I'd come looking for weapons."

"You said there were three chains locking the door?" Eddie asked. "To me, that screams, 'I've got something valuable in here.'" He pointed at a narrow steel rod on the dirt floor. "If I broke through three sets of locks and chains and found an empty shed, I'd start plunging that into the ground until I hit something."

Sure enough, there were narrow holes in scattered places across the floor of the shed.

"He's a prepper," Mercy stated. "It's expected he'd have a stash of guns somewhere."

"They didn't have to murder him in his bed to steal his guns," pointed out Rhodes. "I think the guns were a bonus."

"They?" asked Mercy, her ears perking up.

The sheriff raised his hands defensively. "No proof. Just going by the amount of work I see here and the number of footprints found in front of this shed. The techs are running a comparison on Fahey's and young Toby Cox's boots to see what's left. They'll let us know how many people were here."

"Can't rule out Cox," Eddie pointed out.

Sheriff Rhodes nodded, but Mercy saw the regret in his eyes. She suspected he liked this Toby Cox who wasn't "right in the head."

Mercy mentally placed Toby Cox at the top of her list to interview.

ABOUT THE AUTHOR

Kendra Elliot won the 2015 and 2014 Daphne du Maurier Awards for Best Romantic Suspense. She was also an International Thriller Writers finalist for Best Paperback Original and a *Romantic Times* finalist for Best Romantic Suspense. She lives in the rainy Pacific Northwest with her husband, three daughters, and a Pomeranian, but she dreams of living every day in flip-flops. She loves to hear from readers through her website, www.KendraElliot.com.